One of the b[illegible] April Gardner pulle[illegible] pages all the way to the satisfying conclusion. Through the eyes of a mixed-blood slave, and a scarred and wounded major, you'll encounter prejudice, heartache, loss, and a love so palpable you'll feel it to your very core. Full of grit, realism, and edge of your seat action, *Warring Spirits* is a story not to be missed! ~ *Lynnette Bonner - Author, Rocky Mountain Oasis & High Desert Haven (http://www.lynnettebonner.com)*

Warring Spirits is a tale of loss of pride, civility, and identity; at the same time it showcases the best in humanity and a hope for the future. A must-read for lovers of early American history. *~Lisa Lickel, multi-published author (www.lisalickel.com)*

April Gardner has gone the extra mile to assure accurate and honest portrayals of the diverse characters in Warring Spirits, a human drama played out on the stage of American history. It has been an honor to serve as a liaison between a conscientious storyteller and knowledgeable advisors among modern Muscogee Creeks. The ministry of Warring Spirits is the challenge to examine our Christian practice with clear eyes and new inspiration. ~ *Edna Dixon, Student of southeastern Creek history and culture, Perdido Bay Tribe of Southeastern Lower Muscogee Creek Indians, Inc.*

Gardner's writing and plotting was so well done it left me a bit breathless, but also rewarded for sticking with the story to the perfectly orchestrated ending. She knows how to write with conviction. There is heart-felt love and tension on every page. No opportunity to show God's heart for mankind was wasted. It's impossible not to feel the joy gleaned in the midst of the devastation, and to see God's hand moving in spite of everything. *Warring Spirits* is a wonderful, passionate novel, and one

I won't forget anytime soon. ~*Michelle Sutton, author of over a dozen inspirational novels*

As soon as you pick up this book, you'll find yourself swept away by April Gardner's excellent story-telling abilities. This is one of those rare tomes that make sleep bothersome. With her haunting characters and rich imagery, she has written a wonderful sequel to Wounded Spirits that won't disappoint! Danger, deceit, heart-breaking pain, and finally, God's sustaining power and grace that helps the suffering overcome hardships, makes this a book you won't want to part with until you've finished reading the very last page. April Gardner is a writer to be watched. ~ *Amanda Stephan, author of The Price of Trust and Lonely Hearts*

Warring Spirits completely swept me off my feet! Revisiting characters from *Wounded Spirits* and discovering new ones, this next book in the Creek Country Saga is sure to win author April Gardner new fans everywhere!

From cover to cover *Warring Spirits* is a powerful, action-filled story that's sure to keep you up into the wee hours of the morning! April Gardner is a gem of an author worth sitting alongside the other amazing historical fiction writers on my shelf (Jody Hedlund, Kaye Dacus, and Laura Frantz, to name a few!). Loved every moment I spent in *Warring Spirits* and was sad to see it come to an end! ~*Katie McCurdy, author and reviewer, Legacy of a Writer*

Warring Spirits

April Gardner

Vinspire Inspirations
A Division of Vinspire Publishing
Ladson, South Carolina
www.vrpublishing.com

ISBN: 978-0-9834198-5-3

PUBLISHED BY VINSPIRE INSPIRATIONS, A DIVISION OF VINSPIRE PUBLISHING, LLC

For Jimmy

Chapter One

June 1816

Phillip knew it was a dream. He told himself again, though it did little good. The children's shrieks grew louder. The flaming pickets roared with new life, as though fueled by his denial of their existence.

His legs churned, but he couldn't free his mind of the constant nightmare. At least this time, he reasoned, he wasn't awake. Small blessings.

And then, he saw her.

Adela.

Arms dangling at her sides and skirt undulating in the waves of heat, she stood across the compound. Her lips were motionless, but her voice echoed through his mind. "Phillip."

He rushed toward the vision, and she reached for him. "Phillip, love, you must wake up."

With a cry, he bolted upright.

The silhouette of a woman hovered over him. He stared at her, unblinking, afraid to move and frighten her away.

Sweat poured down his chest—sweat as real as the shadow seemed.

"That's better," she whispered. "You'll be alright."

He disagreed, but if he spoke, he might shatter her. He'd done it before.

Her loose hair swayed as she moved so near, he should feel her heat.

Taking in the comfort of her presence, he held his breath until his lungs burned with need. Refusing to be contained any longer, air exploded from his mouth. The sound ripped through the cabin, and in one blink, Adela vanished.

A moan built in Phillip's throat, and he buried his head in his trembling palms. When his fingers collided with the jagged flesh on his face, he recalled again why Adela was no more to him than a mocking shadow, a figment of his deluded, half-crazed mind.

She had turned him down.

Familiar nausea haunted his gut. With a growl, he threw his damp pillow across the room. The sound of splintering glass sent him scrambling for the musket by his bed. He had the unsteady barrel aimed toward the source before he realized he'd been the cause of the commotion.

He dropped the weapon and backed away from it as though it were a copperhead. Blood pounded in his throat. He swallowed hard, terrified of his own mind.

It had been nearly two years. One more night of this and he would prove the gossip correct. He would go mad.

There had to be a better way.

"Help me." His voice shivered, and for once, he was thankful to be alone. "Sweet Jesus, show me a better way."

***

Sitting as poised as possible in the bouncing buckboard, Milly rearranged her skirt then tugged her bonnet over her ears. Another rut in the road sent her stomach flying.

"You look fine, Miss Milly." Isum transferred the reins to one hand then wiped a palm against his dingy, knee-length trousers. A sideways glance topped his crooked smile. "As fine as any white lady in stole clothes."

Milly squirmed inside her stuffy petticoats. "*Borrowed* clothes, and don't call me that. Milly will do."

"No, miss. It won't. Best make a habit of it now, before we're needin' it."

"I hate admitting when you're right."

Isum chuckled, but Milly pressed her lips and snatched a peek over her shoulder.

"We'll hear somebody comin' before we see 'em." Isum's voice remained steady, his demeanor casual, and his shoulders relaxed. His death-grip on the reigns told another story.

Three years ago, he had been as short and wiry as a plucked cotton bush. Now, his muscular, mahogany frame left little room to spare on the wagon seat. According to plantation gossip, the field girls took to nervous giggles whenever he came around. The master had perked up as well and taken to accepting bids.

There was only one thing Master Landcastle needed more than strong field workers. Cash.

The moment whispers in the big house revealed that Isum had been sold and would leave by dawn, Milly took action. There was no way she would let them take the only true friend she had, so ignoring the consequences, she loaded the buggy with vegetables. And one lady's day gown.

As was their weekly custom, she and Isum set off toward town. Only this time, instead of stopping at the market, they went straight through.

Six miles of red, Georgia clay stretched behind them. Seventeen more before they ran into Spanish Florida. Sixty beyond that, Negro Fort, and safety.

It had been done many times before. It could be done again. But in broad daylight?

Escape stories ran through Milly's twenty-four years of memory. Had there been a single one where a slave had taken to the road while the sun was at its highest? She shook her head.

But I have an advantage...so long as I'm not recognized.

The July sun beat down on her with mocking strength. She pressed a palm across the back of her stinging neck.

Isum reached to the floorboard then passed her the borrowed parasol. "You'll be burnin' if you don't."

Since he first came to the plantation as a skinny tyke five years her younger, Isum had been her responsibility. She had cared for him as meticulously as she did her own flesh. About the time his gaze tilted downward in order to look her in the eye, they swapped roles, and his protectiveness had grown in proportion to his towering height.

She frowned, opened the frilly contraption, and settled it against her shoulder. Immediately, her neck cooled. It did nothing for the bile rising in her throat.

Gripping the side of the bench, she failed to tamp down the regret that swelled within her.

The timing was wrong. They would be caught, and he would be sold. She dare not consider her own fate.

They should turn back. It wasn't too late.

She swiveled and squinted at the road behind them. What options did she have? Mr. Grayson's features, twisting with his customary, terrifying rage, flashed before her mind's eye. *It's too late. We can't turn around.*

They should be moving faster.

Isum pulled on the reins.

"Why are you slowing?" Milly sat forward, resisting the urge to yank the whip from its holder and spur the mare to a gallop.

He swiped the floppy hat from his head and mopped his brow with his sleeve. "We ain't alone. Best we not seem in too much of a hurry." He indicated with his hat then settled it back in place before taking up a deliberate, relaxed posture.

A horseman topped the next slope.

"Oh God, help us."

"What you worried about, Miss Milly? You's armed with the most beautiful smile this side of the Chattahoochee. Ain't no gentleman gonna see past it to doubt your word."

But what if he *wasn't* a gentleman? Milly forced a wobbly smile then swept her hand under her bonnet, securing any strays.

Within minutes, Isum pulled the buggy to a halt as the gentleman came alongside them. The creaking brake nearly sent Milly scrambling for the trees lining the road. Instead, she angled the parasol to shield her face, presumably, from the sun.

"Good afternoon." The man's unfamiliar voice released her pent-up breath.

Easing back the shade, she peered through the lace edging. Long seconds passed before Isum shifted beside her and nudged her back.

Milly lowered the parasol and forced her gaze to the stranger's eyes. She found them friendly and unsuspecting. "Good afternoon to you, sir." Tucking her trembling hands into the folds of the closed parasol, she tried for that beautiful smile but feared she fell short of Isum's expectations.

The man studied her, never once glancing at Isum.

A cold sweat broke out on her upper lip. Like venom, fear coursed through her, poisoning her confidence. Her gaze slipped to the dirt where it belonged.

"You're a might far from civilization. It's not exactly safe out here, even with a strapping young buck such as yours."

Milly's line of sight skittered to the man's chest, then, weighted by years of training, fell back to the ground. "I plan to trade with Creek in the next village. I hear they'll give anything for a little food."

"So they will, poor devils." The man laughed, making Milly's skin crawl. He sidled his horse close to the buggy, and the smell of his cologne wafted down. "I appreciate a woman with a tender heart."

"If you don't mind, we best be moving along. I wouldn't want to be caught out after dark."

The man's silence lured Milly's hesitant gaze. A smile crept up his face. "There they are, those pretty brown eyes." He tipped his hat, bowing slightly at the waist. "It would be my pleasure to escort you, miss."

"No." The discourteous refusal popped out of its own volition. "Thank you, but that's not necessary. We're accustomed to the road."

Eyes darkening, the gentleman reined his horse around, pointing its nose toward the road behind them. "As you wish. Good day."

Milly nodded but doubted he noticed. "Let's move, Isum," she whispered, anxious to leave the man's dust behind.

A brisk mile later, Milly's gloved hand still clutched the parasol in her lap. Tears burned her eyes at the thought of what might have happened. She blinked them away to find Isum grinning from ear to ear.

"We done it. We fooled that dandy."

A strangled chuckle escaped her. "Yes. I supposed we did. He never suspected a thing." Milly laughed, full and long. It unwound the knotted cord in her gut, and suddenly, the road opened before them and filled with possibilities.

Possibilities of a future. With Isum? He had offered as much, and she hadn't exactly rejected him. Neither had she accepted. She found it difficult to move past the years of near-mothering to feel something more toward him. And yet, she couldn't imagine another man on earth who would willingly wed her. And from all indications, he was more than willing.

Taking in a deep, cleansing breath, she turned and found his steady brown eyes on her. All joviality had fled. "Isum? What is it?"

"For half a minute, I thought I was gonna have to kill me a white man, the way he was lookin' at you. Like you's a Sunday pastry."

It was always the same with men. Many women longed for beauty, but for Milly, it was the key to her shackles. Perhaps today would commence the end of her nightmares. Even if it did, it certainly wouldn't erase what had already been done to her. She tucked her chin against the nagging shame.

Isum grunted and slapped the reins across the mare's rump. "Ain't nothin' you can help."

At the sound of thundering hooves, she felt the blood drain from her face. A glance behind them revealed four riders closing in fast.

She gripped Isum's arm, words lodging in her throat.

Jaw clenched, he focused on the horse as he pulled them to a stop. Running was futile. With quivering resignation, she removed her gloves and folded them neatly, just as the mistress had taught her. She couldn't bring herself to look at Isum, to see hope shattered across his face.

"It ain't ova," he mumbled, as Master Landcastle's men surrounded them.

Milly coughed in the horses' dust, and probed her mind for a reasonable excuse.

"I thought you were smarter than this, Milly." Grayson, the overseer, laid one hand across his legs, loosely aiming a pistol in their direction. "A shame what'll become of you now." His false sympathy grated on her ears.

Two of the others dismounted and dragged Isum from his seat. He struggled against their attempt to shackle him and was rewarded with a swift kick to the gut.

Milly jumped from the buggy and scrambled to the side of Grayson's horse. Her nails dug into the leather of his riding boot. "Please, it was my fault. I didn't tell him I planned to run."

He guffawed and kicked her hand away. "He doesn't answer to you, girl. And he'll pay for his own foolishness. Just as you will." He jerked the pistol. "You're riding with me."

The thought of being pressed against the man for seven miles of rough roads sent Milly back a step. He lunged forward, grappling for the fabric at the front of her gown, but he missed and scratched her neck instead.

She barely registered the burn.

His nostrils flared. "Get over here."

Milly shied away from his curses then risked a glance over her shoulder.

The other three struggled against a willful Isum. "Hold him down," one bellowed.

"I'm tryin'!" Metal clinked and rattled as Isum kicked, sending the shackles skidding across the road.

One of the men swore and went after them.

Too late, Milly noticed Grayson's hand as he swiped for her again. She swayed back and away, but he compensated, stretching farther away from his horse. Fisting her blouse, he yanked her toward himself.

With a cry, Milly locked her knees, sending her lower half sliding under the horse's belly. She clung to Grayson's arm, her weight tugging him down with her.

"Let me loose." His breath puffed hot in her ear.

The horse skittered, its hooves striking the ground so close she felt the vibration through the dirt. It bolted away from them, sending Grayson tumbling from his perch.

Just in time, Milly flipped to the side, avoiding his descending bulk.

He landed beside her with a grunt, his pistol coming to rest inches from her hand.

"Merciful, Lord," she whispered through dusty lips.

"Grab it!" Isum screamed. Two held him belly-down, while the third locked one cuff on his ankle. His eyes bore into her, begging her to take action.

Grayson's gaze darted to the pistol the instant her fingers wrapped around the handle. Before he could pull himself to a sitting position, she had the barrel pointed at his head. "Make them stop." Her voice trembled in time with her hands.

He snorted. "You wouldn't kill me."

No, she wouldn't, but she could cripple him. In a way he'd never hurt another woman again. Without a word, she redirected her aim.

Steady. Keep it steady. She scooted back, further of his reach. "You heard me."

Grayson glared at her, his jaw working circles.

From the corner of her eye, she noted the stillness that had settled on the opposite side of the road. Isum flailed once more and managed to dislodge himself from under his captors.

"Unshackle him," Milly called, her eyes never leaving Grayson's.

"I'll find you, and you know it." His voice was gritty with hate.

"Maybe. But not today."

"Grayson, what do you want us to do?"

"Let him go."

The manacles clinked to the ground.

Isum pushed up and trotted to her side, lip bleeding and jaw swollen, but looking better than such a struggle should afford. "I got this here." He took the weapon from her. "Think you can get the buggy into them trees?"

She nodded. If required to get them out of there, she could sprout wings and fly.

The sun had barely moved by the time Isum had all four men bound, gagged, and lashed to the wagon, which Milly had taken as far into the undergrowth as she could.

While he secured the men's bonds, Milly changed back into her comfortable, plain brown frock then scattered all the horses but two. Leading one to Isum, she smiled. On horseback, they could cut through the forest and make better time. At least until the ground grew too swampy.

He gave her a boost then adjusted the stirrups with a swiftness that spoke of a lifetime in the master's stables. Giving her foot a pat, he winked. "Now who's the mastah of himself?"

She fingered the bonnet's ribbon tied beneath her chin and shook her head. "It's a bit soon to be so confident. We have a long trail ahead of us."

Mounted, Isum directed his horse alongside hers. With a quick yank, he loosened her bonnet's ribbons. "You don't need that no more. From here on, we'll be exactly like the Almighty created us to be."

One hand pressed to the top of her bonnet, Milly leaned out of his reach.

He clucked his tongue. "Your feet can run, but your heart, it gotta stop chasin' after lies. It's time you be who you's meant to be."

Who I'm meant to be? "And what exactly *am* I?"

"A child of the King. And my girl. Nothin' else mattuh."

Milly snorted, as he took her mare by the bridle. "We ain't leavin' 'til you know it."

"I know it."

"Then take it off."

She fingered the edge of her bonnet, while Grayson's gaze gouged her back. She was more terrified to remove it than to turn the mare toward Florida. Heart running wild, she lifted the bonnet until a breeze tickled the hair on her forehead.

With a smile born of unending patience, Isum released her horse.

She set the cap in her lap and ran a hand over the braid worked in a circle around her head, its coarse, frizzy texture accusing her of her tainted heritage.

Her line of sight traveled to Grayson. From where he sat tied to the wagon wheel, the hatred emanating from his eyes scorched Milly's weak resolve.

"I can't." With a jerk to the reins, she twisted the horse's bit out of Isum's reach. Gripping the saddle with her thighs, she settled the bonnet back in place. A swift kick of her heel set the mare on the backwoods trail to Spanish Florida.

Isum might be doomed every day to face their reality, but Milly had been blessed with the option to hide.

What slave in her right mind would choose otherwise?

For the third time in an hour, Major Phillip Bailey checked that his musket was properly primed and loaded. The

Apalachicola River wound along on his right, and Creek warriors fanned out on the left. He was trapped. It had only been two years since many of these same warriors had surrendered to General Jackson at the conclusion of the Red Stick War.

The sight of them now, wild in their feathers, piercings, and tattoos, set the hairs on the back of his neck on end. For every one of the hundred and sixteen, blue-coated regulars on the march to Prospect Bluff, there were two—supposedly ally—Creek warriors who slogged across the boggy ground next to him.

The odds were far from comforting. Sweat pasted his silk neck-stock to his throat.

He scanned the surrounding pines for any sign of danger, whether from runaway slaves or friendly Creeks turned hostile. Downriver a ways and set back into the forest, the outline of a dwelling took shape. Like the many other slave-owned shacks they'd come across, the place appeared abandoned, but that didn't mean the owners weren't lurking in the shadows, waiting to ambush them.

Silent as ghosts, a group of warriors split off and swarmed the farmstead. Within minutes, they rejoined Phillip's column empty-handed.

If what was said about the runaway's leader proved true, Chief Garcon wouldn't allow Phillip and his men to waltz into the area without a dandy of a fight. It was no secret the Americans intended to neutralize the fort on Prospect Bluff, the stronghold they called *Negro Fort*. Its name alone struck fear in the hearts of southern Georgians.

General Jackson had jumped at Spain's approval of his crossing the Spanish-American border to defuse the tension and reclaim American property—the slaves. With its swamps, alligators, and prowling Seminoles, *Las Floridas* was wild country. Toss in three hundred armed and desperate runaways, and the place became hell on earth.

Phillip had been the first to volunteer to invade that hell. Alligators and runaways, he could handle. Creek warriors were a different matter altogether. Running into them on the southerly trail had been a surprise to both parties. It just so happened that, this time, Creek and American objectives ran parallel. Or so the Indians said...

Without warning, a regular stepped out from behind a tree blocking Phillip's path. His rifle arm jerked. "In the name of all that's holy, Corporal Higgins, get back in line." Phillip spoke from between clenched teeth.

"Yes, sir. Just taking care of business, sir."

Phillip noted a smirk on the nearest warrior. He scowled back.

The natives might see him and his men as a bunch of untrained idiots, but Phillip knew better. When not attacked on the sly and when properly prepared, there was no equal to Phillip's army anywhere in the Americas. Hadn't they proved it two years earlier by crippling the Creek Confederacy?

He passed Higgins' scrawny frame as he busily fastened his broadfalls. "Didn't mean to scare you, sir." A poorly contained leer plucked at the man's freckled cheeks.

Phillip opened his mouth to refute the charge and put the private in his place, but the gravelly voice of Sergeant Garrigus beat him to it. "Idiot. You can't rattle the major. He's got nerves of iron."

"Is that right?"

"After what he's seen? You bet."

Garrigus's praise sounded sincere enough, but Phillip knew the truth and prayed every day no one else would discover it. "Enough chatter back there. Keep your mouths shut and your eyes peeled." He cast a sideways glance at longtime friend and surgeon, Captain Marcus Buck.

Marcus returned it with a faint smile that raised his flawless cheeks. Eyes, nose, mouth—each feature lined up perfectly. He might be a favorite with the ladies, if he took his nose out of medical books long enough to notice.

Involuntarily, Phillip's jaw twitched, tugging the taut skin around his scar.

"Where's Enoch?" Marcus's gaze skimmed the area.

"Are you enjoying the quiet too?" Phillip subdued a grin and jerked his head toward the end of the loosely formed column. "I put him to work keeping Cook company."

"Indians making him nervous?"

"Him and me both." It wasn't the only thing Phillip and his young slave had in common.

Moisture sucked into his boot as he stepped into another pocket of muck. Swamp water soaked his half-gaiters and spattered his dirty white breeches. He shook his foot, longing for a pair of clean, dry stockings. An arduous, two-day trek behind them, Camp Crawford might have been nothing more than tents and pickets, but right now, it seemed pretty near to heaven.

An Indian, head shaved on the sides, loped from the front of the line toward Phillip. His black hair, collected into a long tail, flipped through the air behind him. His face was a solemn, purposeful mask, and he clutched a tomahawk, as if ready for battle.

A drumbeat sounded from nearby. Or was that the blood pounding Phillip's eardrum?

He strengthened his stance and gripped the musket barrel, ready at any instant to swing it into position. Sweat dripped into his eye, but he refused to blink and miss even one of this warrior's breaths.

The Indians had caught him unawares before. Never again.

As the man neared, the path cleared before him. Ahead, a commotion scattered the column.

This was it. The moment Phillip had been anticipating. One swing of this warrior's blade would be the signal for the rest to attack. By sundown, every last American scalp would dangle from a pole.

Unless Phillip did something to stop it.

The drum increased its tempo. In his mind, he was back at Fort Mims, the fires licking at his heels. The world narrowed to the warrior streaking toward him. Phillip had known better than to trust these savages, but Colonel Clinch hadn't listened.

Phillip should give some sort of call to battle, but his brain went numb. Breath ragged, he raised his weapon to his shoulder and pointed the muzzle at the warrior's chest. His stiff collar dug into the base of his head and his sweaty finger trembled against the cool trigger as he waited for the red man to raise his tomahawk.

Instead, ten paces away, he came to a halt, his brown eyes boring into Phillip. The warrior lowered his weapon and slipped it into a loop on his waistband. Arms limp, his lean body visibly relaxed as he stood before Phillip.

Except for the drum in his ear, silence surrounded them.

Why didn't he attack? Indians never surrendered. Surely, it was a trick.

"Major?"

Phillip blinked, then allowed his gaze to flick to the side.

Marcus laid a hand on Phillip's arm, and he flinched.

"Easy, now," Marcus sounded as though he were calming a terrified child instead of addressing a superior officer. His voice rose barely above a whisper. "The men are watching. There's no call for this. Not this time."

A massive vulture soared above them, pulling Phillip's focus back to the man before him. As much as Phillip searched, he found not a hint of malice in the warrior's steady gaze.

He dropped the tip of his musket and sensed two dozen warriors lowering their bows in response.

As realization of his error took hold, heat crawled up Phillip's neck, burning his scar. He focused on the black ostrich plume trembling in the air above Marcus' bicorned hat as he turned to the warrior.

"It's nothing personal, you see. Major Bailey fought at Mim's place. Next time you're careless enough to run up on him that way, I'll let him have at you," Marcus stated with a half-grin.

The Indian stared at Phillip, long and probing, until his eyes softened and mystified Phillip with their sudden depth.

"No, best stop me, Captain Buck. No sense creating more work for yourself." Phillip's attempt at humor fell flat. He cleared his throat and turned to the Indian. "You have a message for me?"

The warrior nodded. "A white man. We found there." He gestured toward a sandbar in the middle of the river.

Phillip's pulse slowed. He swallowed and willed his voice not to tremble. "One of ours?"

"A seaman. Wounded here." He tapped his shoulder.

"One of Sailing Master Loomis' men?" Marcus asked, his voice rising with disbelief.

Phillip resumed walking at a quick pace. "My thoughts exactly, although it was my understanding that no vessel from the naval convoy was to enter the river until we'd arrived."

"They weren't," Marcus confirmed.

The warrior took up a limping step beside them. "There is more," he said, halting Phillip in his tracks. "Two dead. This side of river."

"Sailors, as well?" Phillip asked, hoping the dead were runaways.

"Perhaps. Their white bodies lie naked."

Marcus hissed a curse, while Corporal Higgins' face lit with anticipation. "We gonna see action?"

"Never mind that," Phillip said. "Did you hear the Indian's report?"

"Yes, sir. I heard."

Phillip pointed two fingers downriver. "Take it to Colonel Clinch, on the double." At the sound of Higgins' scurrying footfalls, Phillip turned to Marcus. "Surgeon, you're with me."

A silent crowd gathered ahead—around the wounded sailor, Phillip surmised. "Clear out," he called as he shouldered his way through the throng. "Give the man space to breathe."

Marcus followed, bumping into Phillip's back when he stopped short. His breath caught in his lungs. Scalped and brutally stabbed, two stripped men lay in a puddle of blood, their features frozen in twists of agony.

Soldiers shifted, allowing the doctor room to press his fingers to each neck. He stood, retrieved a kerchief from his pocket, and wiped his hands, staining the cloth red. "Give me someone I can help, for heaven's sake."

As Marcus stepped over the bodies, a tremble began deep inside Phillip. The quiver grew, moving into his stomach with a painful shudder. "We camp here. Private Davidson, inform Major Collins. Garrigus, set up a perimeter." He tore his eyes from the grisly scene, stepped back, and then turned to Marcus. "Captain Buck, see to the wounded sailor, wherever he is. I'll find you shortly. I'm going to look for tracks before we lose daylight."

Night was falling fast and with it, his composure. The skirts of his coatee slapped the backs of his legs as he quick-stepped toward the shelter of the woods.

He pressed his lips tight and willed his stomach to cease its rebellion. Eyes riveted to a massive cypress twenty yards in, he forced certain images from his mind. Images of Fort Mims, of the dead and dying, of the corpses he had trampled in his fight for life.

Satisfied the cypress hid him, he rested his hands on his knees. His head swam, and the world tipped. Closing his eyes, he focused on keeping his breath even and his army rations where they belonged.

At last, he regained a measure of control—enough to be presentable to his men.

These memories should not hold such power over him. And yet, they did. With more ferocity each passing month.

Furious at himself, he ripped the bicorn from his head and hurled it into the shadows.

A soft cry followed, emanating from the darkness beyond.

Every muscle in Phillip's body froze, as he strained to pierce the obscurity of dusk. He saw nothing, heard nothing—besides voices carrying from the riverbed. Had he imagined the sound? If he had, the fact wouldn't astound him. Not anymore.

The cry had possessed a human quality. Would he go so far as to say feminine? His mind replayed the sound. Yes, he would. Had there been a female with the sailors? Phillip knew of no situation where that might be permitted.

Unwilling to believe he was hearing voices in his head, he set out in the direction his chapeau bra had landed. Musket going before him, he proceeded with carefully placed steps and peered into the ever-darkening forest beyond. This could be a trap, but it was worth the risk if it squelched the notion he was indeed mentally disordered.

Ears finely tuned, he crept toward his cap which lay before a scanty shrub.

The bush shook violently. Phillip jerked his musket up then back down as a woman sprang from concealment.

Her skirt snagged, abruptly halting her flight. As her hands battled to extricate the fabric, she lifted her bonneted head, exposing large, fearful eyes and a face which glowed pale in the waning daylight.

Unless the encroaching night was playing tricks on him, this woman was white. Not the midnight skin of a runaway or the smooth olive of a Spaniard, but white. Nearly as white as Phillip.

He settled the butt of his musket at his feet. “Ma’am? What are you doing out here?”

Her struggle grew more desperate until the sound of ripping preceded her tumble. Mostly hidden by palmettos, she scooted backward on the ground.

Still many yards distant, Phillip reached a hand to her, unable to imagine why she might be afraid of him. “I won’t hurt—”

A black man, large as a bear, darted from behind a thick pine to Phillip’s right. His sprint carried him across Phillip’s path and directly toward the woman.

“No! Get away.” Her words came out a garbled croak.

“Halt!” Phillip flipped the weapon back into position and aimed it at the slave’s chest.

Unfazed, he kept moving and would have intercepted the woman except for the stone she hurled. It thudded off his shoulder and stopped him dead in his tracks.

He swiveled to face Phillip, who had shortened the distance between them, his eye never leaving the musket’s sites. “One more step, and before the night's out, I’ll bury you where you stand.”

The man’s shoulders rose and fell with each rapid breath, but his stony face showed no fear. “Then you bettah do it. Otherwise, it’ll be you what's buried. See, I plan to make it to that fort, and losin’ my life to do it is no mattuh to me.”

Phillip’s brother, Dixon, had often said that a man who didn’t value his own life made the most dangerous of enemies. This one wouldn’t live long enough to become that. Phillip leveled his musket’s barrel at the big man’s heart.

In response, he took a single step forward.

“Don’t shoot!” The woman stumbled forward, placing herself between the runaway and the iron-tipped muzzle.

Reflexively, he skipped to the side to maintain his aim on the man. "Step away, ma'am. Don't want you hurt." *What was she thinking?*

She mirrored his movements, keeping herself between them. "*No one* needs to get hurt."

"Move away from him, and let me handle this."

She faced Phillip, her large brown eyes pleading. "Let him go. Please."

"Woman, are you crazy?" The black man voiced Phillip's own thoughts.

She was either insane or suffering from over-exposure.

Weapon still trained on the runaway, Phillip took a quick step forward and flailed at her, trying to grab her by the arm.

She skittered to the side, and he swiped nothing but air.

"Get out of the way," he snapped. Not one of his men would have dared defy his command, yet this woman stood her ground.

She backed further away from him and dangerously close to the black man. "He didn't run a hundred miles just to be shot down defenseless in the woods a day away from the only chance at freedom he'll ever have." Her voice shook, but her rigid back told Phillip she wouldn't give in any time soon.

With his mind concocting a way to move the woman *and* save both their necks, Phillip was only half-listening. "What are you talking about?"

Although shadows fell across her face, Phillip didn't miss the softening of her eyes or the quiver of her lips. Her passion for this slave's freedom furrowed Phillip's brow.

"If you were fighting for your life, wouldn't you want a fair shot at it?" she asked.

Like a Red Stick's arrow, her soft-spoken question pierced him, immobilizing his thoughts to anything beyond one image—his brother's doom-stricken features and the blood-thirsty warriors that swarmed him.

"Yes," he rasped.

Surprise widened her eyes and parted her lips—a lovely image to return to after his disturbing trip to the past.

For one instant, Phillip would have done anything she asked. He lowered his musket and stretched a hand toward her, but before he could even shift his stance, the slave lurched forward.

He encased the woman in his arms, lifting her and covering the lower half of her face with a massive hand. "Hush, now, or you'll call 'em all down on us." Her startled cry preceded the man's swift backward steps. He hurled a steely glare at Phillip. "You ain't seen nothin'. Ain't talked to nobody. You hear, soldier?" The ferocity in his voice chilled Phillip's blood.

One quick twist of the man's hand was all it would take to snap the woman's neck. Berating himself, Phillip released the barrel of his weapon and let it drop to the ground with a soft thud then splayed his hands in front of him. "No need to hurt her. Let her go, and I'll never breathe a word I saw you. You can go right—"

The slave flipped the woman's legs into the air and caught them under his arm in the same instant that he took flight.

Three seconds into Phillip's pursuit, common sense won out, and he came to a quick stop. If he were going into the wilds after an unpredictable giant, he had better have a squad backing him.

Within moments, the only evidence left of the woman's presence was the dread constricting Phillip's chest that no one would believe she'd even been there.

Chapter Two

Long after darkness had consumed them, Milly clung to Isum, as he held her against his solid chest with bone-crushing fierceness. His long legs covered the forest with a speed that could only be born of desperation.

"Isum." She gasped for breath between his pounding strides. "Isum, let me down."

Either he didn't hear, or he refused.

Running into the soldiers had been unexpected and terrifying, yet they were long behind now. Surely, they wouldn't be so daft as to enter these woods after dark.

The fort on Prospect Bluff should be near. Milly was certain of it. Near enough for runaways to slaughter white men then escape to safety.

Isum leapt over something, jolting her so that her teeth rattled. She dug her fingers into his shirt front and pulled. "Please. You're hurting me."

He slowed and loosened his grasp a fraction. After a quick glance behind them, he brought his speed to a walk then seemed to choose his steps with more care.

His chest, slick with perspiration, heaved against her cheek. He muttered incoherently under his stuttered breath. Catching the faint moonlight, the whites of his wide eyes were the only part of his face visible to her.

"What is it? Do you hear—"

He slid a broad hand over her mouth and froze. The pressure of his arms increased as though he were readying to spring.

She perked her ears to danger but heard only the hammering of his heart—until the distinct sound of a rifle being cocked filled the night air. Others echoed it, coming from all sides.

Isum dropped to a crouch, setting Milly on the ground with a thud. Hidden under blinding darkness and thigh-high palmettos, she felt safe for the first time in hours.

He removed his hand and pressed a finger to her lips, then stood and stepped away. His absence chilled, and a shudder ripped through her. She reached for him, but found only air.

"B'fore you take another step, best you say who you is." The distant, male voice had the familiar cadence of a slave, causing tension to fall from Milly's shoulders.

"Name's Isum. A runaway, same as you be." His voice held a calm authority that Milly hadn't known he possessed.

"You come alone?" asked another, closer this time.

A long pause followed. "I got me a wife."

Milly's eyes widened before she dismissed the lie as necessary. Unless she came in under the unquestioning umbrella of his protection, she might not be accepted into the camp.

Her lids drooped. Fatigue flooded her arms and legs. A mix of races, she found few societies to welcome her. At the master's house, the field slaves eyed her with suspicion—as though she might betray whatever secrets they held. The house slaves treated her with either pity or envy, depending on whether she was receiving nightly visits from the master's friends or a new dress in which to serve them liquor and cigars.

Only Isum treated her as an equal.

"Let's go." His sudden presence beside her pulled her out of her uncomfortable reverie. What had she missed?

He hooked his fingers in the pit of her arm and pulled her up, then swallowed her wrist in his grasp. He was moving before she could register which way they'd come and which way they were going.

Like ghouls—five, six, maybe more—armed men materialized all around them. An armed escort to the fort should have set her mind at ease. Instead, her insides quivered. An image of bloodied, white bodies tossed onto the riverbank resurfaced. She tugged her bonnet forward then buried her free hand inside the folds of her dress.

A few minutes into the frenzied march, they slowed at what appeared to be a checkpoint. Feeling the burning, curious gaze of the sentry, Milly turned her head away from him and toward Isum. His grip on her tightened until they passed through, unimpeded. A hundred paces further they cleared another.

The land grew swampy, and, with each step, threatened to suck her bare feet into the mire. Water and muck sloshed up her legs and weighed down her dress. She tripped over it and would have fallen face-first had Isum's grasp not held her firm.

Not slowing his pace, he gathered handfuls of her dress and shoved the slimy fabric into her free hand. Just as she regained her footing, they were lead onto a makeshift bridge spanning a narrow body of water that extended indefinitely into the darkness.

Ahead, the forest made way for a clearing occupied by squatty huts. The escorts led them through the settlement's cold, lifeless center. The only sign of activity lay ahead behind a massive wall that loomed before them. Hushed voices of women and children carried over the top, and light from their fires illuminated a path that ran the along its base.

Instead of taking the path, one of the men pulled aside a thick layer of hanging vines and banged a series of knocks against the door. Only blackness greeted them until a narrow passageway opened from the other side.

A glow emanated from within. She had yet to step foot inside, but already Milly felt at home. She moved to enter, but Isum hesitated.

"What is it?" she whispered.

He turned to her and grasped her chin. "Them soldiers out there? They's comin' for all them what's here. In the fort."

Milly nodded. "I know."

"Do you?" His voice lit with intensity. "I's willin' to fight for my freedom, but you…you gotta be sure this is what you want. Iffin you don't, we keep on south. Find us another place. Some place safe. You gotta be *sure*. 'Cause there ain't no goin' back. There ain't no surrender."

The finality of their journey weighed her down like a yoke dropped around her neck. *There ain't no goin' back.* That, she understood. She'd told herself the same the moment they'd broken free of Crawford County. For the last two weeks, she'd chosen her own steps, in her own glorious time. Going back to slavery was not an option.

There ain't no surrender. Was she willing to die for her freedom?

Isum was. She heard the resolve in his voice, saw it every day in the proud tilt of his chin and in the way he gripped his pistol. He would die hard, but he would die free.

A handful of seconds passed as Milly wavered. She had a choice—enter, or turn around and try another option.

Was this what freedom felt like? If so, she could never give it up. Not now that she'd tasted it.

She wished to God her first real decision as a freed woman wasn't such a grave one. Still, she smiled. "I'll fight beside you. And if need be, I'll die beside you. There's no going back."

Isum's teeth gleamed as a grin broke his features. In one swift move, he slipped a hand around the back of her head and dropped in for a kiss. With moisture from his lips cool against her cheek, she squared her shoulders and stepped into the opening ahead of him.

Milly ran her fingertips along the interior of the short tunnel and was astounded at the thickness of the earthen wall. This was a place she could feel safe.

A man stood on the other side with a torch in his hand. Impatience creased his brow until he caught sight of her. His lips slackened, and he looked to the man who had guided them to the door. "You brought another prisoner?"

Her body went numb.

Their guide turned. "No, we—" His gaze landed on her as well. He grabbed the torch out of the first man's hand and held it near her face.

She withdrew from the scorching heat and bumped into Isum, who immediately stepped in front of her. "You got it wrong. She's runnin' too."

The man's eyes narrowed. "That's for the chief to decide."

Isum growled. "Take it off." He tossed the command over his shoulder.

Obediently, her fingers searched for the knot of ribbon under her chin.

"Decide what?" A voice emerged from the shadows.

Swinging the torch behind him, their guide revealed a lean figure. "Chief Garcon." He drew himself up. "They's brought a white woman."

A throng of men gathered, creating an impenetrable wall around Milly and Isum, whose taut body radiated tension.

Garcon drew close. His ebony skin glistened. Streaks of gray in his full-bodied hair caught the flickering torchlight. "Another prisoner? Where'd you find her?" His voice was tight, his eyes hot.

Milly fumbled with her bonnet ties. "I'm not a pri—"

"I said, she's runnin' *too*." Isum swiveled then yanked the bonnet straight back. The ribbon cut into her neck as he dug his fingers into the mass of braided hair and shoved her headfirst into the circle of light.

A murmur rippled through the crowd.

Milly remained in Isum's grasp, like a helpless pup held by the scruff of her neck, head bent at an uncomfortable angle. Tears blurred her vision as a dozen men scrutinized her. Tuning out their crass comments, she held her breath for the one that counted.

"I know your kind." Chief Garcon's gaze scoured the length of her as though he saw every handprint of every man who'd touched her.

Isum's clutch on her tightened, but to her dismay, he continued to hold her at arm's length. She shuddered.

Garcon rubbed her hair between his fingers then trailed one from her jaw down her throat. Before he reached the collar of her dress, Isum yanked her back against him. Reaching behind her, Milly grabbed onto his shirt determined never to let go.

"I don't give care who you be. No man touches my woman!" Isum spat.

Even in the dim light, Milly could see Garcon's eyes burn like dual coals. Just as quickly, they dimmed and crinkled with a devilish smile. "We could use a man with such fighting spirit." He lifted his voice. "No matter the color of their skin, every runaway is welcome here."

Isum loosened his grip but did not release her until the crowd had dissipated, leaving only Garcon. Even then, Isum kept a possessive hand on her shoulder. The back of her neck warmed comfortingly with his heavy breath.

"Bed anywhere." Garcon made the invitation sound like a command. "Tomorrow, we'll give you a weapon and put you to work." He left, taking the torch with him.

Soon, they were alone in the dark, and quiet settled around them.

With the cold wall to her back, Milly took in the fort for the first time. Except for in the center where a large building blotted the view, campfires dotted the landscape. Around each, sat a group of people. Some conversed quietly, but most seemed to be settling down for the night.

A baby fussed, and a mother sang a soft African tune. The scent of boiling beans filled the air. Beyond the campfires in the unknown distance, the river hummed in its rush toward the bay.

Their immediate vicinity lay barren, as though forgotten of all but the sentries posted along the wall. In the stillness of the night and their newfound safety, Milly allowed herself to consider sleep.

"I'll scrounge up some grub." Isum moved toward the fires.

"Don't get any for me. I'm too tired to eat." She moved down the wall, away from the gate, and lowered herself to the ground. The chilly, hard earth felt as good as any of the master's cots.

Whether Isum joined her or went in search of food, she wasn't aware.

Her last coherent thought was a vision of the soldier—his form, bent and trembling, the dreadful scar slashing his face, his eyes round with alarm for her.

If only he knew, he had feared for the life of a runaway...

***

"I'm telling you, Marcus, she was white. And that mountain of a Negro took off with her to do who knows what." Having moved to an isolated corner of camp, Phillip felt at liberty to speak his mind.

Marcus nodded slowly, eying Phillip with placating, doctorly concern. "It's been a long day. Why don't you get some re—"

"How can I rest when she's out there somewhere, and no one's concerned enough to do a thing about it?" He thrust his arm toward the darkened forest.

Too many defenseless woman and children had died at another fort in the not so distant past. He'd been helpless to save them.

The color of their skin might be darker, but the runaways' merciless cruelty toward whites was as intense as the Red Sticks' had been. Phillip would see to it that, this time, circumstances ended differently. It would have been foolish to follow the cur through the woods, but he had fully expected to receive permission to take some men and give immediate pursuit.

But when he'd returned to do so, Colonel Clinch had arrived on the grisly scene and been too preoccupied questioning Seaman Long, the surviving sailor, to give Phillip his full attention. By the time Clinch addressed Phillip's concerns, daylight was spent.

"Easy, man," Marcus soothed. "Plenty are concerned, but no one can do anything until daybreak. It's black as pitch out there. Even the natives couldn't find a trail."

To Marcus' credit he didn't remind Phillip that Seaman Long had sworn—several times— that he hadn't seen a white woman in weeks and that had been during shore leave in New Orleans. The sailor had looked at Phillip as if he was touched in the head.

Everyone knew there *were* no white women in this part of the world. Most were smart enough to keep to their side of the American border. Even then, they weren't safe from marauding runaways and Seminoles, which was why the army was doing what it was doing—cutting the Negroes off at their stronghold.

Phillip lowered himself to a log and pressed the heels of his hands against his eyes in an attempt to squelch the growing throb. A fire crackled before him, raising steam from his damp boots. "You think I'm crazy, don't you? Seeing things." He dropped his hands and looked Marcus square in the face, daring him to lie.

In the dark, his eyes were as piercing black as his surgeon's coat, but his reply came without hesitation. "Not at all."

"But...?"

Marcus exhaled then picked up a long stick and stirred the glowing embers. "You've experienced a great deal of strain over the last couple of years. More than most men do in a lifetime." He tossed the branch into the center of the flames and faced Phillip. "And considering that, it's understandable that you might truly believe you saw something that wasn't there."

Opening his mouth to deny it, Phillip jolted as instances of the very nature Marcus described flooded back to him. How many times had he heard an Indian war cry only to realize it was an eagle's screech or a crow's cackle? Or heard his dead brother's voice calling to him in a crowd?

He'd woken countless night, positive Adela had been in his room, caressing his face, kissing his scar, loving him despite it. Each time, her scent was as real to him as the heartache at her rejection and at the thought that she lay in another man's arms and caressed *his* face.

Phillip fingered the broad line of puckered flesh running from temple to chin. Was he so hideous that even the enemy held more appeal?

Marcus' firm hand on his shoulder brought him back to the present. "Give it time. Your heart and mind will heal. But as I've said before, being here won't help. You should have stayed in Nashville behind a desk."

Phillip snorted. "This is the only way to make rank, and you know it." No need to mention it was either get away or go insane.

"Rank is worthless without a sound mind." If Marcus thought his boyish grin would lessen the sting, he was wrong.

Narrowing his gaze, Phillip stood. "You're pushing your luck with your opinions tonight."

Marcus' normally contagious laugh fell flat on Phillip's ears. "I suppose I am, but I would be remiss in my duties as a medical officer if I didn't speak the truth. Especially to a friend." The softening of his tone cooled Phillip's irritation.

He crossed his arms. "Very well. Out with it then. Since you're being so free with your thoughts, is there anything else you'd like to add?"

Marcus' smile faded, and as silence descended upon them, Phillip regretted extending the invitation. At last, he spoke. "As your physician, I've done my best to protect your privacy. However, rumor of your...difficulties has reached Command. Should someone come to me for confirmation of the facts, you must understand that I'll be compelled to be forthcoming with my assessment of the situation."

"And what exactly *is* your assessment?"

"As much as it pains me to say, I suspect you are mentally unfit to see action."

Phillip's fingernails dug into his palms.

"You wantin' your dinner, now, suh?"

Phillip's head snapped toward the voice.

Enoch emerged from the darkness, and Phillip's heart slowed. Luckily, only the boy had overheard the doctor's degrading words.

"I'll come when I'm through here." His stomach lurched at the thought of army grub, but a man couldn't fight without food in his belly. If it wasn't for Enoch, Phillip likely would never remember to eat.

"Already got it, suh. Cook said I's to bring it to you and not come back 'til mornin'. I tol' him you's busy, an that perfect-warmed food would jes go cold. That's what I tol' him, suh, but he got wax fillin' up them big ears a his. Now there it sits, goin' cold jes like I say it would do. What you got here what's more important than eatin' that grub I brought ya? Mastuh, suh." He tacked on the last, as if in atonement for his impertinent remarks.

Phillip turned to him. "That's no way to speak to your master, young man. I've told you to watch your tongue. Don't make me take drastic measures."

Even in the dim light, Phillip noted the shadow of anger that flashed across Enoch's face just before he retreated into the dark without permission.

"That boy loves you. You shouldn't be so harsh with him."

Phillip drew a deep, steadying breath. "I know." He hadn't meant to be harsh, but just now, he didn't have the mental powers to deal with Enoch's moodiness. Another issue clogged his thinking.

Marcus' judgment had always been rock solid, but never before had it struck such a personal chord. "You think me unable to command my troops?" He spoke so low, he was surprised when Marcus answered.

"No, I said I *suspected* you're not fit to fight. Period." His friend held his gaze, his face firm but his eyes gentle.

Phillip struggled for words. Incapable of fighting? Commanding, maybe. But he could always fight. He lived for it. There was nothing else left for him but the army. Shuffling paperwork until retirement would be almost as unbearable as the memory of Adela—learning she was alive, then losing her all over again.

"Fortunately for you," Marcus continued in a lighter tone, "in time of need, the army doesn't remove officers based solely on a surgeon's inklings. So I suggest you keep your nose clean and not push this business with the white woman. No need to confirm suspicions or give Major Collins fuel to flame his personal mission to filch your promotion."

Phillip's lip curled at the mention of Major Jameson Collins. He hated to admit Marcus was right on any level regarding this matter, but, swallowing his pride, he decided to take his friend's advice.

From here on, the captured white woman was Colonel Clinch's responsibility.

Phillip's job was to keep his head screwed firmly in place. If he could.

***

Fingers poised on the tip of the iron latch, True Seeker eased it down and slightly in. He expelled a pent-up breath as the stranger's out-kitchen door opened silently before him. The smell of the family's last meal hung in the air—roasted rabbit, perhaps?

His moccasins carried him over the threshold, along the west wall, and around the barrel of cornmeal. The first time he'd crept through this white man's kitchen at night, the barrel had caught his foot, then his sense of smell. Inhaling its familiar, earthy scent, he had lifted the wooden lid then let the grain run through his fingers, savoring the feel.

As desperation turned his hunger pangs to nausea, he skirted the barrel and slid his palm over the rutted slab of sideboard. His hand connected with the pie safe as the aroma of fresh baked cornbread beckoned memories of his aunt's fire.

His mouth watered, his head spun. He closed his eyes and steadied himself against the counter until the dizziness passed.

He fumbled with the box, cringing at the noise he created. At last, the pone crackled beneath his grasp. He tore it in two and slipped half into the deerskin pouch hanging from a thong at his waist. It would hardly be missed by this thriving family, but could do much good for a small, hungry boy, such as Tadpole.

True Seeker set the other half back into the safe then hesitated for an instant before snatching it back up. His conscience pricked like a bed of pine needles, but there was no remedy for it.

The responsibility to provide for his family weighed upon him, smothered him. Hunger was a cruel task master, and one that did not make concessions for a boy untrained and unproven.

If the traps and snares he had laid along the game trail had worked, he might be skinning a rabbit instead of pilfering food. But, yet again, they hadn't. Had he not disguised the snares properly? Perhaps he had chosen abandoned trails? If only he had someone to ask—an uncle, a father, a grandfather, anyone.

He had tried to craft a bow as he remembered seeing Uncle do, but the project had been a disaster. What he lacked in crafting a bow, he more than made up for in the use of one. If he could get a good bow into his hand, his family might have half a shot at surviving.

Part way back to the door, a gleam caught his eye and he stopped. A shiny object lay on the table.

It had never been there before.

He treaded toward it, captivated by the golden orb. Drawing near, he detected a quiet ticking.

He had seen something similar once before dangling from the shirt front of Benjamin Hawkins, the Indian Agent.

It was a watch for a man's pocket—a way to track time, from longer periods down to every breath a man takes. Why someone would rather watch three miniscule, rotating sticks instead of the sun was a concept that wrinkled True Seeker's brow. But it was easy to see why a man would carry one of these beauties close to his heart.

He slanted his ear toward it and smiled. After a glance at the doorway, he pinched the chain between his fingers and lifted until it dangled before his eyes. It spun and swayed, catching and releasing the glow of the embers.

Its smooth surface fit perfectly inside his grasp. He wrapped his fingers around it and stroked the silky casing.

A faint clunking sound carried from the rancher's house some thirty paces beyond where he stood. True Seeker's fists clenched along with his stomach. The crickets ceased their tune, and True Seeker's heart quickened.

Utter silence followed the slightest rasp of feet against dirt. The rasps were near, each step advanced at a cautious, methodical pace.

He rushed to the darkest corner of the room and crouched behind a chair—hardly adequate cover for a boy on the brink of manhood. The brass buttons on the outside of his leggings scraped the ground. He froze to silence them. Why hadn't he run when he'd had the chance?

He grasped the deer-antler handle of his sheathed blade then forced his hand to release it. Harming a white man was not an option. Theft alone was enough to hang an Indian without question. He could only hope no one would quibble over pone bread taken for a hungry child.

He held his breath, straining to recapture the sounds of footfalls, when the form of a woman filled the doorway. Wavy hair hung across her shoulders in the same bell shape as her skirt. Arms raised, elbows extended, she peered down the barrel of a long gun. With her single step inside, the soles of her shoes clacked against the wooden floor.

Not in nightclothes. She had been waiting for him.

Careless! His mind scrambled for a way to extract himself from this mire he had created. *She is just a woman.*

If a woman was the first one to come for him, did that mean there were no men about? Hope colored his thoughts and strengthened his resolve to return to his aunt alive.

"I know you're in here." Her creamy voice broke the stillness. "And the only way out is past this musket." Her tone rang cold, her words deliberate and uncompromising.

A chill skittered down True Seeker's spine.

Not allowing himself to think it through, he slammed the chair onto its side while flinging himself the opposite direction.

A blast punctuated his landing. Splinters from the chair peppered his thigh.

Unharmed, he shot to his feet and careened into the woman as he would an opponent in a game of Indian ball-play.

His momentum carried her out the door before him. She hit the dirt with a grunt.

He leapt over her sprawled form and kept moving, her shriek of anger in hot pursuit.

With any luck, she wasn't hurt and would choose to put this unpleasant experience behind her, but as True Seeker's feet flew across the forest floor toward the old barn, he reminded himself that in *his* life, there seemed to be no such thing as luck.

Only hardship—hardship by the barrelful.

When his legs were spent and his lungs' demand could not be ignored, True Seeker eased his pace then stopped altogether. His chest heaved as he dragged in air. A brisk wind chilled the sweat that coated his body and soaked through both his trade shirt and his long shirt.

When he grasped the sleeve of his outer garment to remove it, a heavy object dropped to the ground near his feet. The distinct rattle of a chain accompanied it.

The sensation of the watch pressing into his palm was fresh. Too fresh.

Had he truly run off with it? It wasn't possible, yet there it lay nestled among dead leaves, its once alluring gleam now a mocking glare.

A shiver rocked his shoulders.

He couldn't tear his gaze from the watch. How would he cover this heinous trespass? What would Uncle do? And Father? True Seeker shook his head. They would never have found themselves in such a state. Both had been honest and worthy of their callings as warriors and providers. In the end—along with most of their able-bodied clansmen—both had made the ultimate sacrifice for their people and their ancient ways.

True Seeker's nose burned with impending tears. He sniffed and straightened his backbone. Tears had no place in a man's life.

Bending, he plucked the watch from the ground and dropped it into his pouch, intent on finding a way to return it without being discovered.

He broke into a trot, intent on one other thing, as well. With or without a ceremony, from this moment forward, he would behave as a man—with bravery and dignity no matter the circumstances.

No matter the consequences.

Chapter Three

A gentle shake to her shoulder urged Milly from a deep sleep. The sun pierced her eyelids.

"Wake up, girl, or you's gonna miss breakfast."

Cracking open her eyes, Milly squinted into the brilliance and toward the source of the voice. A large woman bent over her. "There's them beautiful brown eyes. I wondered what color they be. And you just as lovely as they say. Um hm. And just as pasty. Like a coffee bean that's in the sun too long." Her belly shook with her own humor.

Milly tried to place her surroundings but failed. "Who said I was white?" Her voice croaked with the first question that came to mind.

The woman clucked her tongue. "Speak white, too. And burnin' to a crisp before my very eyes. Now get that man offa you and let me put some food in your scrawny self."

Still chattering, the woman lumbered off. "He's welcome to come. He *bettah* eat, what with the work my husband's got cut out for him." The woman's jolly laughter faded as she went, the edges of her long skirt dragging the dirt.

Milly's gaze skittered across her dusty surroundings. *The fort.*

She moved to stand but Isum's long arm was slung across her. Had he slept beside her the whole night? "Get off me." She elbowed him in the chest.

He grunted and rolled away, but before she could sit up, he shot to his knees, knocking her in the back of the head with his arm.

She rubbed the spot and twisted to face him.

Eyes alert and searching, he gripped the handle of the pistol at his waist.

"It's just me," she snapped, too aggravated to pity his raw nerves. She glared at him. "What were you thinking, bedding next to me? I haven't said I'd jump the broom with you." The field slaves might all sleep in a pile on the dirt floors of their shoddy cabins, but Milly, being a ladies maid and a favorite, had always been allowed a little room of her own just off the main house. A room complete with a cot.

His nostrils swelled as he got to his feet and jammed the pistol back into his belt. "Well, miss high and mighty, I was needin' sleep, and you was needin' watchin.' And the best way to do both was from right here next to you." He snatched her to her feet.

Feeling the full weight of his reprimand, she winced and massaged the place on her arm where his fingers left their impression. She kept her eyes chest-level. "We're safe now. I don't need watching." Her voice lacked conviction.

Isum exhaled slowly then straightened her sleeve—the closest he would come to an apology. "Not the way them men was eyein' you like you was a slab of meat." He reached for the bonnet hanging behind her and settled it around her face. "You gonna burn." Softness replaced the harsh edge in his voice. After he awkwardly retied her ribbon, he lifted her chin forcing her gaze upward.

"Don't you look down for no man no more. Not even me. We's free. *Free*." His eyes burned with passion. "Whether we live one more day or a thousand, we gonna spend 'em with our heads held high. Like the mastah done when he walk the rows like he was king a' Georgia. We our own mastahs now, and we gonna act like it. You hear?"

How did a woman go about being her own master? Her half-smile shook at the corners, as she patted his chest. "I hear you, Isum."

At her touch, his body tensed. Almost imperceptibly, he leaned closer, his eyes darkening. His chest rose and fell in uncharacteristically large breaths, and Milly wondered if he was aware of the transparency of his thoughts. She had witnessed that smolder in many men, but she had never seen it in him. His strong features wore it well.

Her gaze fell to her hand as it rested against the curve of his well-defined chest. Only a moment elapsed, but in her heart, a thousand memories skittered past. They'd known each other for years, leaned on each other, cried and dreamed together. It seemed natural that they start a new future together.

The sudden quiet of the fort drew her attention. Twenty yards away, groups of people—mostly women and children—gathered and stared. It took a moment for it to register that they were staring at her and Isum. Or maybe just her?

The women wore clean, well-stitched linen clothes—better than any slave she'd ever seen. The children wore only their skin.

Milly scanned the gawking crowd then turned to Isum. "A woman was here. Asked me—us—to breakfast." Her stomach grumbled at the mention of food.

Isum bent to retrieve his floppy hat. "Sound good to me."

"I didn't catch her name." Milly squinted into the mass of people.

A boy of no more than five broke through and trotted fearlessly toward them. His hair stood out from his head like sheep's wool, and he wore no trousers. Dusty knees protruded from a long, sleeveless shirt that hung just below his hips. Stopping beside her, he tucked his pudgy hand into Milly's.

For an instant, she was captivated by their clasped hands—hers paling next to his rich tones. He turned up large brown eyes. A massive smile revealed crooked teeth.

Warmth inflated Milly's heart.

"Mama sez come eat." He took off at a jog, towing her behind him.

The recognizable tempo of Isum's lengthy stride followed.

The crowd parted, a friendly expression on most every face they passed. Milly nodded a greeting to several, but the boy was determined and would not be slowed.

They approached the building Milly had noted the night before. As they skirted its planked, octagonal sides, she glanced through an open door. Her eyes rounded at the barrels stacked floor to ceiling. Beside them sat a pyramid of iron balls. She had never seen explosives before, but these were just as she always imagined they might look.

She slowed to see if the other walls were equally well lined, but the boy pulled harder. "Mama sez t' hurry."

Isum came alongside, his eyes alight with wonder. "You see that? Behind them walls and with that firepower, ain't no white soldiers ever gonna get in here."

Seen in daylight, the towering earthen walls were mighty impressive. Their breadth would give any cannon a run for its powder. Milly's smile came easy. "I'd say we're sitting pretty."

He slammed his fist into his palm. "We'll lick 'em or wear 'em out. Either one works for me."

The boy released Milly's hand and dashed ahead to disappear inside a long rectangular building planted in the center of the fort.

Moments later, the woman who had woken Milly, emerged, hands on her ample hips. "There you is," she called. Knotted in the front, a bright yellow scarf hid most of her graying hair and accented the beaming smile stretched across her face. "Come on now, and eat before there ain't none to be had."

Waving them over to her, she swallowed Milly in a warm embrace. "You's all skin and bones, child. Stick around Mama Tatty," she said, pulling away and slapping her chest, "and we'll see if she can't give your husband something more to grab onto." A great bellow of laughter followed.

Milly's hand flew to the base of her throat. "Oh, you should know. We—"

Isum's blaring voice drowned her out. "Mama Tatty, you won't never find a man more grateful. We been on the trail eleven days. Been too long since we ate proper."

They were safe now. It made no sense to continue the charade. The glare Milly gave him ranked as one of her finest, but it was wasted since he wouldn't look at her.

Mama Tatty hurried them into the dark building.

Milly appreciated the shadows that masked the heat on her cheeks, but she couldn't allow the truth to be equally concealed.

"If there's one thing we got plenty of 'round here, it's food. That and bullets. A hundred for every white man and Indian out there." Mama Tatty waved her hand toward an unspecified point beyond the enclosure.

A cluster of children squatted on the floor, squabbling over a game of some sort.

"This ain't no place for dice. Right smack in the middle of the room. Go find your mommas." She flapped her arms and the children scattered, giggling and squealing.

As Milly's eyes adjusted to the dim light, the forms of women took shape. Some tended children. Some prepared food at a maze of tables. Others tore fabric into strips, but all of them were doing exactly what they *wanted* to do. And if the buzz of chatter was any indication, they were happy doing it.

The hum subsided as the room became aware of Isum and Milly's arrival. Mama Tatty cut a path through the center. "What's the mattah? Never seen a couple a runaways?"

Milly pushed the bonnet off her head and followed Mama Tatty's sashaying backside. She let out a pent-up breath as the volume slowly reached the earlier level.

With a long wooden spoon, Mama Tatty pointed toward an empty table in the corner. "Put yourself there."

Once seated, Milly noticed Isum still standing in the doorway twisting his hat in his hands. Fighting a smile, she angled her back toward him. Wouldn't hurt him to stand there a bit longer looking foolish and out of place.

Mama Tatty placed a bowl of steaming grits beneath Milly's nose and was gone before Milly could express her thanks. Closing her eyes, she inhaled. The scent took her back to Master Landcastle's kitchen, but for the first time since they'd run, she didn't doubt her decision to leave. This was where she belonged.

Thank you, Jesus, for this place of refuge.

"You won't get it in your belly through your nose." A feminine voice accompanied the wobble of the bench.

Milly opened her eyes to the welcoming smile of a young woman joining her at the table.

"My name's Rosie," she said, her words nearly drowned in the noisy building. "I heard 'bout you before bed and could hardly sleep for wantin' to meet ya."

Her smile stretched the width of her thin face. Thick lashes curled above soft, round eyes. "I'm Milly. Thank you for sitting with me."

Rosie's smile broadened. "Eat up. It'll be cold in a heartbeat."

Taking the wooden-handled spoon, Milly dug in. The grainy mush settled into her stomach with satisfying warmth.

Rosie giggled. "As big as he is, your husband's scared stiff of a gaggle of women."

Not looking back at him, Milly shook her head. "He's not my husband."

"But Garcon said—"

"Isum was afraid for me. Thought I'd have a better chance in here as his wife." The woman's eyes bulged, and Milly was glad to set things straight. "But you've all been so kind, I don't see the need to go on letting you believe—"

"You bettah!"

Milly stared at her. "I better what?"

"Garcon, he don't take kindly to bein' lied to. You don't want to get on his bad side. It ain't pretty. Best keep that bit o' truth under your bonnet." Her head moved up and down in long, slow lines. "This here's the best place you and me could be. Chief Garcon, he'd die for any one of us, but his enemies…?" Rosie swallowed hard then leaned in until her breath brushed Milly's cheek. "They got themselves a white man. A prisoner. They gonna kill 'im."

Milly pulled back so quickly, Rosie startled.

"I saw the others. What was done to them."

"You mean the ones killed in the swamp?"

Milly nodded.

Rosie dropped her gaze to the slender fingers twined in her lap. "That was killin' on the run. This'll be for show. To prove to them fancy officers we mean business."

Breakfast took a sick turn in Milly's stomach. "When?"

The woman gave a small shrug.

A tap on Milly's arm drew her attention away from Rosie's haunted gaze. Beside her stood their young escort. "Hello, little gentleman," Milly said, grateful for the distraction.

The boy presented her with his crooked-toothed grin, and Milly couldn't resist tugging him onto her lap and giving him a squeeze. "I owe you a hug for guiding me to my breakfast."

His body molded against her for just an instant before he pulled back and took her cheeks between his sweaty palms.

"Mama sez you's family," he whispered, his eyes large and earnest. Accepting.

Her own prickled with tears, which she hastily blinked away. "Then I think it's best we know each other's names. Don't you?"

His little head bobbed. "Mama calls me Joshua, but everybody else, they calls me Little G."

Rosie cleared her throat. "They call him that 'cause of his daddy."

Milly wondered at the trepidation in Rosie's voice, but decided it best not to question her at the moment. "It's a pleasure to make your acquaintance Little G." Milly used her most dignified tone.

Shoulders hitched up to his ears, Little G covered a grin with his hands.

"My name is Milly. And that is—" She turned to point at Isum, but stopped. Garcon stood just inside, watching them, his black eyes pinned upon her.

"Papa!" Little G was in the chief's arms before Milly had time to make the familial connection.

Garcon's pitted face beamed, as if he'd just been handed unconditional freedom. Noses pressed together, quiet words passed between father and son.

Milly would have given her breakfast to hear them.

She had a vague memory of her mother's vivid blue eyes gazing upon her with adoration. If she focused hard enough, she could still hear her mother's rich southern reiterating that Milly was the most special little girl in the whole of Chatham county. No, the whole of Georgia. No, the *world*.

Every day ended with the same affirmation, in a bed as wide and soft as a cloud and with her mother's pearly skin glowing in the light from the candle kept burning on the bedside stand.

She could still feel her mother's gentle hand stroking her hair, not once recoiling from its rough texture. Milly never gave a thought to her hair and the fact that it was so similar to that of the girl who emptied the chamber pot. Not, that is, until mother's "George, dear" grabbed a handful of it and dragged her out of the house and into the back of a wagon, the word "nigger" prominent on his tongue.

Never allowed to call him "father," Milly had always known George disliked her, but his deep hatred had taken her by such surprise, it wasn't until weeks later that it sank in he had meant that horrible word for her.

Her gaze moved beyond Garcon to Isum and back to the day he had arrived at Master Landcastle's big house. Torn from his family, he had been as scared and lonely as she had been at his age, five years earlier.

She had showered him with all the care she wished for, yet never received. From that first day, he had depended on her, shadowed her. He shadowed her still, albeit for a far different reason.

In recent years, he had taken over the role of protector, but had never learned to reciprocate the gentleness she displayed toward him.

She didn't doubt his dedication to her, but still, there lived inside her a longing she could not stifle—a hunger for physical touch, gentle and selfless—one not concerned with taking, possessing, or even protecting. Milly would have been content with a single squeeze of her hand, if she knew the person giving it had only love toward her in mind. Even slavery wouldn't be so bad if she had unconditional love to see her through it.

Garcon set his son on the ground then took the child's hand. The chief's eyes flashed to Milly for one hard moment before the two left the building, Isum in their wake.

Dread settled in the pit of her stomach as Rosie's words came to mind. *You don't want to get on his bad side. It ain't pretty.* "He seems angry with me. Did I do something wrong?" Milly whispered.

Rosie arched one brow. "You never know what'll rile that man," she said, in an equally low tone. She collected Milly's dish and stood." I s'pect he's takin' your *husband* to wherever it is he's gonna work. Come on. I'll show you where you'll bed down."

Milly followed Rosie to a side table where she deposited the bowl before moving into the already scorching sun. Four steps later, they entered another door of the same long building. Countless pallets, a few still occupied by little ones, lined the floor in neat rows.

"This here's where the women and children sleep. You's next to me. Over there." Rosie indicated toward the back of the room. "Heartless of him havin' you sleep on the hard ground last night without so much as a blanket. We ain't animals, and we ain't chattel. There's no call to sleep like it. If I'd known where you was, I woulda come got you."

Moved by her kindness, Milly reached to lay a hand on Rosie's arm, but froze when Rosie pulled away, her eyes extinguishing their warmth.

Not everyone, it seemed, longed for touch the way Milly did. She withdrew her hand. "Thank you, but I slept too hard to care. Where do the men bed down?"

The sparkle returned to Rosie's eyes as she slanted them toward Milly. "At their posts. Why? You worried about missin' that man of yours?"

"I've always been concerned about Isum." And she always would be, whether they jumped the broom or not.

She spotted him across the compound coming out of the magazine with a musket slung over his shoulder. He strode the opposite direction with confident, purposeful steps. Only freedom could stretch a man's backbone with such speed.

"Mmm, that's a fine piece of work." Rosie's dreamy-eyed gaze locked on Isum's retreating form. "I'm right glad he's not spoken for." She winked at Milly. "And that I'm the only woman who knows."

Rosie was right. Isum cut a fine figure, and in every respect, he was free. What she didn't know was whether she cared that he stayed that way.

***

The scratch of lead against paper replaced the hush in the tent as Phillip feverishly sketched. Last night's dreams had been filled with the face of the woman in the forest. An hour after he woke, her image remained burned into his mind. His fingers would itch until they transferred her likeness to paper.

He couldn't recall all of her features—just her broad mouth and deep, fear-filled eyes. The nose he fabricated from his imagination. The chin, he sketched small and round and the jaw, well defined. He held the drawing at arm's length and tipped his head to the side.

"This place shore is the muddiest I ever seen." Enoch sat cross-legged in the dirt at the foot of Phillip's pallet. Buffing rag in hand, he bent over Phillip's boot and scraped dirt off the sole with his fingernail. "But don't you worry, suh. I'll get 'em spit-shiny clean."

Phillip smiled at Enoch's attention to detail. "Never mind that. Have you had your breakfast?"

Enoch flipped the boot over. "No, suh. Why you askin' me that, suh? I waitin' for you. You know I always wait for you."

"Best not. Make sure you find the time to grab a bite whenever you can. It's promising to be a hectic day."

Enoch polished faster, his long fingers moving expertly over the leather.

Besides the old barn, Enoch was the only Bailey property to survive the Creek War. Phillip guessed the boy's age to be about thirteen. Just coming into manhood, he outgrew his clothes quicker than Phillip could have them made. Since Enoch was the closest thing to family that Phillip had, he didn't mind keeping the boy in tailored clothes. He had, after all, lost his entire family, just as Phillip. No one would ever catch him admitting to it, but he, as he had with Saul, felt a kinship with his slave.

Saul had belonged to Benjamin Tucker, whose bones now rotted in the mass grave outside Fort Mims' old perimeter. Phillip owed more than his life to Saul's quick wit and muscled arms.

Returning his attention to the sketch, Phillip decided he wasn't satisfied with the woman's mouth. He drew a bold line beneath the lower lip, thickening it.

"Find another enchanting butterfly?" Collins' voice grated against Phillip's ear like a dull razor against a whiskered chin.

"I draw birds, not butterflies," Phillip mumbled, aggravated with himself for deigning his tent-mate's taunt with a reply.

"And beautiful women." Collins spoke directly above Phillip's shoulder.

He snapped the journal shut and dropped it into his satchel. "My jacket, Enoch."

"Yes, suh. Right away, but I ain't had time to brush it. You need me to brush it later, you just say the word." Enoch set aside the boots, retrieved the jacket, and held it open for Phillip to slip into.

Collins picked dust off his own jacket then groomed his blond hair forward into an upturned tuft at the center of his forehead. "The mysterious white woman, I presume?"

Phillip brushed aside Enoch's hands and began shoving gilt buttons through their holes. Collins didn't deserve the breath Phillip would expend in even the smallest of conversation.

"The injuns are out again lookin' for tracks," Enoch chirped then quickly snapped his jaw shut at the stinging glance Phillip sent his direction.

"You don't miss anything, boy." Collins chuckled and bent to fasten his half-gaiters. "Have you noticed how your master pines for the lady? He thinks a fine specimen such as her might actually be interested in his ugly mug."

Phillip's scar twitched as he considered the consequences of hurling his fist into Collins' perfect features.

Eyes bugging, Enoch backed up several steps.

"*One a these day, Mistuh Phillip, your anger'll be the end a you*." Saul's voice pinged off the walls of Phillip's mind. "*You gotta let that beast go*."

"Shame he won't be around long enough to find out," Collins continued. "Word has it the good doctor plans to submit a report about our venerable Major Bailey, and it won't bode well for that promotion he's aiming to get." He straightened and tipped his head as though trying to recall a detail. "Something about an impending mental collapse..."

Phillip's hands stilled on the last button. The tent shuddered as Enoch skittered through its opening. The bedding at Phillip's feet blurred as he sucked air in and out of his nose to the time of his quickening heart.

"Ah. You know about this?" Collins shrugged. "I suppose half the camp does."

Phillip wrenched the blade at his waist free from its sheath. He pivoted on the ball of his foot and whipped up behind Collins. Before the man had a chance to react, Phillip possessed a handful of his oiled hair. Throat exposed, arms flailing to the sides, and eyes rolling in fear, Collins had never looked more handsome.

With his knife digging into Collins' hairline, Phillip's hand trembled with the need to slice deep and long. "How about we throw you into a mess of bloodthirsty Red Sticks and see how *your* sanity holds up?"

The tent flap lifted, revealing the Indian Phillip had nearly blown a hole through yesterday. The warrior froze and lifted an eyebrow.

In the distraction, Collins managed to twist away, leaving strands of hair in Phillip's grasp. His face flaming red, the man skipped backward and tripped over Phillip's pallet. The tent canvas impeded his fall but not his wide-eyed fright. He swiped at the nick on his forehead then stared at the blood on his fingertips. "You're as wild as the savages!"

Phillip smirked at the irony of being compared to those he loathed.

"You *are* insane. Would've been better off dying at Mim's place." He flicked a disdainful glance at the warrior filling the entrance to the tent. "Both of you."

Phillip's heart stilled for two beats as his eyes shot to the warrior. This man had attacked the fort?

The Indian's unwavering, black-eyed gaze revealed nothing.

"What? You didn't know Totka, our esteemed Red Stick and comrade in arms, has your family's blood on his hands?" With a smug expression, Collins collected his chapeau bra off the ground and settled it into place. "Well, then, I'll leave the two of you to work it out."

Ears ringing, Phillip barely heard Collins' words as he whipped his coatee off his pallet and strode from the tent.

The warrior took a step inside and let the flap fall back in place. His paisley turban pressed against the canvas top. With a broad torso stretching the fabric of his blue frock and an assortment of weapons dangling from his shoulders and waist, the sight of him would send chills down the spine of any settler. And surely had—right before he'd slaughtered them.

Phillip flexed his fingers around the knife handle still within his clammy grip. “You’re not welcome here. In my tent. In this camp.”

His gaze fell on the small Bible resting atop Phillip’s pallet. “We are brothers of the same Father God.”

Phillip’s chuckle came out as dry as Fort Mim’s fire-baked well. “I sincerely doubt that.”

Seemingly undaunted, Totka drew an imaginary chord from his chest toward Phillip. “Pen has been put to paper. There is peace between our peoples.”

If he wanted reconciliation or forgiveness, he could forget it. “Enough! Why did you come?”

“We share an enemy. The blacks and Seminole muddy our treaty with the White Father. ”

Phillip blinked and shook his head. “Why are you *here*? What do you need from me?”

From a small buckskin pouch at his waist, Totka withdrew a swatch of fabric and extended it toward Phillip. “From your woman’s dress.”

The pale brown muslin covered Phillip’s palm. He enclosed the swatch in his fist, a feeling of vindication coming over him. “Did you find anything else?”

“Two small feet come from the north. They disappear where cloth was found.” Totka nodded toward Phillip’s hand.

“Of course they disappeared. She was *carried*.” He immediately regretted his snippy remark. So far, this man was the only one who could substantiate Phillip’s story. He slipped his knife back into its sheath. “Anything else?”

“All footmarks lead to Negro Fort.”

Phillip had guessed as much, although he had hoped to be proven wrong. His mind flipped back to the sketch. He pitied the beautiful woman and prayed she would last until they broke through and subdued the fort. There was annoyingly little else he could do about it until then.

A long, eerie shriek permeated the tent’s canvas. Totka cocked his ear toward the sound then moved outside. A single column of smoke rose from the bowels of the fortification. “God help him, a man burns,” Totka said confirming Phillip’s own assessment.

Skin crawling, Phillip pitied the soul producing such a sound. The fires of Fort Mims had produced cries equal to the one he heard now. Only then, it had been multiplied by the dozens.

Without another glance Phillip's direction, Totka moved with purposeful steps toward the Creek camp.

Phillip fingered the coarse homespun, unable to reconcile his memories of the bloody Red Sticks to the man walking away from him, a hitch in his step setting his gate slightly off-balance.

A vague recollection tugged at the back of his mind. What was it Lillian had said?

Three months after the war had ended, Phillip had learned of the McGirth's survival. Filled with new hope, he'd returned for the only woman he'd ever truly loved. There had been others—many others—but it wasn't until Adela had been taken away from him did Phillip realize what a treasure she was.

When she had spotted him striding across her yard, she had wept tears of joy, but before the day ended, she had shattered his newfound dreams.

Adela's younger sister, Lillian, had filled Phillip's ears with details that Adela had withheld. Details of their year living as slaves in the Red Stick camp, of the frenzied flight from Jackson's encroaching army, of the winter starving in the frigid wilderness. And then the final twist, the one that still confused and tormented him—Lillian told of the Red Stick that had stolen Adela's heart.

The *crippled* Red Stick.

Lillian had said he promised to return and when he did, he would marry Adela and take her back to live with his people. The thought had horrified Phillip, but he refused to think of her as Lillian did—as a traitor.

Totka's form disappeared behind one of the last tents in the American camp. Could he be the one Adela had been waiting for?

Phillip shook the idea from his head.

Many Red Sticks had survived the massacre, but not without their wounds, surely. Totka could be one of a dozen warriors left permanently impaired from the battle.

Besides, if Totka had won Adela's heart, he wouldn't be so quick to leave her for volunteer service in a distant land. Phillip wouldn't. Could any man?

Then another thought struck him, one he could not so easily dismiss.

A group of Creek women had traveled with their men to cook for them and see to their wounds. They camped not a half mile from where Phillip stood. If Totka was the crippled Red Stick Lillian spoke of, Adela might have come to care for him, along with the other warriors' wives. And if she was the same caring woman he remembered her to be, she would have come.

Half a mile. Could she be that close?

Chapter Four

"You have the best stone-casting arm in the village." Tadpole dashed ahead, swinging the squirrel by one hairless leg. "When Grandmother Mahila sees, she will say, 'Our seeker finds yet another way'." He hurled an imaginary stone into the treetops.

True Seeker grinned as his cousin, with stick-thin legs, scaled an exposed tree root as though it were a mountain. At the top, he faced True Seeker who followed at a more moderate pace. Tadpole puffed out his scrawny chest, fists on his hips. The naked rodent dangled the length of his leg, its nose bumping the ground. "I am a man, as tall as a tree. As tall as you."

"One day, yes. This morning, you rival the shrubs."

The boy stood on tiptoe to reach the strand of beads tied into the hair near True Seeker's ear. "Why do we not live in the village?" He stuck his tongue out the side of his mouth and grunted with effort as he jumped.

True Seeker scowled, then picked the boy up and propped him on one hip.

Tugging at the beads, he whooped in victory then pawed the node on the bridge of True Seeker's nose. The child was the only one allowed to draw attention to it and get away without a scolding. "You do not respond."

True Seeker poked him in the belly. "It is always the same question."

"But you never answer." He squirmed free then entwined his chubby fingers in the decorative, frayed edge at the bottom of True Seeker's long shirt. "Why do we not live in the village? When shall we return?"

"Ask your mother."

"I do."

"And what does she say?" Although he doubted Tadpole would notice, True Seeker worked to keep a disinterested tone. "What reason does Willow Woman give?"

When the boy did not respond, True Seeker glanced down at him.

Color tinged Tadpole's ears. He scrunched his lips and picked at the squirrel's protruding teeth.

"Well?"

"She holds me. And kisses me." With his forefinger, he jabbed at his cheek.

True Seeker suppressed a grin. "As all good mothers do."

He heaved a sigh. "I tire of sleeping under the stars. I miss my bearskin." His plaintive tone struck a chord deep within True Seeker.

He came to a halt and squatted before his cousin, noting how his moccasins strained at his growing feet. There would be no making replacements any time soon. Not while he followed Willow on her endless, bewildering quest. "I do not know why your mother left the village, nor why we travel south. And I do not know when we will return." *If ever.*

Tadpole studied the ground, his black lashes moistening.

True Seeker expelled a burdened breath. If he did not understand what prompted Willow's journey into the treacherous white man's world, how would a boy of four winters? "If it makes you feel better, I also long for my bearskin."

Tadpole blinked and swallowed then raised dry eyes.

Pride filled True Seeker's chest. "You will be a formidable warrior someday."

"And you are a mighty hunter." Tadpole raised the skinned animal and flashed a smile.

True Seeker laughed, relief filling him at this morning's small success. "I try." He ruffled the boy's hair then resumed the jaunt back to the barn and the two women under his care.

"Did Mother make you come with us on this journey?"

"You are my clan and my responsibility. That alone compels me."

"You lie," Tadpole said, his tone light and matter-of-fact. "It is love that compels you. Just as it does Grandmother Mahila."

Unable to refute the child's keen insight, he said nothing.

Only love could compel him to follow Willow on a trail that led to the source of their misery. And only love could lift an old woman from her pallet and into the woods where she would surely die. His great-grandmother's bond to Willow Woman, her granddaughter, was stronger than any ties the woman had to their village. Willow knew this just as well as she knew that a journey into the wilderness without adequate provisions would kill the old woman. Might kill them all.

And yet, Willow had rolled up her blanket, filled her pouch with the last of the parched corn, taken her firstborn's hand, and left—all without any indication of where she was going or if she knew the way.

As True Seeker and Mahila had hurried to catch up, whispers floated through the village.

Willow has gone mad.

The youngest took the mother's sanity with him to the grave.

Old Mahila follows? It is the last we will see of her. A great loss.

True Seeker is a boy of much honor. He will fetch her back.

Their praise turned out to be nothing but meaningless words, for a full moon later, he had been unable to turn Willow's feet. A force greater than reason, greater than love for Mahila, kept Willow's face pointed south.

Agitation quickened True Seeker's heartbeat as well as his steps. He should be preparing for the rites of manhood, along with the other braves his age. How long would Willow continue in this way? Did she seek death? Surely not with her child in tow, but there was no other explanation.

He dug a rock from the dirt and, still moving forward, hurled it into a tree. A flock of birds took flight, and Tadpole squealed with delight.

A sad smile tugged at True Seeker's cheeks. Despite his aunt's seeming insanity, he would not abandon her. She had raised him, loved him, and now he would repay her a portion of that debt.

And Mahila…

True Seeker forced images of his shriveled elder from his mind. Gnawing hunger was no match for the pain her death would bring.

Tadpole slipped his hand into True Seeker's. "Will you teach me to hit a tree with a stone?"

True Seeker forced a full-fledged smile. "Of course. And when we are settled, you and I will scour the riverbanks for the perfect cane. We will make blowguns and darts, and we will practice shooting until we can slay a buck with our eyes closed."

"Kill a deer with a blowgun?" A great bellow of laughter erupted from the boy, but it was another sound, from beyond the woods, that caught True Seeker's attention.

A cry.

Willow.

He grabbed Tadpole by the shoulders and looked him square in the eye. "Stay here. I will be back, but for now, you must *stay*. Do you understand?"

True Seeker could not console the boy's wide-eyed fright nor wait for his acknowledgement.

The path led to the forest's edge where a fallow cornfield rutted the ground. Beyond, sat the barn and the place they had called home for the last week. True Seeker leapt over what remained of a burned down fence and continued across a meadow toward the barn.

Another cry carried on the breeze, slapping True Seeker across the face. Three saddled, riderless horses grazed nearby, their reins dragging the ground.

As True Seeker rounded the structure, he stole himself for whoever might greet him on the inside of the dark barn. What he did not expect to find inside the open double doors was the tail end of another horse.

He came to an abrupt halt.

The horse skittered to the side, its rider pelting him with her gaze. "There you are. I was beginning to think I'd imagined you." Her lips curved into what would be a captivating smile, expect for the disdain coloring her large, brown eyes.

Her voice identified her as the woman in the night, and her wild, free-flowing hair confirmed the fact. She sat astride her horse as confident as any man and clutched her musket with equal authority.

"True Seeker! Run—" Willow was cut short by the violent sound of palm against cheek.

"Willow?" True Seeker darted forward but was intercepted by the woman's horse and the tip of her musket rammed beneath his chin.

"Caesar, I could use your help here," the woman said, never taking her eyes off True Seeker.

He glared back, gathering spittle to lob at her delicate cheek. A black man pulled True Seeker's arms behind his back, tugging him away from his target. "Best you go easy, boy. Won't help nothin' to fight."

True Seeker struggled against the slave. Willow crouched near Mahila who had managed a sitting position. Two white men tore through their meager possessions.

Bonds cut into True Seeker's wrists, but his mind did not register pain—only a single frantic thought. Had he buried the watch well enough?

"What do you seek?" Mahila asked in their tongue, her voice trembling with age. "Do you wish to strip an old woman of her buckskins and blankets?" Willow made shushing noises, but Mahila stretched her weathered hand toward True Seeker. "He is a good boy. Do not take him from us."

Words of assurance lodged between True Seeker's grinding teeth.

"I know it's here. Keep looking." Iron edged the horsewoman's voice.

Willow wrapped her arms around Mahila who would not be comforted. Pushing her granddaughter away, she struggled to rise, but a coughing fit held her captive.

True Seeker averted his gaze, guilt ripping through him like a bone-tipped arrow.

One of the men circled the small mound of freshly disturbed earth, which had once been hidden beneath True Seeker's pallet. "Wait a minute. What do we have here?"

Nausea washed over him as his knees gave way. Why had he not found a way to return it? Discarding it had been out of the question. It was too beautiful, too valuable —the exact value of his life.

While the woman picked encrusted dirt from the watch, one of the men looped a rope then swung the other end over the barn rafter.

"Missy, there ain't no call to—"

"Let me handle this, Caesar."

A mournful wail filled the barn as Willow turned her back.

"I did not intend to steal it. Willow, you must understand."

One of the white men shoved True Seeker toward the dangling noose.

"I am no thief! This thing was in my hand. I ran and did not know that I carried it still."

Willow's shoulders shook with sobs.

He twisted to address the horsewoman in English. "Let my blood cover my own foolishness, but do not harm the women. They did not know I took it."

The woman kept her eyes on the watch, which she wiped with a cloth.

The noose slipped over his head, and the rope snagged the tender skin of his throat.

Caesar stepped up to the woman's horse and took it by the bit. He spoke, but True Seeker could not hear over Willow's cries. Whatever he said, it did not soften the woman's features.

Hands covering her face, Mahila took up rocking and keening as though True Seeker's flesh already rotted in the ground.

Another horse was brought into the barn and the end of the rope was tied to the pummel of its saddle.

So this is how it will end. Mahila would go next, followed in days by Tadpole who would die of hunger, as his younger brother before him. The strongest of the three, Willow, would die shortly after, but of a broken heart. Would things have been different had they stayed in Tuckabatchee? How long would they have lasted? The winter? Did it matter if they died here or there? Now that True Seeker was staring death in the face, he figured it didn't make any difference where they died, so long as they each died with honor.

With his gaze affixed to Mahila's tear-streaked face, True Seeker's heels left the dirt. His eyes bulged, and his ears rang. The desire for breath was secondary to the need to relieve the pressure in his head.

"That won't be necessary, Thomas," the woman said.

Had he heard right, or had the lack of air warped his mental powers?

She settled the watch in her lap and cast a lazy glance Thomas' direction. "Drop him."

"But ma'am, the Indian—"

"My father wouldn't approve of you taking such liberties without his consent." She tugged her horse's reins free of Caesar's grasp and pointed its nose toward the fields. "I suppose the boy's had enough of a fright to cure him of theft. For a few days anyway. Lock him in the corncrib until Papa gets home."

True Seeker's heels returned to Earth with a thud. He dragged in precious air, the skin of his throat aflame.

Thomas grumbled as he removed the rope. While he coiled it, Caesar prodded True Seeker out of the barn and into the sweetest air he'd ever tasted.

"Hold up, Caesar," Thomas called. "Boy, tell the woman she's squatting on Bailey land. The boss won't stand for it, so she best take the old crow and get movin'."

True Seeker swallowed past the pain in his throat. "She understands your tongue, but Mahila cannot be moved. She will die."

Thomas cinched the unused rope to his saddle. "That's not my concern now, is it?" He turned to Willow and raised his voice as if she were hard of hearing. "You got 'til the end of the day to get off this land. You hear?"

Willow consoled a troubled Mahila, refusing to look at Thomas or True Seeker. Her rejection stung far worse than the rope and made him wish the men had finished the job.

He had dishonored himself and brought humiliation upon his clan.

As Caesar directed him across a vacant field, Thomas cursed the white man's god. "Woman, don't make me come back here tonight and drag your sorry hide clear out of…"

True Seeker blocked the man's threats from his mind and focused instead on what he might do if he ever got his hands around Thomas' neck.

Chin held high, True Seeker rehearsed the vow he had made to himself. He would not beg for mercy. He would not bow his head in defeat. With his last remaining dignity, he would suffer the consequences of his imprudence. Whatever they may be…

***

"Get in there." Thomas shoved True Seeker through the entry of the nearly depleted corncrib.

He stumbled to the opposite wall, as the door's hinges squealed like a speared boar. He turned just as Thomas slammed a crossbar in place.

"Shoulda killed you back yonder. Now I got to bake in the sun guarding a skulking Indian until McGirth decides to come home. Only God knows when that'll be. That fence ain't gonna mend itself neither, and if you think Caesar's gonna do it for me, you're stupider than I thought."

Who was the man talking to? True Seeker glared at him through the wide gaps in the logs.

Thomas responded with a swift kick to the door. "Rotten heathen." He hiked up his drooping trousers allowing the sun to catch to his spurred boots. "See that tree?" He indicated a sprawling oak. "That's where I'm gonna set myself. But my eyes? They're gonna stay right here on you. So no sneaky ideas." He marched toward the oak, grouching about women being left in charge.

What did he expect True Seeker to do? Squeeze between the logs? He studied them with a thoughtful eye. It wasn't a completely illogical notion.

He rammed the wall with his shoulder. The structure trembled, but held fast.

Thomas' amusement carried across the yard.

True Seeker narrowed his eyes. He would not provide the man further entertainment.

Sunlight streamed between the gaps in the wall and illuminated the swirling dust and corn powder he had disturbed. The logs were spaced far enough apart to let in a life-saving breeze, but even so, True Seeker already felt faint from the combination of heat and hunger.

It was the end of the blackberry moon, and the crib's stock of corn ran low, but even the few remaining ears did not tempt him.

Sweat ran down his neck, but he did not wipe it away.

One day soon—when he got himself out of this mess and all of them back to their village—he would voluntarily undergo these same conditions during his rite of passage into adulthood. He chose to consider this predicament an exercise in preparation.

Closing his eyes, he drew back his shoulders and inhaled deeply of the musty, lung-broiling air. He welcomed the sting within his throat and chest. It pulled his thoughts from the self-pity niggling at the edges of his mind.

He must hone his focus and remain stoic in the face of whatever circumstance was set in his path. This was a test from the Giver and Taker of Breath, who had the care of all his creation. True Seeker would not cower, and he would not rest until those under his own care had been provided for.

To be closer to the empowering earth, he brushed away scattered kernels and sat cross-legged in the dirt. He must think of a way to escape. Tonight.

It could be days, even weeks, before this McGirth fellow returned. By then, Mahila would be dead and Willow would be long gone. True Seeker hoped that, by then, she would have had her fill of this pilgrimage and would turn her face toward Tuckabatchee. Hers had been a fool's journey, and he had been a fool to allow it.

If he had been man enough, he would have forbidden her to leave in the first place. He would have stood in her path and demanded she see reason. He had the brawn to hold her, but not the mettle. Nor the wisdom to foresee the trials they had faced. Instead, like a deluded child, he had followed on her heels and believed he could somehow protect and sustain them.

If he had loved her more, he would have protected her by not letting her leave. He would have locked her in her house until her insanity passed—

He dug his fingers into the wool of his leggings to stem the flow of thoughts fed by hunger and despair.

True Seeker honored his elders above all else. If Grandmother Mahila had not been able to dissuade Willow, he never would have either.

He dropped his face in his hands, grit on his fingers scraping his sweaty cheeks and forehead.

The day dragged on, punctured only by the arrival of a bucket of water and a bowl of mush brought by a rotund, graying slave. She placed them just inside the door with an expression of soft-eyed pity. "I'd a brung you more, but Missy Lillian say that's all you's to get." The slave fanned herself with her stained apron as she leaned in and dropped her voice to a rough whisper. "But I'll be back tonight. While I'm cook, ain't nobody on McGirth land gonna sleep hungry."

Her kindness warmed a place within him, and he nodded his thanks. The boiled cornmeal passed over his tongue so quickly, he barely registered the taste, but when it hit his stomach, he couldn't contain the sigh that escaped him.

Although his vantage point revealed nothing of the goings on of the place, the sounds of a productive working farm kept True Seeker company. Once, the bubbling laughter of a small child drifted into the confines of the corncrib. True Seeker bolted to his feet, heart lurching, before it occurred to him it couldn't be Tadpole. Heaviness of soul weighed him back to the ground yet bolstered his determination to escape.

Long hours later, night fell and Caesar relieved a disgruntled Thomas of his post.

Quiet settled over the farm.

From the direction of the forest, came the call of a great horned owl. The bird hooted deep and long as though sending a warning of his upcoming hunt.

True Seeker mimicked the bird until other nearby owl calls announced he had succeeded in luring several curious birds.

Corncob in hand, he grinned into the dark. By touch, he located a depression in the earth that created a narrow gap beneath the bottom log on the west side of the crib. As thin as he'd become, he might manage to squeeze himself under and out.

He met each succeeding owl hoot with the scrape of cob against hard earth. Within minutes, he had dug a hole big enough to attempt. He lay with his back on the ground and his head poised to dip beneath the bar when the owls went silent.

The rustle of a skirt passing just outside hastily brought him back to his feet.

A woman fumbled with the crossbar, finally lifting it enough to let one end thud to the ground. The door opened, but stopped short when the hinges began to cry.

A breeze skittered through the corncrib. Moonbeams outlined a woman whose hair hung in wavy disarray and whose body stood in his path to freedom.

Had she not learned her lesson?

True Seeker coiled his muscles to hurtle himself past her and through the door.

"Go. Run." Her whisper released the tension in his body like a bowstring gone slack. "Caesar will not stop you, but you must leave *now*."

True Seeker planted his feet. Despite his mistakes, he was not foolish enough to fall for this woman's tricks.

"I have brought food for your family." She extended a bundle.

Several breaths later, his brain registered her use of the Creek language. "Who are you?"

"A friend."

For ten ticks of a watch, he vacillated. The woman's undulating hair matched that of the heartless Lillian McGirth, but beyond that—her silent steps, her gentle tone, her generosity—there was no resemblance.

True Seeker took the bundle and slipped past. "I thank you."

Her fingers brushed his sleeve as though in benediction. "It is my privilege. Let your feet carry you south until they meet the creek. Follow it east. Between the folds of the second fallen cypress, you will find your family."

"How do you know all this?" he continued in Muskogee.

"Caesar placed them there. Now, go!" She nudged his arm.

He needed no further encouragement.

Before the moon had broken free of the treetops, True Seeker came across the cypress and climbed the massive, fallen trunk. At the top of the ancient decaying cypress, a yawning black hole opened before him. He let himself down, but little arms smothered him before his feet landed.

He lifted Tadpole into a crushing embrace, and although the boy made no sounds, his tears dampened True Seeker's neck. "I knew you would come," the boy said in confident undertones.

Mahila's chuckle washed over True Seeker like the warm, cleansing waters of the big Tallapoosa. "Our able provider returns, like the true seeker that he is." True Seeker detected not a hint of derision in his grandmother's tone—only love and admiration so deep, he felt small in its presence.

"It's true, Grandmother. I took the watch."

"The boy thinks me senile, eh Willow?"

"But I am not worthy of your—"

Willow's hand came to rest on his arm. "A man's worth is found in the value of his word. Yours has never been found wanting. If you say you did not mean to take it, then it is so."

Their forgiveness came as blessed relief to his tortured conscience but could not erase his imprudent actions. The only thing that would ease that guilt would be experience and time to grow into the man Uncle had trained him to become.

"We must be swift. The sun will greet us before we are ready." He set Tadpole down and moved to lift Mahila's frail body, but Willow tightened her grip.

"No. We stay."

True Seeker clamped his jaw to keep from shouting at her.

When his rapid, agitated breath was his only response, she continued. "There is a man. A white man. He will help us. I know it."

"When has any white man helped us?" True Seeker struggled to keep his voice even. "They are self-seeking and greedy. They wish to conquer and overthrow their neighbors, not help them."

"This man is different. He is...he is my...father." The last word rode from her mouth on a stifled sob, as if the utterance of it had cost her great pain.

In the tight margins of the rotted trunk, True Seeker withdrew. His shoulder bumped the edge, and a portion of it crumbled down his chest. "Your father is a white man? Why did you not tell me?" Her dark, native features certainly did not reveal the secret.

Willow's words came out with a weary sigh. "I only learned of this myself—after the war, when he appeared at my lodge wanting to know me. Of course, I turned him away."

Mahila readjusted her old bones, but her grunt was probably more for Willow's benefit. True Seeker wished he could echo it.

"He came again, some months later. But I turned him away again."

True Seeker's memory replayed the last two years and produced the blurry image of an older white gentleman who had called on several occasions, staying only long enough to speak a few words. If True Seeker recalled correctly, the man had come more than twice. It had been three, maybe four times, over the course of many moons.

Then, he had stopped. Shortly after, Little Bear had fallen ill and not many weeks later, the child had crossed into the after-life.

Willow had mourned as no mother before her. True Seeker was certain of it. When, at last, she had opened dry eyes to the dawn, it was with her present, incomprehensible state of mind.

"Is that what this—these *wanderings* have been about? Finding your father?"

"Yes." Willow's soft reply was all but lost in the breeze that stirred True Seeker's hair. "He can provide for Tadpole as I cannot. If he will have me, I will accept his invitation and live with him as one of his daughters."

"Where may I find his lodge?"

"Near the joining of the Tombigbee and Alabama. This is all I know. But you *must* find him. Surely, if any man can speak on our behalf, it is him. We have no other choice but to beg for his help. Mahila cannot travel, and you cannot be caught. Either can only mean death."

True Seeker's chest expanded with new purpose. "Tell me his name, and I will find him."

"McGirth. Zachariah McGirth."

Chapter Five

A massive roar propelled Milly straight from bed and to her feet. With her heart tripping over itself, she braced to flee. Never in all her years had she heard such a brain-shaking sound.

The heart-rending cries of children mounted the room, the first glow of morning light illuminating their terrified faces.

Rosie pushed up on their pallet. "Cannon. Just the cannon."

Another blast shook the walls.

Milly dropped to the ground, pulled her knees to her chest, and slapped her palms against her ears. "Ours or theirs?"

Yawning, Rosie straightened their blanket. "Them soldiers even *got* a cannon?"

"It's General Jackson's army, isn't it?" She didn't imagine there was anyone who hadn't heard of Jackson's victory at the Battle of New Orleans and of his smashing success over the Red Sticks. Such a general wouldn't send his men into battle ill-prepared.

Nervous about removing her hands from her ears, Milly let Rosie work alone to smooth out the wrinkles in their bedding.

"How do you s'pect them soldiers gonna drag a cannon into this swamp? You been through that muck, same as me."

"I suppose you're right." Attempting bravery, Milly released her ears to unflip a corner of the blanket.

Two more concussions rocked their world, and this time, even Rosie lurched. She gave Milly a sheepish smile. "We best get used to it."

As heavily fortified as they were, Milly didn't doubt the battle could go on indefinitely. She'd known that but hadn't anticipated the experience to be so mind numbing. The sporadic gunfire over the last days had been disturbing enough, but the cannons were downright frightening.

She stepped shaky limbs into the skirt of her gown. "Let me take Isum something to eat. I'll be back to help get the children their breakfast."

With a portion of yesterday's cornbread enclosed in her apron, she moved into the cool morning. Tension, together with the scent of gunpowder, hung heavy in the air. Along the eastern point of the fort, the sky lit with the promise of a new day as the first smudges of pink eased above the treetops. A gentle breeze coaxed pillars of black smoke from the fort's perimeter, over the river, and into the remnants of the night.

Isum would be there and due to begin duty soon. Before she could pick him out from the silhouettes of scurrying men, he spotted her and waved.

Refusing to draw any closer to the thundering cannon, she returned the wave motioning for him to come to her.

He trotted to where she was and greeted her with a smile that finished lighting the sky. "They made me the loader," he said, reminding her of when, as a young man, he'd finally been allowed to drive the master's rig from the house to the carriage shed.

Milly worked up a smile for him. "From the looks of you, I suppose congratulations are in order. So what exactly does a loader do?"

"I shove the bag of powder then the ball into the barrel. They told me to watch and learn, but I seen 'em do it a couple different ways." He shrugged. "Guess it don't matter much, 'cept I like things done orderly."

"I would think it's important to be consistent. Powder is too dangerous to be careless. What are you aiming to hit?"

He stared at the activity buzzing about the artillery.

"Isum?"

His head snapped back toward her, as if he'd forgotten she was there. "You say somethin'?"

"What are you shooting at?"

"We're just firing practice rounds. Into the trees. Trying to hit the opposite shore, but it's harder than it seem." He stretched his arm toward the bay. "Navy's comin'. We gotta be prepared."

Milly sucked a breath through clenched teeth. "The army *and* the navy? That can't be good."

With the wave of a hand, he blew off her concern. "It's the Creek warriors we got to worry about. Them blue-coats can't fight in this swamp but the Indians..." He gave a long nod. "They got skills worth reckonin' with."

Another explosion vibrated the air.

Milly jumped, crumbling the cornbread in her grasp. She opened her apron to reveal the fragments. "Drat. I ruined your breakfast."

But Isum wasn't listening. "Something ain't right," he said, turning toward the sound of the explosion. No sooner had he finished speaking did cries fill the air. He left her at a run to join those swarming the farthest promontory.

Only a minute passed before Garcon raced past her, Little G's body dangling limp in his arms.

***

Balancing one foot on a half-submerged log and the other on a patch of dry ground, Phillip stood at the edge of the Apalachicola. A hot wind stirred the ruffled bosom of his shirt as he studied the opposite bank. Before him floated a row of anchored vessels, their skeletal masts protruding against a backdrop of cypress trees over-laden with Spanish moss.

Cannons protruded from the sides of the gunboats, every one of them aimed at Negro Fort...and the woman inside. He grimaced.

Try as he might, he'd been unable to put her out of his mind. The terror in her eyes haunted him, as did her anguished cries. Had she known how close the runaway had been? That he'd intended to take her captive? Is that why she had been so desperate to flee the area?

His mind replayed the sounds—the rattle of the bush in her battle to free herself, the big man's menacing threat, and the absolute silence of the woods after they'd vanished.

The entire episode still confused him, especially considering how others seemed altogether unconcerned. Were they a bunch of calloused oafs, or had he grown selfishly fixated on a situation that might somehow relieve him of residual guilt?

Regardless of whether or not his obsession was justified, the woman's well-being and life were threatened. It was reason enough to be worried. So why weren't they? He pursed his lips into a tight ball.

"Mistuh Phillip, we ain't got to worry about the whens and hows of death. God got it all under His mighty, lovin' hand. It be His job to worry. And He don't, so neither should you." Saul's voice had a way of sneaking into Phillip's thoughts. He took a cleansing breath and let it out along with a prayer for peace and guidance. Even though Saul was half a state away, his wisdom had the same uplifting power.

Phillip scooted over to allow Enoch to join him on the sliver of land along the river's edge. "They're beautiful, aren't they?"

Heedless of alligators and any other unpleasant creature that might be lurking in the calf-deep water, the boy sank his bare feet into the muck. "They sure is. Jes look at 'em, so tall and sleek, like fine racin' stallions. Except these got a bite to 'em, and I ain't planning to be around when them cannon start smoking. You figure they been around the globe? I bet they could sail all the way 'round this big ol' world. I nevah imagined Navy boats was so big."

Phillip grinned at Enoch's round-eyed wonder. "These are the smaller vessels. The bigger ones wouldn't be able to navigate this far up river. Their hulls are too deep, the water too shallow. Even these here risk becoming lodged."

Just this morning, the small convoy had arrived from the bay. Phillip took a moment to thank God his army feet were planted firmly on the ground. He appreciated the sleek beauty of naval vessels, but nothing else about that branch of the military even remotely appealed to him. Their work on this mission, though, would go a long way toward making Phillip's job easier.

Blast the fort for all the navy was worth, then storm the ramparts. That was the plan. But not for a few more days. First, Colonel Clinch would give the Negroes an opportunity to surrender.

Phillip turned and climbed the embankment. "Come along, Enoch, I may need you." Having reached the top, he straightened his uniform then realized Enoch remained with his feet buried in the water, a stricken look wrinkling his face.

"Are you snake-bit?"

Enoch wagged his head. "No, suh."

"Then get on up here."

"You goin' to that Creek camp, suh?" the boy asked, not having budged an inch.

Phillip knew where this was going. He sighed, understanding his slave's fear more than he cared to confess. "Go see if Cook has need of you."

"Yes, suh!" Enoch's feet came unglued from the riverbed. He scrambled on gangly legs over the bluff and set off toward camp.

"If Cook can't use you, find another way to make yourself useful," Phillip hollered at the boy's diminishing back.

Still running, Enoch waved in acknowledgement.

Phillip rolled his eyes. He gave the boy far too many liberties. His father never would have approved.

Finding the newly worn path through the trees, he followed it and the sound of gunfire to the flank of the Creek camp. According to Colonel Clinch's instructions, the natives had surrounded the fort, digging in to hold the position against retreat. Since their arrival, one third of them had kept on the move, firing toward the fort at irregular intervals. It had done little more than keep the runaways on their toes.

In the distance, behind the lines of warriors, a few Creek women sat in front of bark shelters or bent over fires—not the number he'd expected to find. Phillip squinted through the trees but spotted no white women.

At the sight of Phillip, a few warriors adjusted their weapons, their eyes narrowing with disquiet. Or was it simply curiosity?

Repeating to himself that these were his allies, Phillip rested a hand on the hilt of his sheathed sword, straightened his shoulders, and marched through their center. "Good morning," he said to a knot of warriors who stood as he passed.

Most nodded benignly in response.

Not keen on the idea of spending the next hour wandering through the war party in search of their leader, he turned to the nearest man. "Could you direct me to Major McIntosh?"

"The White Warrior is there." The man pointed a long, brown finger behind Phillip.

The mixed-blood was moving toward him, his arms spread wide. The fringes of his dark blue long-shirt danced, and the sheathed sword on his hip swayed with every step. A warm smile lifted his sideburns. "Major Bailey," McIntosh called, still many yards distant. "To what do we owe this honor?"

Phillip grasped the chief's extended arm, at once put at ease by the friendly reception. "Major McIntosh, a pleasure to see you this morning. Colonel Clinch sends his greetings along with a message. A request."

"Aye?" McIntosh tilted his turbaned head, setting the embedded white ostrich feather to trembling.

Phillip could almost guess the thoughts running through the other man's mind. Why not send a private with the message, as usually done? It was a germane question, but Phillip didn't intend to enlighten him with the answer.

"And what is it the good Colonel Clinch requires of me?" McIntosh said, his Scottish heritage tingeing his Muskogee accent.

"He asks that you enter the fort and demand surrender."

McIntosh's eyes lit with excitement. "Done! Captain Isaacs and Mad Tiger will accompany me. The Negroes will not see reason, but we must try to persuade them just the same."

"It will please the colonel to hear it." Phillip bowed slightly at the waist. "How are your women? Are the rations holding out?"

McIntosh stared at him, seeming to falter at the change in subject.

Phillip inwardly kicked himself for the awkward transition.

"Our women are accustomed to war and will use the colonel's gift of rations wisely."

"Yes, of course, I didn't mean to imply..." Phillip laid a hand over his heart. "You must forgive my blundering. I merely meant to ask after their well-being." *Of one in particular, anyway.* Try as he might, he'd been unable to squelch the notion that Adela might be near. "And that of your men, of course."

With a keen black eye, McIntosh scrutinized him.

Pine needles crunched beneath Phillip's boots as he shifted.

"What else brings you?"

There was no fooling this man. Phillip equaled McIntosh's staunch gaze. "I hoped to have a word with one of your war chiefs, Totka. I believe we might have a mutual acquaintance."

A hint of a smile tilted the corner of his mouth. "A woman?"

"Does it matter?" Phillip asked, annoyed at the man's intrusion into his personal life.

McIntosh laughed, setting to jangling the silver trinkets dangling from his ears. "I suppose it does not when I already know the answer. Only a woman could lure such a distrustful man into the midst of his enemy."

Phillip faltered a moment before recovering. "I trust you implicitly, sir."

One of McIntosh's dark brows rose.

"Although, I'll not admit the same regarding Captain Isaacs. You proved your loyalty during the late war, but Captain Isaacs has done nothing to earn the army's trust or to amend for his part in the death of so many Americans." Phillip rubbed the tip of his scar below the jaw. When McIntosh's eyes followed, Phillip lowered his hand, berating himself for his transparency. "If you would direct me to the warrior in question...?"

McIntosh swept his arm westward. "You should find him on the outskirts."

Phillip bowed then set off through the camp and around the perimeter of the fort. As he rounded the northwestern corner, the sounds of artillery increased.

Their faces lined with fatigue, a handful of natives took cover behind pines. Strung out along the entire eastern side, were pockets of Indians, some firing, some moving with agitated strides to a new location. The incessant guns appeared to be doing a number on their spirits, but they held their ground, unwavering in the face of hot lead. Steadfast gallantry seemed their forte. Phillip had certainly seen enough of it in the last years to know.

He scoured each group he passed until his gaze stumbled across a familiar face.

At the same instant, Totka looked Phillip's direction. Keeping his weapon at the ready, he met Phillip halfway, his slightly halting step reminding Phillip of the reason for his errand.

"You find the woman?"

"No. I've come to ask… " Now that he was here, peering into Totka's intense, kind eyes, all the lines Phillip had rehearsed seemed foolish, childish. *Are you the Indian who rescued my intended then claimed her for yourself?* Anger prickled Phillip's skin and sent his heartbeat skittering.

Patience oozed from Totka's countenance, as though he'd been waiting for this moment for a long time. He moved not a muscle and yet sadness poured into his eyes and ran so deep that Phillip felt embarrassment for the man, for displaying his emotions so openly. But when Totka slowly nodded, encouraging Phillip to continue, he forged ahead. "You know the McGirths of Tensaw?"

Another nod, this one abrupt.

Phillip wasn't sure what he'd expected, but the longer he stood before Totka, the longer he sensed something amiss. "You were at Mim's place during the attack. Were you the one? Did you save the McGirth women?"

The most imperceptible dip of Totka's chin accompanied a look so distant, Phillip imagined he was reliving that day. Just has Phillip had countless times.

He knew he should thank the man for saving the woman Phillip loved, but all he could do was wish to dig inside Totka's head and erase all memory of her—every caress of her slender throat, every murmur of love whispered in the dark, every moment he'd stolen what rightfully belonged to Phillip.

"Is she here? In the camp with the women?"

Totka flinched as though Phillip's words had bit into his flesh. "You do not know."

"Know what?"

"She is dead." The words left him as though forced against their will. "Her spirit lives on with our Savior."

Suddenly lightheaded, Phillip flailed for support, his hand connecting with a nearby tree. "When?" It must have been recent, since her father's correspondence from two months prior had made no mention of any illness, much less death.

Without another word, Totka pulled from his pouch a crumpled letter. "Read."

Yellowed and smudged, the letter's creases were deeply worn. He read.

My dearest Totka,

Time has stood still for me since receiving your promise of return. Every day, I have held my breath in anticipation of your arrival, but it seems as though my time of waiting has come to an unexpected end.

The yellow fever has swept through Mobile sparing not even Tensaw its devastation. My quill trembles as I write. Sickness wracks my body, and I fear I am not long for this world.

Should you hold this missive in your hands, it is proof I have passed.

I would not leave without one final confirmation of my love, and one last plea for you to seek Christ while He may be found. His path is beautiful and perfect and should you follow it, we will meet again one day.

Do not grieve me. You have many years ahead in which to live and find new love.

I am yours faithfully and always,

It was signed "Adela McGirth," and yet, as Phillip studied the letter, something about it struck him as odd. The verbiage rang true, but the handwriting was unfamiliar—he would recognize Adela's anywhere. At first he thought someone else must have written it on her behalf, but when his eyes skipped back to the mention her trembling quill, he dismissed the notion.

Pursing his lips, he refolded the page, and it crackled. Exactly how old was this letter? With haste, he reopened it then sucked in a ragged breath.

July 23, 1814.

Impossible! He drew the sheet closer to make certain of the date. There was no mistaking the year.

Lillian.

Evil, spiteful woman!

And yet, her actions gave seed to a hope long dead.

When Phillip had last walked away from his home in Tensaw, he'd sworn never to look back. With his memories of the place more horrifying each day, he had been certain his decision to put his family's land on the market was the correct one. But two years had passed not a single buyer had been interested. He couldn't blame them. Who wanted land tainted with the blood of the nation's worst massacre?

But Adela was available.

Had God withheld the sale of the land for just this reason? Could it be time to go home?

A glance at Totka revealed a man broken and mourning as though he'd received the news yesterday. He had no idea that Adela was alive, that the letter he cherished, had been written by a woman who despised him.

And unless Phillip said otherwise, he never would.

Chapter Six

Like a loaded orange tree waiting to be plucked, the opportunity True Seeker had been awaiting stood before him. Even so, his snugly moccasined feet rocked in the hay. To step out meant the loss of control over his future.

Cool morning air gusted through the McGirth's open barn and stirred the scent of horse manure. The mare in the adjacent stall pawed the ground as though requesting freedom to roam the pasture. True Seeker shared her sentiments.

Yesterday brought Zachariah McGirth home from parts unknown. This morning, he stood saddling a horse not five rods from where True Seeker hid.

For three days, he had kept out of sight and waited for the man to make an appearance. True Seeker's small ration of bread had long since vanished, and he could safely assume Willow had depleted hers as well.

Time was spent.

He stepped from the empty stall intentionally scraping his feet along the ground.

McGirth laid one arm across the horse's neck then lazily turned. With eyes the color of a magnolia leaf, he studied True Seeker. "Did you come back for the watch?" The hint of a smile played around the corners of his mouth.

Heart palpitating in his neck, True Seeker dropped his line of sight to the horse's iron-shod hooves. "How did you know me?"

McGirth lengthened the stirrup of his saddle. "You're the only Indian boy I see around here, and you look hungry enough to steal." His calm voice and easy manner eased a knot in True Seeker's shoulder.

In a nearby stall, the sound of screeching cats sent McGirth's horse skittering away from him and into the barn wall.

On impulse, True Seeker took the animal by the bridle and uttered calming noises. He stroked the horse's velvety nose, grateful for this mundane, distracting task.

McGirth nodded his thanks then dropped the stirrup and stroked his mount's neck.

Taking the man's silence as an invitation to speak, True Seeker met and held his gaze. "I have wronged you and am at the mercy of your justice."

McGirth's hand stilled on the horse, but he did not speak for a long moment. Whatever his verdict, True Seeker at least held the assurance that it would not be delivered in haste.

"The crime of theft is gravely punished in both our nations. Your clan would be much shamed to know of your deeds."

True Seeker's lids widened at the man's fluent use of Muskogee and his meticulous deliberate speech. Such decorum was typical of the ancient chiefs, not white men. It was oddly comforting.

"Your bravery is commendable in one so young. Although you do not ask forgiveness, I am honored to give it."

For five breaths, True Seeker stared at McGirth and waited for the remainder of his sentence. Such offenses did not pass without consequences, but McGirth's impassive gaze revealed nothing more than a man preparing for a day's work. "What are you called?"

"My great-grandmother named me True Seeker." His voice cracked at the thought of her hiding, sick and hungry.

He nodded, admiration warming his eyes. "You prove yourself worthy of it."

True Seeker's brow tightened. He could not agree.

"Lillian is frying up bacon for my breakfast. I'd be pleased if you joined me." He lapsed back into English.

True Seeker faltered, his fingers immobile in the horse's forelock. No tirade? No hanging? Simply an invitation to his lodge?

The animal nudged his chest, and True Seeker absentmindedly resumed scratching. "You are too merciful. I must work to repay my offense." His stomach audibly rumbled, and McGirth's cheek drew up on one side.

"You will, but a boy can't work on an empty stomach." He led the horse into the yard and hailed Caesar, who was exiting a cabin opposite the main house.

The slave gave an answering wave, but when his eyes fell on True Seeker, his movements stuttered. "Mornin' suh. Got him saddled for me, I see."

True Seeker's jaw slackened, parting his lips. The master serving the slave?

McGirth handed over the reins. "He's rarin' to go." He tipped his head toward True Seeker. "You two have met."

Caesar nodded, holding McGirth's gaze. "That's right, but I never would have figured on seein' him again."

"You'll be seeing a lot of him. For a little while, anyway. He's offered to pay for his wrongs, and I'm inclined to accept."

With a tip to his hat, Caesar grinned and mounted. "Sure am glad you's back, suh." The black man had ridden halfway down the lane before True Seeker realized he stood alone in the yard.

A short, crisp whistle drew his gaze to the out-kitchen and McGirth standing in the doorway. "You coming?" he called.

His stomach grinding painfully, True Seeker trotted toward the house and the scent of sizzling pork. Quiet fell over the room at his appearance. When his eyes adjusted to the dark, he found McGirth seated at the table, a curly-haired boy in his lap. Thumb jammed between rosy lips, the child looked as though he'd seen no more than two winters. Droopy-eyed, he rested his head against McGirth's chest.

The crackle of hot grease drew True Seeker's gaze to the hearth and the woman standing before the pan, a fork in her hand. A single thick braid hung down her back and a smile brightened her features.

Surprise rounded True Seeker's eyes. This was *not* Lillian.

Paler and fuller in the hips, this woman didn't possess Lillian's stunning beauty, yet in the captivity of her gaze, he glimpsed the beauty of her spirit.

She winked a green eye, then winced as grease dripped from her fork onto her hand. She swiveled back to her work.

True Seeker smiled. He would seek an opportunity to thank her for setting him free.

With his booted foot, McGirth kicked out a chair. "Take a seat."

True Seeker accepted and within seconds, the woman set a heaping plate before him.

"My name is Adela." Her voice was soft, her Muskogee thick with accent.

"Call me True Seeker," he said, unable to remove his eyes from the biscuits and bacon before him.

"Good to know you. Now, eat before you pass out cold." Amusement tinged her words, as she switched to English. "You must fetch your family. Bring them here, to eat and rest."

True Seeker's gaze flashed to McGirth, but he merely smiled and nodded toward the plate. Maybe he hadn't heard Adela, or maybe True Seeker woke this morning in a foreign land, one found only in his dreams. Perhaps, he had mistakenly returned to the wrong farm?

He glanced around, his heartbeat quickening. Blue and white checkered curtains fluttered in the single open window. A tin pitcher held a spray of vibrant, wild flowers.

Was this the right kitchen? It seemed a different place altogether. But perhaps it was simply the daylight and the welcoming atmosphere that had transformed it.

Like a gust of stormy wind, Lillian swept into the kitchen but stopped short two steps inside. Her eyes blazed.

Yes, this was the right farm.

More wild than usual, her hair appeared half combed. The ivory handled brush she pointed True Seeker's direction confirmed it. "Papa, why is that knob-nosed savage at our table?"

Adela returned to the skillet, her fork scraping violently against it. McGirth stood, his muscled frame towering over his daughter. The child wrapped his arms around McGirth's neck and buried his face in the man's chest.

Lillian faced her father, chin aimed high.

He expelled a heavy breath. "True Seeker has returned to own up to his misdeeds and make things right. I plan to honor his bravery. It wasn't an easy thing he did, coming here."

Eyes slanted True Seeker's direction, Lillian pursed her lips. "Honor! There isn't an Indian alive who has a shred of it."

"True Seeker here just proved you wrong. Besides, I've never seen you own up to your many wrongs."

The clatter of dishes pulled their attention to Adela. Two empty tin plates lay on the ground at her feet, but her wide-eyed gaze was riveted to her sister.

Lillian's face flamed red. Her chest heaved.

No one moved until at last, she slipped the brush into a pocket of her apron, smoothed her hair with her hands, and marched to the opposite side of table. With a swish of blue skirts and haughty airs, she took a seat. "Adela, that smells wonderful. I believe I'll have some if you don't mind."

"Of—of course." Adela collected the plates off the ground.

McGirth slowly settled back into his chair, keeping a leery eye on Lillian—True Seeker's sentiments, exactly.

His neck still burned where her rope had bit into it. He didn't trust her as far as he could toss that fancy hairbrush, but he could no longer resist the food quickly growing cold before him. With one eye still on her, he crammed the biscuit into his mouth, hardly tasting it.

McGirth cleared his throat. "Which village do you call home?"

True Seeker scraped his fork across his plate. "Tuckabatchee."

McGirth shifted the quiet child to one leg and leaned forward. "I lived there once." He spoke with the fondness of one who had loved and lost. "And your clan?"

"Rabbit."

He nodded. "What brought you south?"

True Seeker swept a hand through his straight, shoulder length hair which had long since worked itself free of its dual leather thongs. "I am charged with the care of my aunt, Willow Woman. We have traveled far in search of a man."

McGirth's brows bunched above his freckled nose. "And who might that be?"

"Zachariah McGirth."

The man sat up straight, his brows arching.

Adela slipped to his side and relieved him of the boy, who patted her face. "Hungry, sissy," he whined, but she silenced him with a look.

"Me?" McGirth asked. "Why would your aunt be looking for me?"

Best break the news in one blow. "She is your daughter."

McGirth shot to his feet sending the chair crashing to the ground behind him. "Esperanza? She's here?"

"Esperanza? I do not know—"

Laughter filled the room.

"Stop it, Lillian," Adela snapped.

Lillian wiped her eyes with her sleeve. "I haven't heard that one before. I thought he'd rob us blind, but never expected this. Although I must admit, it's very clever."

True Seeker scowled at her and tried again. "I do not know a woman of this name."

McGirth shook his head then allowed his gaze to travel from one daughter to the next. His silence halted Lillian's laughter.

"Papa?" Adela broke the stillness. "Who is Esperanza?"

McGirth spread his hands wide, as if exposing himself to their judgment. "Your sister."

"What?" Lillian shrieked. "You can't be serious."

Nodding, McGirth seemed to grow an inch with each breath. "It's true. I should have told you long ago, but..." He began to pace the room. "She's from my first marriage, from my time among the Creek. Esperanza is what I—. It's what your mother called her. Of course, she would have been given a different name by her people. It was their—"

"I have an Indian sister?" Lillian's face contorted as though she had been stabbed through the gut.

If McGirth noticed or cared, it didn't show. He halted in front of True Seeker and gripped his arm. "I was wrong to accept your offer of restitution."

True Seeker shook his head to deny it, but before he could utter a word, McGirth withdrew the familiar watch from his pocket and placed it in True Seeker's hand.

He clamped his large hand around True Seeker's, digging the chain into his palm.

"I'm the one who owes a debt. Take the watch. As a token of my gratitude."

True Seeker stared at their hands—McGirth's large, worn, and freckled; True Seeker's smooth, slim, and kissed by Father

Sun. Two more different hands did not exist and yet a bond passed between them as sure as any clan, as sure as blood.

Like a flock of crows before the boys in the cornfield, every doubt True Seeker had owned since following Willow into the woods, scattered and fled. "I humbly accept your gift and will carry it with pride." His gaze floated through the open door. "Willow was right to come. I will take you to her now."

Before the watch's shortest stick completed one rotation on the dial, True Seeker approached the old cypress concealing his family.

Adela and her father followed steps behind. No one had shown disappointment when Lillian refused to come.

True Seeker's practiced redbird call brought Willow from the bowels of the tree. Her onyx gaze landed on her father and took root. Fear, insecurity, desperation—all marred her delicate features for the briefest of flashes.

Like a doe alerted to danger, she froze in a crouched position, the ruffled edge of her soiled blue dress draping across the crumbling wood.

McGirth brushed past True Seeker and extended a hand toward her. "You are welcome here." His Muskogee came out rough and raw.

Willow's jaw trembled and her gaze faltered, skipping from his face to his hand then to some point in the distance. "My white father, I—I have come only because…" She glanced down at Tadpole who peeked with sunken eyes from over the edge of their hiding place.

True Seeker's heart constricted in his chest.

"Because you need help," McGirth finished for her, his hand still outstretched. "I remember a time when life in Tuckabatchee was full and carefree, but now, I fear for *any* child of mine who chooses to live there. But no matter the reason, I am grateful you have come. You are my blood. I offer my love and protection, expecting nothing in return."

Willow's chest expanded with her slow, deep inhale. With an uncertain smile, she placed her hand into his.

From behind True Seeker, Adela sniffled and rested a light hand on his back. "Thank you," she whispered, "for bringing my sister home."

True Seeker nodded in acknowledgement, but inwardly, he cringed.

As kind and gracious as these people were, this was not home, nor would it ever be.

***

"The colonel's right. This is our best bet. Here." With a stick, Major Collins jabbed at a map crudely drawn in the dirt. "It's the only half-way solid ground around the whole blasted fort."

Phillip rubbed his roughened jaw. "They'll be expecting it. And assuming the naval guns manage to penetrate the wall allowing our men passage, the Negroes will concentrate all their fire at that point. It's a narrow gap. We'll be slow getting through, especially once men start to fall."

Rolling his eyes, Collins glided a manicured finger over the embroidery skirting a button hole on his coatee. "They're a ramshackle band of runaways, not a trained military. They can't think for themselves, much less aim their weapons strategically. They've been firing their artillery for three days and have yet to hit anything."

"It's a foolish army that doesn't respect its opponent."

One side of Collins' face lifted with the smirk that twisted his lips. "Do my career a favor and when he gets back, tell Colonel Clinch you think he's a fool."

Sergeant Garrigus appeared out of breath before the tent opening. He touched the edge of his shaggy brow in a hasty salute while stepping inside uninvited.

"Sergeant Garrigus." Phillip returned the man's salute with exaggerated precision. "Only a ghost sighting would justify that lack of decorum."

"My apologies, sir. I haven't seen a ghost, but I may as well have. There's a woman. A *white* woman." He whispered the word "white" as though too reverent to speak at normal volume.

Collins straightened at the report, his unbelieving gaze darting to Phillip then back to Garrigus.

Surreally calm, Phillip relished a silent moment of vindication before pushing past Garrigus' bulk and plunging into the dusk. "Where is she? Is she well?" A quick scan of the camp revealed a commotion on the far side where a large group had gathered. Around the woman?

Garrigus joined Phillip. “Yes, sir. She seems to be, but she’s...”

“Out with it, sergeant.” Phillip forced himself not to rush like a crazed lunatic into the midst of the crowd.

“She’s asking for a doctor.”

“Did you notify the surgeon?”

“No, sir. It didn’t seem right.”

“How could a woman requesting a doctor not be *right*?” Phillip snapped.

Sweat ran from Garrigus’ temple onto his stubbled cheek. “Well, sir, she wanted to take the doc.”

“What in God’s name are you talking about?” Collins asked.

“To the fort, sir.”

Phillip’s mouth hung open for a moment before he snapped it shut.

Collins chortled. “Beautiful *and* crazy. Bailey. The two of you should get along splendidly.”

Angling himself away from Collins, Phillip addressed Garrigus. “Bring her to me. And keep the gawkers at bay.”

“Yes, sir.” Garrigus swiveled on his heel.

“Sergeant?” Phillip stopped him. “Send for Surgeon Buck.”

Silence followed as Garrigus did nothing more than stare at him.

“Is there a problem with your hearing, Sergeant?”

“No, sir. It’s just that...well, the captain’s in the Indian camp.”

“How is that a problem?”

“It’s not...”

“Then send for him. *Now*.” Phillip waited for Garrigus to leave then turned to face Collins.

Arms crossed, the man’s expression was nothing if not amused. “This ought to be interesting.”

For once, Phillip couldn’t disagree, although he’d rather Collins not be around to watch how interesting it might become. Reentering the tent, he lit the sole candle and searched for a legitimate reason to send Collins away but came up blank.

"You want I should make some coffee for her, suh?"

Phillip turned at the sound of Enoch's voice. He'd forgotten the boy was there. Enoch had been exceptionally quiet of late. "That would be nice. Thank you."

Coffee tin in hand, Enoch left Phillip alone with his racing heart—and Collins.

Under the man's unnerving scrutiny, Phillip smoothed his uniform front feeling his heart pound against it. He fought the urge to angle the ugly side of his face away from the tent flap. Instead, he faced it head-on, clasped his hands behind his back, and planted his feet shoulder width apart.

Collins ran a palm from crown to forehead then straightened his tall collar, his smile as oiled as his hair. "She's a lady. Not a visiting dignitary."

Phillip knew that fact better than anyone. Wasn't it *his* pocket that carried a fragment of her dress? He slid Collins a sidelong glance. "And you'll respect her as such, or you'll have me to answer to." He yanked his gaze toward the sound of approaching footsteps. Expelling a deep breath, he consciously eased the tension in his shoulders, while mentally bracing himself for how she might look and behave after being held prisoner for so many days.

Garrigus had said she was uninjured, but Phillip couldn't imagine the woman to be without scars of some sort. He feared for her mental state, and willed Marcus to speed his arrival.

Garrigus' gruff voice carried through the opening. After a moment, he entered, a sheepish expression crumpling his face. "She won't come in, sir."

Phillip pushed passed him and stepped into the quickly darkening night. Some yards away, she stood, half-concealed beneath a hooded cape. Only her nose and mouth were visible in the waning day, but it was enough for him to recognize her.

The sight of her, calm and unharmed, lifted a burden from his chest. Every muscle in his body loosened, and he fought to keep a smile of relief from his voice. "Miss? Won't you come inside? Coffee will be ready shortly."

He stepped toward her, but she backed away an equal distance, her head dropping a few inches in a motion Phillip recognized—one all too familiar. This woman had something to hide. Her own scars maybe? Phillip's heart went out to her, and in a gesture of respect, he gave her more space.

"You have nothing to fear from me. I understand."

Her head snapped up, and for an instant, just before she dropped it again, Phillip glimpsed her eyes, soft with question.

"Clear out. All of you." He waved his hand in a dismissive gesture, and within moments they were alone. Even Collins, surprisingly, had vanished.

"My name is Major Phillip Bailey. And yours?"

"Milly," came the hushed reply. "Miss Milly...Landcastle."

"It's a pleasure to make your acquaintance, Miss Landcastle."

He stretched his arm toward a log lying before the fire. Except for Enoch, who tended the coffee pot, the place was deserted. "Please. Won't you sit?"

She wavered a moment before inching closer.

Phillip caught himself from taking her by the elbow and instead gave her a wide berth. Choosing to remain standing, he kept enough distance between then to give her breathing room, yet permit him to study her as opportunity afforded.

He was determined to allow her to speak first, but she said nothing for long minutes. Was it the flickering light, or was she trembling beneath her layers of clothing? She kept her attention affixed to Enoch.

Phillip shifted on his feet. "Enoch's a good boy. He won't hurt you, but if you'd rather, I can send him away."

She turned toward him then. The firelight flickered across her high cheekbone. "He doesn't frighten me."

The rich texture of her voice almost startled him. It was deeper than he'd expected, but it was the cadence that gave him pause. Something about it rang familiar yet seemed out of place.

He squatted nearby, resisting the urge to place a hand on her arm, to attempt to ease whatever nightmares lived in her mind. "No one here will hurt you. You have my word. Whatever you've been through, it's over. You're safe now."

"He's your slave?" she asked, still eying Enoch.

The boy's jaw tightened, but he kept his eyes trained on the kettle nestled in the coals.

"I—yes. Of course," Phillip said.

"Of course," she repeated, the words dead on her tongue.

Expelling a heavy breath, Phillip dropped his hands between his knees. He couldn't be handling this worse if he tried. "Miss Landcastle, I can only imagine what you must have been through, but if you'll allow me, I'll do my best to make you comfortable. You're welcome to my tent for as long as necessary." He spread his hands wide. "I'm afraid I don't have much experience with women in camp, so I'll need a little help. Are you hungry? What do you need?"

Maybe it was his humble tone or maybe his bumbling speech that broke through to her. Regardless, Miss Landcastle withdrew her hands from their pinched position at the base of her cape, pushed it back slightly, and faced him. Large eyes peered at him from the shadows. As though making a conscious effort to trust, she leaned toward him, jaw quivering, eyes beseeching.

Phillip dropped to one knee, his body drawn toward her by force of compassion. "What is it? Let me help you."

"I need a doctor. You have a doctor?"

"The surgeon is on his way. He should—"

A nearby shot rang out behind the woman, followed quickly by another—too close to be part of the on-going skirmish surrounding the fort.

Phillip sprang to his feet, as did Miss Landcastle. She swiveled and back-stepped into him.

He shoved her behind him. "Enoch, my rifle," he ordered, but the boy was already halfway to the tent.

"I got one!" A jubilant voice blared out from the woods beyond the forest's edge, which lay some thirty yards distant. Although muffled, the sounds of a struggle ensued.

While he scoured the darkness for incoming danger, he marveled at the oddity of the moment. For the first time in years, the fight didn't beckon him. His usual longing to be in the thick of action was absent. News would have to come to *him* this time.

He tossed a glance over his shoulder, becoming aware of how close she stood, how she clutched the back of his jacket.

She hadn't moved an inch from where he'd placed her, directly behind him. Shoulders hunched, she gripped the base of her hood in one hand and with the other, clung to his uniform.

An all-out battle would be hard-pressed to persuade him to leave her.

***

"Whatever happens, stay with Miss Landcastle." The officer spoke, but it took Milly a moment to realize he addressed his slave.

"Yes, suh. You goin' somewhere, suh?"

From beneath her stifling hood, the sharp clicks of a musket hammer reached Milly's ears.

"Don't plan to." He raised an arm so suddenly, Milly jerked. "Soldier! Figure out what's going on, then report back."

"Right away, Major."

Major...who? Bailey, was it?

Since she'd stepped foot in the camp, her fear-frazzled brain had refused to process a coherent thought. The one thing she had noted was this officer was the same one who had stumbled across her outside the fort. A woman didn't soon forget a scar such as his.

Milly rocked on her heels, anxiety crushing her chest. The image of Little G's perspiring face and hard, distended belly pressed upon her, urging her to hasten her task.

If only she hadn't been so fearful of the soldiers, so distracted by the major's kindness...

Never mind whatever ruckus was playing out in the woods, she *must* get a doctor. Untangling her fingers from the scratchy wool of his coat, she took a small step to the side to get his attention.

Without warning, he threw his arm behind him, and grabbed a fistful of the front of her cloak.

Instinctively, she wrenched away, the motion flinging the hood's rim to the edge of her forehead. Terror flooded her. She flailed one arm to regain her balance and with the other groped for her covering.

But the major got to it first.

With a quick yank, the world was reduced to only what she could see at her feet—a pair of boots reflecting the firelight.

Hands clasping the hood to the sides of her face, Milly trembled with the knowledge of what had almost happened.

"Forgive me," he said, his voice laced with regret. "I didn't mean to upset you."

No man had ever apologized to her. If this is what it meant to be a white woman, she could never voluntarily give it up.

He straightened her cloak then rested a hand on her shoulder—its weight the burden of guilt. If he knew of her deceit, he would offer irons instead of an apology.

"I lost you once and don't plan to do so again. I'd be grateful if you stick close so I don't have to worry. At least until we know what's going on out there." He waited until she gathered her wits enough to acknowledge his request with a nod before he turned back around.

As if in response to his mention of it, the commotion from the woods increased. The bushes shook then parted. The forms of two men emerged, one of them calling for a doctor. They dragged a third who could barely keep his footing. Several more, their weapons drawn, followed at close quarters, their taunts and verbal prodding carrying easily through the night.

As they neared, Milly recognized the groans of pain—the same that had brought her to tears time and again. Her breath came in shallow puffs, as dread filled her to brimming. Before she thought to stop them, her feet carried her at a dead run toward Isum.

Still ten strides distant, he crumbled, holding his side.

"Isum!" Her frantic voice reached her own ears with shocking strength. Holding fistfuls of her skirt, she propelled herself toward him, closing the gap far too slowly.

Heavy footfalls sounded behind her. "Ms. Landcastle, don't!"

Falling to her knees, she pressed her palms against his side. Sticky warmth gushed through her fingers. "Foolish, foolish. What were you thinking? I told you not to come." Her words bubbled from her lips between sobs.

He cried out at her touch and swinging an arm, knocked her face-first into the dirt.

Too stunned to move, Milly laid there, soil gritty against her teeth. In all his gruffness, Isum had never struck her. The pain in her heart outshone the pain in her shoulder.

Someone grasped her around the waist and hauled her to her feet and away from Isum. Orders were given in regards to him, but Milly couldn't process them.

Without conscious thought, she placed one foot in front of the other, going where led then sitting where told. Through her tears, the fire blurred. How had this gone so wrong?

It had been a simple mission. Get the doctor and bring him to the fort—she had promised Garcon there would be no trouble. No doctor could turn away a woman requesting aid for a child. With her hair covered, they would trust her white skin and her motives. But if she had known the price she would pay in exchange for the chance to save Little G, would she have volunteered to come?

The major lowered himself to one knee, took her hand, and poured cool water over it. Red-stained water spattered the ground between them. "You know him, don't you?" he asked without lifting his eyes from his task.

What use was there in lying? "Yes."

He ran his fingers down her palm then flipped her hand, inspecting it. "Is he yours?"

"Mine?"

"Your slave."

An irony-laden chortle escaped her.

Isum's moans carried from where he lay. She clenched her fist and cringed. Would no one help him?

"If not your slave, then what? Your lover?"

Her gaze flashed to the man so fast, she caught his unguarded, sickened expression just before he quickly smoothed it—all except his left eye, the skin drawn taut by the puckered scar.

She withdrew her hand and settled it in her lap—its cleanliness a stark contrast to the one polluted by blood and debris. If only she could wash away her tainted heritage as easily as this man had rinsed her hand...

"I'll gladly take that as a no, but after that display, no one will believe your association with the Negroes to be innocent. Were you sent as a spy? Maybe they're holding someone you love, threatening to—"

"No. I came to you because a little boy is in desperate need of a doctor's care. He's dying. I'm sure of it." With each word, Milly's voice grew stronger, more confident. She lifted her gaze from her hands to his chin. "I promised his father I could bring help. Told him no doctor would refuse it. Please, if you could just—"

The major held up a hand to stop her, as his gaze ran to somewhere behind Milly. Without a word, he rose and, handing the pitcher to Enoch, strode from her view.

The boy rushed to her as if he'd been waiting for just such an opportunity. "It be the doc. He finally here," he offered, extending his hand as a request to take her own. "He'll help your man."

Extending her stained hand, she searched for the courage to look behind her but found none. "He's a good doctor, then?"

"Yes'm. He don't care 'bout color the way most do. He see right through skin to a person's heart, and I don't mean the one that goes thump. But he do care 'bout that one too, him bein' a doc and all."

The boy poured while she rubbed her hands together beneath the flow. "I'm glad to hear it. Do you think there's a chance he'll come with me?"

Enoch set the pitcher down and scooted toward her on his knees until they bumped her feet. Turning large, animated eyes on her, he licked his lips. His eyes darted about before landing back on her. "Can I come wid you? Back to the fort?" he rasped in a low voice. "I know all 'bout rifles, how to clean 'em, load 'em. And I can fight these white soldiers. As good as any man."

Milly carefully arranged her features into a scowl. "Awfully brave of you to speak of escape and sedition to a strange white woman. Or foolish maybe?"

Enoch shook his head, his brow furrowing. "You're as black as I be." He hammered his chest. "In here."

Isum cried out, and Milly's stomach lurched, her head turning instinctively toward the sound. A man knelt over him, working diligently. *God, give the doctor wisdom. Don't take Isum from me.*

Nearby, several soldiers kept their weapons trained on Isum. The major stood to the side, arms crossed, one hand at his jaw. His body was square with those on the ground, but he aimed his gaze her direction. Unable to read his expression, she could only pray he wasn't angry with her, that he hadn't deciphered her as easily as Enoch had.

A touch to her knee brought her attention back to Enoch's grinning face. "See? No regula' white woman would give that slave the time 'a day."

Milly let out a weary breath. "I don't know that they'll let me return, much less let you go with me."

"But if they do—let you go—can you get me in? Some way? I won't be no trouble."

Drying her damp hands on her skirt, she considered his request fully understanding his yearning for freedom. Could she deny him the chance to fight for it? Her shoulders drooped. "There's a gate on the eastern side, just beyond the footbridge and hidden behind a tangle of vines. Tell anyone you happen upon that Milly sent you."

With a flurry of nods, he scrambled to his feet. "Yes, miss. Thank you, miss. Thank you!"

Her slight smile lifted cheeks tight with drying tears. "Best keep it down. Find yourself something to do to look busy."

He picked up the pitcher moving away as he spoke. "Yes, miss! You wantin' mo' water? I'll get you mo' water."

She watched him disappear into the darkness beyond the crackling fire and wondered what kind of a master the major was to the boy. Without a doubt, he was better than Master Landcastle. And yet, Enoch longed for freedom...

"She's been asking for you since she arrived. Something about a boy in the fort and you going to help him."

At the sound of the major's voice and approaching footsteps, Milly jumped to her feet, her hand automatically going to her hood. He walked briskly toward her. At his side strode another uniformed gentleman, scrubbing at his hands with a cloth.

"How is he? Will he live?" Milly asked, not attempting to hide the wobble in her voice.

The man Milly assumed to be the doctor, bent in a crisp bow. "Captain Marcus Buck, surgeon, at your service, miss. To answer your question—barring infection, yes, I believe he'll live."

Milly's chest heaved with a sigh of relief.

Captain Buck's tall, stiff collar gored his check as he tipped his head to the side. "He is...a friend?"

Unbidden, Milly's gaze flicked to Major Bailey who stood rigid and unreadable. His patient stare unnerved her.

"Th-that's right."

He narrowed his eyes, as though straining to see through her insipid skin to the lies buried within. "A friend? I got a closer look at him. Tell me, Miss Landcastle. Why are you protecting him? And what business does a *friend* have grappling a lady and hauling her through the woods in such a—"

"Enough, Phillip. This isn't an interrogation. Leave the poor woman alone." Captain Buck spoke with the quiet, gentle authority of a trusted friend.

Phillip fell silent, but his shifting jaw told her he wasn't satisfied.

Swallowing hard, she silently willed the man to let his questions die unanswered.

Captain Buck placed the tips of his fingers on her elbow and motioned back toward the log. "Our accommodations are far from comfortable, but please, won't you sit?"

She moved to obey, then stopped cold. "No. I've waited long enough. I thank you for helping Isum, but there's a child who needs you now. He's hurt, and unless you help him, he'll die. I know it." She forced her gaze to the doctor's eyes—eyes burning with the responsibility to save life. In an instant, she knew that, if it was in his power to do so, this surgeon would not deny Little G the doctoring he needed.

"Chief Garcon sent me to fetch you. He said that if you save his son, he will negotiate surrender."

The officers exchanged looks, their eyes round.

"Please," she whispered.

Captain Buck focused on Milly, urgency intensifying his gaze. "What happened to him? How long ago?"

"For heaven's sake, Captain. You can't go up there." Disbelief cracked Phillip's voice.

Captain Buck's fist tightened around the belt crossing his chest at an angle. "Think of the life we might save. Not just this one, but dozens—hundreds!"

Phillip gave Milly his back, positioning himself to speak in the captain's ear, but she heard every terse word. "Use your head. You can't go, and you know it. You don't even know what's wrong with him, or if you'll be able to help."

"Does it matter? I have to try."

"And what if you can't save him. Then what?" Major Bailey didn't wait for the surgeon to reply, but turned to her, his stiff military bearing causing her to shrink inside. "You understand, of course, that Colonel Clinch must approve of our surgeon going to the child's aid." He paused as though waiting for acknowledgement.

Although she didn't understand, she afforded him a brief nod.

"However, the colonel is indisposed at the moment, and it might be close to dawn before he comes and a decision can be made. I suspect he will not authorize such a venture but assure you it will be brought before his attention as soon as possible." He waved a hand toward the nearest tent. "You must be tired. Allow me to see to your accommodations."

"You should let the captain go." A new voice joined the discussion.

Major Bailey's face went rigid as he stepped aside, revealing another bicorn-crowned officer just behind him.

The gentleman joined their circle, probing Milly with his gaze. He was handsome, far more so than the other two. The upward tilt of his chin, confident set to his shoulders, and seductive half-smile lifting one corner of his mouth sent a wave of disquiet through Milly's middle.

The silver tassels on his epaulettes glimmered in the firelight, and she lowered her eyes, keenly aware that she didn't belong here, surrounded by such important men, addressing them as if anything she said was worthy of their consideration. She sucked in a slow, deliberate breath and drew back ever so slightly.

Major Bailey matched her move and slipped a hand to the back of her elbow. She suspected the touch meant to be one of support. Instead, she felt trapped.

"Miss Landcastle, may I present Major Jameson Collins?" Major Bailey's voice was clipped tight, and Milly feared he was beginning to see through her façade.

The sound of rattling chains stemmed from the shadows and her eyes darted toward it. Any minute these officers would realize she should be shackled, as well. Could they see through the shadows of her hood to the pulse pounding in her neck?

Her mind snapped back to her role and she hastily dropped into a courtesy. "A pleasure, Major Collins."

"At last we welcome the elusive lady. Miss Landcastle, the pleasure is all mine." Eyes riveted to her face, Collins bowed more deeply than was usual in such a casual setting. "I'm certain we'll find a way to help the boy."

Fearful of his scrutiny, she turned her head blocking his view with her hood. Something about him sent shivers down her spine, which was a direct contradiction to the fact that he seemed to be on her side. She forced her gaze back. "Thank you, Major."

Almost imperceptivity, Phillip's hold on her tightened.

"Regarding her request," Collins addressed Major Bailey. "Captain Buck is correct. With an offer like that, Colonel Clinch couldn't refuse, and every minute spent waiting for him lessens the captain's odds of helping the boy."

Phillip released her and took a step forward. "Have either of you even considered that this might be a trap?"

Major Collins lifted his chin a notch further. "I don't make it a habit to question a lady's word."

Phillip's fingers curled into a fist at his side.

Milly took another step back, but Major Collins simply shrugged.

"You confound me, Major Bailey. Why put in for promotion if you can't handle the responsibilities your current rank requires?"

Phillip's arm twitched, and the doctor stepped forward as if to intercept an assault. But Phillip held fast, his broad shoulders and fisted hands gradually easing into a more relaxed posture.

"I feel very strongly, sir, that I should go to the child," the surgeon said. "And I will do so with or without your approval, although I'd much rather it be with."

Phillip swiveled away from the men and stared into the night behind Milly. Anger tightened his lips and set his scar aflame.

"Please," she whispered, bringing his flashing eyes to her face.

His gaze bore into her until she dropped her own and prayed he wouldn't lash out at her. At last, he expelled a heavy breath. When she chanced a look, she found his distorted eye beaming anguish. He quickly concealed it and spun on his heel. "Then go. Take Sergeant Garrigus, and if you're not back by dawn, I'm coming in after you."

Chapter Seven

Milly followed in Garcon's wake as he hurtled through the shack's door. The structure shook as the door slammed against the wall. Right behind her, Captain Buck caught the door as it bounced back on its hinges, nearly striking her.

Melting onto an upright barrel, a candle flickered with the gust of wind Garcon created. The single flame lit a corner of the room where Mama Tatty sat on the floor next to a low cot. Her arm lay across Little G's chest, and her head shared his pillow. In a fractured voice, she hummed an unintelligible, mournful tune.

Little G lay so still that Milly might have thought him dead, except for his shallow, raspy breaths. Garcon dropped next to his wife, bumping the cot and swallowing Little G's hand in his grasp. "Milly done brought you a doctor, Little G. He gonna look at you now. Make you better. You wait and see."

The boy made no response.

Pressing her back against the open door, Milly wondered whether he had lost consciousness.

"Let me see him." Captain Buck's voice gentled as he laid a hand on the big man's shoulder. "I'll need plenty of space to work. There will be time to talk to him later."

When only Garcon moved, Captain Buck peered over his shoulder. "Miss Landcastle, if you don't mind?"

Milly crossed the small space and settled an arm around Mama Tatty's shoulders. "The doctor will take care of him now. You can rest for a bit. Just a bit, then you can come back." She patted the woman's arm then gave a small tug. "You're exhausted. How about a bite to eat?"

Mama Tatty turned glazed eyes on her. "You're right. He'll be hungry for his breakfast." With Milly's help, she pulled herself off the ground, but before they reached the door, she shrugged off Milly's arm. "I don't need no help."

"Let me walk with—"

"Let her be." Garcon's command was a bone-chilling growl.

Milly stayed put while Mama Tatty shuffled out the door mumbling about boiling water as she went.

"Let her cook the boy some oats."

The woman would wake the whole camp with her clattering pans, but at least her mind would be occupied. With a nod, Milly stepped toward the threshold. "I'll be right outside if you need me."

Garcon stood over the foot of the cot rocking on his heels. Captain Buck pressed his ear to Little G's chest. Neither man seemed to notice her exit.

The fort stretched out before her as still as death. Hardly a sound could be heard. Even the campfires dotting the premises had dwindled to embers, seemingly forgotten. Milly imagined most everyone laid on their pallets in dreaded anticipation of Little G's fate.

Darkness consumed Mama Tatty as she plodded toward the kitchen. For half a minute, Milly considered following after the woman despite Garcon's order.

"Don't even think about going after her, Miss."

Jumping inside her skin, Milly spun toward the sound of the hushed voice. "Major Bailey, I forgot you were here."

At first, he had refused to let her return to the fort, but when she insisted she must show Captain Buck the way, he had relieved Sergeant Garrigus of his duty and stepped in his place. He'd insisted that if anyone was going to be put in harm's way protecting the doctor, it would be him.

Milly's hand flew to her hood. It was still in place, but did it matter anymore? Not really. She was safe, and the doctor was tending Little G.

Soon bullets would fly between her people and the major's. Enemy lines had been clearly drawn, but she could not bring herself to expose those lines to Phillip. In a few days, either one of them could be dead—or both. It didn't matter whether or not he knew she was another man's property, ruined in every way a woman could be. She refused to be the one to tell him. This sense of value and equality was too precious to willingly forgo.

The building creaked with the release of Phillip's weight. "Forgive me. Again. I'm afraid my manners are a bit rusty." He chuckled and the sound ran through her like sweet, warm milk.

Another soft laugh—this one rancid— came from several yards beyond the major. As Milly's eyes adjusted to the obscurity, she made out the man assigned to guard Phillip, standing with rifle at the ready. She bristled, irrationally afraid he would reveal her secret.

If Phillip recognized the mockery in his guard's laugh, he didn't let on. "How's the boy? Can Marcus help him?" His apparent sincerity over the health of a black child caught her off guard.

She expelled a tremendous breath. "I'm afraid we're too late."

"He's dead?" His muted voice made it difficult to discern whether or not it was relief or alarm that heighten his tone.

"No, but he's much worse than when I left. I should have come to you sooner."

Phillip leaned toward her as if straining to hear. "You say that as if you had a choice." The incredulity in his voice sluiced her with guilt.

He thought her a captive when she was among her own kind, and she had aided that belief. "I did have a choice."

Phillip greeted that information with a space of silence then placed a gentle hand on her arm. "You've been held against your will. No one could possibly blame you for any part of the child's difficulties."

Too comfortable in his nearness, Milly turned and left him, but six steps away, an inexplicable yearning stopped her short.

Although she was under no obligation to continue any sort of relationship with him, Phillip was the only man who had ever treated her with any real tenderness.

Her hand still held the memory of it.

Her ears, the pledge of protection.

Her heart, the warmth of thoughtful consideration.

None of which he would have offered if he'd known the truth.

Every respectful "Miss" and offer of comfort had been meaningless, and always would be.

But maybe, under the blanket of darkness where bloodlines blurred and everyone's skin was a shade of black, maybe for one minute longer, she could play the part. Pretend they were equals and glow beneath the warmth of his gentility.

She sucked in a lungful of air thick with humidity and let it out in a gust. "I didn't come sooner, because I was afraid." *Of being found out, of being caught*. The last bit lodged under her tongue.

He came up behind her moving in so close the heat of his body radiated against her arm. "I can imagine the terror you've experienced here. But you don't have to be afraid anymore."

Milly pushed back the side of her hood to hear his whispering.

"It's over. Marcus and I will take you out of here. Back to where you belong."

What arrogance for a man, in the midst of his enemies and stripped of his weapons, to think he owned power of any sort. Even his rank held no bearing with Garcon, a chief with a penchant for cruelty. Milly's first day in the fort had taught her that lesson, and she wouldn't soon forget it.

"Where *do* you belong?" he mumbled, as though not expecting she a reply.

Arrogant, yes, but his tenderness had set her so at ease, that his hand appearing at the corner of her eye seemed the most natural of movements. With the back of it, he eased aside the edge of her covering.

Unflinching, she drew in a soft breath as his fingertips traced a line down her cheek. Men always grew bolder in the night, but Milly did not draw back. In fact, she swayed, resisting the urge to lean into his touch. How many men had touched her? Yet, never once had she craved more. With a shuddering breath, she coaxed her face away from him.

Inexplicably, Isum's burly features flashed before her mind. If he were here, he wouldn't have allowed this man near her. She was shocked to find herself relieved Isum wasn't in the fort. She squeezed her lids tight. Was she that desperate for acceptance and affection? *God, forgive me. I am.*

She edged away from him, and when the hood once again obscured him from view, she found her courage. "This is where

I belong. And where I'll stay." She prayed the hopelessness that permeated her spirit did not seep into her voice. "There's nothing to rescue me from."

The ensuing silence was so complete that for an instant Milly wondered if she had missed his retreat. Then his breathing resumed, closer and faster, startling her. His seizure of her arm expelled any thought of fleeing. "What are you talking about?" The normal volume of his voice roared in her ear.

"Get your hand off her." The unyielding command came from over her shoulder. The guard?

Milly tried to peer behind her, but Phillip's solid hold and the wall of his frame didn't allow it.

Undaunted, Phillip tightened his possession. "You're no one to give me orders."

The guard snickered. "I'm the one holdin' this rifle to your back and hopin' you'll give me an excuse to use it."

Tension hung in the air, tingling the back of Milly's neck.

When she slid her hand over the knuckles clapped around her arm, Phillip responded with the slightest jolt.

The feel of him, warm against her cool fingers, sent a mournful ache to her core. "You didn't come to help me." She whispered to hide the knot in her throat. *Would wish to God you had.* "You came for the surgeon. But you can't protect him if you're dead." At the first sign of his fingers relaxing, Milly tugged free and kept moving.

That treacherous yearning in her spirit would have to go unquenched.

***

Hours passed and still Marcus worked over the boy. Phillip remained at his station just outside the door, his ear strained to any change in the situation.

He had yet to see Milly since she left him standing with a half dozen questions and the guard jamming his rifle into Phillip's back. Darkness had consumed her, but he imagined she hadn't gone far. She seemed to have formed an attachment to the child and would probably want to be near.

At first, he considered that she might have gone after the distraught mother, which made him nervous.

Garcon was a loose cannon, and Phillip didn't want Milly on the chief's bad side, especially with his son at death's door.

When the mother had scurried back across the compound with a steaming bowl in her hand, Phillip had been surprised Milly didn't return with her. Maybe the child didn't mean as much to her as he thought.

What was she doing running free anyway? What kind of prisoner was allowed that liberty?

He let out an exasperated huff and paced the length of the exterior of the shack, his eyes peeled for Milly, as well as for the guard.

Some time ago, the man had moved into the shadows seeming to have lost interest in his duty. Phillip had no doubt the rifleman was still out there, somewhere. He suspected the guard hoped Phillip would do something rash, but he didn't plan to oblige.

The cabin opened and Marcus' form filled the doorway, silhouetted by the candlelight. His normally squared shoulders drooped, and as he stepped into the night, he massaged the back of his neck.

"I'm here," Phillip called softly, grateful when Marcus came away from the door, allowing them to speak privately. "How is he?"

"Not good. He has a slow abdominal bleed. I thought I might be able to help him, but..."

Phillip had seen Marcus in such a state countless times, but he didn't expect it here, among runaways. "How long?"

"I pray God takes him soon."

Phillip laid a hand on Marcus' shoulder but caught himself before uttering the words "he's just a slave." It seemed the obligatory thing to say—what everyone said when a slave died. He had heard his father voice the same words on any number of occasions. But Marcus wouldn't agree with the statement. He was a doctor, and all deaths intimately affected him. He had a vested interest and saw any death as a professional failure.

As the seconds ticked past, an uneasy feeling burrowed into Phillip's belly. His hand on Marcus' shoulder felt heavy, out of place, and...false. He removed it and stepped back.

With a weary sigh, Marcus returned inside.

Phillip strode to the end of the cabin and leaned a shoulder against the corner, wishing more than anything they could leave this place. Dawn fast approached, and they would be needed in the camp. What had he been thinking to allow this?

A dozen cannon were aimed his way, and all Phillip and Marcus had was a runaway's promise they would be allowed to leave at some point in the future. Phillip shook his head. That wasn't entirely true. Milly had promised, as well, but against such a chief, her words surely carried no weight.

He ran a hand across his face, his thumb bumping against his scars. He snorted. Two years ago, when his molten flesh was still an angry red, he would have scoffed if someone had told him he would willingly place himself inside another doomed fort. Yet here he was. Because of a lady. *And not Adela.* He pondered that fact, surprised to find that through the entire night, he hadn't once thought of her and Totka's letter. Only Milly had filled his mind.

Milly and her crazy notion to stay in this God-forsaken fort.

A slight sound around the side of the shack drew his ear. He stilled and listened. There it was again—the rustle of fabric.

He squinted and made out a heap of something—tarpaulin?—stacked against the building. He moved nearer but paused at the sound of a sigh that could only come from a woman. Picking up pace, he followed the sound of deep, even breathing. He could see her now, curled into a fetal position, the signature hood covering all but her nose, lips, and chin.

She stirred, then bolted upright and scrambled to the back of the pile.

He reached toward her, but froze when she lurched away. His gut wrenched. What would cause to a woman to posses such inbred fear? "It's Phillip." He blinked at the automatic use of his Christian name.

She stilled then her hand flew to her hood.

"You're still covered," he assured.

She took in a ragged breath before scooting to the edge of the pile. "Is Little G...did he die?" The last word caught in her throat.

If she cared as much about her own safety as she did about the slave child, she would be a lot better off. "No, but Marcus said it won't be long."

"What has he been able to do to help? Anything at all?"

"I'm not sure, but whatever it is, it isn't enough."

She slumped and let out a sigh that seemed to come from the depths of some dark place within her. "Another wasted life. And so young."

"I don't understand you. Taken prisoner, but willing to stay—help them, even. Have they so quickly won you to their cause?"

A short, bitter laugh burst from her. "I'm sure I present a rather mystifying picture, but trust me. Some things are best left in the dark." She rose to leave, filling him with disturbing dismay.

He reached out but stopped short of touching her. "Don't go." As an officer under oath to protect the nation's citizens, there were things he could not allow. "I can't let you run off again. Marcus and I will be leaving soon, and if I can't find you, I can't get you out of here."

She paused but didn't face him. "I already told you. I won't be going back. You don't need to bother yourself with me."

"Bother myself?" Phillip's voice rose as did his agitation. "If you think I'm going to leave you here with this band of lawless—"

She snapped her head toward him, and the whites of her eyes became slits in the dim moonlight.

He forced his tone back to a hushed level. "I don't understand what the Negroes have done or said to persuade you to their cause, but you must understand how cruel and desperate they are. They ransack every white homestead they come across taking no care for the blood they spill. Not an American within a hundred miles is safe. These runaways must be reckoned with, and I promise you that before the week is out, they will be. My men will be in possession of this hill, and the taking of it will be bloody. Even if it was at your own request—as unimaginable as that is—I'm not the sort of man who would leave you here to witness it and possibly come to harm."

Unable to read her expression, he could only hope he had gotten through to her. At least she hadn't turned away, and the longer she held his gaze, the more his hope grew.

In a surprise gesture, she lifted a hand and took a tentative step toward him. At the realization that her hand was aiming for the marred side of his face, he flinched then braced himself for the first touch he'd received in years.

Her breath came irregular, and when her fingertips touched his temple, they trembled. As gently as a butterfly landing, they skimmed the uneven surface to his chin in a mirror stroke to his earlier touch.

He sucked in a sharp breath and held it. Had his fingers blazed this hot against her skin? Had her blood run this fast? He hadn't considered how his touch might have affected her. He had simply satisfied the urge to reach out to her, to connect in some small way. If her body had responded even a fraction of the way his did now, there was little wonder she had fled. He had been too bold, too selfish.

With his skin growing warm beneath her lingering touch, he withdrew slightly, fearful that the tingle of his skin might transfer to her fingers enlightening her to the desire escalating beneath.

Stiffening his back, he clamped his hands behind him. He had just said something but for the life of him, he couldn't recall what.

"How did it happen?"

His thoughts lodged in his brain. "How did what...I'm sorry. I don't follow."

"Your face. How did—" She ducked her head. "Forgive me. I forget my place."

Ah, yes. The question everyone thinks but no one asks. Her candor was refreshing. It appeared their unique environment emboldened her, as well. "You've heard of the massacre at Mim's place."

"You were there? I thought everyone died." The awe in her voice rang clear.

"A few survived, and more than originally thought. I was shot outside the walls and fell unconscious onto smoldering timber. Except for the quick actions of a neighbor's slave hiding in the river cane, I would be counted among the dead."

"A *slave* saved your life?"

The question gave Phillip pause. Was that so unusual? "Saul did more than that. For three months, he nursed me back to health in a cabin out in the middle of nowhere—a useless swamp, really. Red Sticks came prowling several times, but they weren't interested in Saul, and he hid me well. He's a good liar, that one." Phillip chuckled, fondly recalling the months spent in the man's company.

They were the most painful, in body and spirit, he'd ever endured, but he wouldn't trade them for a lifetime with Adela. If not for Saul, Phillip might never have learned to connect with Christ on a soul-searching level. He might never have learned that there was more to a man than a handsome face.

A deep sigh pinched off Phillip's laugh. He lowered himself onto the stack of tarpaulin. "Saul was God's gift to a rotten man."

"Where is he now?"

"In his swamp, determined to live alone but free. It was my gift to him, keeping his survival a secret from his dead master's kin." He cocked his head toward Milly as she settled down beside him. "I trust you won't tell anyone?"

"Of course not, but," her slim shoulders lifted into a self-deprecating gesture, "may I ask you something?"

He angled his body toward her. "Please do."

"Enoch...he's your slave."

"That's right."

"Why? When you seem to understand the value of freedom, why do you own a slave?"

Phillip's insides bristled. "Not every black man is meant to be free. Enoch could never survive on his own. He needs me."

"Have you asked him what he wants?"

She had no right to question Phillip's morality. He was a good person—a good Christian. "He's well cared for, and I have only ever treated him with kindness."

Voices within the cabin rose and carried through the wall. There was no mistaking the mother's agitated tone. Had the child reached the end?

Phillip and Milly said nothing until the voices died down. When Milly spoke, it was with tears clogging her voice. "Little G will die a free boy tonight. He is blessed above so many others."

Finding no way around that ludicrous statement without being downright rude, Phillip kept a tight seal on his lips.

"It's in your power to see that Enoch lives free. What a gift that would be to a young man." She cleared her throat. "Freedom is a treasure that those born with don't appreciate. Those who live without it can't fathom it—not until they've experienced it. And then, *then*, they'll do everything in their power to keep it. This fort won't be as easy to conquer as you imagine."

Uneasy with her keen perception and the direction the conversation had taken, Phillip stood and walked off a few steps. "I admire your compassion for the human plight, but your own freedom is the more pressing issue."

"I see." Her flat tone clearly said that she was lying. But what was there not to see?

He twisted and stared at her. "I don't believe you do."

"Who else survived?"

"Excuse me?"

"The massacre. You said there were others?"

Had she not listened to a word he'd said all night? Apparently, there was no reasoning with her. Swallowing a huff of frustration, he whisked sweaty palms down his trousers then crossed his arms. "My fiancé," he quipped, "but one look at me after the fact, and she promptly turned me away." As the words left his mouth, the Spirit whispered that it was time he stop believing that lie. But believing the truth meant admitting she'd turned him away for reasons that went deeper than his external scars.

When Milly met his declaration with silence, he continued, "In exchange for a Red Stick."

A hand flew to her mouth. "How beautiful! She married an Indian. And the enemy, no less."

Phillip bunched his lips then rubbed eyes that burned with fatigue. "There's nothing beautiful about rejection. And I didn't say they wed. He thinks she's dead."

Soft footsteps neared, and when Phillip dropped his hands, he found Milly standing toe to toe with him. She laid a cautious hand on his arm.

"I know the pain in your voice. Rejection for any reason hurts, but it only lasts a moment. Something you can't change such as...your skin," her hand fluttered across his cheek, "...well. That is a wound that cuts deeper than most. One you cannot hide."

Again, he wondered what lay beneath that hood.

Too soon, she expanded the distance between them. "But you're a good man, Major Bailey. You'll do the right thing."

The right thing? Isn't that what he'd been trying to do these last years since God gave him another lease on life? Yet this woman seemed to have a different concept of what that was. It confused and fascinated him.

The squeal of a door sent Milly dashing around the corner of the shack. Phillip followed in time to see the last of her skirt as it whipped around the doorpost. He would have followed her through, except for Marcus intercepting him with a hand to his shoulder.

"The boy's dead. It's time to go." Although weary, Marcus' voice held a brusque, no-nonsense tone.

An unfamiliar, mournful tune floated from the cabin. Only a grieving mother could sing in such a way.

"You negotiated Milly's release?"

A shake of Marcus' head sent his mussed hair into his eyes, but he didn't brush it away. "Forget it, Phillip. It's no use."

"That's ridiculous. We have to try." Phillip tried to muscle past, but bumped against Marcus as he stepped further into Phillip's path.

"I did. Now, let it go." He raised his voice, his patience already spent, confusing Phillip, boiling his blood.

He struggled against Marcus' hold on his arms. "No way. We risked our lives coming here. For his *son*. The least he owes us is a prisoner release." He directed his heated words over his friend's shoulder and toward the open door.

Moments later, Milly appeared in the doorway, head lowered and face obscured. "Garcon says you have minutes to leave, or he will tar you and burn you alive as he did the other," she said, her voice devoid of emotion.

Without another word, she closed the door in Phillip's face.

"Milly! Miss Landcastle!" He freed an arm and pounded a fist against the door.

"Enough." Marcus shoved hard, propelling Phillip away from the cabin

Chest heaving, he ground his teeth, but didn't resist further.

There was still time. He would bring the matter before Colonel Clinch. If official negotiations didn't work, when they stormed Negro Fort in a few days' time, Phillip would make it his personal mission to seek Garcon out.

Grieving father or not, he would pay his debts. If not with a prisoner exchange, then with his blood.

***

In an array of oranges and pinks, dawn streaked the sky. Its beauty would have been lost on Phillip, except that he kept his eyes glued to it as he stood at attention before Colonel Clinch.

The field officer paced, the skirts of his coatee flapping wildly. As he listened to Marcus debrief him on the night's unauthorized mission of mercy, the colonel's normally soft jaw firmed into a rigid line beneath his long sideburns.

Major Collins, his lip raised in a barely concealed sneer, stood on hand to witness their dressing down.

"If you think to sway me with stories of suffering children, you're quite mistaken." From the narrow shadow cast by his chapeau bra, Clinch's clear blue eyes pierced Phillip with their displeasure. "For an officer to enter the fort at all, much less without at least informing me, is foolish beyond words. For it to be the unit's only surgeon is unthinkable!" His meatless lips thinned even further as he stopped before Phillip, inches from his face. "What you deserve, Major Bailey is a demotion."

"May I speak, sir?" Marcus asked.

"If you think it will do either of you any good, then please do."

"Major Bailey was not in agreement with my going to the fort, sir."

Phillip suppressed a growl. He would return to Tensaw and push cattle before he allowed Marcus to tarnish the bright future that he had ahead of him. "Sir, if I may—"

"No, you may *not*." Clinch's jaw turned to steel.

Marcus continued with hardly a hitch. "When I determined to do so with or without permission, he consented but refused to let me go alone. I take full responsibility."

Major Collins shifted his stance. He blinked in rapid succession.

"Is this true?" Colonel Clinch's gaze burned a hole in Phillip's cheek.

"I did not approve of the idea, sir, but neither did I forcefully detain the surgeon, as I might have done. Captain Buck has no cause to assume all responsibility."

For an interminable minute, Colonel Clinch continued to breathe down Phillip's stiff collar. When at last he turned away, it was to stare at Major Collins, who immediately straightened his posture.

"Captain Buck," Colonel Clinch began, his back to Marcus and his gaze still pegged on Collins. "It has come to my attention that you believe Major Bailey's mental health to be in question. Can you deny this?"

Phillip's wind caught in his chest. His gaze darted to Collins whose cheek twitched.

The confusion rumpling Marcus' brow confirmed what Phillip already knew—his friend wouldn't betray him. No, this was all Collins' doing. The only question was how he'd come across the information.

His mind flashed back to the night Marcus had spoken his mind. The only other person who had been present was—

Enoch.

Phillip brushed away the thought. The boy would never be disloyal. Their bond was too strong.

When Marcus didn't respond, Colonel Clinch turned on his heel, setting his epaulettes to dancing. A single eyebrow arched toward the canvas stretched above them.

Marcus' mouth hung open for a moment before he boldly spoke. "Sir, when your source slandered Major Bailey, were his motives for the good of the unit or for the betterment of his own career?"

Laughter bubbled inside Phillip's throat. He restrained it, but Colonel Clinch was not as successful. He let loose a short, amazed chuckle. "I asked myself the same question."

"They're back, sir." Collins comment redirected the colonel's gaze.

Captain Isaacs and Major McIntosh approached. If their stoic faces were any indication, their request for the fort's unconditional surrender had been rebuffed.

Excellent timing, eh, Collins?

"Finally," Colonel Clinch muttered. "Gentleman, we'll revisit this topic when I have the time to deal with such petty squabbles. It goes without saying you will not attempt another such reckless undertaking."

"Yes, sir," Phillip and Marcus chorused with a crisp salute.

"I'll thank heaven for that. Dismissed." The morning sun caught the spotless white of Clinch's pantaloons as he strode toward the approaching warriors.

The natives greeted him in terse tones.

"I'll wager the navy will be priming their artillery within the hour," Marcus confided to Phillip, as the two took their leave. "I best ready the clinic."

They parted company, and as Phillip passed McIntosh, the chief acknowledged him with a respectful nod. Phillip returned it, but his thoughts carried him beyond the half-Scot chief to another warrior—the one with the hitch in his gait and the grief in his eyes.

Phillip held the power to change it to the latter, but could he wield it?

"You're a good man. You'll do the right thing." Milly's confident statement slammed against his conscience.

Why did her approval mean so much? He didn't care what anyone else thought of him. But for some inexplicable reason, it mattered that Milly looked down on him for owning a slave, that she held out hope he would "do the right thing."

At some point during the last few days, thoughts of Milly had overlapped—then overtaken—thoughts of Adela. It had been refreshing and given him a new sense of motivation. They were different thoughts, those of Adela being filled with love unrequited and those of Milly simply being an obsession to fix and protect. If nothing else, it proved Phillip could let Adela go, that he could move on.

Throwing his shoulders back, he aimed his steps toward his tent and lengthened his stride.

"Enoch, fetch my tablet," he called, still ten steps away.

He threw back the tent flap and was surprised to find it empty. *Blast, there isn't time for this!* He rummaged through his things determined to get this done before he was obliged to rally his men to prepare for battle.

At last, he came across writing paper buried beneath his extra pair of trousers.

He might be a slave-owner, but he *wasn't* a liar and a thief. And with one letter, he would prove it.

Chapter Eight

With the missive in the hands of the Indian courier, Phillip returned from the Creek camp feeling as though a tremendous weight had been lifted. His purse was lighter, that was certain, but a clear conscience was worth every silver coin he owned.

No more than an hour had passed from the time he sat down to pen the note, but as he returned to camp he noted that it had taken on a different tone—one of expectancy. Men geared up for assault. Some cleaned their weapons. A handful knelt in prayer. Others placed bets on how long it would take to blast a hole through the earthen wall. Two days seemed the most popular answer.

At the very least. It would be days before the army was called into action. *Don't rush it, boys. Let the Navy do her worst.* As the thought crossed his mind, he prayed he might have a chance to approach Colonel Clinch about Milly's situation. There was still a chance he could return for her before the balls began to fly.

Clinch was angry, but he wasn't heartless. If there was a white woman in the fort in need of rescuing, he would do his best to help her. And there *was* a white woman. Phillip had confirmed it with his own eyes, and Marcus would back him up. He hoped.

As Phillip passed his tent, he took a glance inside. It was empty. *Where is that boy?* With Cook, perhaps? Or Marcus?

On his way to Cook's station, he stopped in the clinic, which consisted of no more than an open-sided tent and several rows of pallets primed to receive the wounded.

Isum laid on his side facing away, his massive shirtless torso glistening with sweat. The droplets clung to a mess of scars that crisscrossed his back and snaked around his side, over which Marcus worked.

He wore no coat, and the ruffled front of his linen shirt lay in a mass of damp folds against his vest. He lifted weary eyes from peeling away the old dressing then nodded toward a basin of water just beyond his reach. "Scoot that toward me, will you, sir?"

Phillip moved the bowl a few feet closer. "Has Enoch been through here?"

"Haven't seen him since yesterday."

A smirk slid up the side of Isum's face. "Lose your boy?"

Marcus' hand stilled in the bowl of water an instant before he caught Phillip's eye. He sat back on his haunches. "What do you know about it?" he asked the slave.

Isum jerked one shoulder. "I mighta given him a few pointers. What he did with 'em was his own business."

A sinking sensation filled Phillip's gut, but he shoved it aside.

"What did you tell him? Did you send him to the fort? Is that where he is?" Marcus demanded.

Lids narrowed and jaw clenched, Isum didn't utter another sound.

"He's just a boy! Do you have any idea the amount of danger you've placed him in?" Marcus lurched to his feet accidently kicking the basin. Bloody water sloshed Isum in the face, but he did little more than blink.

Phillip jumped aside as Marcus pushed past him. He had never seen his friend so riled. "There's no call for this. We both know Enoch would never run."

Marcus stopped at the tent's edge, his eyes fixed on the distant fortified bluff. "With all due respect, sir, you're a fool." He spun and left Phillip with his mouth gaping and his ears turning hot.

Anger burned his insides and zinged his cheeks. As he was turning to demand an explanation, a flutter caught his peripheral vision and brought his attention back to the fort.

At its most promontory point at the river's edge, two new flags flapped in the wind. The topmost being the Union Jack and the one beneath, a solid red flag.

Red, for blood. For no surrender.

How many would die before the fort was subdued? How many wounded? Marcus had every reason to feel strain, but was he correct in believing Enoch had left Phillip? That he had intentionally placed himself in a position which would force Phillip to fire upon him? The thought was too difficult to dwell on. "Enoch, where are you?" he muttered.

Across the river, a single cannon boomed sending a red-hot ball streaking in a high arch over the water. The center gunboat rocked in the waves it created by the blast.

Urgency to reach Milly coursed through him.

White, blinding light filled the sky. An instant, later a bone-jarring concussion hurled Phillip through the air and turned his world black.

***

Ears ringing, Phillip cracked open his lids.

A clod of dirt thudded to the ground inches from his head, pulverizing and spraying into his eyes. Instinctively, he covered his head with his arm.

The heavens opened and a shower of debris rained down. Phillip curled into a ball as dirt, rocks, and shards of wood pelted his body. He held his breath until the storm ended, then did a quick assessment of his condition.

Arms, legs, torso. He ached from the landing, but aside from a few small cuts, he wasn't hurt. Fighting a wave of dizziness, he struggled to his feet and tried to orient himself.

Smoke filled the air, making Phillip's eyes water and his lungs burn. It cleared in pockets revealing surroundings that he barely recognized.

Rubble plastered the tents, some of which bubbled and moved as their occupants sought escape. Men sat or stood in various stages of confusion, but none seemed seriously hurt.

An eerie quiet filled the daylight. Nature had hushed, so that only the wind and the faint crackle of fire could be heard.

Behind him, Marcus was sitting up, rubbing his ears.

Phillip squinted into the immediate area looking for the center of the blast. He found nothing. His line of sight widened its circumference, up to the river's shore then around to the forest's edge behind him. Gray haze hung in the air like a cabin with a blocked chimney flue.

A strong breeze kicked up whisking away some of the smoke and exposing the blood stained top of a fallen tent canvas. Phillip grimaced at the blood still dripping onto it. His gaze followed the droplets into the pine towering above the tent, and his mind stumbled upon an object that did not fit its surroundings.

Hooked in the tree's branches and still swaying with the force of its landing was a black arm, its ragged end draining.

Phillip spun. "Isum!" he called.

Marcus stood, a bewildered expression scrunching his features. "What happened?" he nearly shouted while mashing his ears with the heels of his palms.

"I don't know, but your patient is missing an arm." Phillip pointed toward the tree then began pulling back canvas, tossing it up to look beneath.

The sight yanked Marcus out of his daze. He turned a circle where he stood and scoured the wreckage. "Where is he? He was just here."

A moan led them to a bulge beneath the canvas. Together they flipped it back exposing Isum who sat up looking perplexed, but perfectly whole.

Phillip's mind reeled. If the arm wasn't Isum's, then...

"God have mercy." Marcus' face went pale, his jaw hung open.

Following Marcus' horrified gaze, Phillip rotated.

The wind shifted the smoke toward the north and cleared their view of the bluff, but he couldn't find Negro Fort. It was gone—razed to nothing but charred ground and a few burning timbers.

Where once had loomed thick earthen walls, now only rubble remained. Nothing moved. Not a human was in sight, wounded or otherwise.

What force could possibly wreak such devastation? Phillip struggled to wrap his mind around it and failed.

Then in one painful twist, her name lodged in his throat.

"Milly!" Isum jumped to his feet, his long cry matching the one caged in Phillip's heart. Blood pumped from Isum's unbound wound. He stumbled five steps before either Marcus or Phillip had the presence of mind to stop him. It took both of them to tackle him to the ground.

"There's nothing you can do," Marcus hollered above Isum's wails. "You're not well enough to search for her. There will be others to do it."

Beneath the weight of Phillip's body, the man writhed and cried, his distorted, agony-stricken face raising the hairs on Phillip's arms.

"I'll find her," he shouted in Isum's ear. "Do you hear me? I'll find her and bring her back." Even as he said it, Phillip didn't know how he would bring himself to step inside the flattened fortification. If the sight of two corpses had sent him reeling, how would he face hundreds?

The man calmed.

"Captain Buck will bind up your wound so you will be fit to help her when she gets here."

Quiet now, Isum blinked and nodded.

"Good." Phillip rolled off the man and patted his shoulder. "Pull yourself together then get this place back in order. We'll be needing it for the wounded."

Isum nodded again, "Yes, suh."

Relieved at his compliance, Phillip looked toward the fort's remains and wondered how many had died. Had it been a single blast or had more explosions occurred while Phillip was unconscious? Was there any chance that Milly had survived, that *anyone* had?

"We come to help." Totka stood to the side, his hand extended.

It was the first time he had seen Totka without his turban. Tied back only at the top of his broad forehead, blue-black hair blew around his face. His chiseled jaw was slack, his lips turned down.

Beyond him, warriors poured through the trees and filled the clearing. Many stopped and gawked at the destruction. Their presence tightened the knot in Phillip's stomach.

He grasped Totka's proffered hand and allowed himself to be pulled to his feet. He nodded his thanks then swatted red dust off his pantaloons. "If you're offering help, we'll take it." He repositioned his bicorn on his head then turned to Marcus. "Do what you can for Isum but follow us up. We'll need you." *I'll need you*.

"I'll be there as soon as I can, sir, but I might need to tend some of our own wounded first." Already pressing wadding down on Isum's side, Marcus peered at Phillip out of the tops of his eyes, assessing him as only a doctor could.

Phillip glanced away. "Fine." His face heated with the thought that his weakness was so obvious that Marcus felt compelled to assess it. Phillip's head went light at the thought of failing his soldiers or humiliating himself in front of them. He couldn't allow it. He wouldn't. Fort Mims would stay in the past, where it belonged.

Totka left with the warriors, and Phillip called to his sergeants and instructed them to organize their men into squads and send them to different quarters of the fort. Their only orders were to bring any wounded to the clinic for medical attention. He left with the last squad.

If a severed arm had made it this far, he dreaded learning what the interior held. Except, for the driving need to find Milly and Enoch, Phillip might not have found the mental stamina to scale the bluff. As he picked his way through the glowing embers of the fort's perimeter, images of Fort Mims flashed before him. He squeezed his mind shut against the onslaught, but the scent of burning wood smarting in his nostrils sent pain ripping down his cheek.

Keep your mind on task, keep your mind on task... His gaze combed the grounds for movement of any kind.

A cold sweat broke out on his skin and sent shivers through him despite the scorching heat. He stepped over unidentifiable scorched flesh as his insides gave way to trembling.

Creek warriors fanned out across the blackened ground. Phillip's molars ground against each other as he staved off a wave of nausea.

Beside him, a private leaned on his knees and retched.

Swallowing his own bile, Phillip waited beside him until he was done then clasped his shoulder. "No harm done, Private Gilroy."

The young man wiped his mouth then his dirty, tear-streaked cheeks. "They're all dead, sir."

"We might find some alive, yet. Focus on that. It'll help."

He moved on, but found nothing even remotely resembling a complete body. His breath grew heavier. Death surrounded him, mocked him, and tried at every step to drag him into history and disgrace him. Legs going numb, he feared he might stumble.

A mound of dirt rose before him. The upper half a woman's body protruded and appeared unharmed. The rest of her was hidden beneath the rubble.

He dropped to his knees and patted her cheek.

The woman groaned. Her lashes fluttered.

A wobbly smile curved his lips. Frantically, he began scraping away soil. "Hold on. I'll get you out," Phillip said while praying the rest of her was in one piece.

Private Gilroy fell to the ground beside Phillip and joined him in digging. Within minutes, she was free. The bone in her lower leg protruded from her flesh, but everything else seemed intact. It was incomprehensible how she had managed to come away virtually unscathed considering the carnage around her.

Grateful the woman had dropped back into unconsciousness, Phillip sat back on his heels and wiped at the sweat dripping into his eyes. "Have you seen Captain Buck?"

The private pointed a crusty finger toward the front of the fort. "Saw him head back that way a few minutes before we found her. Want me to fetch him?"

Phillip shook his head. "I'll get him. You stay with her. If she wakes up, try to keep her calm. Take off your jacket. Use it to give her shade."

As the private worked the buttons of his coat, Phillip rose to seek out Marcus.

Upon reaching the center, he stopped, unable to rationalize why a crater would have been dug in the middle of the fortification. The basin was blackened and empty, except for the debris that had fallen, littering it. Smoke rose from the earth itself as if the crater had been baked in a massive oven. The destruction went out and away from the depression in a perfect circle. *The center of the explosion*. Only the munitions store could cause such a blast and wreak such havoc.

Skirting the singed hollow, he swallowed a knot of fear. Odds of finding Milly and Enoch alive were next to nothing. Then again, he hadn't reckoned on finding the one alive, and if there was one, there might be others. He picked up his step.

All throughout, groups of soldiers and Indians burrowed through the wreckage. The closer Phillip grew to the front of the fort and the river, the more serious the search, and for good reason. This section seemed less affected by the blast. Spotting two, then three survivors being aided to their feet, Phillip allowed a spark of hope to ignite.

Through swirling dust and smoke, Marcus' tall, thin frame caught Phillip's eye. Across the compound, he pushed himself up from the ground as two warriors tugged a man to his feet then slung his arms over their shoulders.

As the Indians neared with their charge, Phillip squinted into the sunlight hopeful his mind was playing tricks on him. The warriors turned to take the path from the fort, and although covered in soot, their prisoner's wild, wiry hair couldn't be confused for any others' than Garcon's. The children lay in tatters, while their ruthless chief walked away whole.

Ire singed Phillip's throat and propelled him to find others, to be a part of recovering lives worth saving.

He signaled to Marcus, but another patient had already snagged his attention. Phillip began to trot the final yards to his friend, but a flutter halted his step.

A portion of fabric protruded from beneath a pile of planks. He knew that pale brown well, carried a snippet of it in his shirt pocket. His heart lurched then dropped with a crash to the pit of his stomach.

Atop the material, lay an arm stripped of its sleeve. Though scratched and streaked with blood and dirt, it was unmistakably white. The rest of her was buried beneath the ruins of whatever building had stood above her.

"Milly?" Phillip called, his voice clogged with dust and tears. He staggered toward the site, unable to reach her without scaling half the mound. "Milly, can you hear me?"

Not one of her fingers so much as twitched.

Swallowing grit and fear, he quickly circled the pile and assessed the situation.

Boards crisscrossed in a tangled mess as high as his chest. Jagged edges stuck out at all angles, and there seemed no good place to begin clearing. Perhaps if he went in from the other side…?

The wind kicked up and whistled through the heap causing it to shudder.

It was more unstable than he'd thought. One wrong move and the whole thing would topple.

Jesus, where do I start? he prayed.

Sweat poured between his shoulder blades. He ripped off his jacket and tossed it to the side.

When he summoned help, several soldiers joined him. He worked alongside Sergeant Garrigus, orchestrating every move, monitoring every board they touched and when. As the pile diminished, Phillip's dread grew. The image of the arm in the tree haunted him with every board he tugged free and tossed aside.

His muscles trembled with fatigue and his stomach lurched with trepidation.

"This is where I belong." Her hushed words floated through his mind as real as if she'd just uttered them. They jabbed at his heart with stinging precision.

He wanted to scream at her. This *is where you belong?* He wanted to scream at himself for not dragging her out when he'd had the chance.

More than that, he wanted to hold her—needed to hold her, to assure her that she would never have to look at this place again. If he found her alive, he would get her as far away from it as possible. He would take her wherever she wanted to go to get this horrible fort and all its memories as far behind her as he could.

Splinters pierced his hands as he grunted and lifted the last slab. Chest deep in the rubbish, Sergeant Garrigus ducked to peer beneath the wood Phillip had raised. "She's all in one piece," he declared.

Praise, God! Phillip tossed the wood to the side and picked his way overtop the rubble to the hollow they had uncovered.

"Surgeon, you're needed here!" Garrigus shouted as he moved toward Milly's head then out of the wreckage, allowing Phillip a partial view of the situation.

If not for the depression in which she lay, the timbers' weight would have surely crushed her. Her skirt, tattered and singed, was twisted about her waist. Her legs were scraped and caked with dried blood. Draped over a sideways board, her upper body hung lower than her legs, concealing the rest of her from full view.

Near her feet, Phillip crawled into the hollow. "Is she alive?"

"I think so." Garrigus reached his thick hands to lift Milly's head.

Phillip yanked her skirt down over her legs then stretched forward and burrowed one arm under her knees and another under her back. Although she made no response to his touch, her body felt warm and alive.

"Is she free? Can I take her?"

"Hold up," Garrigus said. "Her sleeve is stuck under this..." He groaned as he shifted rubble with this shoulder. "Got it! Take her. Quick."

Phillip pulled her to his chest then straightened his knees and lifted her free of the wreckage.

Her upper body hung at an awkward angle, and her arms dangled and bumped his knees.

He adjusted his hold by bouncing her slightly and scooting his arm further up her back and beneath her shoulders. The move flipped her head up landing it against his chest.

Coarse hair rubbed his chin. He peered down at the top of her head then missed his footing. He caught himself just before sending her flying from his arms.

"Steady, sir!" Garrigus crawled backwards off the mound. "Corporal, get yourself over here and help the Major."

Was this not Milly? Panic took hold, squeezing his throat like a vice.

Higgins plodded toward him and held out his arms. Phillip passed her off then climbed out just as Marcus arrived on the scene.

A smile touched his weary eyes. "You found her." He pressed his fingers to her neck and nodded. "Just unconscious. Lay her down. I need to examine that gash on her forehead."

When Higgins dropped to one knee and settled her on the ground, Phillip gained a glimpse of her face. His gaze traveled from her parted lips to her slender throat, and his thoughts ground to a halt. It was his first real look at her in the sunlight and without that cursed hood, but even through the dirt-clotted blood staining her features, he couldn't deny this was Milly.

Dark lashes fanned out from her closed lids, and tiny sable freckles spanned the bridge of her nose. Except for the wound on her forehead, he found not a single blemish, just smooth, perfect skin. Its silky feel still registered on his fingertips. She was more beautiful than he'd believed her to be, but... "She's black," he whispered to himself.

Marcus looked up from picking debris out of the wound. "Yes, she has African blood," he said, as though he'd known all along.

The world tipped, and Phillip dropped to the edge of the pile that once held Milly captive. He sank his head to his hands and dug his fingers into his sweaty hair. *She's a slave.* Part black. How much didn't matter. One drop was enough to condemn her.

Phillip took a tentative glance at the wound on her forehead and the mass of black hair beyond. Kinky tufts had pulled loose from the braid that worked a circle around her head.

The hood had hadn't concealed scars. It had concealed her bloodline.

Marcus was right. Phillip was a fool.

Chapter Nine

"I said I'll take her." Phillip stepped between doctor and patient. He had a promise to fulfill—to Isum and Milly. He would personally get her out of this fort if it killed him doing so.

A protest written in his eyes, Marcus opened his mouth to speak.

Phillip cut him off. "I'll leave her with Isum then come back to search for Enoch. He's still missing." He was as eager to be away from her as Marcus was for him to be. His friend closed his mouth then expelled a slow breath through his nose. When he backed up, Phillip collected Milly in his arms. He had not gone far before Marcus called to him.

"Major, the clinic will need several sentries. Would you mind seeing to that before returning?"

"Not at all," Phillip lied. How could he place Milly under guard as if she were a common criminal? He pulled her tighter to his chest and hunched up one shoulder, tilting her body so that her head didn't slip and loll.

Isum needed a gun pointed at him at all hours, but perhaps they could make an exception for Milly. Phillip would give up his tent until she recovered and...*and what*? What would happen to her once she was well? His mind leapt forward to what would become of the runaways, then in one stupefying blow he connected the dots.

His leg buckled and one knee went down, slamming into dirt and rocks. Pain shot up his thigh and into his back, but only one thought registered.

Milly was a runaway. Just like the rest of them. Once well, she would be a flight risk. And just like the rest of them, she would be returned to her owner. *Her owner...*

Phillip squelched any further thought on that subject. He pushed his foot back under him and focused on getting her to the clinic and out of his arms. He would request an assignment to fort detail, settling matters with the Creek, record keeping, serving gruel—anything but handling matters with the surviving runaways.

As he neared the clinic, he spotted Isum. The tent had been re-erected and a few of the wounded brought in. As of yet, no guard had been placed over them, but Phillip wasn't surprised. The camp was in chaos. There was no protocol for a situation such as this.

Isum could have run off, but he had stayed. For Milly. The man loved her, and he had every right—unlike Phillip.

Each moment, Milly felt heavier. She was long but thin and easy enough to carry. It was the suffocating burden in his heart that made each step an exertion. She was alive, and he was grateful. Beyond that, he couldn't cope with more. He would hand her off, then force himself to wipe her from his mind.

Several Indian wives had arrived and were tending the wounded, one of those under their care being the woman Phillip had unburied earlier. She seemed alert and responsive. Isum knelt nearby listening to her speak, but she lost his attention when he noticed Phillip's approach. His eyes grew round and spilled tears quicker than Phillip would have imagined possible.

In three bounding strides, Isum reached them. Like a possessive child, he pulled Milly from Phillip's grasp.

"Easy with her," Phillip snapped. "She's taken a blow to the head."

He responded with garbled wails as tears and mucus streaked down his face unchecked. He crushed her to his chest pressing her head against him at an odd angle.

"I said take it easy. You're going to snap her neck."

Isum gentled his hold then wiped at dried blood on her neck. "She gonna be alright? Where's the doc?"

"Captain Buck said she's just unconscious. He'll see that she's healthy before she's sent back to her master." Bitterness twisted his tone.

Another wail peeled from the big man's throat as he pressed his cheek against hers. It was the sound of broken hopes and dreams, the sound of the condemned.

It shattered Phillip's nerves. "You're bleeding again. Go put her down. See if you can cool her with a little water." He swiveled and quickly put distance between himself and the tragedy unfolding before him.

He stopped the first two men he came across and assigned them guard duty, then mechanically, set his sights on the fort. On the way back, he encountered six male slaves prodded forward by a sober-faced warrior brandishing a rifle. Phillip stepped aside to let them pass on the trail. Judging by the slaves' half-lidded, tear-stained expressions, they'd lost the will to fight, and the armed warrior was a mere token.

Totka came down the path, his breath coming fast and his eyes boring into Phillip, searching. "Your woman, she lives?"

Phillip loosed an abrupt exhale. "She's not *mine*, but yes, she was found alive."

"She is chattel?"

"Appears to be." He dusted his hands together, then propped them on his hips.

"Why do you leave her now?" Totka jutted his chin toward the American camp.

Phillip's head jerked back. "I don't understand your meaning. She's unconscious, and there are others who need my help. My boy, Enoch, for one."

Totka's brows bunched. "The boy is wounded?"

"I think he was at the fort when it blew. No one has seen him since yesterday afternoon. Captain Buck thinks he's a runner." His throat closed around the last two words, and he looked away, anxious to renew his search.

"I will find him," Totka said, giving Phillip a nudge toward the camp. "Go to the woman. She has much need of you."

A half-strangled laugh popped from Phillip's mouth. "She doesn't need me. She never did." With emptiness filling his chest, he took possession of the narrow path and resumed the trek up the embankment.

Milly might not need him, but Enoch would. If he was still alive.

***

"Five hundred swords in scabbards, five hundred carbines, four hundred pistols, one hundred eighty-seven rifles, and two thousand five hundred muskets." Sergeant Garrigus ticketed the items off his list with an ink-stained finger. He squinted at the paper, then scratched his chin, smudging it black. "Plus one hundred, sixty-three barrels of gun powder."

The armory at the backside of the fort had survived the blast and the cache of small arms found inside had been brought to camp. It lay in piles before Phillip, who had been charged with its collection, inventory, and distribution.

He walked the line and compared Garrigus' numbers with his own.

"Find the boy yet, sir?" Garrigus asked.

Worry over Enoch had taken up permanent residence in Phillip's mind. "Not so much as a shred of clothing."

Garrigus clucked his tongue and ran a thick finger behind his leather neckstock. "Shame to lose a quality slave."

"Shame to lose a quality friend," Phillip retorted, his gaze pegging a stunned Garrigus. Enoch had left a larger hole in Phillip's life than he ever would have imagined possible, and it had nothing to do with his shoes no longer being brushed to a shine.

Needing to redirect his thoughts, he jabbed a finger at the paper in his hand. "Our numbers match."

A moment of silence passed before Garrigus wagged his head and dropped his voice to a hushed growl. "It's a heck of a lot to give them Indians, sir."

He quirked an eyebrow. "You suggesting we should go back on our agreement?"

Garrigus visibly withdrew. "No, sir. I'm just sayin' that it won't be the last time we see these arms. And when we do, they just might be pointed at our bellies."

It took everything within Phillip not to heartily agree with his sergeant. The Creek warriors had been invaluable to the United States Army over the last week. With their random continuous fire, they had kept the Negroes busy and on their toes. After the navy's hot shot rolled into the magazine and obliterated the fort, the warriors had toiled alongside the

Americans to rescue the twenty-five survivors and bury the dead.

Colonel Clinch chose a plot beyond the demolished village for the communal burial, and the Creek women had keened as if they'd interred their own.

When the American sailor's scalping, tarring, and burning had been confirmed, Clinch had handed eagerly Chief Garcon over to the Creek to do with as they pleased. His execution had been swift and, to Phillip's way of thinking, too merciful.

The two nations' mutual goal to subdue the fort had been achieved. Neither the Creek nor the Americans had wished for it to end as it had, but when it did they pulled together as brothers—an unexpected, yet not entirely unpleasant, twist.

As it was, a man had no grounds to mistrust these Indians...unless that man had seen his loved ones slaughtered by them in a previous engagement.

The sun's scorching heat pressed on Phillip's shoulders and, in the blink of an eye, he found himself just outside the burning pickets of Fort Mims. Shrieks of terror and the roar of flames enveloped his senses. *"Captain Bailey!"* someone screamed for his brother, Dixon, just before he went down. His wild eyes flashed before Phillip's face, then dimmed as life ebbed from a hole in his gut. Another warrior came at Phillip from the left, engaging him while Dixon bled out alone.

"Major Bailey?"

Phillip blinked rapidly. He focused on the stream of sweat running down his neck while forcefully clearing his mind. He licked dry lips and for five beautiful seconds allowed himself to dwell on Milly's beautiful image, to think of what it would be like to hold her and love her back to health. *Love a slave*?

"Major, you alright?"

Phillip blinked again, and Milly's delicate cheekbones were replaced by Garrigus' sun-crinkled eyes as they burrowed into Phillip's. His meaty hand shook Phillip's arm. "Are ya in there somewhere?"

Phillip shoved the man in his broad chest. "Are you trying to dance with me, sergeant?" His forced smile felt more like a grimace.

Garrigus flashed his yellowed teeth in a wide-mouthed grin. “You were a thousand miles away. Nice of you to rejoin us here in this tropical paradise.” He slapped the back of his neck and examined his hand. “Blasted creatures gonna suck me dry before the day’s through.”

Wiping his palm on his coat front, his gaze caught something of interest behind Phillip. His lip curled at the edge in a barely concealed snarl. “Don’t look now, sir, but the devil’s on a mission and his pitchfork is pointed straight at you.”

There was only one person in camp to fit that description. Phillip caught the laughter barreling up his throat then peered down his nose at Garrigus. “You will address your superiors is a respectable manner, or pay for it with your rations.”

Another grin. “Yes, sir. Good to know we’re on the same page, sir.”

To hide his smile, Phillip reexamined the list in his hand. “Speaking of pages, see that this gets to the colonel within the hour. We’ve taken too long as it is.” He folded the sheet and handed it off.

Garrigus made a hasty exit just as Major Collins marched up, his head cocked at a haughty angle. A chip had sprouted on his shoulder the moment Colonel Clinch gave him charge of overseeing the surviving slaves. It had grown steadily ever since. Overseeing slaves was a thankless task, but Collins would jump at anything he thought Phillip might want. What disturbed him most was how close to the mark Collins had hit this time.

Phillip had initially been assigned the same position, but requested an alternate duty. For the last three days, he had alternated between regretting that move and being thankful he’d made it. His hands might have been working inventory, but his mind had been back at the clinic next to Milly’s cot.

She had yet to wake, and he had yet to visit her. Periodically, he attended Rhody’s bedside. He felt a strange pull toward the woman he had unearthed, to see her through to full health, or death. But the additional ten steps to reach Milly might has well have been a thousand.

She had misled him, but he couldn’t blame her that. His inability to lay eyes on her again rested solely in the fact that he didn't care to possess even one more memory of her. The ones he already had would be difficult enough to forget.

Marcus had been certain she would wake within no more than two days. Now on her third, he spoke freely of his concern. She needed fluids and the amount Isum managed to trickle down her throat wasn't cutting it.

If she pulled through, she would inevitably suffer at the hand of slavery, and Phillip would be powerless to stop it. He did another quick mental calculation of how long it would take him, on army pay, to save up to buy her. Milly's type didn't come cheap. Even using conservative numbers, the years were staggering.

Since the explosion, Phillip had nearly worn through the knees of his trousers on his face before God. He asked the Almighty to show Himself real, to show His purpose in this disaster, if even in a small way.

"False modesty isn't your strong suit, so don't stare at me like that and expect me to believe you have no idea what I'm talking about." Collins crossed his arms over his chest.

What had Phillip missed?

"Half the men in camp can't scratch their name in the dirt, much less draw. The Colonel insists this get done as soon as possible, and you're the only one that could sketch a person's likeness with any accuracy." With forked fingers, Collins fluffed the tuft of hair that in the heat drooped against his forehead. "Trust me. I've asked."

Sketch? Was Collins asking him to—? *Not a chance.* Phillip wanted no part in handling the slaves. Staying clear of Milly was the least he could do to make up for not hauling her out of that fort when he'd had the opportunity. No matter that it had seemed impossible at the moment. He should have tried harder. He should have spoken with Clinch immediately instead of waiting for him to cool down.

"Don't make me take this to the colonel." Collins' voice dipped low with threat.

"Do what you want. I'm not sketching those slaves unless I hear the order from Clinch's own mouth." Phillip turned, but when Collins caught him by the arm, he spun back, his hand spasming into a fist.

Collins quickly released him then let out a rushed breath. "We don't have a choice in this, and you know it. Now make it easier on us all, won't you? The sooner those sketches get done, the sooner we get out of this God-forsaken wilderness."

Phillip scowled. Like it or not, the man had a point. The sooner they were out of these wilds, the sooner he could start forgetting and moving forward in his life.

"I'll start today," he said, hating each clipped word. At least he wouldn't have to sketch Milly. He already had one of her. *Small blessings.*

Later that afternoon, journal in hand, he knelt beside Rhody's pallet. Two days ago, the woman's leg had been removed below the knee, but Marcus suspected infection had set in. They would know soon enough.

The sight of her, sweating and trembling with pain, tore at Phillip's heart. Tears stung his nose. He tried to swallow the lump in his throat but gave up and spoke around it. "How are you, Rhody?"

Contrary to other times, she didn't attempt a smile. "I been bettah." She gripped her bedding.

Show your purpose in it all, Lord. I beg you. It hadn't been until months after the tragedy, but, through Saul, God had shown His hand in the Mims massacre—at least as far as Phillip's own spiritual welfare was concerned. Surely, He would do it again.

Tossing the journal aside, Phillip scooted closer to her and wiped sweat from her brow just before it spilled into her eyes. "How about some water?" He uncorked his canteen and settled the wooden rim against her lip. "I'll be sketching your likeness." He refused to believe she wouldn't make it, that her portrait wouldn't be posted with the others. Although the thought of her returning to face her master made his insides shudder.

Such matters would never have affected him in such a way before. The change was baffling and a bit unsettling.

"I nevah seen a picture a myself. Heard you's good."

He smiled, flipped open the book, and settled in more comfortably. "I'll let you be the judge of that."

Rhody wrinkled her sweaty forehead. "You gonna put my face up with the rest? In them newspapers?"

His fingers whitened on the wood-encased pencil. She hadn't been so delirious that she didn't know what was going on. "Those are my orders, but I'll draw one just for you too."

She closed her eyes and a shiver tore through her body. From fever, or the thought of returning to her master?

"It's in your power to see that Enoch lives free. What a gift that would be to a young man. What a gift that would be..." Milly's words echoed through his mind and carried his thoughts five rows back and two pallets over.

He hadn't so much as peeked at her since that day, but his artist's eye had long ago captured every curve and divot of her face and locked them away in a place he dare not linger.

Her words haunted him as well. Words that before seemed absurd and naive now seemed...

God, forgive me. She was right.

***

Over the last week, life had taken a drastic turn. Living in the McGirth home felt almost surreal. True Seeker never would have imagined such a situation, much less content to be in it.

Adela stepped from the kitchen and rang the dinner bell.

With a whoop, Tadpole dropped his small whittling knife, grabbed Charlie by the hand, and whisked the smaller boy toward the smell of food.

Shoving two fingertips between his teeth, True Seeker let fly a sharp whistle.

Charlie covered his ears, and Tadpole screeched to a spinning halt.

Using his own blade, True Seeker pointed at the one abandoned in the dirt.

With a huff, Tadpole stomped back to where True Seeker was just getting to his feet. The boy collected his knife and plopped it into True Seeker's open palm.

"Have a care, little chief. A good leader must create a path that is straight and true to keep his people safe as they follow behind him." At Tadpole's scrunched nose, True Seeker nodded toward Charlie who cast admiring eyes at Tadpole.

His chest puffing, Tadpole grew a hand's breadth. "Come, Charlie. The women await."

Although Zachariah's youngest didn't understand a word of Muskogee, he mimicked Tadpole's dignified march, his reddish-blond curls bouncing with each snappy step.

By the time True Seeker had secured the carving tools in the work-shed, washed, and entered the kitchen, the boys were on a rampage around the room.

Holding a bowl high in the air, Adela ventured toward the table. Tadpole rounded the corner and became tangled in her skirt. She laughed. "Who invited the war party?"

As Charlie darted past Lillian, she swatted at his backside with a long-handled wooden spoon, but missed. "Get yourself in that chair," she hollered above the ruckus, indicating with her spoon.

Charlie cackled and kept going, but made the mistake of entering the reach of True Seeker's arm.

Grabbing the boy by the back of the breeches, True Seeker lifted and dropped him into the nearest chair. "The war is won. Now the victory feast," he said in English as he ruffled Charlie's hair.

"Tadpole, do you wish to trample Grandmother Mahila? Find a chair," Willow ordered from her place at the fire.

"What a tragedy to reach my age and die trampled by my own brood." Mahila chuckled from the doorway.

Pleased at how well she looked, True Seeker took her arm and helped her totter to her pallet against the far wall, then he held her slight weight until she eased herself to the floor. When he bent, the watch slipped from his pocket but was caught by the chain pinned to his long shirt.

She settled herself then with a gnarled finger, tapped the dangling watch. "What does this shiny thing tell you?" Her fragile voice was barely audible above the noise in the room.

He fingered the silky object aware that Grandmother did not seek the obvious answer. "It tells me that times are changing." He ended the sentence with a slight, uncertain raise of voice.

She gave him a toothless grin and tapped a yellowed nail against the watch's face. "With its every tick, remember that in a world of mixed races and warring spirits, all things are possible." She patted his hand. "You are a good boy."

Self consciously, he stroked the side of his knobby nose. "Thank you, Grandmother. Adela bring you some bread."

"Sounds like at least two people are happy it's dinner time." McGirth's broad shoulders filled the doorway. Hair and shirt damp with sweat, he made it not two paces inside before Lillian pointed a stiff finger at him.

"You're filthy. Wash up."

Examining his fingers, he grunted.

"Take Tadpole with you?" Willow asked. "He forgot the backs of his hands."

McGirth swung Tadpole over one shoulder. "We are dirty men and not welcome here," he grumbled as he plodded toward the door. On his way out, McGirth intentionally moved too close to the lintel. Tadpole squealed and ducked his head. Their laughter continued until they returned, looking only a trifle cleaner.

Lillian's lips twisted, but she said nothing. Even *she* seemed more content the past days. Perhaps she had come to terms with Indians living under her roof? True Seeker wasn't certain, but even if he was, he doubted he could ever bring himself to trust her.

In the morning, McGirth was due to leave for Mobile again. There was no telling what Lillian might do or how she might behave without his authoritative presence. True Seeker would sleep with one eye open for the duration of the man's absence.

According to Zachariah, True Seeker and his family were now part of the McGirth clan and were welcome to stay as long as they pleased. Although he found himself at ease, he could not see himself staying for any length of time. He missed his own people and their ways. Other boys his age would be preparing to earn recognition as hunters and warriors, able to provide for and protect the village—all opportunities escaping True Seeker.

But how could he leave Willow and Tadpole? And what of Grandmother? Even with her improved health, she would not live many more moons. If True Seeker left any time soon, he might never see her again.

When all were settled at the table and a prayer of thanks had been offered to their Great Spirit, Adela began dishing pork and beans onto their plates.

True Seeker glanced around the table, letting his eyes fall on every face. It had only been a week, but it felt as if he'd known these people a lifetime.

A mother to them all, Adela overflowed with kindness and generosity of soul. She tended every one of her family's needs whether physical or emotional. Even Willow blossomed under Adela's gentle authority. More than once, True Seeker had spotted the half-sisters deep in conversation, Willow's head bent and Adela's arm about her sister's shoulders. After all, she'd been through at Fort Mims and during the war, it was a mystery to him that she was not resentful.

Learning the sisters' recent history had given much insight into Lillian's sour disposition, and almost made him pity her. Almost. She wasn't the only one that had lost much during the war. True Seeker's own family had been all but wiped out.

Since arriving, Tadpole had asked only once about returning to their village. Willow had responded that they would be staying at the McGirth place indefinitely, and he seemed at peace with her answer.

When Adela leaned over True Seeker's shoulder with a full ladle, he lifted his eyes to her. "Sister, Grandmother Mahila would like a bit of pone bread."

A smile split her face into a lovely display of pleasure. From the first day, she had asked he call her sister, but until this moment, he hadn't. "I'm glad to hear her appetite is stable. I'll get it for her as soon as it has cooled from the fire."

True Seeker loved Adela already. Everyone did.

He returned her smile then dug into his bowl and emptied it before she finished serving everyone else.

"Someone is making up for lost time." McGirth's weathered features lit with amusement.

Adela laughed and refilled True Seeker's dish. "I imagine there's still plenty of growing left in him too. It's alright. We made plenty."

What a comfort it was to have food enough to fill the hollow space inside his middle. True Seeker remembered a time, before the war, when food was abundant. Since the years of want and hunger had monopolized his mind, shriveling his earlier life to a distant echo, as though his uncle and father, mother and siblings had only lived and died in a dream-turned-nightmare.

The return to Tuckabatchee would mean a return to hardships, but his people needed him. Every man and boy was vital to the rebuilding process. There were fields to prepare for crops and small, new herds of cattle to tend and butcher for meat. There were fences to build and schools to erect. If they were to have any chance at surviving the onslaught of American settlers, the Creek must adapt. The swifter, the better.

"Where's Hester?" Zachariah asked, crumbs of cornbread lodged on his rough chin.

Lillian dabbed at her mouth with a linen cloth. "I gave her the night off. With Willow here and so eager to help, Hester is hardly of use anymore."

A hush fell over the meal. Even the boys quieted.

True Seeker had been surprised to learn that Hester and her husband, Caesar, were not slaves at all, but beloved servants. To state that Hester's place in the household had been rendered irrelevant seemed almost a profanity. True Seeker knew this, and he had just arrived.

He set his spoon into his bowl, not the least surprised by Lillian's backhanded compliment to Willow. The next days would prove to be interesting, indeed.

"We got us a visitor, suh." Every head at the table turned at the sound of Hester's voice. The large woman fanned herself with her apron as she stepped into the shade of the kitchen. "He's in a awful hurry. Caesar's tendin' his horse. Poor beast's plumb wore out."

McGirth's chair squealed against the floor as he rose. "Who is it?"

"An Indian. Ridin' a government horse, Caeser say."

Before Hester could utter another word, a warrior, tall and sinewy, pushed past her into the kitchen, his eyes searching. "I am Crazy Fire. I carry a letter for Zachariah McGirth." He spoke in their native tongue, stumbling over Zachariah's name. Sweat matted his hair, which seemed to have been dyed the deepest black, along with his eyebrows.

"I'm McGirth." Zachariah rose and took the proffered letter then turned to Adela. Seeing her dish up a new bowl, he faced the warrior. "Please rest. Eat." He broke the seal on the missive.

"I accept." The warrior pulled out a chair and took the food Adela offered. He nodded at True Seeker then ruffled Charlie's hair and smiled. Few could resist his bouncing locks.

Charlie responded with his usual friendly grin.

"It's from Major Bailey." Zachariah's gaze flicked to the other end of the room then back to the single sheet. Which of the sisters would be interested in this Bailey?

Bailey… Ah yes, the owner of the barn whose rafter nearly snatched True Seeker's life. His line of sight followed the path McGirth's had taken.

Lillian shifted in her chair, her gaze glued to a crack in the table that she scrubbed with her forefinger. She had certainly been protective of the man's property…

Adela's hand stilled on the dirty bowls she had stacked. Her green eyes softened. "Oh? What a pleasant surprise."

Was there competition between the sisters over this officer? Had one of them been spurned for the other? That would explain the subtle tension between them.

The room hushed of all but Crazy Fire's noisy slurps and the crackle of paper beneath McGirth's grip.

As his gaze ran across the page, red splotches bloomed on his neck. His lips tightened into a rigid line. When he reached the bottom, he flipped the page over, expelled a snort, then went back to the beginning and started over.

Adela crossed the room and settled a hand on his forearm. "Papa, what's the matter? Is he alright?"

McGirth hastily folded the paper.

She withdrew her hand, as if stung. "What can you not tell me? Is he married? You know that if he is, I would be happy for them bo—"

"He isn't married," McGirth blurted, holding the letter between his fingers as though it were contaminated.

Lillian stood. "Then what is it? Did he ask for Adela's hand again?"

True Seeker did not miss the hopeful timbre of her voice, which smothered his notion of rivalry between the sisters.

"Oh, Lilly, what a ridiculous thought!" Adela hissed the words.

Zachariah shoved the letter into his shirt front, but before he removed his hand, his shoulders slumped and his eyes drifted closed. With a sigh, he withdrew the envelope and passed it to Adela. Was it the flicker of firelight, or did his hand tremble?

Without another word, he ducked through the door and out of sight.

As though herding flies, Willow steered the children outdoors. "A bit of sunlight remains. Go play. And do not disturb Father," she called after them then returned to see that the courier was satisfied.

Taking a deep breath, Adela slowly unfolded the letter.

"Read it aloud," Lillian said.

Yes, read it out loud.

Adela began.

Dear Sir,

I pray this letter finds you and yours healthy and well. It has recently come to my attention that Miss McGirth has succumbed to a dreaded illness and passed, but I have every reason to believe the one communicating the tragedy to be mistaken.

She paused and looked up with a wrinkled brow and unfocused gaze. "Does he mean Ellie?" she mumbled. "No, no, he knows better."

Jaw loose, Lillian rose. Her eyes bulged, not with surprise but with…fear?

My unit's current assignment has brought me to Las Floridas to subdue Negro Fort. A large party of Creek warriors met us on the path. It appears they have the same intention as the United States Army. In an odd twist of fate, my men now fight alongside their former enemy, one of which is an acquaintance of yours to whom, I understand, you owe a great debt.

Adela's voice dropped to hardly more than a whisper.

This acquaintance bears the ranking warrior's name—

She sucked air as though about to plunge beneath water. Tears pooling, she clutched the letter to her chest. "It's Totka." Tears warped her voice. "Phillip has found Totka, and he thinks I'm dead."

Only love could melt a woman's composure as Adela's did now. She loved an Indian? And a former enemy? Despite the gravity of the moment, a smile tugged at True Seeker's lips.

Adela's gaze shot to Lillian. "He thinks I'm dead! Why would he think I'm dead?"

Lillian jammed her hands into the crooks of her elbows. "Why would I know?" But she did know. It was written in the lines burrowed into her forehead.

Willow crossed the room, carefully eying Lillian, but going to Adela and wrapping an arm around the small of her back. "Perhaps the letter will explain. Yes?"

Adela nodded and, dashing away tears, continued to read in silence.

The watch in True Seeker's pocket ticked away the seconds as she finished the letter. Then, in a burst of action, she clutched Crazy Fire's shoulder and shook the crumpled paper before his nose. "Will you take me to the man who gave this to you?" Her English accent was at its thickest.

The man shoved the paper away, his pitch black eyebrows meeting in the center. "No."

"Please, this man—I've waited so long. He must know. I must see him!" Her knuckles whitened on his arm and twisted True Seeker's heart.

The man unhooked her fingers. The thick silver crescent suspended about his neck swung out then slammed back against his chest as he abruptly stood. "Are you sick in the brain? The soldiers would turn me out. The battlefield is no place for a soft white woman."

True Seeker jumped to his feet, inexplicable anger zinging his cheeks. "Tell that to the hundred warriors who assaulted her at Mims' place. This woman is no stranger to blood and courage in the face of death."

With tears filling her eyes and tremors shaking the paper in her hands, she did not create the picture of courage True Seeker had attempted to paint. But, no matter. If this man refused to take her, True Seeker would.

"What are you all talking about?" Lillian demanded, obviously lost in their dialog. No one so much as glanced her way.

With one raised brow, the warrior studied Adela. She lifted her chin and returned his steady gaze. True Seeker inwardly applauded.

When the man's silence affirmed his refusal, True Seeker squared his shoulders. "The soldiers do not frighten me. I will find the path and escort her."

Willow moved toward the counter. "You will need provisions."

A smile crept up Crazy Fire's cheek as he shifted his gaze to True Seeker. "What do they call you?"

"True Seeker."

His head dipped in a slow nod. "You are shrewd for one so young. I do not doubt you would make a worthy guide, but there is no need." He jabbed a thumb at his chest. "Crazy Fire will take her. We start tomorrow, before the sun lights the sky."

When he left, Adela released a breath. She gave True Seeker a brief, shaky smile then skittered to Willow's side.

"What are you doing?" Her father's voice boomed through the room.

Adela whirled to face him, strips of jerky protruding from her fist like kindling.

Stepping inside, McGirth filled the place with his charged presence. He pointed at her hand. "Put that back. You're not going anywhere."

Anger simmered in True Seeker's gut. His eyes darted back and forth between father and daughter. There was no way, McGirth would forbid her from going to the man she loved. It wasn't like him, but then True Seeker had known the man but a week.

"But Papa, what if he dies in battle without knowing—?"

"No!"

Adela's entire body jolted. The dried meat littered the floor. She backed against the sideboard, planting her palms on the surface.

McGirth's neck glowed red. "If Totka loves you enough, he'll find you. Adela, you will listen to me in this. You will *not* go against my wishes. I will not have you traipsing through the wilds again. Do you understand?" His shouts rattled the inner ear.

Tears streaming down her cheeks, Adela stared at him and nodded. "Yes, Papa."

"I won't lose you again." His tone softened.

She reached into her sack and began setting items back on the counter.

With a grunt, he turned to leave then stopped. "And no sending letters either. I'll write Phillip tonight and thank him for informing us of the misunderstanding. I'll let him know that we will address the issue in the future. As I see fit." He peered at her over his shoulder. "I never should have let you read it. If I had known you would…" Like a dog whose meal was threatened, a low growl rumbled from his throat.

"Thank you, Papa," Adela said between sniffles. "For letting me read it. For letting me know why he has not come for me. It is enough. For now."

Lillian snorted and brushed past True Seeker on her way out the door.

Eyes crinkling with a hint of remorse, McGirth swallowed hard. "You best start considering forever, in case he won't settle down around these parts. He's welcome here, but I won't have him hauling you off to starve with his people."

That night, True Seeker chose to sleep under the stars instead of between McGirth walls. He chose a level, grassy spot just off the riverbank, then removed his long coat and balled it beneath his head. In the nearby woods, the cicadas sang their last stanza before relinquishing the song to the crickets.

Overrun by galloping thoughts, sleep eluded him. McGirth had opened his home to them as readily as any clansmen had, but it had been Adela who had warmed their bellies with food and their hearts with a sense of family. To see her spirits so beat down—and by her own father... It jarred True Seeker to the core.

Cheeks sleek and shining with tears, the spectral of her face danced in and out of his semi-conscious, the luminous green of her eyes magnified by moisture and anguish. They seemed to call to him. *True Seeker, what will you do for me?*

Against such a powerful man, what could he possibly do?

True Seeker, you must help. True Seeker...

A hand jiggled his shoulder. "True Seeker, wake."

He bolted upright, his heart thrumming a crazy rhythm against his ribs. A blackened form crouched beside him. "Adela?"

"Yes." Fatigue scratched her voice.

A quick glance at the sky showed the moon two hands beyond its pinnacle. The night was more than half-over.

"You offered to take me to Totka. Are you still willing?"

"Your father—"

"He said nothing of carrying a message by mouth. Will you do this for me? Will you travel back with Crazy Fire?" Her nails bit into his forearm.

He slid a hand over her cool, taut fingers. Didn't she know that, after all she had done for them, his debt was so great he could deny her nothing?

If she didn't, he would prove it to her.

Chapter Ten

Like an angry child demanding attention, Milly's heartbeat pounded against her temples attempting to push her into consciousness. It had done the same before, but each time, she had refused and let herself slip back into the darkness. At last, even in that black world, hammering pain had found her.

When the light beckoned again, she followed, drawn by a thirst that shriveled her throat and fastened her tongue to the roof of her mouth. Squinting against the light that penetrated her lids, she moved her mouth to speak but stopped when her lips cracked. She tried to lick them but her tongue refused to obey. Had someone shoved cotton in her mouth? She would spit it out, if she had the strength.

Her mind grasped for the reason she felt half-dead. Had Master Landcastle finally followed through with his threats and beaten her senseless?

Voices, mostly male, drifted around her. She recognized none of them. No, wait. That deep, throaty murmur belonged to Isum.

Where was she, and why did her head feel as though it might burst? The tiring race from the pain had left her unable to process a coherent thought. Now that she had given up running, these questions demanded an answer.

Isum would know.

She worked at lifting her lids until they gave way to a slit of blinding light. A groan eeked from her parched throat. If her hands had responded properly, she would have blocked the light. Instead, her hand made it only as far as her chest before its weight became more than she could bear.

"Milly?" Heavy footsteps slapped the ground, each one a knife in Milly's ear. "Milly? Capt'n, she's movin'. Doc!" He plucked her hand from where it rested and gave it several brisk slaps. "Come on, girl. Don't go back to sleep. Wake up for me, now."

He might slap her face next if she didn't respond. She opened her mouth to ask for water, but before she could find her voice, cool liquid spilled across her teeth and down her throat. It found her lungs, choking her.

Her eyes flew open as she spewed the water back out. Isum knelt beside her, a mixture of worry and joy flashing across his dripping face. He scooted an arm beneath her and lifted her back from the cot. "There, now. You forget how to swallow?"

Slipping her lids shut, she slumped sideways against him and found her tongue had loosened. "What...happened?"

"Well, look who's decided to stick around a while longer." The chipper voice was familiar.

She edged up one lid at the corner. The army doctor peered down at her, his eyes sparkling. *What was his name?*

Details of the last weeks flashed through her memory. The escape. The fort. Garcon. Little G. *The major...* Her heart quickened and drove nails through her brain. She couldn't contain a whimper.

"Headache? You'll have it for a while yet, I suspect," the doctor informed, his voice sympathetic.

Through the distracting pain, she worked to piece together her last memories. *That night*—the night Little G died...and Major Bailey had nearly gotten himself killed in his absurd attempt to rescue her. His logic would have made perfect sense, if his assumptions about her had been correct.

Grimacing against the torturous light, she took in the canvas above, the putrid scent of infection, the rows of bedding—each with an occupant, twenty or thirty in all. She was in a clinic. Had the fort succumbed to disease? The doctor was more than kind to nurse them all, and the army generous to spare him.

The doctor sat on the edge of the cot, hers being the only one in the infirmary, she noted.

"Tell me your name." His gentle voice contrasted with the stabbing pain he caused when he lifted first one lid, then the other.

She gasped and pulled away. "Milly."

He lifted a bandage on her head that until that moment, she hadn't been aware that she wore. Something else she noticed was her missing hood, not that it mattered anymore. She was safe in the fort with Isum, and the doctor had learned about her heritage before he'd ever left Little G's bedside.

"Your owner's?" The doctor's hands stilled as he waited for an answer.

Isum tightened his hold on her, and she melted into him gleaning from his strength. "I don't have to tell you that."

"Your mind appears to be working properly." The doctor failed to hide a tiny smile, as he resumed his inspection of whatever offense lay beneath the dressing.

Her gaze followed the line of his nose which led a straight path to firm lips, just a shade on the thin side, but which spread into a charming smile.

"In case you were wondering why it feels like a gnome is hammering inside your head, you have a concussed brain. To be truthful, after a blow like that, I'm surprised you were still breathing when the major found you. The fact that you're sitting up and in your right mind is a miracle we can only attribute to the Almighty."

Milly held up a clumsy hand to halt the flow of words. "Someone hit me?" She fumbled with the bandage.

Isum pulled her hand down. "*Somethin'* did, but it's anybody's guess what."

Did someone sneak up on her? Strike her with something and leave her for dead? Had it been outside the fort? If not, how had Major Bailey come across her? So many questions, but so little strength to ask. Fatigue lolled her head.

Isum caught it and settled her back down. "No sleepin' yet. We gotta get somethin' down you, then you can let them eyes close."

Her empty stomach roiled at the thought of putting anything in it. "Just water," she mumbled, but doubted she would stay awake long enough for him to put it to her lips. The weight of weariness pulled her head to the side. The instant before her eyes drifted shut, she caught sight of army blue at the opposite end of the infirmary. How many soldiers were here, and why did Isum seem not to have a problem with it?

She strained to focus blurry eyes down the length of the pallets to the uniform. The man stood facing her, one foot stretched out before him as though he'd stopped mid-stride. She recognized that cropped, ash blond hair, silhouetted against the bright daylight behind him. Phillip hadn't left the fort, after all.

Expecting him to come to her, she was surprised when he changed course and marched the opposite direction. Confusion and disappointment curved the corners of her mouth downward.

"Haughty white boy got a bee in his drawers," Isum mumbled. Crooking two fingers at her chin, he pulled her face toward him and held a tin cup to her lips. "Gotta get this in the right spot this time. No spittin' it back in my face." He grinned, but when his gaze slid back to Phillip, it vanished.

Milly might have a bump on the head, but she didn't miss the hatred spilling from Isum's eyes.

As sleep fought for possession of her, one gut-wrenching thought battled back.

He knows. Phillip knows...

No wonder he had turned his back. How he must hate her.

***

An insuppressible craving for water dragged Milly from semi-consciousness. Running her tongue over dry teeth, she opened her eyes to blessed darkness.

Her head still throbbed, but at a slower beat. Afraid to move and renew the onslaught, she lay perfectly still, stared up at the black canvas, and absorbed the sounds of her environment. Fort noise was greatly subdued. Either night had just fallen or dawn approached.

From her left, several strands of snores floated on the stifling breeze. From outside the tent, a man coughed relentlessly. The river ran nearby, all but covering laughter stemming from somewhere beyond her immediate surroundings. Nearby, a woman wept, her sobs muffled but still heartrending.

Had someone died? If the fort was suffering from an epidemic, deaths were likely. *How many, Lord?* Milly prayed

Rosie and Mama Tatty hadn't been affected by whatever malady plagued them.

Deep, even breaths sounded from the ground next to her cot. *Isum.* She swung an arm over the cot. When her fingers grazed only matted grass, she walked them until they connected with a warm sleeve, which she gave a slight tug. "Isum?" she whispered, not wishing to wake anyone else.

The breathing came to a quick stop as a strong hand flew out of the darkness and enveloped her wrist.

Just as quickly, it let go, but the damage had been done. Pain rocketed between her temples. Gasping, she clamped her jaw and longed to cry, but the effort would cost too much.

The cot shifted slightly as someone hovered over her, his body warming her arm. Fingertips settled against her cheek, their uncharacteristic gentleness drawing open her eyes.

She blinked. This man was not Isum.

The doctor maybe? His name continued to elude her.

"You're awake." The hushed voice carried a hint of awe and hurtled Milly back to the last night in her memory.

What was Phillip doing sleeping by her cot? Now that he knew the truth, he should hate her, be repulsed by her tainted blood…and her deceit.

That Isum had allowed him here was enough to befuddle her already sluggish mind.

Phillip stretched, reaching for something out of view. "Would you like some water?"

"Please." Her voice creaked, rusty from disuse.

He pressed a cup into her palm, and a slipped a hand beneath her head. Except for her intense thirst, shame at his touching her hair would have driven her away from him. Instead, she allowed him to guide the cup to her mouth.

Sweet water passed over her tongue, one manageable trickle at a time. It ran in a soothing stream down her throat and cooled her stomach like a dip in the lake on a hot July afternoon. Her need now fully awakened, she clutched the sides of the cup and gulped.

"Easy," he murmured, but didn't stop her from finishing the contents.

"Thank you." When she released the cup to him, he wiped her mouth with the backs of his fingers. Her instinct was to withdraw from his touch, but he was done and gone before she could react.

His shadowy form moved to the edge of the tent where he mumbled terse words to someone just outside then returned and squatted next to her. "Marcus left me with orders to get some broth in you, should you wake. I hope you're up to it, because no one defies Doc's orders." A grin lightened his whisper. "Cook will warm it up."

Marcus. That was his name. Captain Marcus Buck.

"Why are you here? Where's Isum?" she croaked, finding it difficult to control her volume. The sniffles across the way abruptly ceased.

Phillip continued in hushed tones. "A certain ensign was caught pilfering rum and earned himself a flogging. Marcus is seeing him through the night."

He hadn't answered her questions. "Why are you with me?" She touched her hair. "Now that you know—"

"Never mind that. You were fighting for a little boy's life, and he deserved a fair shot at it." He parroted her own words back at her. "We all do what we must to survive. And the doctor asked me to stay, because I'm the only other man that you know here. It made sense that it be me you see first when you woke."

Now, he spoke nonsense.

She would recognize plenty of men in the fort. Something wasn't right. Confusion and panic compressed her chest. She sucked in a frantic breath. "What do you mean, *here*? Where am I?"

Silence engulfed them before he expelled a series of brief incomprehensible murmurs—swearing or praying, she wasn't sure which.

"Forgive me. I didn't realize you were unaware of what happened. I thought they told you when you woke last time."

It was as if she had gone to sleep and woken in a twisted world. Where was her rock? "Is Isum sick too? Is that why—?" In a collision of memories, she spied Isum on the forest floor, his blood pumping between her fingers. Next, he lay in chains, captured. "But he was just here. I saw him."

It didn't make sense that he was back in the fort, but Phillip had let Isum go once before. Perhaps, he had done so again.

"Milly..." He scooted closer and draped an arm on the cot behind her head. He fumbled in the dark until he found her hand. "Milly, there was an explosion, a rather large explosion."

"Where?"

"The fort. That's how you came to be unconscious."

Dread sank to the depths of her stomach like a lead ball down a musket barrel. Her gaze flicked into the dark to the rows of sick—no*, wounded*. She tried to sit up, but he pinned her with the arm holding her hand.

"Rest easy," he murmured, stroking her cheek. "There's nothing anyone can do about it now."

She shook off his hand. "How big an explosion? How many dead? Isum?"

"He's fine. Kept under strict guard at night. You can see him in the morning."

Her head swirled a cyclone of thoughts and pain. If Isum was still under guard...but he had been by her side when she had woken, right?

She gave a quick tug and freed herself of his grasp. "Was the fort overrun? How many died?"

"You're too upset. I think that's information enough for now."

"Tell me! How many died?"

A breathy growl met her ear followed by a lengthy silence. "Those you see here are the only survivors."

She stole another glance across the clinic. "That's not possible." One explosion couldn't kill hundreds spread out over so many acres.

"I would have said the same, except I saw it with my own eyes."

"How? The walls—they're so thick."

"A red-hot ball rolled into the magazine."

She well remembered the magazine, and when she opened her mind to the possibility of its explosive power, the truth barreled down upon her. With it came grief at its usual suffocating speed. It wrapped its fingers around the back of her throat and tightened into a merciless fist.

"Cook's on his way, sir," a masculine voice called from just outside the clinic.

"Coming," Phillip replied then squeezed her hand and moved to stand. "I'll be right back."

Cook? She was in the army camp. Under guard. It was over. Most everyone was dead, and she may as well be*. They'll take us back*.

"No!" She bolted upright, gathering strength from a place she didn't know existed. The shadowed world spun, but she ignored it and swung her feet to the ground so fast she kicked Phillip.

Still pulling out of his squat, the blow tumbled him backward.

She leaned forward and swung her weight to her feet. Grays and blacks smeared together. Up became down, and her forward motion continued even when her mind insisted it stop. She expected to greet the hard ground. Instead, she toppled onto Phillip. Her knee sank into his belly, and he exhaled sharply.

He achieved a fistful of the fabric at her thigh. "What are you—?"

"I can't," she cried, the pain in her head increasing her terror. In a flurry of arms and legs, she scrambled to free herself from him, the baffling urge to flee driving her on. One side of her skirt, still firmly in his grasp, sank beneath her hipbone.

"Enough, Milly! Stop struggling," he hissed in her ear and wrapped a restraining arm around her, nailing her arms to her body.

Sapped of strength, she gave up the fight. Above the rush of blood in her ears came her own sobs. "Please. I can't go back."

"Don't worry, Major Bailey. I got her," a voice announced moments before rough hands grappled her waist and lifted her off Phillip's chest.

"Stand down, Private," Phillip ordered, not relinquishing his hold.

She fell back onto him and wished she could think clearly, think something, *anything* besides what awaited her at the Landcastle Estate. "I can't go back. I can't. Not now. I can't."

On the off-beat of the pounding inside her head, shushing sounds filled her ear and grated against her nerves. Each moment proved more difficult to process a coherent thought.

"Let me help you, sir. She'll wake the whole camp with that racket."

"Back off," Phillip's voice boomed next to her head. His chest caved, and he tightened his hold. "Hush now." His lips moved against her ear. "You're safe. I won't let anyone hurt you."

Unable to cope with the truth, she let herself believe his lie. He couldn't hold her and ward off evil forever, but for tonight, for this moment, she was safe. The wailing quieted to a whimper, and Milly expelled a shuddered breath of relief. Fatigue washed over her, and she went limp.

"That's better. Everything will be all right. You'll see." He pressed his cheek against hers and for ten pounding thumps of his heart against her back, she pretended she didn't own a head full of frizzy hair, that she wasn't a runaway, that this man could really carry her away from this nightmare and make everything alright. It calmed her and numbed the pain.

"Good work, Major. Want some help now?" The guard stumbled over something in the dark behind them. "Can't see a thing, a dad-blasted thing," he mumbled. "The doc's gotta have a candle around here, somewhere."

Phillip held her tighter, and his hot breath moistened her ear. "Whatever happens, don't lose hope." He spoke so low, she almost missed it beneath the guard's bumbling search.

Hope? It already died—along with hundreds of her fellow runaways. She swallowed a new sob that rose from the darkening pit of her soul.

The guard continued his grumbling. "The sun'll be up in an hour or so, but you'll need light sooner than that if you're gonna get any of that broth down her before the doc gets back. Hold on...found it!"

Lifting a lethargic hand, she grazed a patch of the damaged skin on Phillip's neck.

He had seen his own share of troubles. Maybe that was why he seemed to take her plight so much to heart. Why he had chosen to forgive her. She could never utter the words aloud, but running her fingers along the prickly line of his jaw, she prayed he would understand how much his concern for her wellbeing—as bleak as it was—would sustain her in the coming days. To know there was at least one white man in the world who hadn't seen her as mere chattel, or a warm body to satisfy a base need.

The strike of flint threw sparks. "Come on," the guard coaxed.

Milly dropped her hand. Phillip unwrapped his arms and rolled her to a sitting position.

The next set of sparks caught the wick and cast wobbly beams of light across the clinic and illuminated a row of dismal, black faces. She didn't recognize a one of them.

"Looky here," the soldier quipped. "We got us an audience. Back to bed with the lot of you."

Without a sound, they withdrew into the gloom.

Keeping a palm against her back, Phillip got to his feet. "Let's get you back to bed." He tucked his hands under her shoulders, and pulled her up.

She let him ease her onto the cot while inside her skull, the gnomes drummed a hellish lullaby. Eyes rolling shut, she longed to escape the horrors of her new world.

Isum's uncompromising vow echoed through the haze of her mind.

There ain't no surrender and there ain't no goin' back.

As she sank into the blessed oblivion of sleep, she made the same pledge to herself and God. She wouldn't go back. The soldiers could shackle her, beat her, put a gun to her head, but she wouldn't go.

They would have to pull the trigger first.

Chapter Eleven

Before the courier, Crazy Fire, rode on toward the American camp, he had directed True Seeker toward a group of men at target practice. Totka's paisley turban could be seen from where True Seeker tethered his horse.

As he wound his way through the Creek war camp, he felt every pebble and twig through the worn soles of his moccasins. After four days of hard riding, his skin felt equally thin, his bones brittle and sore.

"My mare is lame. You must take Lillian's," Adela had insisted when True Seeker balked at the offer. "She owes me this."

Throughout the journey to Prospect Bluff, he'd wondered if Adela had discovered her sister was involved in Totka's confusion regarding her supposed death. How could Lillian not be? Heartbreaking and cruel, the incident bore all the markings of what the raven-haired witch was capable of.

The warriors' rifle blasts punctured the air, jolting True Seeker's insides. They laughed and carried on, congratulating and teasing each other as the occasion demanded. He stood apart and watched, admiring their skill and smiling at their camaraderie. It had been far too long since he'd seen such carefree spirits among Creek men.

Crazy Fire had spoken of the American victory at Negro Fort. As tragic as the event had been, True Seeker, was grateful it had ended so swiftly and effectively with no loss of Indian life. Perhaps the same brush painted the smiles on these warriors' faces?

Dressed as every other warrior in a long calico trade shirt and buckskin leggings, Totka's height alone set him apart. That, and the aura of quiet authority that floated about him. He wore three feathers in his hair dangling over his right shoulder, just as Uncle had.

The last years of loneliness and oppressive responsibility suddenly weighed more than True Seeker could bear. His heart seized with the longing to know and be known.

Although he hadn't moved a muscle in the last sixty ticks of his watch, Totka's head snapped toward him as though True Seeker had waved his kerchief in the air above his head.

Totka stared and tipped his head to the side, drawing the attention of the other two.

One not much older than True Seeker, waved him toward them. When he approached the young warrior asked, "How did you come to be here, boy?"

His pride kicking up, True Seeker stretched his backbone to its full length. "I rode in with Crazy Fire. Moments ago."

An older warrior, a thick silver band about his upper arm, gave a knowing laugh. "You must be the lazy nephew that fills Crazy Fire's evenings with tales." He turned to Totka. "I did not know he went to Tensaw by way of his village."

Totka's brows tucked together, suspicion darkening his eyes. "I did not know he was going to Tensaw at all."

Unwilling to converse before these other two, True Seeker hastily attempted to redirect Totka's thoughts. "Crazy Fire is of no relation to me. I am my own protector and provider. Uncle and Father have passed into the spirit world. Taken during the Red Stick War. I am here of my own will, bearing a message."

Silver Band drew toe-to-toe with True Seeker. "What message? Why did Crazy Fire not bring it himself? Is the message for one of us?"

Of their own accord, True Seeker's eyes shot to Totka's.

In one intake of breath, his towering body went rigid.

When True Seeker compressed his lips, Silver Band pressed for more, but Totka nudged him in the arm. "Let him be. He will speak when he is ready."

His gaze shifted to True Seeker. "Come. Try your hand at this rifle. I believe it strays to the left. Tell me if you disagree."

Hating that these seasoned warriors would soon learn what an inexperienced shot True Seeker was but finding no way around it without opening his mouth and admitting to it, he took the loaded weapon and aimed at a scrap of brightly colored fabric nailed to the trunk of a tree. When the smoke of his blast cleared, he saw that he'd missed the target entirely. Shame burned up his neck.

Totka took the rifle and handed it to Silver Band. "Did I not tell you? It strays to the left. Keep it. I will find another." His long legs took to a westerly trail. Even with a hitch in his step, Totka covered the ground with amazing speed. Half-turning, he caught True Seeker's eye and motioned for him to follow.

Grateful he wasn't asked to reload and try again, he jogged to catch up.

Totka dropped his gaze to True Seeker, and in one sweeping glance, seemed to assess, conclude, and approve. A smile bent his lips. "The soldiers have gifted us with many weapons. I could use a keen eye such as yours to help me choose one for myself."

"Rifles are a mystery to me. I am better suited to throwing stones," he blurted, then threw a hasty smile on his face and hoped it distracted from the bitterness that leaked into his tone.

Totka didn't appear to notice. "What of a bow, then? Have you trained?"

"Yes, I prefer it."

"But you have none?"

"I tried to make one before—" True Seeker fumbled for words to express how his irrational aunt had a notion to join the white world. "But I lacked guidance. The war was hard on Tuckabatchee's Rabbit Clan."

With an abrupt spin, Totka stopped short. "Tuckabatchee? You did not come from Tensaw with Crazy Fire?" Emotion played in the backs of his eyes. Fear? Desperation? Anger? The man was nearly shaking with it.

For all his rehearsing over the last days, True Seeker was unprepared for this moment, for the pain that the mere mention of Tensaw would bring Totka, for the instant kinship True Seeker would feel toward him.

But prepared or not, it was time to end the man's suffering. "My home is in Tuckabatchee, but, yes, I have come from Tensaw with a message. For you."

"Tell me." The demand was swift and as hard as the sinew protruding from his tense neck. "Is it from McGirth?"

"No. From Adela. She wishes you to know that she is alive."

Totka's face went slack. For interminable moments, he stared at True Seeker, his eyes blank. His hand flew to a pouch at his waist. From it, he yanked a crumpled sheet of paper and stared at it as though he had no recollection of it. "It is true."

"What is true?"

"Bailey...he read it. His eyes—I suspected something foul, but never...this. I would not allow myself to believe." The parchment began to tremble. Totka slowly pulled it into ball inside a fist white with strain. His eyes turned to flint, and on a hiss a single word rode from his lips. "Lillian!"

Anger rose from his flesh like steam, and True Seeker pitied the woman the day Totka reentered her life. And reenter, he would.

"Adela said—"

"Adela." With the rapid utterance of her name, the stone in his eyes disintegrated. He seized True Seeker's arm. "She is well?"

"Well? She is beauty itself."

A slow smile took residence on Totka's lips. "Isn't she?" His eyes twinkled as he gave True Seeker's arm a brisk punch. "Have I lost her to you? I fear I must fight you for her."

True Seeker laughed. "I loved her from the first, but she would not have me." He sobered. "Her heart belongs to only one. She awaits him, still."

Totka's smile wobbled, and his eyes instantly brimmed with unshed tears.

True Seeker turned away.

"You will camp with me and tell me everything you know." Totka took up step again, his voice controlled and bright. True Seeker joined him. "And when you and I are through with this swamp, we will go to her, together. After I return with her to Koosati, you must visit. I will guide you in making a strong bow."

The idea appealed to him. "Very well. In exchange, I will teach you to toss stones."

Totka burst into a hearty laugh, but judging by the sudden far-away look in his eyes, True Seeker suspected his mind was not on the bow or the stones, but some place quiet with Adela.

"I must warn you, though. McGirth will not take kindly to your taking her to live as one of us. He has spoken very strongly against it."

Totka's smile wavered only for an instant. "God has strengthened me these last trying years. He will not fail me now. If McGirth chooses to shoot me in the back as I carry my wife to her true home..." He shrugged. "So be it."

***

Standing outside his tent, Phillip cracked open his journal. Despite the cooling evening temperatures, sweat dripped from his nose onto the paper, blurring a thrasher's bill. If only he were still drawing birds.

He flipped through the pages until Milly's big, brown eyes stared up at him. He ripped out the sheet and added it to the others then stalked into the tent and slapped the stack onto the portable table that stood before Collins. The papers fanned out, exposing Rhody's broad forehead and hollow eyes. He had tried not to transfer any of the slaves' dark emotions to paper, but he saw now that he'd failed.

Rhody glared at him, accusing. Such a beautiful woman, empty. Like the crater left by the blast, her spirit had been gouged out and spattered across a hundred acres. Only God knew if she'd ever find it again. Or if she would live long enough to try.

The candle on the desktop danced as Collins' slender fingers pushed the pages around exposing one black face after another.

Uncle Jeremiah's image surfaced. The old man was toothless and mostly deaf, but of all the slaves, his were the only eyes that still held a bit of sparkle. At first, Phillip had thought him senile and unaware of what had transpired, but a short time into the task, he had squelched that notion. The old man's mind was as sharp as Phillip's guilt over leaving Milly in the fort.

The journal's leather grew tacky beneath his sweaty fingers. He tossed it onto his rumpled bedding, and Enoch's absence bore deeper. The boy's was the only image that remained in the book. Phillip had drawn it from memory, and of all the slaves, it was the only face he never wanted to forget. The others, he prayed God would wipe from his memory as soon as they were driven out of this wasted swamp.

All, except Milly.

Last night—when she'd woken and he'd held the cup to her lips, when she'd flung herself from the cot and he had seized her to himself, when she had run her fingers along the ridge of his jaw—it had been as if he was born for that very moment. As if God had saved him from the fires of Fort Mims and the thousand bullets that had flown at him since, for that purpose. For Milly. For *them*.

When he'd uttered seemingly ludicrous promises, he had meant every one of them and what was more, he'd sensed God's blessing over them. Their calming effect on Milly was proof that the Spirit had been present.

Phillip was practically penniless and restrained by a law that prohibited a white person from marrying anyone of African descent. But there was one thing he was certain of—after all he'd suffered in his life and after all the heartache he'd witnessed, he knew without a doubt that his God was bigger than a sack of coins or a ridiculous law. Phillip hadn't a clue as to how it would happen, but it would. Even if it meant abandoning his commission, Phillip would free Milly. Then he'd marry her. Rank and wealth were meaningless without the woman you loved to share it with.

Collins continued to shuffle through the sketches, covering Uncle Jeremiah's mischievous eyes with as little thought as he might a pile of dung, but when he reached Milly's, he paused then scooted it free from the rest. "She had us all fooled," he murmured, running a thick finger over her lips.

Phillip's teeth bore down on the inside of his cheek. He would walk away, except for his inability to abandon Milly to Collin's lustful eye.

He eyed it more closely, a smirk twisting his lips. "Of course, her not being a lady does have its advantages. Too bad she's laid up. If she can't fight back, I'm not interested." His husky laugh nearly sent Phillip over the top of the table, but reacting would only encourage Collins to attempt something. Phillip's jaw tightened, and he tasted blood. Forcing a deliberate speed, he turned and stepped toward the tent's opening.

"You got the eyes right, but the rest of her is all wrong. Her master would never recognize her. And I wonder…"

Phillip halted, a cramp knotting painfully in his rigid back.

"Did you think I wouldn't know this was the sketch you drew that first morning? That I wouldn't figure out what game you're playing?"

Phillip spun, his fists tingling with the urge to strike. "I don't care what ideas your deluded brain concocts! You have what you asked for."

One of Collins' eyebrows shot up. "I do?" He stepped away from the table and touched the corner of Milly's sketch to the candle's flame. The paper blackened and curled and in seconds littered the ground with ash.

The muscles in Phillip's punching arm quivered, but he rooted his feet in the dirt. Methodically, he drew air in and out of his nose, seeking control from a Power higher than himself.

"Colonel Clinch asked for thirty-three sketches. It seems we only have thirty-two." Nails scraping wood, Collins gathered the sheets back into a pile. "The colonel's patience is waning, Major Bailey. Best get on it."

***

The three-legged stool squeaked beneath Phillip's weight as he adjusted his legs and leaned toward Milly's cot. It was just as well she refused to look him in the eye. He wasn't certain he could sustain a full dose of her grief and not do something rash—like pull her into his arms and assure her that God had big plans for her. For them.

Standing just to the side, Isum responded to Phillip's forward motion by shifting his wide stance. Beefy arms crossed his chest, and muscles swelled beneath his shirtless, glistening flesh. It was an unnecessary show of brawn. Did either of them really doubt that given half a chance, he could whip Phillip, hands-down? Phillip didn't, but thankfully the fact remained that he held the weapons and wore the uniform, as well as the correct color of skin.

He shot Isum an answering glare, then refocused on Milly's eyes. Or tried to. "Look at me, Milly."

She lifted her lashes and centered on some point below his chin.

He could have drawn her from memory, but then, hope-filled idiot that he was, he would have had to pass up possibly his only opportunity to reassure her that he was searching for a way to get her out of this situation.

There had been few legitimate reasons for him to pass through the clinic, so Phillip decided to thank Collins for providing this windfall. Not that Phillip would actually put voice to the words.

"Private Gilroy," he called, not taking his eyes from his sketchpad.

The young man stationed just outside the infirmary turned, brow raised. "Sir?"

"The boys working supply could use some help distributing rations to the Indians. Take Isum here and put him to work. He looks healed well enough now and a little bored, if you ask me."

Eyes narrowing, the slave uncrossed his arms, exposing the bandage spanning his ribcage. Best get rid of him before Marcus returned from consulting with the naval surgeon.

"It's time you pulled your weight around here." Phillip jerked his head. "Go on."

Isum stalked out, arms swinging, and Gilroy rushed to catch up.

Slowly pulling herself erect, Milly gazed after them. "It isn't wise to rile him. He's been known to act first and think later, but he has yet to be the one to come out on the losing end." Her closed lips curved into an almost sassy smile, heating Phillip's core.

If it made her mouth react that way, he would aggravate the big man every chance he got. He bit back a grin. "Thanks for the warning, but I'll be fine. It's good to see you on the mend." The dressing remained, but her eyes were lucid and her pain seemed lessened.

Ignoring his reference to her health, she closed her eyes and tipped her face into a stream of sunlight that angled over her cot and lit the pinprick freckles across her nose. The smooth skin of her throat beckoned Phillip's touch.

He dropped his gaze to the paper, steadied his hand, and shaded in the line of her neck. The freckles, he would record only in his memory.

Having regained some color since the explosion, Milly's skin had taken on an attractive tone and was darker than he'd originally thought. Still, she could pass for a southern belle at any Savannah social event—except for that hair. Although braided tight and neat against her scalp, there was no escaping its decisively African flavor.

It was a far cry from Adela's auburn waves, but Milly's style and texture added a uniqueness and depth of character that Phillip didn't imagine she recognized, or appreciated.

Shoving the wood of his pencil between his teeth, he studied the drawing. Something about her eyes didn't satisfy. "I sent off a letter. To Adela's father," he said around the pencil in his mouth.

Her gaze zipped to him, and he observed that he'd made the distance between her pupils a smidgen too narrow. He couldn't fix that now, nor did he care to.

When he looked up from darkening the circle of her iris, she was still staring at him, her expression blank. "What did you tell him?"

Phillip closed the journal and rested his forearms on his knees. "The truth."

A smile was born on Milly's lips and slowly matured until it stole Phillip's train of thought. He'd never seen her smile, and although it didn't quite reach her eyes, it transformed her face into a thing of beauty that sucked the breath from his lungs. Heaven help the man that received a full dose of her approval. For her own well-being, it was probably best she had precious little reason to smile.

She held his gaze—another first. "I knew you would do the right thing."

Except for her, he might not have.

"Can I see?" She pointed at his journal.

He flipped to the correct page and passed her the book.

After a moment of scrutiny, she looked at him through the tops of her eyes. "I wouldn't have minded if you'd made my nose flat or my teeth crooked. Or both." Her lips twisted and drew up on one side.

"I sort of tried. With an earlier sketch." When she cocked one brow at him, he shrugged a shoulder. "One I drew...before."

"What happened to that one?"

"It didn't pass inspection." He slanted his chest toward her and slid a smirk up the smooth half of his face. "What Collins doesn't realize is that no likeness can come close to the original beauty." The words came out huskier than he'd intended, his desire more exposed than was prudent. He quickly straightened, expanding the distance between them.

Conversation in the clinic continued as usual, but Milly wasn't as oblivious. Lashes fluttering, she inspected the fingers curled on the dingy brown of her skirt. A rosy hue tinged her throat. The hollow at her neck pulsated, and her chest rose and fell with each heightened breath.

It might have been years since he'd seen them, but he knew the symptoms, had witnessed them often enough in women who had succumbed to his onslaught of charm. On cue, his skin burned and his thighs tensed.

He stood and rubbed sweaty palms down his trouser legs.

Chin still tucked near the base of her throat, Milly held out the journal. "You're very good at what you do."

He took it and tapped its binding against his palm, wishing he could saddle a horse and ride her away from this place. "Unfortunately, for you."

"Your sketch matters little. I told you I wouldn't go back, and I meant it."

Phillip scowled down at the top of her head. "That's awfully big talk, but there's only one man in this camp who cares about what you think or want, and he's powerless to do anything about it."

"Don't tell Isum," she said, flippantly. "Just to prove you wrong, he might turn you over his knee and give you a sound whipping. He was never one to consider consequences."

He studied her guileless, downturned face and realized he would have to be more obvious. "I wasn't talking about Isum. Or the doctor." He sat back down, plucked her hand from her lap, and dropped his voice to an intense whisper. "If I had the means—the money, Milly, I'd get you away from here. I'd buy you and—"

She snatched her hand back and her eyes went cold. "Don't fool yourself. If you had the money, you'd spend it on a woman who deserved it. One that was pure and unsullied. The way I imagine...Adela to be."

He rose and, turning his back to her, glared at the blue bird which perched on the lower limbs of a nearby tree and attempted to brighten the day with his song. "She wouldn't have me, or did you forget?"

"There will be another. Save your money for her. You'll be glad you did."

"I know as surely as God placed you in my path what my purpose is in your life."

"Your purpose? Just like that, just like every other white man, you take possession of the course of my life? I don't need you." The quiver in her voice weakened her bold statement. "I got away once. I can do it again."

Fear pivoted him on the ball of his foot. "Keep your voice down and your ridiculous notions to yourself." No sooner had the heated words shot from his tongue did he regret them.

Like a book slamming shut, her eyes flattened, and she closed in on herself.

He deliberately calmed and lowered his voice. "I couldn't bear to see you in shackles, and if anyone hears you talking like that, that's exactly where you'll be."

***

Milly lay back down and willed Phillip to leave. If he spoke another tender word or touched her again, she would be undone. She could barely stand the acute brown of his eyes. If it wasn't for the fact that he breathed and sweat like an average man, she would swear he was an other-worldly being capable of burrowing into her carefully guarded soul.

He'd said he would buy her if he could, and although he probably believed he cared for her well-being, she knew better. If she had a dollar for every brainless thing spoken to her in the heat of lust, she'd have enough cash to buy her own freedom. Knowing they could never be held accountable, men spoke foolishness her presence.

Phillip had made his own longing abundantly clear, but men's desires were like steam—scorching hot and fleeting...at least until the next boil.

Milly's more closely resembled a carefully prepared dish that baked slow and steady. But her life hadn't provided the ingredients for a dish worth baking, much less tasting.

She lay on her side, curled her legs, and tucked her hands under her head. From her periphery, she sensed him edge toward her. Lids dropping, she feigned the desire for rest.

His steps halted near her head. He seemed a decent man, but even daydreaming that a man like Phillip could care for rubbish such as herself was a dangerous venture that her heart wouldn't survive.

"Milicent, did you know you're the most special little girl in the whole of Chatham county? No, the whole of Georgia. No, the world. *To me and God both."* Her mother's phantom voice floated through her mind.

Phillip's hand hovered just above her head, skimming her hair and tickling her scalp.

"Did you know he keeps an account of every one of your hairs?"

The air above her suddenly grew cold, and when Phillip's steps moved around her cot and kept going, she swallowed a sob. God might number the hairs of the whites, but He had cursed hers.

Phillip's muffled voice carried from the back of the clinic. He'd spent hours at Rhody's side, his distress over her condition growing more obvious.

It was also growing more obvious that the woman would not survive. Her cries, though quiet, had kept Milly awake through the last several nights, and her heart broke at her inability to go to the woman.

Today had been the first that Milly had managed to move without grinding her teeth in excruciating pain. With it now a low throb, she felt she could visit Rhody's bedside and be in enough control of her faculties to actually offer her some measure of comfort, or at least companionship.

As soon as Phillip left, Milly would go to her. He had said nothing of the loss of his own slave, but Milly suspected he'd been deeply affected. She felt as though she should beg his forgiveness.

Going to the fort had been Enoch's idea, but she shouldn't have encouraged him. Giving him directions had been like handing him a death certificate. Negro Fort had been an indomitable safe haven, but in a single breath, it vanished. Flattened to nothing but mounds of rubble.

Despair eked from the corner of her eye, surmounted the bridge of her nose, and fell into the palm beneath her cheek. Long ago, Isum had told her that God stored his people's tears in a bottle. She imagined a massive glass jug labeled "Black," but her tears didn't belong in it. Her tears didn't belong anywhere.

Terse voices drew Milly to a sitting position.

Major Collins had entered the tent through the rear. He stood before Phillip, his hand outstretched, palm up.

With his back to her, Phillip's movements were hidden, but the ripping of paper could not be mistaken for anything other than what it was—betrayal.

Although she hadn't believed him, Phillip had assured Milly that everything would be all right, yet he had sat before her and, without apology, sketched her likeness. If she wasn't so taken with the man, she would hate him. She *should* hate him.

Collins studied the page then lifted lust-filled eyes straight at her.

She whirled back around, feeling as though she had been stripped. Clutching the front of her bodice, she quickly lay back down and wished more than ever Isum wasn't taken away each night.

Collins left and the day dragged on. Waiting for Phillip to leave proved a futile effort. Through the day and into the evening, he never left Rhody's side.

Isum returned from laboring, his wound broken and seeping. Judging from the daggers the doctor's gaze hurled into Phillip's back, Milly was certain he would have given the major a piece of his mind, except for Rhody's life slipping away. Instead, Marcus changed Isum's dressing and ordered complete rest for the next three days.

Milly didn't see Marcus again the rest of the evening, as he kept vigil next to Phillip. Only one Indian woman remained of those who had come to give aid. Every soul in the clinic seemed to hold its breath until at last, Marcus stood, mopped his neck with a kerchief, gripped Phillip's shoulder, and left with his head hanging.

One by one, the slaves reclined on their beds. The candle was snuffed, and night fell heavy and oppressive.

Isum, along with several other able-bodied slaves, were taken to be chained to a tree for the night. Milly had heard it told they were the greatest flight risks as well as the most desperate and dangerous. She believed it. Once she was back to her feet, the soldiers would be wise to shackle her as well.

But for tonight, she could only long for Rhody's new-found liberty.

Sleep eluded till the last, and when light finally split the sky, it was to the morbid sound of shovel slicing earth. Milly sat up and rubbed her burning eyes.

Phillip had left in the night, but Rhody's body remained stretched on the floor, hands crossed on her chest.

Determined to say her goodbyes to a woman she never knew, Milly pulled herself up. The world tipped then righted itself. She waited for a light-headed sensation to pass then shuffled on unsteady legs toward the back.

Moving from one tent post to the next, she followed the stench of infection down the center of the infirmary. Thirty-one slaves lay to her right and left, but Milly had yet to know them. Now on the mend, she would remedy that, beginning by discarding the cot and joining them on the ground.

Somewhere far beyond the tent, the shovel continued to slam into dirt. Thud, scrape, toss. Thud, scrape, toss. A familiar sound, it usually always heralded the conclusion of a slave's misery.

Rhody had suffered so much toward the end that Milly expected to find it frozen on her face. Instead, her brow was smooth, and her lips bent slightly upward. Between fingers gray with death, she clutched a crumpled sheet of paper.

Uncle Jeremiah hobbled up next to Milly. "That's what freedom look like. Even these old eyes can see."

Taking in Rhody's peaceful expression, Milly nodded and batted at fresh tears. "What's she holding?"

"I told ya, girl. Freedom. In black and white." He sucked in wrinkled lips, worked his toothless jaw, and turned to move back to his bed. "Don't reckon she need it no more, but there it be."

Phillip had freed her? Could he even do that? If so, had he changed his views about owning human chattel? No, this was merely selfishness on his part—give a dying woman a useless piece of paper and appease a guilty conscience.

But if this was proof that he'd changed his views on slavery, it could mean he also meant what he said about working to free her...

No, she dare not think it. It didn't matter what the man's motives were. He could never be anything to her, other than what he was—her jailor.

Milly shrugged internally, but the memory of his rough cheek against hers taunted her solid reasoning. She touched where his lips had grazed her lobe, where his soothing voice had struck her resolve with the accuracy of that single heated cannon ball.

No! Such thoughts were forbidden. She gave her head a firm shake.

Sharp pain shot through her eyes to the back of her skull and lodged there. A cry ripped from her throat. One knee turned to water. Vaguely aware of movement around her, Milly flailed through blurring vision for the nearest tent pole.

Hands reached for her, but she slipped through their grasp and hit the ground with a jarring crash.

Darkness crept in and dragged her into a black abyss.

Chapter Twelve

Rain beat against the tarpaulin, stirring Milly to wakeful consciousness. She floundered through the murky waters of her mind to orient herself. Light penetrated her closed lids. Was it morning? No, she had blacked out. There was no telling what time it was...or what day.

"I could only guess at why." Someone nearly shouted above the downpour. *The doctor*? "Head wounds are a mystery, but we do know that absolute rest is essential for complete recovery. She cannot travel. Traipsing with us through the forest would—"

"What would you have me do? Leave her for the Seminole?" Phillip asked.

Milly slatted her eyes. A set of muddy, black boots shuffled in front of her face. Just beyond, was another set and beyond those, the bottom edge of a tent disappeared behind a row of scraggly grasses.

Not the clinic. Uneven earth bit into her shoulder, but afraid to drive the tips of the knives back into her head, she resealed her lids and lay as though etched from marble.

"She might prefer the Seminoles to us!" Marcus snapped. "They all might."

"Since when does what *they* want matter? You had your orders to get her well. Now, I have mine to get her out of here."

The slaves were being taken back so soon? Milly bit the inside of her lip to keep from reacting. How long had she been out this time? Surely not long, since she hadn't woken thirsty enough to drink from a trough.

"It's not just about Milly," Marcus continued. "There are at least a half-dozen of them still unfit for travel. At the very least, you should be concerned with returning damaged property."

"Me? *I* should be concerned?" Phillip nearly shouted. "That's your job. Not mine."

He had been concerned before. At least, he'd told her he was. Even though Milly had advised herself not to believe him, hearing the truth spoken aloud cut deep.

"Have a heart, Phillip!"

"My heart deceives me, as does yours. If we listened, the army would put us both out on our backsides. Lift a hand to help those slaves, and you'll spend the rest of your life regretting it." Phillip's biting tone made Milly's skin burn icy-cold. She braced against a shiver.

"This is bigger than you or I or our blasted commissions. It's the opportunity of a lifetime to *do* something. To help their cause, if even in a small way."

"Stop speaking as if we have a choice!"

"There's *always* a choice," Marcus bellowed back. "Think of Saul. What would he want you to do? What would you do if he was the one out there in shackles?"

"This has nothing to do with Saul, or with me, for that matter. It's about you, Marcus, and what will become of you when this ghastly plan of yours falls through."

"I can take care of myself." The remainder of Marcus' reply was so quiet, Milly failed to make it out.

After a lengthy pause, Phillip spoke in a raspy, disbelieving bark. "Are you truly suggesting insubordination?"

The sky lit with a flash of violence.

"I'm suggesting we do something, *anything*. That we fight for what's best for the patients, for all of them."

Phillip's short dry laugh followed. "The day the army cares more for Negroes than it does its own men is the day I let you sacrifice your career. These runaways have deluded your thinking. It bears repeating, *Captain*. You're an officer in the United States Army, first and foremost. If you want to take up anti-slavery dealings, do it on your own time. Not the army's. Any more talk of this, and..." He released a growl that meshed with a rumble of thunder. "Just...keep a cork on your rebellion, and let me do my job. As ordered, when we leave, they leave with us."

Moisture seeped through Milly's clothes as the storm howled. She wished it would drench her and cleanse the grime of repugnance. Even the tossing rain held more appeal than being in close quarters with such a charlatan. She curled her toes to keep from scrambling to her feet and dashing into it.

"How do you plan to move her?" Marcus finally spoke.

Phillip responded but his words were lost.

"He can't—" The doctor's words were clipped short by Phillip's grunt of anger.

"He'll do what needs doing."

Who will do what? Milly sorted through the bits of fact she had collected. Had one of them said something about the Seminole? Isum would want information about the local natives, but she couldn't think around the single revelation pervading her mind—Phillip was no different than any of the other hot-blooded white men she'd known.

Memory of her romantic notions about him warmed her body with shame.

You're just another useless darkie! George's voice and curling lips were the only part of him she remembered, but it had been enough to convince her she was worthless.

Momma had said she was the most special little girl in all the world, but Momma must have lied.

Momma, do you remember your little girl?

"I'll come for you, baby! I swear it!"

Not a day had passed since Milly was dragged away that she hadn't been haunted by the memory of Momma hurling her promise from the upper story window. She might have hurled herself after it had George not restrained her.

During her first years as a slave, Milly had lurched at the sound of every approaching buggy, thinking it would be Momma coming for her. As she grew older, she consoled herself with the idea that Momma would have been powerless to save her, even if she had known to whom Milly had been sold. In these last years, though, Milly had matured enough to realize what a relief it must have been for a gentlewoman to be freed of her illegitimate quarter-breed.

And the man who sired Milly? He had swung from the big oak in the front yard long before Milly entered the world. No slave ravishes a white woman and lives to brag about it.

That left Isum. Together, they had survived the unthinkable. And through it all, over and over, he had insisted they were valuable in the sight of God, as valued as anybody with a surname. If only she could believe it.

The fingers of her mind scratched at George's snarling image. They plugged her ears to his accusing voice which had been her constant companion.

In the tent, such a long period of silence passed between the men that she began to wonder if she had been left alone. Finally, when her shoulder screamed louder than the torrent above her, she eased onto her back and blinked grit from her eyes. Above, the oiled canvas undulated beneath the storm's assault. Lighting flashed instants before a clap of thunder rattled her bones.

Near the small tent's open flap, Phillip's broad shoulders and rigid back faced her. Feet planted wide and hands clasped behind his back, he looked every bit the guard.

Slowly, she pushed to a sitting position, grateful that the world stayed still. The buzz of a headache lingered, but it was nothing compared to before. A smooth role of the head released burning kinks in her neck.

"How long have you been awake?" In three strides, Phillip knelt beside her, eyes probing.

She clamped her heart and stared at his chin. "Where are you taking us?"

He grimaced and his scar twisted into a tangle. "That long?"

A fire lit inside her and blew heat up her throat, igniting her tongue. "Long enough to wish it had been Captain Buck whispering promises in my ear instead of a sham like you."

She hardened her backbone in anticipation of the slap she deserved, but he simply stared at her, impassive.

He opened his mouth to speak, then paused and ran a tongue over his lips as if tasting the words before they left his throat. "I've been assigned to take you all to Camp Crawford. We hit the trail as soon as this storm lets up. I'm sorry you had to hear all that with Marcus, but you must believe that anything I do is only for his good and yours."

Your own good, more like. She knew his type. Most men took from her without qualm. Others, to ease their guilt, pretended to care first. She turned away.

"We have a long trail ahead of us. I was worried about you. Still am." He ran a palm against her forehead then cupped her cheek and forced her face toward him.

Trained not to recoil, she gnashed her teeth and dug her nails into the folds of her skirt. Wind blew into the tent bringing with it spitting rain. The canvas fought its moorings.

His eyes dropped to her lips a breath before he took them between his own and severed the meager thread holding her together.

Recoiling, she struck out and cracked her knuckles against his jaw. His head whirled to the side then back around just as quickly. Mouth agape, he stared at her as if she had grown an extra head.

There might be a few people in the American South unaware of the consequences of a slave striking a white person, but Milly was counting on this officer not being one of them.

Blood rushed in her ears as she shoved her feet beneath her and pegged him with a look of challenge. "Touch me again, and I'll see to it you're obligated to hang me from the nearest tree just to save face," she screamed above the rain and the pounding of her own heart.

His jaw slammed shut and hardened.

She shot to her feet and darted on unsteady legs toward the opening.

"Milly!"

Just short of stepping out, she halted and took a fistful of the thrashing tent flap. The front of her was instantly soaked through. Rain stung her cheeks and drove into her mouth.

Across the camp, tarpaulin and stakes littered the ground. The tents that remained erect bulged with men who sought shelter beneath them. Across the way, her fellow slaves, at the mercy of the storm, huddled together. Several hunch-backed guards dotted the perimeter of the group.

From the outer edge, Isum stepped out. The sight of him comforted her. How long had he been watching Phillip's tent?

"Milly, please don't." Phillip called into her ear from just over her shoulder. "Fighting back will only make things harder on us both. Let me handle it."

His buttons scraped the back of her bodice, and she stiffened. For one purpose or another, he should have his hands all over her by now, but he didn't.

Isum took another step, and a guard shouldered his weapon, shouting soundless words. Isum didn't even glance his way.

Milly locked gazes with him, the only person who had ever been faithful to her. He loved her unconditionally, and she had all but spewed it back in his face. Muck squished between her toes as her feet carried her toward him and into the downpour. It hit her with such ferocity, she gasped.

Phillip stepped into the rain right behind her. "Milly, where are you going?" Was that panic in his voice or anger?

Fist balled and elbow bent, she faced him and squinted through the rain. "I won't go back. Do you hear?" She spit out a mouthful of rain and spun her heel in the mud. "I won't go back!"

***

Milly ran into Isum's arms, and relief uncoiled the muscles in Phillip's back. For one interminable minute, he had been certain she was going to break for the woods.

If she had run, he would have been obligated to take drastic measures. If she had struck him in public... A shudder throttled his spine. She *hadn't* struck him again, and for her sake, he was grateful.

Rivers coursed down his shirt and poured from the fingers dangling at his sides. Even beneath the stinging tempest, Phillip's jaw still smarted for her swift fist, but he would take a hundred more such blows if it meant not shackling her.

Milly's slim form almost disappeared inside Isum's muscled hold. Even through the rain-darkened haze, Phillip didn't miss the other man's barefaced possession of her. If he fisted the back of her dress any tighter, the worn fabric would surely rip. Over the top of Milly's head, Isum glowered at Phillip then turned, shielding her from his view. It was a lucky slave that got away with such blatant insolence. If Isum kept it up, his luck would run out— about the same time as Phillip's patience.

He hated that she let another man hold her, that she thought Phillip as much a wretch as the next foul-blooded male. He needed to see her again, to set things right. Tonight, he would find a way.

On his knees inside the tent, he curled the end of his pallet and began rolling. Clods of hair hung forward and dripped onto the bedding.

With few provisions left and the path to Camp Crawford, their supply base, blocked by warring Seminoles, it was either break through the thick enemy cord or die trying. Either way, they would be driving the slaves into the open arms of their most eager ally. Phillip would bet his next promotion that there would be at least one escape attempt.

He yanked the blanket to release a wrinkle then dug his fingers deeper into the fabric and rolled quickly past the warmth that remained from Milly's body.

It had been his forceful handling of her that set her off. A curse fouled his breath. Its reappearance in his vocabulary didn't surprise him. In the fort, when he had indulged in the feel of her skin, he had turned the handle on the door to his past. Since then, each look her direction opened the door a little wider. Up to now, he hadn't been willing to shut it, but just before her knuckles connected with his jaw, the terrified, half-crazed look in her eye had plowed sense back into his thick skull.

The blow was well-deserved. Just like Collins, Phillip had no right to any part of her. One day, Lord-willing, he would, but first God would have to reveal how and when.

As it stood, his only asset lay in Bailey land on the outskirts of Tensaw, but despite McGirth's noble efforts, it wouldn't sell. Two years after the massacre, folks still skirted the area, as if it were cursed. As if the Red Sticks' very skeletons would rise for a final reckoning.

With a fierce exhale, Phillip blew away unwanted images. Tensaw dredged up nightmares aplenty. He wouldn't settle there, so how could he expect others to? Oh, that someone would just take the place off his hands! Free him of it, and provide a way to purchase Milly.

Whether through the sale of his land or, like Jacob of old, through fourteen years of labor, the day would come when Phillip would free her. In Mississippi Territory, laws didn't hold the sway that they did in the States. If he could get to that territory, he was certain he could find a minister who might marry them.

The blood heated in his veins at the thought of waking next to her each morning. In his mind, he ran a finger down her neck felt her pulse race under his touch, just as it had quickened at the suggestive quirk of his lips.

One day, she would be his. To his thinking, she already was, but until the rest of the world agreed, he would do what he'd vowed and keep her safe while it was still in his power to do so.

Let her escape. Phillip shook his head and reached for the leather thong to secure his bedroll, but the Voice was insistent. *Free her.*

He snatched the strap from the dirt and whipped it into place. He was hearing wrong. There was no way God would task him with her protection, teach him to love her, then demand he let her go. Not after having already taken from Phillip everything and everyone he held dear. The Almighty wouldn't deny him this one request. Surely.

Like a father's reproving glance, a whisper brushed across Phillip's soul. *Am I not enough?* In that one hushed truth, the Spirit stripped him of every ambition and hope. Phillip found himself naked before a God whose Voice pricked Phillip's conscience. *Let her go.*

He dragged air in through his nose. *Oh, God, don't ask it of me. Not Milly too.* God had taken everything —family, community, fiancé, slave, and, at times, his wits. Phillip burrowed his fingers into the damaged skin of his cheek. God had even taken his face. Why *not* ask for Milly too?

He sank back onto his thighs letting the tight bedroll spring away from him. He watched it unwind, then treated himself with the memory of his bed cocooning her. Running frantic fingers over the fabric, he was met with nothing, but cold, damp wool. The chill seeped into his bones, cracking them from the inside, out.

Through obedience, he had already let one woman go. Before he willingly released another, he would do any number of things—give up his career, beseech her master for mercy, work until the skin sloughed from his fingers. God knew he would. What he could *not* do was free her to perhaps never see her again, to allow her to wander the wilderness to find her own way, to never know if she had escaped, died, or suffered a worse fate. Panthers and alligators aside, the basest of men dwelt in this desolate country, and she would be defenseless against them.

She is ever under my Eye.

A growl hummed in his throat. “No,” he croaked. Phillip had entrusted his family’s care to God, but now their bodies rotted in a mass grave. *No*—this time unyielding.

Rain pattered against the canvas, as though the heavens wept at his choice.

God would have to find another way—a way that included Phillip in the plan. The Great Creator was capable, was He not?

Tilting a squinted eye heavenward, Phillip dared Him to prove it.

Chapter Thirteen

The clink of shackles startled Milly from the hazy borders of sleep. Beside her, Isum shifted to rub the chafed skin beneath the iron clamps. As had the other able-bodied males, he had worn the irons the whole long march from Prospect Bluff, and the sun had already tucked in for the night by the time the soldiers allowed them to rest for the night.

A groan slipped from Isum's throat.

Milly sat up and rubbed comfort into his shirtless back.

He wrapped an arm around her and folded her in beside him, the weight of his arm locking her in place. The familiar musk of his labor and the steady thump of his heart drew from her a long sigh.

He kissed the top of her head. "How you feelin'?" he asked, not bothering to reduce his volume.

The guard's shadowy figure shifted their direction. Next to them, Uncle Jeremiah grumbled about needing sleep.

"I'm managing fine." The dull, lingering headache was nothing of concern.

He rested his chin on her head. "You know I love you, girl."

She inhaled filling her lungs to capacity. Although he had never spoken the words, she had always known it to be true. She let out her breath in a rush. "I know."

"When we get ourselves free," he said in a gruff whisper. "It'll be just me an' you. Like before, 'cept this time, I won't wait. Before God, I'll make you my own."

Milly nodded. Although rough around the edges, Isum would cherish her—spirit, body, and soul. She could never find a more loyal partner in life, nor a better guardian. Either join her life with his *in* freedom, or die fighting with him *for* freedom. Considering the alternative, neither prospect appalled.

She cocked her ear at the sound of approaching footfall. A soldier picked his way through the sleeping crowd, pausing at every odd step to poke at a slumbering body.

Isum went rigid, and his heart thrummed his ribs. Pulling her down with him, he dropped to the dirt and slipped a finger over her lips.

The prodding soldier stopped at her side and nudged her with the toe of his boot. “Get up, wench. The major wants you.”

Isum shot to a sitting position, his muscles coiled as though ready to pounce.

“No, Isum. It’s fine.” Milly pressed a hand against his quivering breast and turned to the guard. “The major wants me?”

“That’s what I said. Now get up.” His boot found Isum’s leg. “Hands off, swine.”

Isum lunged over her and caught the man by his calf, but the point of a rifle jammed under his chin abruptly halted his attack. His head twisted to the side, and he had no choice but to ease back.

“That’s right,” the soldier said, a sneer in his voice. “You’re not invited to the party.” With the rifle keeping Isum at a distance, the soldier pulled Milly to her feet.

“Don’t give in to him, Milly. Fight like you’s worth it.”

“The major’s a gentleman. If he wanted to hurt me, he would have done so by now.” Her voice remained remarkably steady and seemed to calm him. “I’ll be right back.”

Not waiting for Isum’s response, she went with the soldier in the direction of the main camp. A dozen or so yards from where they started, he came up beside her and shoved the butt of his rifle against her arm, nudging her. “That way.”

She stumbled, confused as to which direction he meant. The river ran to the right. The camp’s dim fires dotted the clearing ahead, and there was nothing to the left, except an endless sea of black, fathomless woods.

“Go on,” he hissed and shoved her again. Clearly left.

She balked and shook her head. There was no way she would enter those trees with this man. Then again, his feet were planted as if expected her to go in there alone.

Her heart stuttered. "Where's Major Bailey? I want to speak with him." The previous steadiness of voice was nowhere to be found.

The soldier took her by the arm and flung her toward the trees. Arms flailing, she staggered several strides before her hip hit the forest floor with grinding force. At the sound of his weapon being cocked, she flipped onto her seat. Terror clogged her throat, and pine needles gored at her palms as she quickly scooted backwards.

Rifle shouldered, he stared her down from just outside the tree line. "Don't make me say it again."

She scrambled to her feet and took several halting steps into the shadows. If she took a few more, the dark would render the guard's aim nearly useless, but the unknown evils that lurked beyond the boundaries of the moon's weak light were paralyzing.

Her eyes strained the darkness until they hurt. Why would Phillip meet her here, and why did he not call out?

She forced herself to take a dozen more carefully chosen paces then stopped. The woods around her felt like a cavernous mouth ready to snap its jaw and eat her alive. Rapid, shallow breaths sucked the moisture from her throat and the last shred of courage from her spine.

"Major?" The trees muffled her call. She raised her voice. "Major, are you there?" As livid as she had been at him yesterday for his advances, she would deposit a kiss on his lips this instant if he would just show himself.

When no response came, a whimper escaped her. Never had she felt more alone. "God, help me. What do I do?"

One yap of a coyote led to another closer by, followed by a chorus that seemed to come from all directions. She froze to the spot and weighed her options. Return to the relative security of the camp—and the business end of a rifle—or plunge further into the unknown. She slid her lip between her teeth and glanced behind her. Like stationary fireflies, the campfires winked between the vegetation. Ten more steps. She would take ten more, then go back.

One, two—

To her immediate left, something rattled the undergrowth. She caught the wind in her chest and waited. A chill prickled the skin on the back of her neck. When the suffocating night closed in tighter, she took the next step, eager to be done. An animal screamed and zigzagged across of her path.

She choked on a cry and darted through the brush, heedless of direction. A branch sliced the old wound on her forehead and warmth trickled into her eye. Something snagged the crook of her elbow, arresting her flight. She pivoted, swung around, and slammed against a hard, warm chest. Her shaky fingers became entangled in the ruffled front of a linen shirt. "Thank heaven, it's you." Her forehead dropped to his shoulder.

"I'm glad to hear it." Collins' voice sapped the strength from her legs, but his unyielding grasp on her upper arms kept her aloft. "It'll make things so much easier."

***

A blur of voices and muted laughter swirled about Phillip. He had told himself he would join his men around the fire to rally them for tomorrow's battle, but after two mugs of weak coffee and not one word uttered toward them, he finally admitted that he'd come hoping to get her out of his head.

It hadn't worked.

He couldn't help but think that every breath he drew was air that might have, moments ago, passed between her lips. It wouldn't always be so, not unless he found another way, and he *must* find one.

Gaze riveted to the ruby coals, Phillip slurped then winced at the flavorless brew. No coffee at all would have been preferable. Tomorrow night, if he was still alive, that was exactly what he would have. Not that he had a choice. Breakfast had exhausted their rations.

Fires were banked low. Not for concealment's sake, but to spare the men the heat. The sun was well beyond set, and still, perspiration trickled past Phillip's limp collar. The motionless air, heavy with moisture, brought no relief. Sleep would be hard to come by.

Through his shirt, he fingered the key dangling from a thong about his neck. It had appeared in his boot that morning, a bit of suture thread knotted about its shank. Marcus' fingerprints were all over the none-too-subtle suggestion.

How easy it would be to pass the key to any one of the slaves. That Marcus hadn't done it himself was proof of his loyalty and obedience.

Phillip slung coffee dregs onto the embers and watched it go up in steam to a chorus of hissing and popping. A log cracked and sparks shot into the air. He flinched. Like an adder bite, pain gripped his jaw and spread up his face through his spoiled skin.

At the snap of a musket cock, he spun, his hand flying to the hilt of his sheathed sword.

All conversation ceased. Several slanted their bodies away from him.

Corporal Higgins, oily rag in hand, dropped his disassembled weapon in his lap, and raised his hands in a gesture of surrender. "Just cleanin' her up, sir."

Phillip blew air through distended nostrils. It had been so many days since he'd suffered a flashback that he'd begun to hope they were over. Impending combat must have his nerves on edge.

"You expecting a surprise attack tonight, Major Bailey?" someone asked.

Phillip's gaze flicked to the sparsely whiskered sergeant. "Not likely." He slid the exposed steel of his blade back into the sheath.

A short laugh rose from the opposite side of the fire. "Nah, it's that half-breed filly what's got him all fired up. She's got us all aching with the want of her." Bawdy laughter spread.

Bitter hot rage billowed in Phillip's gut. His joints burned inside the ball of his fist. "The slaves are off limits. You'll keep your hands on your weapons and your trousers buttoned, or you'll pay for your pleasure with the lash." The growl in his voice should have been enough to silence them, but Higgins plunked down his half-cleaned musket and rose, one hand on his hip.

"Beg pardon, sir, but it just don't seem right officers should get their fill while we sit guardin' their naked backsides. Officer or not, regulations are regulations."

Those gathered chorused their agreement to the ghastly tune of Phillip's ignorance.

In three snappy paces, he was nose to nose with Higgins. "What's going on that I don't know about?"

"Major Collins, sir. That's what," he said under his rancid breath.

"What about the major?" Phillip tried to remember when he'd last seen the man. It couldn't have been more than an hour ago.

With an edgy glance into the night, Higgins clamped his lips.

Phillip's gaze raced to where the slaves had bedded down, but their fires were too weak, the darkness too thick to make out any activity. An insane urge to check on Milly sent a spasm into his calves. Heart lurching, he fisted the front of Higgins' jacket and jerked, ripping fabric. "What about the major?" Phillip roared.

Eyes bugging, Higgins flapped his arm in the direction of the woods. "There, over there! He's beddin' that eye-catchin' gal of yours. It's like I said, sir. It ain't right the officers not sharin—"

Phillip's fist snapped Higgins' jaw shut and hurled him backward over the log at his feet.

Swiveling, Phillip raked each man with his gaze. "Keep your hands to yourselves, your breeches up, and your mouths *shut*." He turned to the nearest soldier. "Take me to Major Collins. Now."

Moving quick-time toward the woods, the soldier glanced over his shoulder at Phillip. "He told Conyers to keep watch. Should find him somewhere along here." His sweeping hand encompassed the stretch of forest between where the slaves slept and where the Creek camped.

Phillip overtook the man. "Go on back. I'll take it from here." After a quick glance to confirm the soldier obeyed, he darted into the trees and ran as stealthily as possible just inside the break. When he caught sight of Conyers' silhouette leaned against a pine, he dove into the yawning depths of the forest.

Like the coward he was, Collins would do his dirty work a safe distance from prying eyes.

An opposing force, the darkness thickened and pressed against Phillip's eyes. Urgency nipped at his heels, but he forced himself to slow then stop. Steadying his erratic breathing, he strained to listen above the blood hammering his eardrums. The wind soughed through the needled canopy. From behind, the persistent river marched on dampened feet toward the bay.

He attuned his ears to anything abnormal and prayed he wasn't too late. Milly had been back on her feet just two days, and already she was a target. If the other men found her even half as alluring as he did, they certainly *did* throb at the sight of her. But Collins! Of all people, an officer should exercise restraint. No doubt this assault was a personal affront to Phillip. The fact plunged the guilt-knife deeper.

What had he been thinking to leave her unprotected? A muscle in his jaw bunched and cramped. With his palms itching to strangle the man, Phillip began picking his way through the underbrush. He whipped his head in every direction, methodically scouring every square yard he passed.

A gruff, masculine voice muttering incomprehensive words spun Phillip on the ball of his foot, and an all too familiar whimper propelled him through spiny palmettos. Hackles raised and fingers choking the leather grip of his sheathed sword, he sprinted toward a clearing bathed in moonbeam and evil.

He broke through the trees not ten strides from where Collins pushed off Milly and rose. Phillip's next footfall clattered against a sword belt abandoned near a shrub. Not breaking his stride, he snatched it off the ground. Breath erupted from his nose with each exhale as he focused on Collins' back.

"Conyers," he muttered, not looking up from fastening his gaping broadfalls. "You couldn't wait a few more minutes? I told you I'd come get you when I was done." A torrent of curses poured from his mouth.

With a heart-wrenching moan, Milly flipped onto her side then got to her hands and knees.

"Who said you could move?" Collins kicked her hip and sent her sprawling, the air exploding from her lungs her only response.

The hiss of the sword leaving the sheath in Phillip's hand compensated for her silence.

Collin's torso wrenched at the sound, his hand grasping at a weaponless waist.

Phillip pitched the scabbard aside "Looking for this?" He rammed the pummel into Collins' cheekbone. With a strangled grunt, he stumbled two steps then teetered.

Phillip dropped the sword and snatched Collins by the shirtsleeve just before he went down. No sooner had he regained his balance did Phillip land a knuckle-splitting blow to the same cheek.

Collins hit the dirt with a whoomph and a groan.

Arms trembling with rage, Phillip dropped to his knees and straddled the other man. "What did you say, Collins? A couple more? Good idea. We'll match."

"Enough, already," he panted. "You can have her."

Phillip growled and struck again then again, shocking every bone in his arm.

Head flopping, Collins succumbed to Phillip's powerful, repeated blows.

"Stop it," Milly screamed in his ear as though she'd said it many times already. She pounded his shoulder with her fist, suspending his hand mid-swing. "I'm not worth killing a man over."

Sultry air skidded down Phillip's throat, one heaving chestful at a time. He licked dry lips and stared at her in an attempt to recuperate a decent frame of mind.

The top of her blouse flopped open to one side, and the swell of her breast flashed bare in the pale light. The full implications of her ordeal sank in, and his heart cracked within him.

"Milly..." He flung his leg over Collins' writhing form and reached for her.

Clutching her blouse, she hastily backed away, the whites of her eyes brilliant in the moon's glow. As though influenced by the slight wind, she swayed then took another small step back and stole a glance over her shoulder.

Feet rooted, Phillip shook his head. "Stand still," he commanded too brusquely.

She flinched.

Dread that he would have to tackle her knotted his throat. He swallowed uselessly then forced the growl from his voice. "If you run, I'll be forced to catch you. And it won't be pretty for either of us."

Collins held his head and staggered to his feet, his breath coming hard. "Just take her down. You know you want to."

"Shut up, Collins."

The man neared, searching the tall grasses—for his weapon, presumably.

Milly's foot lifted and tentatively sought adequate placement behind her. "I told you I won't go back. Please...let me go." The last word fractured her voice.

"Let's talk about this, Milly. Come here." Keeping an eye on Collins, Phillip thrust a blood-tacky hand toward her.

Spooked, she hiked her skirt and ran.

Collins' mocking laugh sounded close by. Too close.

Phillip spun to face him, tracking Milly out of the corner of his eye. Her long legs ate up the ground quicker than he'd expected, and in seconds, she vanished into the woods on the opposite side of the clearing.

Collins could hardly keep himself erect. A glint of moonlight against the sword lying in the grass some yards distant drew Phillip to it. He tossed it at Collins' feet. "Your savior just took off, so unless you want me to finish pounding you to mush, I suggest you get out of my sight."

"Always said you were rabid." Collins bent to collect his sword and blood pattered against the foliage at his feet. "Don't think we're through, Bailey." The nearest tree caught his weight as he stumbled into it.

Not sparing the man a response, Phillip took off after Milly. She wouldn't escape on his watch. Not this way.

Her noise trail was easy enough to follow. A short distance into the woods, a fallen tree loomed out of the murk. He skirted it then made out her dim outline running some twenty yards ahead. He lengthened his stride and soon came within arm's length of her but balled his fists to keep from seizing her. "Stop, Milly. You can't run. Not this way," he called, coming alongside.

She angled away from him. "Let me go!" The sharp crack of wood preceded a gust of pine-scented air and a series of awkward thumps.

A branch whizzed past his face. He ducked then scanned the black ground for her. "Milly, are you hurt? I can't see a thing. Where are you?" If she had been rendered unconscious again, he wouldn't cease blaming himself for not tackling her when he'd had the chance. Remorse already burned the back of his throat.

He waded through heavily shadowed underbrush then dashed toward the sound of rustling leaves. He found her on one knee, pulling up on a trunk. Relief whooshed from his decompressing lungs as he slumped against the same pine. *Let her go*. The simple words came at him in a rush, and he struggled to find the justification to fight them any longer. She was no safer with him than she would be without him. The realization that he couldn't protect her—*hadn't* protected her—brought acid to his throat.

Although unsteady, she achieved her feet unassisted. Her ragged breath spoke of masked pain. "That beast took...what he wanted. There's no one to stop you from doing the same, but when you're done, either let me go or kill me. If you don't, Master Landcastle will. One way or another he'll suck the life out of me. I won't go back to him. I won't!" She took a wobbly step back then released her grasp on the tree and took another.

Phillip winced. She would run until her legs gave out, or her heart exploded.

Sticky evergreen bark embedded itself under his nails as he affixed himself to the tree to keep from reaching for her. Even as he wished to hold her, he gritted his teeth. He could mop at the blood and bind her scratches, but only God could soothe the jagged edges of her spirit. And if He, who loved her so much, wanted her to escape, who was Phillip to stand in the way?

He blinked long and slow then swallowed a gagging mouthful of his own desires. "I understand. But we'll do it my way, so just..." He dragged air in through his nose. "Just stop running."

Her breath caught. "What...do you mean?"

"You'll need to go back tonight, but there's a good chance that tomorrow you'll be able escape." *Isum*... Phillip repressed a grumble. If she was going to make it, she would need that obnoxious, muscle-bound guardian of hers. When God asked for something, He didn't go easy on a fellow. "Isum too."

"You can't be trusted."

"After what you've seen and heard, and knowing everything you've been through, I don't blame you. But right now, trust is a luxury you'll have to forgo."

One of her knees buckled, but he leapt and caught hold of her elbow before she crumpled to the loam. Stiffening at his touch, she made an attempt to reclaim her own weight, but her legs refused. "I just need a minute to rest," she said, tugging at his grasp and trying to sit.

"We don't have a minute." He slipped his arm around her back. Her sharp intake of breath and the recoiling muscles beneath his hand said more than a scream ever could. A curse on Collins rose to his tongue, but he bit it back and infused gentleness into his voice. "In all the times I could have hurt you, Milly, I haven't. I don't plan to start now."

The tension in her back released ever so slightly, encouraging him to push her a bit further. "They'll be looking for us soon. We need to get moving, and I intend to carry you." Without waiting for a response, he scooped up her knees and lifted.

There must have been some element of trust left in her, because she didn't fight. Instead, she emptied her lungs and slowly wilted against him. When she did, a coziness, like coming home, enveloped his senses. With soul-shattering force, it collided with his God-ordained task to let her go, to free her to build a new life with Isum.

As Milly's fingers clung to his neck and her breath warmed his throat, he realized how wise she'd been to demand he not touch her. Letting her go now would be all the more agonizing.

Chapter Fourteen

Silence settled between them as Phillip painstakingly picked his way through the thickets.

Each footfall jarred Milly's aching joints to the point she almost opened her mouth to beg he put her down, but the blessed—albeit fleeting—security she found in his arms outweighed the discomfort.

Isum had physical strength, but Phillip—when he was present to do so—held the real power to protect. And there wasn't another man like him within a thousand miles who would. She already grieved the moment he'd set her down and the day he marched out of her life. According to him, that would be tomorrow.

When they reached the clearing, his labor eased, and she felt more at liberty to address the obvious issue at hand. She licked her lips and tasted iron at the swollen split where Collin's mouth had crushed her lip against her teeth.

"So...you'll help us escape?"

"That's the idea, but whether or not it happens is going to depend on how the battle fairs and how fast you can run, although that last doesn't worry me so much anymore." The moonlight cast a shine on the dry smile molding the perfect half of his face. *A most perfect half...*

It had been his disfigurement that had captivated her at first, his attentiveness a close second. Now, with his chin inches from her view, she could note and truly appreciate his rugged beauty—the strong jaw whose stubble portended a morning shave, the thick neck whose jutting tendons shimmered with exertion. Adela must have loved her Indian deeply to abandon Phillip for him.

His eyes flicked down at her and widened. He cocked his head then stopped and pivoted until the moon faced her head-on. A storm spread across his features, working his jaw in a tight circle. Without a word, he resumed his march, each step more forceful than the last.

She raised cold, shaky fingers to her mouth. “That bad?”

“Let’s just say, you would have done yourself a favor to let me finish what I started.”

She had discovered long ago that struggle only produced regret, but with Collins, good behavior had not benefited her at all. Her fingers moved to the gash on her forehead which was sticky with sap and blood. If she hadn’t run, she might look a sight better. “I brought a good deal of it on myself.”

“Forgive me. I didn’t realize you chose slavery or asked to be dragged into the woods to be used in such a vile manner.” His sarcasm didn’t seem directed at her, but he was right.

Tears distorted her bleak world and ran down the back of her throat. She played the part well—that which was so deftly engrained in her and most every other beautiful slave in these twenty United States. “I should have done what Isum said and fought back.” Earned a few more bruises—just to prove she possessed an ounce of dignity and the right to preserve it. But to fight for it, she’d have to believe it. Isum would be disappointed. Hadn’t they sworn to never surrender?

Her comment earned her another raw glance. “Even against such a spineless snake, fighting would have done you little good. It was my responsibility to see no harm came to you. I failed, and you’ve suffered for it. Milly, I’m sorry. I should have paid closer attention. I should have—” A catch in his voice halted the mad rush of words, breaking her heart.

She settled her hand against his cheek and stroked his mangled features with her thumb. “Enough. What’s done is done. Only Major Collins is to blame, and he’s paid for what he’s done. You saw to that.”

An abrupt puff of air signaled Phillip’s disagreement, but when he said nothing, she rested her head against his chest.

“About what I heard what you say to Captain Buck—”

“You weren’t supposed to hear that.”

“Do you have something to hide? The real Major Bailey, perhaps?” As soon as the ungrateful questions left her mouth, she regretted them. Hadn’t he just proved the sort of man he was?

“We all have something to hide. Don’t we, Miss *Landcastle*?”

She tucked her chin against the gentle rebuke and the sting of truth. That he didn't hate her for such deception was a miracle.

He shifted his hold on her, and the laceration across her collarbones burned hotter.

A tremor built in his arms, but he didn't slow his march. They couldn't be far from camp now.

"Marcus has a heart of pure gold, but he lets it steer him instead of his common sense."

"What do you mean?"

"Once, he spent his last coin on a broken nag due to be put down. He was convinced he could nurse her back to health. Went hungry two days before I pulled the story out of him." A gust of exertion punctuated each sentence. "Put him in a clinic full of wounded runaways doomed to return to their masters, and there's no telling what he'll do."

Yes, Milly could believe that about the man. She had seen his eyes water, then harden in resolve at the mere mention of Little G's suffering. That night's mission of mercy had probably earned him a reprimand. "Was he right? Did the horse live?"

"Surprisingly, he got another year out of the old bones. He has a head for stitching. But strategy? God love him, if I had let him follow through with whatever half-conceived plan he'd formed, he would have botched the whole thing and landed himself in the clink. If anyone is going to sacrifice his career, it'll be me. Marcus is the best this army has to offer by way of doctors. He has a promising future and too much to lose."

"More than you?" Her quiet voice bounced in time with his rapid stride.

With the edge of the tree line just ahead, he slowed to a stop, his gaze seeming to roam the campfires speckling the grounds just beyond. "After tonight, I will have lost it all anyway." The utter barrenness of his tone struck deep and lit a passion within her.

"That's ridiculous. You'll always retain the rights to your own body." Impulsively, she ran the fingers that were hooked behind his neck deep into his hair. Its silky quality caressed her fingers and mocked her own state. "God gave you the gift of being born white and free. Don't squander it on self-pity."

He angled his head toward her, drawing close. Too close.

"From that first encounter in the woods, I've searched for a way to give you the same gift, to free you from one situation or another—the Negroes, the army, your master. In the beginning, it was duty that compelled me, but then…" The tremble in his arms increased. "I never imagined the impact you'd have on my life or that it would be less of a chore to free you from bondage than to free you from my mind." His chuckle emerged crisp and tight. "It's been a long time since a woman so completely commandeered my faculties."

A rush of blood made her bruised cheekbone throb. There was generally only one thing about a woman that ever controlled a man's thoughts. She had read it in Phillip's eyes just as easily as she had any others, and although he possessed rare self-control, he was, after all, still a man.

His chest hardened against her arm for an instant before he released a somber breath that chilled the moisture at her hairline. The tempo of his breathing kicked up in that pattern familiar with men, and Milly feared that, like the rest, he would follow the drive.

"It's time. Do you think you can stand?" He pulled back and slowly lowered her feet.

What sort of man was this? She was so stunned he hadn't taken advantage of her that it took her a moment to prove she wouldn't topple when he let go of her.

"Ready?" He removed himself and raised pinpricks of dread across her body.

She peered through the foliage at the forms of soldiers standing over their slumbering chattel and couldn't find her tongue to answer. She had escaped before and hadn't been this terrified. The possibility of another assault on her person was nothing new, nothing that should create this level of fear. The only variable from past situations was Phillip. And the thought of never seeing him again.

"Milly? Are you ready?" He rested a hand on her shoulder. "You're trembling." The tenderness in his voice was too much.

"Don't speak gently. I'll shatter."

Without a word, he pulled her to him.

Taking possession of his shirt front, she buried her face against him and used his chest to absorb her sobs. She emptied into him every foul touch, every terror she'd felt that night. His strength was comforting, but she couldn't take it with her to see her through the inevitable impending horrors. As her shoulders shook with silent tears, he massaged her back, and mercifully spared her the utterance of empty platitudes.

"We need to go," he finally said, the night's strain evident in his voice.

A quiver ran down her frame as she reluctantly pulled back.

He removed something from around his neck then shoved a long, cool object into her hand.

"A key?"

"Tuck it away for now, but give it to Isum when you're settled. Tell him we expect to engage the Seminole around noon. He'll know what to do with it."

Yes, he would. She rolled the key into the fabric of her waistband. "I don't understand why you would help me," she whispered around the anguish lodged in her throat. "Why you would concern yourself at all."

Labor-worn fingers bracketed the nape of her neck and inclined her face upward. His thumbs brushed at her wet cheeks. Moonlight spilled across his face and illuminated a deep valley etched between his brows. "How can you not understand? I'm far too selfish a man to do this for just anyone."

Awe at his intimation shackled the breath in her lungs. Was it possible he could care for a woman tainted with black blood and the feral mark of more men than she could count? If he did, it was best she run long and far. Her curse was hers alone to bear, and she'd spend the rest of her days in chains before she allowed Phillip to ruin himself with it.

Through the inflexibility of his arms and the irregularity of his breathing, she sensed a battle playing out in his mind. Whether desire or pity, she wasn't certain. She had no interest in the first, but his nearing mouth told her they were not in agreement on that point.

She stood immobile, willing him to be strong, to be different than the rest. To not disappoint her.

When he drew so close that his breath warmed the inside of her parted mouth, he hovered for three gasping breaths then twisted away with a groan.

Relief slumped her shoulders. Only a man who truly cared would practice such denial. As everything he'd done for her that night flashed across her memory, the thought that he might love her tiptoed into her mind.

Without warning, he took a sudden pinching grasp of her arm and, with a single-minded stride, broke into the camp's clearing. It was all she could do to keep her feet under her as he dragged her behind him.

"Conyers!" he called, not slowing.

The man trotted out of the darkness. "What can I do for you, sir?" At the sound of his overeager voice Milly shrank inside herself.

"We've got a runner. Bring me an extra set of irons."

He hadn't said anything about being clamped, but if it protected him from suspicion, she would wear them any length of time.

"She got away from you?" Conyers laughed. "Yeah, I'd shackle the hussy too."

At Phillip's quick stop and pointed stare, Conyers clipped off the end of his chortle.

"Who was the half-brain that hauled her into the woods in the first place?"

Conyers' head swiveled toward Milly then back to Phillip. He took a step back. "I'll go find out for you, sir."

"Sure you will."

Conyers spun on his heel, but Phillip snapped his fingers to recapture the man's attention. "Shackles."

"Yes, sir. Right away." Conyers melded into the night.

"It was him," Milly whispered.

"I know. He'll get what's coming to him." He released her and pointed to the ground at his feet. "Sit."

She obeyed, thankful to be off her watery legs.

"Milly, you alright?" Ten yards distant, Isum's frame towered over the other slaves, most of which probably feigned sleep.

"Shut up, already." A guard grumbled as though weary of repeating it. "I'll clout you again. Don't think I won't."

The jangle of chains preceded Conyers reappearance. Phillip took them. Without looking at her, he flung her dress to her knees, grabbed a calf, and dropped her ankle onto the open cuff. The hinge creaked as he snapped it shut.

She winced. The cold weight biting into bone was as unfamiliar to her as cotton-scarred hands.

With the cuffs secured, he stood and turned his back to her. "Get her back with the others and keep her there. Remove the irons in the morning." There was a sound of keys passing hands. "I take it you've heard my hands-off order?"

"Yes, sir, but..."

"Speak up."

"It's just that I heard maybe the colonel's wanting to speak with you."

"You heard *maybe*?"

Conyers shuffled his feet. "Actually, sir, he's got men out looking for you."

Milly's heart squeezed off a prayer that Phillip might be spared any backlash from helping her.

"Fine." He started off, then stopped and pointed a finger back at her. "If I see any new marks on her or any of the others, I'll hold you personally responsible."

The subordinate stiffened into a tart salute.

Without a backwards glance, Phillip walked out of her life, her only mementos of him the vanishing impression of his fingers on her arm, the key pressed against her stomach, and the undeniable, gut-wrenching awareness that he loved her.

Conyers rapped his knuckles against her head. "You heard him. Get over there."

The shameful clack of chains accompanied her down the row of resting slaves to Isum's side. "What they done to you?" Anger roughened his voice and hands. When he gripped her arm and angled her chin toward him, Milly blessed the passing cloud cover.

"I'm fine." Hoping the tremor in her voice didn't betray her lie, she wriggled from his grasp and sank to the ground to ease her aching hips.

Isum harrumphed then lay on his side, arranged her back against his chest, and hung his arm over her. The gash across her chest protested fiercely, but she swallowed the cry in her throat.

His tender kiss at the curve of her jaw brought a trembling smile to her lips. Isum was a good man, and he loved her. More than that, he was her reality. Not Phillip.

Together, Lord willing, she and Isum would hack out a new life together with the Seminole. She would contentedly bear him children. Children born free.

His lips ran up her jaw to the base of her ear. "Won't no man ever touch you again but me. And I'll kill that Bailey for you. As sure as I'm layin' here, I'll kill him."

She flipped inside the cage of his arms and glared at the crook of his neck. "That man did nothing to me. You owe him a debt of gratitude, so I expect I won't hear any more talk of killing." She lugged his hand to the bulge of fabric on her stomach.

His fingers explored. "What's this?"

She untwisted her waistband and delivered the key. "He gave it to me. Said you would know what to—"

A growl ripened in his throat. He swung his arm in an arch over their heads. A rustle and thump announced an object had landed in the outlying shrubs.

She launched into a sitting position and pried open his calloused hand only to find it empty. Surely, he hadn't tossed out the key. Her mind went numb. "What did you do?"

"I don't need that dog helpin' me take care a you."

Someone coughed and the guard walked their direction.

Four feet away, Uncle Jeremiah eased onto his side, the whites of his eyes full on them.

Shocked speechless, she didn't resist when Isum pulled her back into the circle of his arms. "I ain't blind, Milly. I see your face, what he done to you. How he hurt you. And I'll die a slave before I take any favors from his hand."

Had he gone mad? "You, you don't know what happened. He—"

"Hush. You don't gotta talk about it."

Her mind scrambled for a way to retrieve the key. She vaguely remembered what direction it had flown. Perhaps in the sunlight, she could excuse herself for nature's call and search for it.

Disgusted by his rash behavior, she tried to curl away, but his arms and the manacles allowed minimal movement.

His lips found her temple. "You don't need that white boy. It's me that'll take care of you."

"Don't you ever listen? I said shut up," the guard shouted.

The sound of shuffling feet came just before a dull thud that vibrated through Isum's chest to her back. He ground his teeth in her ear.

"One more word and you'll find yourselves on your feet the rest of the night."

Fear pinching off her throat, Milly gagged, then swallowed the vestiges of her hope.

***

Phillip stretched out for the night at the edge of camp, as close to the slaves as possible without drawing questioning eyes. From the woods, five yards from where he settled, an army of crickets chirped their chaotic symphony.

He longed to kick off his boots but wouldn't risk removing them and being caught unprepared. Not with the Seminole so near.

The night was half spent. Mind and trigger finger on full alert, Phillip doubted he would be able to take advantage of the portion that remained. He decided he'd spend the rest of the night replaying every sensation of that almost-kiss. It was a foolhardy pastime, but it was better than seeking out Collins and finishing what he'd started.

A broad shouldered, trim-waisted silhouette approached at a tramping pace. It was a rare occasion that merited his friend's anger.

With a grunt, Phillip collected his aching muscles and rose to meet him.

"Nice handiwork tonight." Marcus kept his voice to a gravely whisper but the biting tone came across loud and clear. "Next time, you should get a later start, so I have more moonlight to stitch by."

"Since when do you care what happens to Collins?"

"To the devil with Collins! It's your sorry hide I'm working to keep out of—" He bobbed a foot behind him and leaned back. "Are you hurt?"

Phillip plunged his chin to his chest. Large, dark splotches tarnished the front of his white shirt. He splayed his fingers across it. His chest constricted at the memory of her tarnished face. "It's Milly's. She was scratched...cut. Not sure what else. Collins ravished her. That much I do know."

Marcus jutted his chin. "And her blood ended up on you, how?" Was that accusation spiking his voice?

Phillip's pulse surged, but he hedged at self-defense. Exactly how did one say that he'd held another man's property? Soothed her terror? Fallen in love with her?

An exasperated burst of air shot from Marcus' mouth. He took off toward the slave holding area, his arms chopping the air at his sides.

"Marcus!"

He stopped and twisted at the waist.

Like a reeking carcass, silence lay between them. At last, Phillip released a slow, leaking breath. "She's fine. Leave her be."

"From what I hear she's far from *fine*. No thanks to you."

Eyes narrowed to slits, Phillip obliterated the space between them. The lie Collins had reported didn't infuriate him half as much as the thought that Marcus believed it. His fingers curled. "Tell me you didn't fall for that weasel's lies."

"There's never been a doubt in my mind that Collins' tongue is split right down the middle. I'm merely voicing the questions you're bound to hear shooting through camp come morning."

Phillip uncoiled his heart. "Rumors, I can deal with."

"Probably, but it's Command you have to worry about. You're sure Milly doesn't need me?"

He shook his head. Her wounds ran deeper than a needle's reach. "I doubt there's anything you can do for her. She's exhausted. Let her rest. You can examine her in the morning." For half a second, he considered confiding in Marcus about the key, but decided he didn't want to bring his friend down with him should the whole thing blow up in their faces. For her sake, he inwardly whispered another prayer that it wouldn't.

"So, what did the colonel say?" Marcus asked.

Caving under the weight of impending ruin, Phillip eased his creaking joints to the earth. He rested his forearms on his propped knees. "Suspended garnishment of wages." One more misstep, and he'd be stripped of three months' pay.

"Could be worse." Marcus sat beside him.

"Would have been, too, if it had been anyone other than Collins."

"Clinch said that?"

"May as well have."

"Well, there's a boon for you."

A small rustling from the woods behind Phillip spun both men that direction. The cool wooden grip of Phillip's pistol greeted his sweaty palm. Prickles ran the length of his spine. It would be just like Collins to shoot a man in the back.

A moth fluttered clumsily into Phillip's face, and a mosquito feasted on the back of his neck.

"It's nothing," Marcus said, after a minute. "An animal."

Phillip held his breath a moment longer before reluctantly allowing it to resume a normal pattern.

"Did Collins suffer any repercussions at all?"

"Clinch didn't say, and I didn't ask," Phillip replied, continuing to probe the black forest with his gaze.

The shrubs shook violently.

Phillip whipped sideways, making himself as small as possible. Pistol arm going before him, he took two quick steps toward the sound. He sensed Marcus just over his shoulder mirroring his moves.

Another crack and snap pinpointed his aim. The click of his pistol's hammer echoed back the sound.

"Don't shoot," a small voice quavered. "It just me, suh."

Phillips arm fell to his side, his thumb releasing the hammer. "God almighty, Marcus. It's Enoch!"

The boy emerged from the inky woods and took a few faltering steps toward them.

Phillip finished the distance.

Enoch's legs gave way, and as Phillip caught him, the boy's ribs bumped past Phillip's fingers like thin fabric on a washing board. He reacted quick enough to tighten his grip and snag Enoch under his emaciated arms.

He turned his overly large eyes up to Phillip. "Mastuh, I done wrong and come back to see if you'll have me."

"What kind of foolish talk is that?" Phillip said, attempting to mask his horror at the boy's loss of girth. That he was alive at all was a fact that had yet to fully register.

Marcus backed out of the way, while Phillip ushered Enoch out of the trees and onto the grassy stretch between the woods and the riverbank.

"But I run off. Been hidin' out." His knees folded, so Phillip helped him to the ground where he stood.

He swept a hand across the boy's sweat-dampened brow. "This whole time? How did you survive the blast?"

Marcus squatted beside Enoch, urged him to lie down then commenced examination.

"I nevuh made it in. Couldn't find that dad-gum door."

"What door?"

"The one Isum told me 'bout. It was secret. Hidden-like."

Phillip should be angry. No, furious. He should wear out the boy's hide for running off, not to mention for letting him believe he'd been blown to a dozen unidentifiable bits. The chuckle that blossomed in Phillip's stomach took him off guard, but felt so good, he let it stem into a full-blown laugh.

"T'ain't funny, suh. But I can't say I ain't pleased as pumpkins to be alive."

"Barely," Marcus stated, leaning to rest his ear on the boy's chest. "Now shut your trap so I can listen."

Phillip wiped his eyes. "Enoch, you couldn't find your way to the outhouse in plain daylight. How was it you thought you could locate a *secret* door in the black of the night?"

"I found you, didn't I?" Even Enoch's saucy attitude couldn't wipe the smile from Phillip's face.

"True enough. And a worthy feat it was." It might take Phillip a few days to figure out exactly how the boy had accomplished it. Phillip's strongest soldiers had crashed that night, completely worn out.

Marcus sat up. "Well, from what I could hear over your yapping, your heart seems to be doing a proper job. You hurt anywhere unusual?"

"My stomach's been gnawing at me somethin' awful."

Marcus waggled Enoch's head. "That's what happens when you camp out for two weeks with no rations. We've about run out ourselves, but being the doc, I'm entitled to special privileges." The customary smile lit his voice.

"Got any of them priv'leges you willing to split with a no-account slave boy?"

Marcus patted Enoch's shoulder then rose. "I'll see what I can do."

When Enoch and Phillip were alone, Phillip sat next to his slave, more grateful to see the boy again than he would have thought possible.

"I'd sit up, suh, if it wouldn't knock all them stars off kilter."

"Best not do that. You'd destroy the view." Phillip eased his back to the grass and joined Enoch in gazing at the heavens. Uncountable stars winked at them as though in possession of a secret soon to be revealed. Like a soul streaking to eternity, a falling star coursed across the dark canopy. Since the start of this mission, two hundred and seventy souls had passed into the hereafter. Tomorrow untold more would follow.

Would his be one of them? A scowl warped his lips. He knew his eternal home and wouldn't mind seeing it on the morrow, but if God took him, who would see that Milly escaped? Who would care for Enoch, so recently returned from the dead? Unless he found his way to the Seminole, he would be taken to auction and sold into only God knew what sort of evil.

Like the whisper of a butterfly's wings, Milly's soft voice flitted across his mind. *"It's in your power to see that Enoch lives free. What a gift that would be to a young man."*

Eyelids drifting shut, Phillip smiled.

What a gift, indeed. A gift that would do the boy no good, if it came one day too late.

Chapter Fifteen

A single heavily-bottomed black cloud obstructed the sun and brought blessed relief. True Seeker trekked just behind Totka from the right flank to the center of the loose, yet alert, American column. Seeking the author of Adela's letter, Totka weaved in an out of sober faced white men, each clutching their weapons with white-knuckled intensity. Eager to blend in, True Seeker followed the warrior's blue frock and mimicked his every move. Even without his turban, Totka's height made him hard to lose.

True Seeker kept his eye on the bow slung over Totka's shoulder and was comforted in the way it rose and fell with each of the man's steps. The way he handled that bow, one would think it was a part of him, an extension of his body.

"When battle begins, stay by my side," Totka had commanded earlier that day.

True Seeker wouldn't have dreamt of doing otherwise. A young man must be prepared to prove himself when the opportunity came, and, ready or not, this was True Seeker's.

When the short hand of his watch neared the six, Creeks, Americans, and slaves had resumed the march north. As the sun neared its zenith, scouts reported spotting the Seminole moving en masse to intercept them within the hour.

Since numbers were not in American and Creek favor, the American chief increased the tempo of their march and gave orders to use speed and intimidation to break through the Seminole line then keep moving until they reached the relative safety of their camp.

Speed, True Seeker could manage. Intimidation was another matter altogether. His slippery fingers repositioned their grip on the handle of the pistol that Totka had supplied him with. His free hand again flitted to the hefty shot bag. It didn't bring as much reassurance as he would have hoped. He might have better luck pelting the Seminole with the lead balls.

What he wouldn't give for a sturdy bow...

True Seeker's stomach knotted. He was nowhere near trained for all-out battle. It was not death that worried him but the possibility that through ignorance or carelessness, he might cause another's. If it were possible, he would allow himself to be scalped a dozen times before endangering Totka's life through any foolish action on his own part. He had come to bring Totka back to Adela, not get the man killed.

The sun reappeared at the same time that a light rain began to fall. It tumbled against True Seeker's blazing skin with a refreshing, calming effect. An inner resolve to bravely face whatever lay ahead overcame him.

They reached the heart of the soldiers' column where the rattle of chains was at its loudest. Soldiers prodded the gaggle of slaves to a heartless tempo. At least seven wore shackles. A couple of them were old enough to be their tormentors' great-grandparents, and others, with their assortment of bandages and splints, still struggled against wounds inflicted during the explosion.

One in particular ensnared his eye. A woman. Even in the tattered brown dress, she carried herself with a willowy strength and grace that did not belong in setting such as this. The tangled mass of frizzy hair crowning her head betrayed the reason for her bondage. Her skin might be as fair as Adela's, but it was hard to tell around the purple and red blotching her face. Her injuries were fresh, and True Seeker winced at the thought of the heavy hand that had applied them.

As though privy to his thoughts, her eyes flicked toward him. No, not at him, but at the officer just in front.

Totka sidled up to the officer, who could be none other than Bailey. He angled his head and cast a sidelong glance at Totka, effectively widening True Seeker's eyes. Totka had made no mention of the man's deformity.

True Seeker was already fascinated by a man who would give up the woman he loved to his enemy—former enemy, he amended. The scarring further enriched True Seeker's curiosity.

The rain swelled and ran crooked trails down Bailey's disfigured flesh. "Totka. What can I do for you?" The edge of his mouth lifted in the slightest of smiles as he transferred his rifle to his left hand and reached across his body to extend an arm in greeting.

Totka grasped it without hesitation. "I wish to draw my bow here, to defeat our worthy foe at your side."

Phillip's arched brow tugged at the taut lines of his skin. His brown eyes darted over his shoulder. In one sweeping, unreadable glance, he took in True Seeker's presence then turned his head to the front.

So, Totka wished to subtly repay the white man for the gift of Adela? It was a laudable cause and Bailey, even being unaware of Totka's reasoning, would be thickheaded not to accept.

Totka's beaded bandolier strained against the sculpted muscles of his chest and arms. He wore no face paint, claiming he did not need to draw on the natural powers of the earth. His God would supply all he needed, or so he had said. Even taking that, as well as his slight limp, into consideration, Bailey would be hard-pressed to find a man in either camp more suited to battle than Totka.

At last, the officer dipped his head in a nod. "I'm honored." Indeed, he should be grateful to have such a fine warrior guarding his flank.

The cloud lumbered across the sky taking with it the afternoon shower and allowing the sun to resume its scorching duty. Steam rose from the major's wool jacket, and the air saturated True Seeker's lungs. Sweat tingled his scalp, and swarming gnats caught in the sticky perspiration on his throat.

Bailey jerked his head toward True Seeker. "Who's your shadow?"

"True Seeker has come to us from Tensaw."

"Oh?" Bailey twisted and studied True Seeker more fully before returning his gaze to the encroaching battlefield. "The boy just arrived?" Did he suspect anything? It couldn't be often someone from his small settlement crossed his path.

Totka replied with a terse nod. With a flick of his finger, he summoned True Seeker to walk between them.

He obeyed.

"Welcome," Bailey said, surprising True Seeker by once again stretching his arm in greeting. "And how's Tensaw these days?"

After one glance into Bailey's firm, yet humane eyes, True Seeker knew the man wouldn't have minded he and his family taking refuge on Bailey land. What might he say if he knew his barn had nearly been the site of a hanging?

"Much ash remains. Empty land. It is rumored the whites are still fearful of settling it."

"So I hear." Bailey's demeanor remained guarded, impassive. Except for his eyes, which, for the second time in as many minutes, darted toward the slaves—who struggled across the swampy ground some thirty paces to their left.

"You seem the strong, capable type. I could use an extra set of eyes today, if Totka doesn't mind my borrowing you."

Totka adjusted the strap supporting his powder horn then shrugged. "He is his own man. He will decide."

Tentative warmth filled True Seeker at Totka's confidence in him, but it was misplaced. "I am not a man," he confided in Muskogee.

Totka appeared nonplussed. "Would a mere boy care for his family as you have? Would he travel many leagues to help a man he does not know? You will prove today that ceremonies do not make a man."

True Seeker internally winced. A boy was capable of much when a desperate situation required it, but that did not mean he was a man, nor did it mean he could wield a weapon with experience enough to do more than cause trouble for the warriors fighting next to him. Totka's trust in him was misguided. And now, this major had been deluded, as well.

True Seeker took a leaping step over a pocket of muck thinly disguised by a dusting of pine needles. Surely he would disappoint, but how could he turn down such a request for help? He slid his gaze to Bailey. "What would you have me do?"

"You are aware that the Seminole and the blacks are allies?"

"I am." It was part of the reason the Seminole were just minutes away—to free the slaves and exact retribution for the fort's destruction.

"It's my responsibility to see they make it back to their masters unharmed, but I expect to be a bit distracted today," Bailey said, cynicism drying his voice. "There's also a good chance they'll attempt escape during battle. If any of them break free, I need someone who can track them."

True Seeker had much to learn, but surely he could track a slave in a headlong scramble toward freedom. "You want me to bring them back?"

"No," Bailey replied, a bit too quickly.

True Seeker quirked an eyebrow.

"Don't interfere. Stay on their trail. Hidden. Then bring *me* word."

He nodded, catching Bailey's emphasis on the word "me." "I can do this thing you ask."

"Good." The clipped word released a taut cord in Bailey's neck.

"He leaves much unspoken," Totka added in Muskogee. "I am not certain, but I believe his heart to be attached to the white one." He jutted his chin toward the slaves, and True Seeker's gaze traveled again to the woman.

Her rain-laden dress clung to her curves. She held handfuls of her heavy skirt, exposing bare feet and shapely calves spattered with filth.

"Do not stop her from running," Totka continued. "And do not bring her back. Just see that she is unharmed and you will fulfill your duty. But listen well." Intensity blazed in his eyes as he leaned toward True Seeker. "Unless there is no other recourse, do not raise your hand against a white man."

"I understand." And he did. More than Totka would probably ever know.

"Take this." Totka flipped his bow off his shoulder and held it out.

True Seeker's jaw hung open for three breaths before he found words. "I cannot take your bow."

"Take it. Your hand is more suited to it than to a pistol." His rigid gaze told True Seeker he would brook no argument.

Still, to take a warrior's bow from him... Would that be worse than insulting him by refusing the offer?

Rendered speechless, True Seeker wrapped his fingers around it. The feel of the smooth hickory against his palm infused in him a much needed dose of confidence.

Before Totka released the bow, he spoke the name he had oft repeated. "Lord Jesus, bless this man and this battle. May he seek your guidance. May your strength be his. May his arrows fly swift and true."

At the warrior's hushed, reverent words, a force, a presence swept over and around True Seeker. As real as the hot wind ruffling his hair, its existence could not be denied. It struck him with awe and fear, prickling his skin.

His gaze flicked to the men at either side. As before, Bailey diligently scanned the trees. Totka fiddled with the straps of his quiver. Had they not sensed it? Who was this invisible God-man who could be summoned with a simple invocation, and why would He care to make Himself known to one as lowly as True Seeker?

As he slipped Totka's full quiver over his head, he swore to himself that he would not let these men down. If the major wanted the stunning slave to escape, True Seeker would see to it that she did. The trick would be staying alive long enough to make it happen.

His mouth curved into a smile. Carrying the blessing of such a God, how could he fail?

***

The race to Camp Crawford grew more frantic by the yard, but an army of angry Seminole stood in their path. The Indians' presence didn't scare Milly, not too much anyway. It was the thought of bullets flying...and her traipsing through the midst of them.

There was no need for surprise, no need for quiet, yet for the last ten minutes, the only sounds Milly had heard were clinking chains and the shouted whisper of nearly five hundred feet scurrying through brush. If anyone was talking, she was too on edge to notice.

When the arch of her foot found the jagged edge of a broken stick, she bit the inside of her cheek, as if crying out would summon a stray arrow to her heart.

Isum caught her before she went down, but her stumble created a wrinkle in the line.

Brandishing his rifle, a guard was upon them within moments. "Get moving! You want the savages to fall on you?"

Milly scowled. Of course, she did. Since Isum had decided to lose his mind and toss out the key, the Seminole were her only hope.

"If you value your scalp, you'll pick up your feet!" The guard continued. It was *his* mangy, blond scalp he should worry about.

The first gunshots rang through the trees ahead. Milly instinctively tucked her head between hunched shoulders.

A flock of black birds took flight, momentarily blacking the sun.

More explosions filled the air, followed by shouts. At once, the forest was filled with the sound of the blood-curdling war cry of what must be a thousand Indians. The treetops seemed to lift with it, along with the hairs on Milly's neck.

A few of the soldiers in front crouched, their rifles raised, their blue-coated backs stiff. Someone screamed an order for everyone to keep moving.

Isum shoved a hand between her shoulder blades and pressed her forward.

A doe materialized from the woods. Eyes bulging, she skittered through the thickets and past Milly, who balked.

Red faced and sweating, a soldier appeared at her side. "Stop again, and I'll shoot you where you stand," he yelled above the increasing din. His frantic eyes injected terror into Milly's bloodstream. What had he seen to scare him so?

Metallic fear flooded her mouth, coating her tongue, and stiffening her legs. Isum's steely grip on her arm yanked her forward forcing her knees to unlock. She floundered to regain her footing and Isum's speed.

The ring of clashing steel echoed through the trees coming from all directions. Sunlight flashed against slashing swords, careening her thoughts to Phillip. She twisted to locate him in the spot he had occupied over the last couple of hours. Just *there*, over her right shoulder.

But this time, her glancing eye brushed only a young Creek, pistol drawn and at the ready. His gaze raked the surrounding area then snapped her direction. His steady, black eyes connected with hers, and for an instant, calm washed over her, dousing her with the strength to take a few more steps into the encroaching melee.

Ahead, the battle frenzy increased. Then, from the gray haze of gun smoke, a bare-chested warrior emerged streaking toward them. Milly might have thought him Creek, but for the blood lust on his face and the war club he flourished toward heaven.

She veered away from him and collided with the damp wall of Isum's body. He halted and wrapped a strangling arm around her, but the warrior seemed oblivious to their presence. He sprinted past and made a leaping bound toward one of their guards. Shouts slammed into her ear. A shot discharged at close range.

Shielded by Isum, she was unaware of the warrior's fate, but it was almost irrelevant as five more flocked the area, engaging every guard.

The slaves instantly scattered, leaving Milly, Isum and the other shackled men standing in a huddle. Uncle Jeremiah hobbled to a large rock and eased his old bones onto it, as though prepared to wait out the madness and extend a greeting to whatever outcome awaited.

"Now," one of the slaves shouted. "Get it out. Hurry!"

"Give me room," Isum demanded. When he shrugged out of Milly's grasping hold and thrust her a few feet away from him, she realized he had been speaking to her.

Surrounded by nothing but screeching air and whizzing bullets, Milly fought panic and the urge to run. Slapping her palms against her ears, she fell to her knees and hunkered down.

Ten feet away, a soldier pitched under a warrior's hacking blade.

Milly squeezed her eyes against the flow of red. When next she opened them, it was to Isum squatting before her, jamming a long rusty key into the lock of his shackle.

"Where did you get that?" she asked, incredulous. That morning, it had been made clear to them that none of the guards had been given keys, rendering futile an attack on their person.

With one snap of his wrist, a cuff fell away. "The major."

How had Phillip managed to give Isum—? Milly gasped. There were *two* majors. But why that hideous Collins would care to help them escape didn't make sense. It seemed to Milly, he would want her around, for personal convenience.

Free now, Isum tossed away the irons then passed the key to the other men. He stooped to relieve a dead soldier of his rifle and bullets. "Run, Milly!"

She took off toward the main body of Seminole, which suddenly scattered. *Where are they going?* The battle was far from over. She picked up her skirt and lengthened her stride. A swift runner, she would catch up to them in minutes.

***

True Seeker stood in the open, feet planted apart, weapon at the ready. The battle churned around him but did not approach, and he felt the oddest sensation of being in a time and place not his own. His heart seemed to race outside his body, and his eyes, darting toward every slight movement, functioned independently of his sluggish thoughts.

No one noticed him, a boy out of season—not even the slaves that had produced a key from thin air.

When the fray had reached them and the huddle of slaves dispersed like troubled ants, True Seeker had latched his gaze onto the woman. Although it was becoming more obvious by the moment that she would not be parted from the big one.

A frown bent True Seeker's hardened lips. If she was going to get away, she needed to start running. *Now*. As the thought crossed his mind, she took off on a clear path toward the disbanding Seminole line.

A blur flashed in the corner of his right eye, and instinct swung his body down and away. Simultaneously, he snapped his neck and pistol arm toward the threat.

The enemy, tomahawk raised, was only a single great bound away. His silver earbobs reflected the sunlight into True Seeker's eyes. He squinted against it as the Seminole let loose a shriek that was promptly cut short by a blast. His shirtless, painted chest ruptured. His legs folded, and like a felled tree, he toppled, arms extended.

True Seeker's chest thudded with the rhythm of a half-crazed war drum, but it was a cramp in his crooked trigger finger that connected him with the deed. *First kill.*

The earlier surreal effect dissolved placing True Seeker squarely in the heart of this battle, making it his own. The heat became more intense. The war cries amplified. Acrid gunpowder sullied the air that whizzing over his teeth and into his starving lungs. His eyes burned with it.

He blinked away the welling moisture and honed his thoughts. *The woman*. Only seconds had passed. She should still be visible running through the long gap in the trees. But she wasn't.

He spun. The big black man was half-dragging her away from safety and into the thick of the fight. Is this what Bailey had feared?

True Seeker jammed the spent pistol into his waistband and set off after them. He had been prepared to follow her into the midst of the enemy, but unless the two turned immediately, there would be no reaching the Seminole.

Skirting a dwindling fight between several Creek and Seminole warriors, True Seeker slipped the bow off his shoulder and snatched an arrow from the quiver. The fletching brushed his finger as he notched the arrow against the sinew. His eyes did not waver from the black man's expansive back and the rifle he gripped.

To True Seeker's left, a Seminole loped away from the field of battle. Another followed some paces behind him. True Seeker trotted past a soldier standing with blood dripping from his sword onto his dead foe and looking in vain for another to fight. Where were the vast Seminole numbers that had been promised to them?

Soldiers regrouped, but the black man either didn't notice or didn't care. He swiveled his neck in search of something or someone. Not given much choice, the woman trailed him, her free arm working to disentangle her skirt from her legs.

Abruptly, the slave stopped and dumped the woman behind a shrub.

True Seeker followed his gaze to Major Bailey, who, in a flash of blue, disappeared behind a thick trunk. Moments later, he emerged on the other side, his arm crooked around a Seminole's neck.

In five long strides, the slave shortened the distance between himself and the major. He dropped to one knee, and began loading the rifle, his head pointed firmly in Bailey's direction.

True Seeker jerked the bow into position. *Lord Jesus...*

Surely, he did not intend to kill the white man, but a slave waiting to kill his oppressor made more sense than wanting to protect him, which as the only other reason the black man would be where he was instead of fleeing to freedom.

I seek your guidance. He drew taut the string.

Bailey's opponent thrashed and the two spun, exposing Bailey's back.

Nearly done loading, the slave's hands moved faster.

...each moment, your guidance... Totka's prayer echoed in his mind. *Bless this arrow, may it be swift.*

Then, in one yank of Bailey's arm, the warrior ceased struggling and slithered down Bailey's front.

The slave had the rifle to his shoulder almost before True Seeker could register his movement.

A woman's scream pierced the air.

May it be true.

The bowstring burned the pads of True Seeker's fingers as the arrow took flight. The thump of the bone-tipped shaft slamming into the man's ribcage was lost in the blast of the slave's rifle, but the fletching protruding from between his shoulder blades spoke of a true shot.

Eyes searching, Bailey spun and crouched, his hand going to his powder horn to reload the pistol he snatched from its holster.

The rifle barrel tipped from the slave's hand. A blackberry bush caught his forward tumble.

Taking in the arena, Bailey's eyes flashed anger. Blood dripped down the good half of his face and over his lips.

"Oh, God, no. Isum!" The woman stumbled to the slave and began futilely to pull at his massive frame to free him of the briar.

True Seeker ran to her and wrapped an arm around her waist. He backed away, taking her with him.

A sob lashed her chest as she lunged toward the lifeless body.

Digging his heels into the loam, True Seeker hardened his muscles against the strain. "You can do nothing. He is dead. Leave him."

Immediately, she relaxed, but the wet splattering onto his arm told him her grieving had just begun.

Bailey had eased his stance, but not stirred. His gaze rested on the woman, and even if True Seeker were a half-wit, he could not deny the love he found written across Bailey's battle-stained face. Instead of going to her as True Seeker expected, Bailey set his jaw. After a curt nod to True Seeker, he turned his back and collected the dead Seminole's weapons.

The situation became as clear to True Seeker as the spring that bubbled in the hills near his Tuckabatchee home. And it was just as bone chilling.

"You must run," he murmured in her ear. "The battle is almost over and there is not much time. Go east. You will find the Seminole *east*." He hoped she had enough sense to know which direction that was and how to find it. If she did, she should have no trouble locating the war party.

He released her.

Miraculously, she found her feet and, after one last glance toward the dead man, moved away in the correct direction. At first, her steps were too slow to give True Seeker any hope that she might make it, but when, just a stone's throw distant, a soldier straightened from a fresh kill, she startled then seemed to remember her purpose. Within the minute and with a speed True Seeker did not anticipate, she disappeared from sight.

Chapter Sixteen

Sergeant Garrigus picked up his discarded coatee and slung it over his shoulder. "Where to next, sir?"

"There should be newer growth along that stretch." Phillip waved his knife toward a stand of trees and took off that direction.

It was their second morning back at Crawford, and after a filling breakfast of coffee and biscuits, he'd taken it upon himself to choose the lumber for the new palisade.

During the Fort Negro expedition, Camp Crawford had proved its worth as a border outpost. With the Seminole threatening war, it would be even more needful to have this post well stocked and well defended.

In the weeks that Phillip had been at Prospect Bluff, the camp had undergone surprising growth. No longer a field dotted white by tents, Camp Crawford now boasted several buildings—a cook shack, an infirmary, and barracks for the officers. The pickets were several dozen yards from completion.

Clamping his knife between his teeth, he spanned with his hands the sticky circumference of a young pine, sizing it. Satisfied, he gauged an X into the bark with his blade.

A ways off, Sergeant Garrigus moved from tree to tree, choosing and marking. Men would follow later with axes and mules, but this almost solitary work, away from the hubbub of camp, suited Phillip just fine. He'd be hacked and staked before he was caught sitting around waiting for the slaves to be rounded up and returned.

The Creek were seeing to that task, and already, several groups of runaways had been ushered at rifle point into camp. So far, Milly wasn't among them. *Father, let her make it.* The prayer was constant on his heart—right alongside the selfish hope that today he might lay eyes on her again.

An investigation into their escape was underway, but so far, no slave had been found that could—or would—explain how the slaves had come across a key. Phillip could only pray it stayed that way.

He was confident that Milly, if found, wouldn't give him up, and thanks to True Seeker's quick thinking and steady bow, Isum was dead. It was a shame, but given the alternative, Phillip wasn't going to complain about the outcome.

Whether or not the man had blabbed about Phillip's involvement in the escape was the worrying question on his mind. He wouldn't have thought it possible before, but *before*, the slave hadn't inexplicably turned on the very man who had given him the key to freedom.

Using the back of his sap-coated hand, Phillip caught a trickle of sweat at his hairline. "That's all of them, sergeant," he called. "We'll have to move further north."

Garrigus lifted a hand and turned to notch his last tree.

"Suh, suh!" Enoch raced toward Phillip, his spindly legs a blur.

Phillip smiled at the sight of life, full of hope and headed his way at full speed. For the last twenty-four hours, Enoch had gone full speed everywhere his feet carried him.

Like the recoil on a rifle, after a few substantial meals, he'd bounced back from the brink of starvation. He had yet to stop bouncing. The scrap of paper in his pocket had more than a bit to do with it. When he wasn't springing around camp annoying the soldiers with his crooked-toothed grin, he was sitting stock-still tracing with his eyes the letters on the parchment. They were the only words he could read, and that was only because he had memorized them the hour Phillip had quoted them.

As soon as he reached civilization, he would find a lawyer and make the emancipation official. In the meantime, he had written a detailed document and stashed it among his possessions. That single act of liberation had filled him with more joy than he had ever experienced. It was dampened only by his inability to do the same for Milly.

"He's back, suh!"

Which one? True Seeker and Totka had gone opposite directions, with True Seeker trailing Milly, just as he said he would. Phillip ground his teeth to keep from shouting the question. He would race back to camp to see for himself, if he was certain the act wouldn't rain suspicion on him. He locked his knees.

"Brung more runaways back with 'im." Enoch hollered as he ran.

Phillip's heart sputtered then lurched. A sharp twinge jolted his gaze to his hand. Blood dripped from a slash across his thumb where he inadvertently gripped his blade. He forced his knuckles to relax and stared at the trickle of red.

Enoch came to a panting halt then leaned over, propping his hands on bent knees. "I knew you'd want to know, mastuh."

"You don't need to call me that anymore, remember." It was inconsequential, but saying it delayed asking the question burning on his tongue...and receiving an answer he didn't want to hear. The trouble was figuring out which answer he wanted to hear *less*. He filled his lungs with muggy air then buried his bleeding thumb inside a tight fist.

The boy straightened and jerked his shoulders in a sloppy shrug. "I know, but sayin' it sometimes makes things bettuh when you's angry at me."

"What have you done?"

"I'll be a three-legged mule if I know, but I seen them cornrows between your eyes b'fore. Last time was when you found me catchin' a few winks behind the general's drapes."

A chuckle bubbled in Phillip's throat, but he coughed it away. "I'm not mad at you, and even if I was, calling me *master* wouldn't fix it." *Not anymore, at least*. "Now, what did you come out here hollering about?" Enoch might suspect Phillip had feelings for one of the slaves, but he wasn't about to confirm it. Not with the boy's jaw being so loosely hinged.

"That Indian's back. The one what walks funny."

"*Who* walks funny, and there's no need to insult the man. Use his name."

Enoch's eyes began an impudent roll then stopped. With his toes, he snipped the yellow head off a dandelion. "It's Totka, and he brought slaves back with him."

Phillip's eyes widened at Enoch's perfect use of the English language. "How many did he catch?" He tried for an indirect approach.

"I didn't count."

Phillip suppressed an impatient sigh. "Make a guess."

Enoch's tongue popped out as he scrunched his face. "Couldn't say, suh. A goodly number."

Would he have to drag the information out of the boy? Glancing away, Phillip cleared his throat. "Was Milly with them?" Blood squeezed from between his fingers. *God, give me strength.*

"I knew you was sweet on that gal! Was wonderin' how long it'd take you to ask." A self-satisfied grin split Enoch's cheeks.

Phillip advanced a step toward Enoch, effectively wiping the grin from his face. "And I'm wondering how long it'll take you to answer my question."

"No, suh. She ain't been found."

Disappointment coupled with hot guilt burned through Phillip's veins. He stared through the trees in the direction he had last seen Milly. Enoch kept talking, but none of it registered as more than jabber.

Phillip's mind carried him back to the night she had woken from unconsciousness—the night he had promised her everything would be all right. The feel of her molded against him still emblazoned on his chest, the silky skin of her neck still warm on his fingertips. These sensations still as real to him as God's rock-solid command to let her go.

The Almighty had pulled him through the horror of Fort Mims, then, with the hands of a loving Father, set him back on his feet. Still in awe at God's mercy and grace, Phillip wouldn't start questioning His plan now. God would see him through whatever the future held, and the last couple of days, the niggling thought whispered that perhaps he should return to Tensaw to pick up ranching on his family's land. Only God could instill and nurture such a notion. The why of it was just as confusing to Phillip as the idea itself. Perhaps it was simply proof of God at work calming the spirit that warred within him.

"Suh? You alright?"

Phillip's gaze floated back to Enoch. The concern softening his dark eyes touched a place inside Phillip that he was just discovering existed. Milly might be lost to him, but his latest calling stood before him now, on fire and eager to explore his new freedom. And wasn't Phillip the perfect man to open the way?

Phillip could almost feel Saul's hand of approval coming to rest on his shoulder. The slave's broad, broken-toothed smile flashed before Phillip's mind, and a confident assurance crept into place in his soul. "It's time you learn to read, young man."

Enoch's brows shot up. "Come again?"

"Read. I plan to teach you. A free man needs employment and good employment requires the knowledge of letters and numbers. Unless you intend to spend the rest of your life cultivating tobacco for some stingy white farmer…?"

The skin on Enoch's face went slack. "You don't want me no mo'?"

Wondering where Enoch's proper English had gone, Phillip laughed and laid a hand on the boy's shoulder. "Of course I do, but someone as bright as you has the potential to be far more than a soldier's valet. You could save your money, go north, start your own business. I've heard tell of free black men opening barbershops and forges. You're free now. Free to choose any number of jobs. What's the one thing you've always dreamed of doing?"

"I nevah had no dreams. What would a slave do with one of those?"

What indeed? The smile faded on Phillip's lips.

"Don't send me away, suh." He blinked rapidly. "I just wanna be wid you."

Phillip had said too much, too soon. He squeezed Enoch's shoulder, still boney from his extended tramp through the wilds. "You're not going anywhere." As if Phillip could actually part with him. "Truth is you've been lolli-gagging long enough. You're well now, so you'll be earning your keep around here, same as the rest of us. You can continue as you always have. I'll keep track of your pay and owe it to you when we get back to Nashville."

Enoch's eyes brightened at the mention of cash. It wouldn't be long before a dream sprouted into the promise of a future.

But what of Phillip's future? It stretched out before him like a fog-coated meadow, impenetrably gray and eerily lifeless. Once clear, his path was now obscure. If only he could find it again. But even if he did, he wasn't sure he could walk it alone.

Not without Milly.

***

A brilliant sun beat against True Seeker's closed lids. Dried grass crackled beneath his ear. He squinted and blinked to clear the haze in his brain.

Lids flying wide, he shot to a sitting position. How long had he slept? Judging by the slant of the sun's rays, it had been far too long.

While clambering to his feet, he raked away the dead blades stuck to his sweaty cheek. He was only supposed to have dozed for a few minutes, not hours. Three days of steady foot travel and two nights of little sleep would hardly excuse his lapse in duty.

He moved on swift, silent feet a short distance across the field to where he had last seen the woman sleeping, but his stealth was for naught. All that remained of her presence was the indention of where she'd slept in the switchgrass. For the span of two beats, his heart stopped. Pinching the knot on his nose, he sucked in a long, steadying breath then knelt to feel the spot. Not surprisingly, it was cold.

In a steady lope, he set out on the wide trail she left through the grasses. Fortunately for him, she and covertness were not bedfellows. The last days, she had hacked her way through nature as though she wished to be found, and it still amazed True Seeker that soldiers had not yet overtaken them.

At least, not as of the early hours of this morning. Only Totka's Jesus knew if she still walked free…or even lived. Any number of wild animals could have easily taken her down.

How was it that his foolishness unceasingly cost him the safety of those in his care? If there were time, he would stop and kick himself for his irresponsibility. His neck blazed at the remembrance of Lillian's abrasive rope, but it was his conscience that felt the suffocating squeeze.

The woman had spent yesterday moving at a brisk pace and that with no more than a fistful of berries from the brambles she had stumbled upon along the way. Her feet had churned until nightfall when exhaustion dragged her down. Sleep had swiftly overtaken her.

He'd been certain she would sleep like the dead and not wake until the sun scraped the top of the sky, but he'd had her confused for himself. The aggravating thought etched a grimace into his brow and infused speed into his steps. He reentered the woods and invoked the God-man to guide and protect the woman until he reached her. He could only hope Totka's Jesus also had ears for True Seeker's prayers.

A crushed sassafras sapling told of her passage. Briefly, he slowed and inhaled. The plant's fresh, citrus scent reached his nose giving him hope that he was not far behind her.

Bailey had told him to stay hidden and not intervene, but last night, True Seeker had decided that if the woman did not cross paths with the Seminole by this nightfall, he would make himself known to her and guide her in the correct direction. Whether by accident or design, for the first day and a half, she had followed the Seminoles' trail. But sometime yesterday, to True Seeker's utter frustration, she had taken an abrupt turn.

The war party had been swift. Even with her long legs and admirable speed, the woman would have been hard-pressed to eliminate the gap in any reasonable amount of time. With each passing hour, her chance at a life with them dwindled.

A shadowy form moved just ahead. The woman's brown skirt, now familiar to him, fluttered from behind a tree. Cheek crammed against its trunk, she studied something in the distance.

True Seeker stole toward a cluster of bushes. He put a hand against his watch chain to stop its faint jangle then strained to listen. Above the whistle of the wind came the rumble of men's voices.

Needles raced down his arms and before his next breath, he placed an arrow against his bowstring. He whipped his neck about, scouring the landscape behind them.

The men's native dialect was impossible to differentiate from where he crouched, but there was little chance they had come this close to the Seminole without being detected. That was well for the woman, but he'd had no intention of practically entering the bear's den himself. Getting out of here with his scalp still attached would be a delicate matter. Sweat burst from his pores, soaking his upper lip. A bead scurried down the back of his neck.

Eyes dead ahead, the woman licked her lips. Her breast swelled with a great intake of breath.

True Seeker could only imagine her fear. No matter their race, rank, or ambition, these were men whose path back to their women was likely very long and lonely. He would not leave until he was certain they would not harm her.

Before she could make a move, a broad-nosed warrior stole from behind a tree under ten paces to her left. He wore several colorful kerchiefs loosely knotted about his neck, but neither his brilliant attire nor his movement caught the woman's attention. What must have been a deliberate snap of a twig beneath the man's foot brought her gaze around.

With a small startled cry, she shrank from him.

The murmurings went silent.

Although his hands were empty and his fingers loose, the warrior maintained a firm stance. His hard gaze dared her to run. "Where do you come from?" he asked, in a familiar Muscogean dialect.

True Seeker's jaw hung. This man was as Creek as Grandmother Mahila.

There could be only one reason a group of Creek warriors would be here—to capture and return the runaways. And this woman had no idea.

As a slave, she would have been isolated on her master's plantation. Most likely she'd only encountered a few natives in her life, certainly not enough to recognize the differences between tribes.

Before she could recover enough to respond to the warrior's question, True Seeker shot to his feet, his arrow pointed at the forest floor.

The warrior merely glanced True Seeker's direction, unfazed.

True Seeker squared his shoulders and lifted his chin. "I am True Seeker of Tuckabatchee."

The woman's gaze whipped between them, as she backed away from the tree. "I've run away from the soldiers." Her voice shook, and if her rustling skirt was any indication, so did her legs. "Can you help me?"

Broad Nose's only response was to swat an insect from his ear.

Within moments, they were surrounded. True Seeker counted six, none of them wearing the typical Seminole red leggings and patchwork clothing. They closed the ring, but did not press in.

The woman hugged herself, and turned a jerky circle, taking in her situation with more aplomb than True Seeker would have expected. "Do you speak English? Will you help me?"

"You are Totka's charge." The statement came from a warrior whose blood-red turban was secured to his head by a silver band. Red half-circles decorated the flesh beneath his eyes.

True Seeker nodded once. "I am."

"He was trailing the woman," Broad Nose said.

Red Turban took time to absorb the information. "You know her?"

Know her? He knew that she was brave in the face of adversity. That she was swift but reckless. That hunger and thirst were less fearsome to her than slavery. That she had loved deeply and that her grief was just as intense. He knew the set of her shoulders when on alert and the slack of her face when she slept. "I do not know the woman."

A voice rose from behind True Seeker. "She is a slave. I saw her with the rest."

"Then why does she not run from us?" another asked.

True Seeker stepped forward. "She believes us to be Seminole."

From behind, someone snorted a chuckle. "What a surprise she will have when we tell her—"

"You will tell her *nothing*." Red Turban directed his glare behind True Seeker then softened and shifted it to him. "Why is she of interest to you?"

"I gave my word that I would see that no harm come to her."

"To whom is your word bound?"

True Seeker hesitated. "An American."

Red Turban eyed True Seeker, seeming to understand he would divulge no more. Of course, if any of these warriors wished to know *which* American, they had simply to follow True Seeker when he went to report his failure.

"As you must know, we are on the hunt for fugitives, although I did not expect one would find *us*." A wry half-smile lifted Red Turban's cheek as his amused gaze traveled to the woman.

Arms still wrapped around her waist, she quietly waited.

"You understand that we must return her to the soldiers."

"Can you not let this one go? She has suffered much and journeyed far."

Over the last days, the purpling on her cheekbone had lightened, and the gash on her forehead had sealed. The swelling on her lip had decreased but thirst had cracked her lips in several other places. Fatigue rimmed her eyes and hunger deepened the hollow in her neck. She was a shocking sight to behold, but unfortunately, not a one of the men present could possibly deny the beauty that lay beneath.

Red Turban studied her. The edges of his mouth and eyes eased almost imperceptibly and lit within True Seeker a tiny spark of hope.

The senior warrior flicked an index finger at Broad Nose. "Give her something to eat." He turned back to True Seeker. "Your unease is warranted. Her face is painted with misery, and her eyes speak of the hardship of her people. But just as you, we are under oath, and our word with the American chief will not be broken. Not while breath resides in my body. You have done as you promised and kept her from harm. We will not touch her, but you are welcome to travel with us to complete your vow."

With stomach-clinching certainty, True Seeker knew he would not be able to dissuade the man from his purpose.

Chewing on a bit of dried meat, the woman now sat cross-legged, her calm, grateful gaze aligned with True Seeker. If she knew the full truth—that it was True Seeker's hand that had taken the black man's life and True Seeker's incompetence that had allowed her to walk into this hornet's nest—he imagined quite a different expression would dominate her features.

Waves of pity, sorrow, and shame crashed over him. He could avert his eyes today, but soon, he would be forced to own up to the truth.

Chapter Seventeen

Colonel Clinch joined the group of officers congregated outside their barracks. He planted himself before them then meticulously adjusted his collar until its fold created a perfect line against his throat. "At ease, gentleman," he said at last.

As one, Phillip and Collins, along with Captains Buck, Delaney, and Littleton clasped their hands behind their backs and moved their feet shoulder width apart. A gap remained where their lieutenants would be if not for the skirmish that took one and wounded two others.

From across the semi-circle, Collins spent the first three minutes of Colonel Clinch's address burning a hole through Phillip. Face still a swollen pulp, he was far from intimidating.

"Within the month, our outfit is to be relieved of duty at this post," Clinch said, a rare smile pushing his cheeks heavenward. "The Twelfth Infantry will be replacing us. Only one obstacle keeps us from returning to Tennessee with the satisfaction of a job well done."

He peered beyond the camp's enclosure toward the open-sided tent that had been erected for the recaptured runaways. Phillip refused to look.

"By the end of August, every slave must be either collected by his master or taken to auction. Because of Creek assurances that all twenty-three will be rounded up and returned, their names and portraits have already been forwarded to Savannah for distribution in state papers. So far, our allies have performed beautifully. Not including the buck slaughtered during the battle, only three remain unaccounted for." He paused, his attention riveted elsewhere. "Make that two."

On the outskirts of camp, at the edge of a field of switchgrass, a small group of warriors emerged. A woman's skirt swished in the midst of them, and although Phillip had yet to see her face, he knew by her gait that it was Milly.

His heart soared then sank, and he forced himself to remain where he stood.

"It's that sorceress," Clinch muttered, his quill-thin lips turning down as he leveled his eyes first on Collins then Phillip. "Any man found molesting her will answer to me. Questions? Good. You're dismissed." Before the words had finished spilling from his mouth, Clinch was already marching toward the newly built headquarters building.

Collins' greedy eyes and sliding smirk said he had just taken Clinch's order as a challenge. Anger smoldered in Phillip's gut, but a shriek snapped his attention back to Milly.

Like a woman possessed, she thrashed inside the grasp of one of the warriors. Unrestrained, her arms and legs beat the air. Another reached for her, but she lurched, elbowing him in the jaw.

Fire ignited in the warrior's black eyes, and his payback came swiftly. As Phillip raced toward them, the slap reverberated painfully against his ears.

Silenced, she went limp and nearly slithered out of the first man's grip. He hiked her up for a better hold, as the second withdrew a thong and tugged her wrists together. If the man struck her again, Phillip wouldn't hold himself accountable for his actions.

Her head slowly shook as though she were regaining her bearings.

Sluggishly, Phillip's feet churned beneath him. "Put her down," he ordered, still twenty feet away.

The one holding Milly, glanced toward Phillip then spoke to his companion.

Suddenly, she sank her heel into the gut of the one in front, doubling him and sending him back two steps.

Had she lost her mind? Phillip would lose *his* if he couldn't stop what was sure to follow.

The affronted warrior yanked himself erect, his arm raised.

"Stop it!" Phillip's throat stung with the shout.

Before the warrior's hand could re-connect with Milly's face, someone rammed into him, blind-siding him. In a blur of raven hair and chestnut skin, the two flew across Phillip's path.

He swerved to avoid the scuffle then turned his back on it and pinned Milly's captor with a hot gaze. "I said put her down." He ground the words between his teeth.

Out of the bottom of his eye, he caught the release of tension that slumped her shoulders. He refused himself the privilege of dropping his eyes to her, but like liniment on a smarting wound, the feel of hers against his face soothed the edges of his raw heart.

Black eyes flashing, the native's white-fingered hold on her upper arm seemed to tighten. "You treat your slaves like animals. You are the savages." The man spat out the last word.

If anyone knew the correct definition of "savage," it was Phillip. Blood began to pound behind his scarred eye and heat crawled up his neck. A flame licked at his cheek and crackled in his ear. His pulse accrued speed. *Dear Lord, not now. Give me strength.*

He dropped his lids in a long, deliberate blink and dragged air in through his nose. When he opened his eyes, Fort Mims was gone.

After a pause to gather his thoughts, he flung a pointer finger toward the warrior who had slapped Milly. "And what do you call his behavior? A lover's caress?" The man in question was back on his feet and shouting in his attacker's face.

Phillip took a second glance. It was True Seeker that faced the quick-tempered warrior. Shoulders thrown back and spine straight, the boy looked older than Phillip remembered. He turned back to the one in possession of Milly.

"Her master is due any day. Should he object to these fresh marks you've left on her, the United States will be obliged to demand you pay for the damages to the man's property."

"I have not damaged her. The blood runs too hot in Three Fists' veins." The apology in the warrior's voice raised Phillip's brows. The warrior rushed on. "But until this hour, no man has touched her." He thrust her forward so that Phillip could have easily stretched an arm and pulled her against him. But he would have to look at her first.

"Look," the man insisted. "You will find no fresh marks."

Phillip clamped his hands behind his back. Only then did he allow himself a fleeting perusal.

The warrior had been correct. No recent wounds marked her face. The bruise on her cheek had faded to almost nothing, and the old lesion on her forehead was clean and healing. Where her torn collar hung limp the slash across her chest still shone an angry red, but the glistening salve smeared across it spoke of the care she had received. Her hair was neatly plaited, and her skin was fresh.

Except for the paling evidence of the warrior's swift hand across her cheek, she looked good. His breath solidified in his chest. Better than good.

Of their own will, his eyes traveled to hers. Even had he braced himself, he never would have been prepared for what he found. A corpse's eyes could not be more lifeless. Even their deep coffee tone seemed faded.

She stared at him—no, through him. Did she even know who he was? She had been through so much that he couldn't help but wonder if this last turn had carried her over the brink of sanity.

Sweat puddled inside the palms still clasped behind his back. His arms trembled with the urge to drag her to himself, his hands with the need to stroke life back into her face, and his lips with the desire to utter more useless promises.

"We're certain you've taken excellent care of her. The United States thanks you for your service." Marcus' voice cut through the muddle of Phillip's mind. "I'll take her from here."

The warrior huffed and released Milly to Marcus, who immediately moved her out of Phillip's reach. Marcus never stopped, but continued guiding her in the direction of the slave enclosure.

Gratitude swelled Phillip's lungs. With his insides still churning, he determined he would find a way to thank his friend. What, if anything, he could do for Milly was another matter altogether—a matter that left him feeling more powerless than ever.

Short of the miracle of his land selling and filling his pockets with ready cash, there was absolutely nothing he could do to help her.

His gaze locked on her slender back. If it was possible, she had lost more weight. He would see to it Cook provided adequate nourishment for her…for them all. The decision bolstered his spirits. Seeing they were well fed was precious little, but it was something.

Apparently, he'd been mistaken when he'd believed God wanted him to free them.

Trust me.

Phillip recognized the Voice flitting across his heart. His instinct was to curl his lip in doubt, but God had carried him through enough pain the last years for Phillip to heed Him. Where Phillip could not, God could. But that simple faith-filled knowledge couldn't stop the questions from pounding his mind. *How*? And more importantly, *when*?

Of Israel's Jacob, He had required fourteen years of labor. What would He require of Phillip?

***

Shoulder throbbing, True Seeker raised his voice to match that of Three Fists'. "I was assured no harm would come to her."

Three Fists took yet another step forward and jutted his chin, presenting True Seeker with a clear view up the man's flared nostrils. "Was I to let a woman, a *slave*, strike me?"

"She is a formidable creature. I understand how you feared for your life." True Seeker drenched his words in sarcasm.

Eyes flashing rage, Three Fists towered over True Seeker. "If you were a man I would unsettle the teeth in your skull."

Spittle landed on True Seeker's cheek as alarm washed over him, but he narrowed his eyes and firmed his stance. "If I were fully grown," he said, equally hot, "I never would have let you pull your miserable carcass out of the dirt." It was a preposterous statement, but since ducking his head in submission was not an option, he chose the ludicrous.

Three Fists' chin jerked. His eyes bulged, and True Seeker mentally braced himself to counteract a blow. Instead, he was awarded a half smile that burst into all-out laughter.

The warrior gripped True Seeker by the shoulder and gave him a hearty shake. "One day I will be seated in the round house on a cold winter night listening to stories of great deeds, and I will hear tell of a mighty knot-nosed warrior who defeated his enemy through cunning and extraordinary bravery. And I will say to my chief, 'This is a man I am honored to know. This is my brother.'"

Stunned speechless, True Seeker allowed the man to clap arms with him. Still chuckling, Three Fists took his leave. The others trailed behind, leaving True Seeker to stand alone and wonder exactly what had happened.

Major Bailey stood off a short distance and addressed a black boy. Milly was nowhere to be seen, and True Seeker immediately felt a loss and disturbance of spirit at the thought of what might become of her.

For three days, she had believed herself free. It had made for quicker, more compliant travel, but it had been a hard blow they'd dealt her when they'd emerged from the woods and she had come face-to-face with the truth. Up to that point, she had been composed, quiet, capable. None of them could have foreseen her explosive reaction. It had been one of True Seeker's more shameful moments.

She was only in her predicament because he could not stay awake long enough to keep her out of trouble. He had been a child not to foresee a situation in which she might confuse Creek for Seminole.

Guilt sickened him. Perhaps Totka would know what to do. He might even beseech his Jesus on Milly's behalf.

True Seeker's racing heart was still slowing when a young slave trotted up to him. The boy was close to True Seeker's height but had yet to muscle up.

"Major Bailey says you's to meet him down by the river come noon. There's a big oak what's got a drooping branch. That's the spot."

True Seeker nodded and started toward the camp. "Tell your master I will be there."

The boy skipped to True Seeker's side. "He ain't my mastuh no more!" He grinned, fished a dirty piece of paper from his pocket, and flapped it in the air. "He gave me this paper that says I'm as free as you be. I'm gonna earn cash dollars. Get me some learnin'. Be a right smart man one day. The major says so."

In such a grim world, Bailey's unusual kindness was refreshing. "Your major is an honorable man."

The boy's bushy eyebrows met in the middle. "Weren't always so. But those of us what survived the Red Stick war was all changed. Some for worse, some for bettah."

"Were you at Mims' place with Bailey?"

The spark left his eye and his voice grew dim. "Just Momma and Daddy. Daddy was tied to a post ready for a lashin' when hell swung its gates. I found Momma beside 'im, an arrow in her heart. Least she went quick-like."

As they passed the first tents of the camp, they fell silent.

After a long moment, True Seeker knocked his fist against his chest. "I am True Seeker, and I mourn with you."

A sad smile tipped the boy's lips. "I'm Enoch. Enoch Bailey," he said, his eyes taking on a faraway look as though he were listening to the sound of his own name.

"It is a proud name." A name connected with honor and benevolence toward those in bondage, as was the McGirth name.

McGirth…

The man's reaction to Totka reentering Adela's life had confused True Seeker, but he could not deny that if ever there was an advocate for the weak, it was Zachariah McGirth. He had forgiven True Seeker a great crime. He'd provided shelter, food, and love for an old woman and a boy. And at a time when hatred for the Creek ran hot, Zachariah had openly declared a Creek woman his daughter.

It was a shame McGirth did not own Milly, for he would have freed her long ago.

As True Seeker fingered the watch chain dangling from his shirt front, his mind began to whir and tick. Perhaps there was a way to help Milly, after all.

Chapter Eighteen

As had become his custom, True Seeker made his way to the half-empty slave's tent. Most of the men had been put to work building more barracks. Earlier, when he'd passed the creek, he had seen a good number of the slave women washing uniforms or beating them against the stones.

Legs crossed, Uncle Jeremiah sat in the corner gumming his wrinkled lips. The way he unceasingly rocked and hummed a person might think him feebleminded. True Seeker wondered if that was the old man's intent. He turned his rheumy eyes toward True Seeker who raised a palm in greeting. The old man dipped his whiskered chin in a reply.

Hands clasped in front of her chest, the woman named Eva stood in her usual corner and looked in the direction of the trees and the river not far beyond. Did its distant rushing sounds sooth her, or did she envy its freedom? Perhaps it was the mere act of turning her back to the slave tent and the camp itself that kept her in that position. Denial was a compelling force.

At the far edge of the tent, Milly lay on her side on the thin blanket that separated her from the dirty, matted grass. Hands tucked beneath her cheek, she stared into nothingness. A fly buzzed about her face. Another crawled along her jaw. Full sun beat upon the back of her neck.

He went to her, but it wasn't until he squatted within her line of sight, that she blinked and shifted her gaze to him. Her eyes crinkled around the corners as a lazy smile formed. "I was just thinking about you. Wondering when you'd come."

Remorse sliced through him. He almost hadn't. Each visit was more painful than the last, but an hour ago, the white medicine man had confided that True Seeker's visits were the only thing keeping the poor woman alive. Why, he might never understand.

The first visit had been the most difficult. Tears spilling over her cheeks, she had refused even to look at him, but he had stayed and quietly told her everything he'd intended—Bailey's request and True Seeker's task. How he had taken Isum's life and the sorrow he felt for having to do it. Their shared journey through the brush, and True Seeker's failure to keep her safe.

He did not ask for forgiveness, but before he'd left that first day, in a broken voice, she had freely offered it.

"Forgiveness is my only possession," she had whispered. "And no man can stop me from giving it away as many times as I please."

It was a gift True Seeker shamefacedly cherished, but since that day, he had reminded himself that more than forgiveness, she possessed an abiding love. Her grief went beyond Isum, beyond her slavery, and to a place no black woman dared go.

No one had spoken the words, but True Seeker knew as plain as the crooked nose on his face that Milly had emptied herself loving Bailey. It was that emptiness that stared True Seeker in the eye every time he sat before her.

He forced a smile. "Tomorrow, I will come sooner." There was no need to mention that tomorrow she might be gone. "Let me help you move your blanket. You will burn." Already her pale skin blazed red.

"Oh." Her fingers flitted to the back of her neck. "You're right."

When he had moved her to the shade, they settled down, and she shared memories of Isum as a child. True Seeker listened politely, all the while wishing *he* was still a child, so he could run from her and the heartbreaking reality that he had killed her only friend and spoiled her last chance at freedom. Hang Bailey and his order to stay hidden! Looking back, True Seeker admitted that he should have revealed himself to her from the start, provided for her, taken her by the hand, and guided her to the Seminole.

Her reminiscences were blessedly cut short by the doctor's arrival. Captain Buck wore a sober expression, and Enoch, who followed the doctor, had left his usual chatter behind. Spotting

True Seeker, Enoch hurried over and joined him and Milly on the blanket.

Black bag in hand, the doctor stood at the edge of the tent looking at no one in particular.

"Who has he come for?" Milly's tone held not a shred of hope.

"Eva." Enoch had the good sense to mouth the word.

Milly reacted with neither relief nor sorrow, but went and stood beside the other woman. She remained there, statuesque, even when Eva's owner arrived to observe the medical examination and sign a paper.

Enoch leaned in close to True Seeker and whispered, "Doc told me that paper says the army is sendin' her back in good shape. It's so's the owner can't get angry later ovah damages, like missin' teeth and the like."

Disgusted, True Seeker took his leave. As was the Creek habit, he had bathed that morning, but another plunge in the river might be what he needed to cool his anger.

"Are you off to battle?"

True Seeker stopped midstride.

Totka trailed him at a moderate, uneven trot. "Such a gait as yours can only mean battle." The older man's smile was grim.

"No, I—I thought to take a swim."

Before he'd even come to a halt, Totka was studying True Seeker's countenance. "What disturbs you?"

"It is nothing," True Seeker responded a bit too hastily.

Totka pursed his lips. "Very well. We leave for Tensaw at first light. Make certain you are ready." He turned to go, but True Seeker snagged him by the arm.

"We cannot leave."

Totka raised a brow.

"I sent a messenger. To McGirth."

A spasm bunched Totka's jaw. "Why? When did you do this?"

"When I first returned. Five mornings past."

"You sent Crazy Fire," he stated, seeming to click a puzzle piece into place in his mind. "You have no silver. How did you pay for such a thing?" He grabbed True Seeker's forearm in a pinching grip. "What message did you send?"

Although he did not waver or flinch, on the inside, True Seeker felt tenfold the fool. "Zachariah McGirth is a wealthy man, and his heart is soft toward slaves. He has freed many and treats blacks as equals. I have seen it myself."

"You did this for Milly?"

True Seeker nodded.

The intensity eased from Totka's eyes as he released True Seeker, allowing blood back into his fingertips. "What exactly did you ask of the man?"

"That, for Bailey's sake, he come and purchase her from her master."

"This is no small thing you ask."

"I understand."

The lines in Totka's forehead deepened. "Do you? A slave such as Milly is worth more than a year's earnings for a white man."

Stunned, True Seeker analyzed the parched grass between Totka's beaded moccasins. "I did not know she was so costly." He lifted his gaze and his chin. "But such knowledge would have changed nothing. I failed in my duty and owe her more than the value of McGirth's opinion of me, more than the value of my pride."

The dour lines of Totka's face smoothed. His eyes warmed. "And so, you become a man."

If only what Totka said were true. True Seeker's faults were too many, his worthy accomplishments too few. But he said nothing, simply passed Totka a look that he hoped portrayed pleasure at such praise.

With a barely suppressed sigh, Totka nodded. "We will stay until either McGirth or Milly's master arrives." Understanding what the warrior sacrificed by delaying his reunion with Adela, True Seeker spoke his gratitude.

"Have you told any of this to Milly?" Totka asked.

"I would not do such a thing."

"Good. Adela's father did not attain his wealth by spending it on slaves he has never seen." The soft tone of Totka's voice did not dispel True Seeker's irritation.

"You do not know him as I do. He *will* come." Even as the adamant words left his lips, he remembered the fire in McGirth's eyes at the mention of Adela starting a life with Totka. Unease settled into his gut. There was a good chance that neither Milly's nor Totka's dreams would ever be realized.

Totka tipped his head to the side as though attempting to read True Seeker's thoughts. "God saddles each man with burden enough. Do not encumber yourself with another's load, or your back will break under the weight. Do not fret over what you cannot control. Trust your Maker. In His almighty plan, one day, whether in this life or the next, all will be well." Totka's voice hummed with ageless wisdom and confidence, and True Seeker wondered how much of it was due to this Jesus of whom he perpetually spoke.

Dare True Seeker trust and find out for himself?

***

Milly lay awake long into the night. She had witnessed every subtle change of the evening sky, noted the last strains of bird song, and tracked the meandering flight of the night's first moth as it wandered toward the stoked campfire. Not one element of this last night in Camp Crawford would slip past her.

Tomorrow would mark the beginning of her journey to the auction house. Why Master Landcastle had not sent for her and how her spirit had lasted this long without cracking were mysteries she had no interest in solving. The auction block held terrors all its own, but it was nothing to Mr. Grayson's punishing whip.

Starting in the morning, she would be completely alone. Isum's painful absence would be more acute. As it was, she could hardly breathe at times just for the grieving of him. Being alone in the woods had been bad enough, but when she took her leave of True Seeker and Phillip, the loneliness would surely suffocate her.

Hours ago, another slave had been repossessed by his master, leaving only Milly, Uncle Jeremiah, and another named Toby. Phillip had come to supervise the earlier discharge and assure her with a sad, warm look that he had not forgotten about her.

His visits were few and fleeting, precious yet excruciating. Each time she caught a glimpse of him, fear nearly squeezed off her air. Heaven forbid he do something rash and place himself in danger of suspicion. He had risked much by slipping her that key, and although it had not been his that had unlocked the shackles, the threat of blame falling to him was still just as real.

Even so, after nearly a month of fruitless investigation, it appeared that the matter of the slaves' escape had been given up as pointless. At least, Milly prayed it had…for whatever her prayers were worth.

Lately, God seemed to have taken special delight in toying with her life, stripping from her everything that could have been and dangling what should be an arm's reach away.

If He chose not to remove her from this miserable existence through freedom or death, the least He could do was make her lame giving Phillip a better shot at affording her reduced value. But, no. God chose to keep her perfectly whole and desirable.

Amazingly, prayers still flickered within her, but she no longer had the faith to believe her pathetic pleas for mercy reached further than the boundaries set by the ever-present guards.

On the opposite side of the tent, Toby grunted and shifted on his pallet, most likely disturbed by Uncle Jeremiah's gurgling snores. In her periphery, a guard moved alongside her and paused.

Fearing that the fire glittered in her eyes, she dropped her lids and feigned sleep. After a moment, the sound of his plodding footstep continued.

Milly let out a slow breath, but the weight of her lids against her eyes felt too good to negate. Her muscles relaxed and sank into the rutted ground.

As sleep enveloped her, she was yanked straight out of it by a suffocating weight against her mouth. Her eyes flew open to pitch black.

A hand blocked her air passages and the scream that clawed for release. She scraped at the hand with her nails, her need for breath increasing along with gallop of her heart.

"Easy, girl." Collins' purred. He hovered over her, pinning her to the dirt with his body. "We're old friends. There's no reason to act like this." His breath slid across her ear, and she jerked away, budging his hand a fraction.

A trickle of air slid into her nose. Frantically, she sucked. *God, help me*!

He eased his hand down and the cool night filled her burning lungs. "See? I can be reasonable. Unlike the treatment you'll get at the auction shed," he rasped, as he wrenched up her skirt and slid a sweaty palm up her leg and over the curve of her hip.

Bucking, she freed her knee and thrust it into his groin.

He growled a curse, but her paltry attack lacked the strength to alter the course of his hand.

The noise of Uncle Jeremiah's sleep continued uninterrupted, and Milly didn't need to look to know that if Collins lay on top of her, the guard would be nowhere near. The night was blinding. The ever-present fire had been put out.

"Milly? You alright?" Toby's sleep-scratched voice drew near.

She stilled, fearful he might needlessly entangle himself in this mess.

Placing his weight on the hand that mashed her face, Collins' twisted his upper body backward. The cock of pistol filled the night. Toby's soft gasp chased it.

"Take a walk, won't you boy?" Collins spoke as though asking the man to pass the cream and sugar. "If you're not back in ten minutes, you'll swing before dawn. Understand?"

A rush of retreating footsteps signaled Toby's obedience.

She was alone. Again. *Where are you, God*?

Collins released the hammer and turned back to her, never once removing his vise-like clamp on her mouth.

Blood seeped onto her tongue, and tears pooled in the crooks of her ear. The fingers of her heart reached toward God. Her mind grappled for a single shred of evidence that He cared for her even a whit. *Do you not see me?*

Collins released a deep, satisfied breath that sluiced her face in a repugnant wave. "On to more pleasant business," he said, but before he could make another move, a deep thud sent a jolt through his body.

His hand slithered from her face, his elbows caved, and his full weight crashed upon her. Oiled hair slicked her face as he landed cheek-to-cheek with her. His movements were sluggish and meager, in his semi-conscious state.

Someone heaved his torso angling it off her.

"Milly, are you hurt?" True Seeker's voice spilled over her senses like a rain shower in a desert. Just as quickly, it ran dry and left her soul parched. "Get out of here," she hissed. "Run!"

As she wriggled out from under Collins' bulk, her hand connected with the back of his head and came away sticky. Fear mingled with the taste of blood in her mouth.

She shot to her feet and pushed against True Seeker's chest, taking care not to stain him with the evidence on her fingers. "Go!"

He balked. "A voice woke me, and I knew I must come."

"A voice? Whose?"

"I know not. When I rose, there was no one."

A tingle raced up Milly's spine. She sensed they were not alone.

"I was told to come to you, and I will not leave."

"Don't you know the consequences of striking a white man? You came and now you must go. If they learn what you've done, they'll kill you."

Collins moaned. His rustling about increased.

"So be it. I will not leave you."

"I cannot allow another man to die for me." Resolved, she beat his chest with her fist.

"What you got, Indian?"

They turned toward the sound of Uncle Jeremiah's worn voice. The old man shuffled to where they stood then manipulated True Seeker's hand. "Nice hefty stone, eh? I expect I'll keep it. You move along, now. Get outta here."

"Give it back." True Seeker reached, but a smack stopped him short.

"Woman?" Collins' groggy voice carried like a roar. "Where are you?"

Uncle Jeremiah shoved up chest-to-chest with True Seeker. "Now, you listen to your elder. There ain't no reason for you to die tonight. Not when them woods be right there for the takin'. Get yo'self gone." He jabbed at True Seeker with such shocking force that he took two quick steps back. "Get! Then you stay put 'til this be through."

True Seeker stood his ground. "I will not let you take this on your shoulders."

An odd chuckle escaped the old man. "Be too late to stop that. Already got blood on me from that stone. Hands are stained. Clothes too."

True Seeker responded with a low growl, but did not move.

Milly wedged herself between them. "You would dishonor an old man by denying him this?" Anger sizzled on her hushed tongue. She hated for Uncle Jeremiah to take the fall, but mercy might be found for an old man where it did not exist for an upcoming Creek warrior.

The rigidity began to ease from True Seeker's body.

Collins' stumbling gait raised the hairs on Milly's arms. "I hear you, wench. Don't think I won't find you."

She rammed herself against True Seeker once more and to her great relief, he relented and noiselessly left them to their fate.

***

A brusque whisper dragged Phillip from slumber. Someone had called his name. The cot squeaked as he sat up and squinted at a featureless silhouette. "Who is it?"

"Rise. Quick. Bring your medicine man." The ragged voice belonged to True Seeker.

Tasked with keeping a watchful eye on Milly, the young man had come to Phillip at this hour for only one reason. He swung his legs to the ground. With one foot going into his trousers, he took a wide step across the narrow barracks and jostled Marcus' shoulder.

His friend was on his feet and half-dressed before Phillip left the building, alarm urging his feet to a run. No one need tell him which direction to go. He buckled his sword belt as he ran. The sheathed blade slapped his leg with each footfall, bringing to mind a similar night not long enough ago. His stride lengthened. This time, he would run Collins clean through.

True Seeker appeared at his side, easily matching his pace. "Collins lay on her. He would have taken her. There was no guard. He had to be stopped. I had to stop him." The words rattled off his tongue.

"What happened? What did you do?"

"Nothing I would not do again." His reply came swift. Confident. "The man is a spineless thief."

"Did you kill him?" *Lord, please let the snake be alive.* Phillip would be grieved to lose True Seeker to a noose. As it was, he was probably in more trouble than Phillip could get him out of.

"No." Regret lanced True Seeker's tone.

"Good." That way Phillip himself could kill him. "Say no more. To me or anyone else."

Ahead, someone stoked the slaves' campfire. Its flames burst to life and revealed Milly sitting by herself hugging her knees to her chest. Although glistening with tears, her face portrayed calm.

Ten yards away, Sergeant Garrigus held a rifle on Collins, who ranted about the sergeant's audacity and the lashing he would receive because of it.

Before they entered the light, Phillip slowed and motioned for True Seeker to stay hidden. He huffed his displeasure but did as told.

Marcus pulled up alongside Phillip, and the two moved ahead. At their approach, Milly lifted her gaze and connected it with his. Even through the flickering light, he saw anxiety fall from her body.

He knelt on one knee before her and took her face in his hands, but was unable to voice the hateful question.

Her eyes watered and overflowed onto his fingers. "I'm fine," she whispered.

"Did he…?"

Her head moved back and forth in taut little shakes. It was all he needed to know. For now. He brushed a kiss against her forehead, and stepped aside to give Marcus room.

"Sergeant Garrigus, good to see you have things under control."

Garrigus kept the rifle butted against his shoulder. "Me and the major here, were having ourselves a chat, sir. About the old man." He brandished the rifle toward a darkened corner. Marcus perked at the comment and rushed to the shadow crumpled on the grass.

"Forget the old coot," Collins snapped, holding the back of his head. "He assaulted me. Had it coming."

"Save your excuses for the colonel." Phillip spat. Uncle Jeremiah, it seemed, had taken the fall for True Seeker—quite literally.

Garrigus cleared his throat. "And then, sir, there's the matter of Major Collins spreadin' the girl's legs when we all got orders to steer clear of her."

"Old man's dead," Marcus' flat tone shot through the dark. "Neck snapped."

Collins shrugged. "What can I say? I'm a merciful man."

Phillip's insides seethed with the knowledge that Collins had again laid a malicious hand to Milly, but he'd be shocked if the man suffered repercussions from it or for killing Uncle Jeremiah. He was merely an unclaimed slave, and one who was believed to have attacked an officer of the United States Army.

"Get him out of my sight. Keep him under guard until I've had a chance to speak with the colonel."

Collins sputtered. "You can't detain—"

"Just a minute, sir, if you don't mind?" Garrigus held up a hand. "There's something eating at me, and I aim to figure it out. When I found him, the major was so busy trying to keep his straddle on the woman he didn't know I was there. Shoot, I snuck up within spitting distance before he wizened up."

Phillip crossed his arms. "What are you getting at, Sergeant?"

"What I'm getting at, sir, is that things were said between them. Things, I reckon Major Collins would rather keep shut up."

Collin's jowls went slack, instantly piquing Phillip's interest. "What things?"

"Well, I don't know for sure, but the woman said she'd blab about something if the major didn't get off her right quick. And the major, he said, she'd never have the guts to tell. That's when he noticed Betsy aimed at his backside." Garrigus patted his rifle.

Feeling as though he was about to sink his teeth into something delicious, Phillip turned his attention to Collins. "I'll give you one chance to tell me. What are you hiding? What does she know?"

Collins arranged his lips into a smirk. "The minx doesn't know anything except how to be a whore. Pretty good at it too. You should get a taste. What do you say, Bailey? I hold her, you take her?"

The muscles in Phillip's jaw bunched in a spasm, and his fingers twitched with the irrepressible urge to strangle. Fire coursed through his lungs and into his legs. A man who would take a life or a woman's body without a moment's compunction didn't deserve to live one more day, to take even one more breath.

"Phillip!"

Marcus' frantic voice gave him a jolt. He blinked.

An arm's width away, Collins' eyes bulged from their sockets, as Phillip throttled his throat.

Garrigus stood beside them, his burly hand gripping Phillip's forearm. "You gotta let him go, sir!"

Instantly, Phillip released his hold and backed away. As though he'd just finished a footrace, his chest rose and fell in great heaves. His gaze drifted, finally landing on Marcus. Concern dug deep ridges into his brow.

Phillip flexed his trembling fingers and tried to recall what they'd been discussing, what had set off his attack. While his brain scrambled, he wondered, like a dunking in an icy lake, if Marcus had been right all along. Perhaps he truly *wasn't* fit to command.

Fort Mims had irrevocably changed not only who he was, but who he was destined to be, and for the first time since that fateful day, Phillip took a deep breath and allowed himself one moment to consider a life outside the army.

"Major Bailey? Can I speak with you?" Milly spoke above Collin's coughing and sputtering. She approached with hesitant steps. Was she afraid of him?

He smoothed his hair into place and forcibly eased the strain from his facial muscles. "Certainly." He cleared his throat to disguise the treble. "Should we find some place private?"

Her gaze skittered to Collins who rubbed his throat and eyed Phillip with raw fear. She straightened her spine. "No. I want the sergeant to hear."

"Go ahead then."

She licked her lips and drew a deep breath. "It was Major Collins that gave Isum the key. He was the one who encouraged us to escape."

"That's absurd!"

"Shut up, Collins," Phillip snapped, although he'd had the same thought himself. Collins giving Isum a key was an absurd thought. Milly was his prize. There was no way Collins would willingly give her up before it was necessary. "Captain Buck, I think the major popped some stitches on his cheek."

"I believe you're correct, sir." Marcus took the weapon from Garrigus then nudged Collins' arm. "Let's go. To the fire, so I can see."

Collins passed Milly landing her with a glare that could freeze the Spanish Florida sun.

She shivered but held his gaze.

Phillip inwardly applauded. She was a strong woman, but he couldn't have her lying to deflect a bullet meant for him. "What's this about the major giving Isum a key? What reason would he have to free either of you?" Phillip asked the same question Colonel Clinch would voice when Phillip took this unlikely story to him in the morning.

"Because he wanted you dead, and he knew..." Her throat bobbed with a hard swallow. Again, her tongue flashed over her lips. "He knew Isum would do it. Especially after Major Collins lied to him about who—" Her gaze plummeted.

His pulse sputtering, Phillip gulped down a deep, steadying breath. "About who defiled you."

She nodded.

Isum had certainly taken his best shot at Phillip's back. Had he done it at Collins' request—at his *goading*? Phillip wouldn't put it past the scoundrel to lie to a desperate slave in order to get what he wanted, but would he go so far as murder?

Yes, he would. Which meant Isum died for a lie. That fact must have compounded Milly's grief ten-fold.

Phillip settled his gaze on the top of her bent head. Tufts of hair protruded at odd angles from her normally tidy braid, evidence of her struggle. A sigh built within him and left his lungs in a surge of frustration. He could fight her battles tonight, but next week, she'd be on her own.

"Thank you, Milly." *For so much more than I can express.*

Her admission took courage, but it was just a slave's word against an officer's. He doubted much would come of it. Unless... he scanned the area. "Where's Toby?"

"Major Collins sent him on a walk, but told him to be back in ten minutes or he'd be found and hung." Milly surprised Phillip with her sudden candor.

"Sergeant, when Toby gets back, take him aside. Question him and see if his story lines up with Milly's."

Garrigus touched the brim of his hat with his fingers in a hasty salute. "Yes sir. Glad to. Still want me to put a guard on Major Collins?"

He gentled his hand against Milly's back and began guiding her back toward the slave tent. "The man wants me dead." Phillip tossed the words over his shoulder. "Make it two."

Chapter Nineteen

While the escort readied their mounts for the journey to Savannah, Milly was put to work scrubbing bowls from the stack by the washbasin. The last of the men had just finished eating their morning gruel, but holed up in the kitchen cleaning, she mercifully hadn't had to face a one of them.

Her jaw was tender where Collins' fingers had dug into it, but the Spirit-infused resilience straightening her backbone all but masked the pain. God had heard her cry and come to her in her dark, shameful place.

And He'd shown Himself real.

He had given her the strength to speak out against Collins last night and again this morning. If she wasn't blurry-eyed from lack of sleep, she might have trusted herself to believe that the commander had actually accepted her story as fact. A slave's voice held no weight in such matters, but Lord willing, it was enough to keep the colonel's eye on Collins and off Phillip.

Cook smacked her on the rump. "Stop dawdling. I want those clean before you leave."

She startled, but with a stubborn cock of her jaw, continued at her previous speed.

The clop of boots sounded behind her. "Cook, Captain Buck would like a word with you."

Milly spun, slinging water across the dirt floor. Her gaze collided with Phillip's.

"You'll find him just outside the infirmary." He addressed the cook, but kept his focus on her. Eyes rimmed with fatigue and loosely masked sorrow. No one need voice what Milly read there, that he'd come to say goodbye.

Cook tossed a rag onto the table and, grumbling, left the building.

Phillip swept the door closed behind him, but not before she caught sight of Enoch stationing himself just outside.

He turned to her then, his brow creasing into a hundred folds. His body pulled in on itself as though shot through with pain, then shook with a tattered breath. Eyes flashing with an unknown emotion, he seemed at war with himself.

Over what, Milly could only guess. His distress stabbed at her heart, and she opened her arms.

In three strides, he crossed the room and crushed her to himself. "I tried. By God, I tried!" He buried his face in her neck, and his breath puffed hot against her skin. "I failed you. Again. I'm sorry." His voice cracked. "I'm so sorry."

Her eyes pegged the closed door, and she knew that somewhere on the other side was one of Master Landcastle's men. Mr. Grayson, most likely. Waiting to get his clammy fingers on her, so he could triumphantly drag her back. Would he lay the whip to her first or wait until the master had seen her?

Her future stretched out before her in the form of one long, sun-scorched cotton field after another. But none of it, not one moment of the horror that awaited her could be laid to the charge of the man who shook in her arms.

She dug her fingers into his hair and pushed his head away so she could pin him with a commanding glare. "This isn't your fault, and I won't leave here knowing you're torturing yourself over something you have no obligation to do anything about. This is my lot in life. Always has been. Always will be, and unless God sees fit to change things, there's nothing you or anyone else can do to stop it. With God's help, I'll be fine." She clapped her palms against the sides of his face. "Are you listening?"

Hard with obstinacy, his eyes bored into her. The muscles of his jaw bunched beneath her hands, and his fingers dug into her ribs. But he said nothing.

Time was short. Cook would be back, and she would need to be taken to Marcus for her medical clearance. At the thought that she might forever live with the knowledge that Phillip could not forgive himself, panic took root.

"It's not your fault. You can't spend the next months, years, blaming yourself. You've given me a gift, Phillip. The knowing that there is at least one white man in this world who is selfless, generous, and *good*." Her voice dropped to a whisper. "It's enough."

"How can you say that's enough?" He stared at her as though she'd lost her mind. "That man who's come for you? I saw him. And the things he said, the look in his eye, Milly I can't—"

"I know." She slid her fingers over his mouth. "But none of it is new to me. I'll be fine unless I leave knowing you're *not*. You must promise you'll let this go. Please. Promise me."

"You want a promise? Here's one for you." He enveloped her jaw in his grasp, hardening his gaze with resolve. "I promise that no matter the cost or the time it takes, I'll find you and free you. I won't leave you there to be beaten and pawed at by every man who takes a liking to you. I won't! And *that's* a promise you can consider sealed."

He whisked his fingers to the base of her head and dug them into her hair. When his gaze skipped to her lips, her pulse tripped and sent rivulets of anticipation down her throat and into her belly.

His arms flexed then went rigid as he bent toward her, and for the first time in her life she eagerly parted her lips in reception to a man's. Tears prickled her eyes as his mouth possessed hers, feverishly branding her with his promise.

Arms clutching his neck, she stood on tiptoe and pressed into him, accepting what he offered and deepening it with trust.

This was a man who would never hurt her, would never take what wasn't offered. Hadn't he proved it time and again?

She tipped her neck and let his lips explore the length of it. Tingles raced down her spine, arching her back. She dug her nails into his shoulders and knew with mind-boggling certainty that if he but asked, she would gladly give him her all. Her heart, her body, her every sunrise and sunset, if he required them.

But he wouldn't ask. He couldn't.

She belonged to another.

A slight rap at the door stilled his lips at the hollow of her throat.

Her fingers constricted against him arms.

Again, the rap. Enoch would never be able to keep at bay whoever approached.

Phillip's exasperation saturated her blouse with the balmy gust of his breath, and her pulse quickened its throb against him.

He came back to her lips and tasted them briefly before settling his forehead against hers. "I don't care what Grayson or his legal document says," he muttered between catches of wind. "God's given you to me, and as soon as He allows, I'll claim you as my own."

He spoke with such confidence that if she allowed herself, she could almost believe him. But with belief came hope, and with hope, the inevitability of pain.

The knocking resumed, more urgently this time.

Along her throat, splotches of cool marked where he'd sampled her. Milly lamented that it was already warming. In heartbeats, all she would have was memories. And anguish. Could God truly fill the hollow Phillip would leave? Last night, His promise had filled her to the depths of her soul. It was enough. It would have to be.

With his eyes locked on hers, Phillip's hand trailed her cheek and throat. It brushed over her shoulder and down her arm. Then, in one blink, he wiped every emotion from his face, stunning her with the callous glaze of his eyes.

He gripped her by the elbow, whisked her through the kitchen, and opened the door to her wretched future.

***

Phillip caressed his mare's velvety muzzle and pampered his bleeding heart with the memory of Milly's supple mouth expertly coordinating with his own. Their kiss had been flawless, as if they'd composed, rehearsed, and mastered the art in the first attempt.

The entire episode had been so powerfully seamless it could have only happened in a daydream. But it *had* happened. As proof, his senses still tingled from the gale of her abandon.

Discarding every reticence, she had plunged headlong into desire, catching him off guard, albeit not indisposed. Never indisposed.

Was there anything he wouldn't give for an isolated cabin and one night with her? No, he didn't imagine there was—not that he had anything left to give. God had taken most everything already.

The last two things Phillip possessed he'd already bequeathed—to Milly, his heart, and to the Almighty, his vow to that he'd marry her if He would simply rearrange their circumstances to make it possible.

Simply? Nothing was simple about this situation. The prayer of surrender that he'd been repeating the last weeks suddenly failed his memory. With unsteady hands, he yanked on the mare's bridle straps while trying to loosen one of the stubborn buckles. She snorted at his rough handling.

Totka appeared beside him. "Let me."

Phillip gratefully released the task to him, an unexpected sense of brotherhood filling his chest. If anyone knew the heartache of separation, it was the man whose deft brown hands readied Phillip's mount for the long road ahead.

Totka's own, personal road had been lengthy. And yet, after two years, he somehow managed to continue to place one foot in front of the other. His breath still entered and left his body in the same monotonous pattern. How? When already several times over the half-day since Grayson had ridden out with Milly, Phillip had wondered if his chest might explode with the effort of expanding and contracting without her.

Silently, Totka saddled the horse while Phillip could manage little more than look on. True Seeker stepped in and strapped on the cantle bag. Had the young warrior just arrived, or had he been there all along and Phillip had been too blinded by gloom to notice?

He took a ragged breath.

Totka stroked the mare's shoulder then turned to Phillip, his black brows tipping inward. "Time will make it easier."

"Make what easier?"

A knowing smile warmed the man's eyes. "To breathe."

Yes, he understood, and he deserved to know the truth. Now.

As worthy a man as McGirth was, he might never find it convenient to apprise an Indian of his daughter's, no-doubt, willing availability.

A nicker drew Phillip's attention to a loaded Indian pony tethered to a post behind him. "You're heading out?" The rest of the Creek war party had taken to the trail weeks ago. On several occasions, Phillip had restrained himself from asking if he and Milly had anything to do with Totka's decision to tarry. If the man wanted his business known, he would share it.

His gaze moved to True Seeker who, with hooded eyes, busied his moccasin with something in the dirt. "There is no purpose left us here," Totka said.

True Seeker snatched a stone from the dirt and hurled it with dead aim at the post to which the pony was tethered. It reared but was stopped short by its rein. With drooping features, True Seeker went to the animal and calmed it with a gentle hand.

"I will return him to his clan."

It didn't appear the boy was in agreement with the journey. Perhaps, he'd run away, and loathed being returned. There was much that had been left unsaid between Totka and Phillip, and he was surprised to find how deeply he regretted it.

The man's destination finally clicked in Phillip's mind. "You're going to Tensaw," he said, deliberating on how to break the truth to him.

Totka jerked his chin in a brusque nod, and a feather dangling from his hair fell across his shoulder. Strange how Phillip could stand across from a warrior whose hands were stained with the blood of his loved ones and not blink at the thought of encouraging his pursuit of Phillip's former intended. Then again, he never dreamed he would fall in love with a slave, much less one many times his better.

For being so straight and sure, God's path held quite the assortment of twists.

Phillip glanced at the activity around him. The company was geared up and ready to march north within the hour. Across the field, a squad of his soldiers began to scrap. Phillip might need to intervene, leaving but minutes to spit out what needed saying.

He shifted his gaze to Totka's fixed, black eyes. "There's something you should know. About Adela." The waver Phillip expected to see in Totka's emotionless face was strangely absent.

Phillip's tongue rushed ahead of him. "She's not dead. I notified McGirth that you've been under the assumption she passed on. I left it up to him to contact you, but I suspect he's waiting for...well, I can't say what. Who knows what goes through a father's mind at a time like this?" He shrugged and stared past his men to the half-butchered forest beyond the fort. "You should go to her. Take my blessing with you."

A deliberate smile cracked Totka's façade. "These things, I have known, but your blessing gives joy to my journey."

"You knew?"

"McGirth followed your counsel." Totka's smile morphed into a boyish grin that lit his face. "And my love sent True Seeker to assure me of her faithfulness." Without warning, he pulled Phillip into a chest-crushing embrace.

The warrior pounded him once then pulled away. "My debt to you is a great chasm, and all my days will be too few to cross it. Until the Great Maker stills my heart, it will beat in gratitude to Him for setting your feet against my path."

Shame stained Phillip's conscience. "You owe me nothing. I should have told you the truth the moment I discovered it."

Totka clucked his tongue then swept his fingers toward the sky. "Our God does not toil at man's bidding. I do not question His choice of timing. Neither must you. Wait, and you will see."

God's timing... As Totka had done, Phillip would accept it as perfect.

Hours later, on the northbound trail and with Enoch on foot keeping pace with Phillip's mare, he and his troops broke free of the tangled forest. They entered a vast field blooming white with cotton. The bowed backs of slaves dotted the expanse, and he wondered about the lives of those who tirelessly labored without pay or proper care. Would it always be this way, at every cotton field between here and Nashville? This new feeling of pity toward them was none too pleasant. He couldn't help them all. He couldn't even help *one*.

He peeled his eyes from the sight but could not shut out the mournful spirituals wafting upon the heat-drenched breeze.

The horse's hooves hit upon a road rutted by the passage of countless wagons. For a man born and bred on the frontier, the sight of a bit of civilization shouldn't bring such relief, but it did. The red road stretched out before him like an arrow shooting toward Nashville.

At a time in his life when he most needed a steady income, quitting the army wasn't an option, but he was through pretending Fort Mims hadn't irrevocably changed every course of his life, including his military career. As soon as he pocketed the last penny to purchase Milly, he would tender his resignation. Until then, he would station himself behind that desk Marcus had prescribed.

"Somebody comin', suh." Enoch pointed toward a dust cloud billowing into the cobalt sky. "In a hurry too."

A group of riders—five or six—approached at a trot. A woman's skirt billowed from the side of one. The flounce and flare of her hat were plainly visible from where he sat. What business did a lady have out here, so close to the border?

"They sure are. Stay with the troops. I'll see what they're about." Phillip reined his mare to face the rear of the column. Off to the side, Colonel Clinch stood in his stirrups peering down the road ahead. He caught Phillip's eye and nodded.

Phillip raised an acknowledging arm then squeezed his heels into the mare's flanks and rode to intercept the riders. As he neared, he discerned the lady was of some means and that she rode center to four men, who were, judging by their rugged attire and the weapons strapped to their hips and saddles, hired protection.

Almost to them, Phillip steered his horse into the grasses along the road's edge. They followed suit, the woman breaking away and closing the distance. Her horse skittered at something unseen in the grass, and she struggled to maintain control.

Phillip thrust his boots into his animal and lurched forward to grab hold of the lady's reins. "Whoa there," he soothed.

When her horse responded accordingly, Phillip led them to a single pecan tree and the shade it offered.

"I thank you kindly, sir," she said breathily, while gathering the reins and readjusting her skirt to cover her ankles.

"Not at all, ma'am." He tucked his hat beneath his arm and, still atop his mount, bowed at the waist. When he lifted his eyes and peered beneath her bonnet, his heart leapt in his chest.

He captured his breath in his gaping mouth. The high forehead and defined cheekbone, the wide mouth—though not quite as full—the graceful manner in which she smoothed her skirt...all of it belonged to Milly.

This woman was *not* Milly, but in a number of years, Milly could easily be this woman. She lifted dark lashes and startled Phillip with brilliant, blue eyes. A strand of silky, auburn hair fell over the alabaster white of her cheek.

Methodically, he breathed through the annoyance constricting his chest. For the next undetermined number of years, he couldn't allow himself to see Milly in every female he passed. Still...the resemblance was uncanny.

He eyed the men traveling with her. Not a one had followed or appeared the least interested in aiding her in a proper introduction. He shifted in his saddle.

An indolent smile played around her lips. "Being as we're a stone's throw from the wilds, shall we dispense with proper etiquette and introduce ourselves? I'm Charlotte Davenport, wife of Mr. George Davenport of Noble Oaks Plantation."

The names didn't ring any bells. "Major Phillip Bailey of the Fourth Infantry. A pleasure to know you, ma'am, but may I ask what business brings you this close to the border? The Indians are riled, and I don't advise travel any further south."

Mrs. Davenport's back straightened and her dainty nostrils sprawled. "I have good reason to be here. I'm on the hunt for a certain slave. One of the survivors of that despicable Negro Fort tragedy."

Phillip replaced his hat and quirked an eyebrow. It was generally referred to as a success, not a tragedy, but the exultant tone of her voice sent mixed signals. Did she approve of the fort's demise or not?

"The army placed an announcement in the paper," she continued, her chin raised so that she looked at him through the bottoms of her eyes. "To whom should I speak regarding the matter?"

Phillip crossed his wrists over the pommel. "I'm the man you're looking for. You must have come for Toby. I wondered why no one had shown up to claim him, but you missed him by a handful of hours. He's on the road to Savannah's auction house. If you hurry, you'll catch him before sundown."

"I'm actually looking for a female. There was a sketch in the paper." She loosened the strings of a small reticule hanging from her wrist.

Phillip speculated about her shaky fingers. She wouldn't be the first to arrive claiming a slave that didn't belong to her, although her fine breeding didn't fit the pattern.

Mrs. Davenport withdrew a slip of paper and passed it to Phillip.

The knotted reins slipped from his hand. They landed on his thigh with a thump that equaled the drop in his heart. From between the span of his fingers, Milly's heartrending eyes stared up at him.

The gentle slope of her neck brought her scent sharply to mind, and the curve of her lips, her absence.

"I believe she now goes by the name of Milly." Mrs. Davenport's voice sliced through Phillip's thoughts. "Although she was born Milicent."

His gaze snapped toward her. "Milicent...Davenport?" He had always assumed her mother to be a slave, and her father, the woman's craven master. But he'd assumed wrong.

Her eyes widened at his bold question, then she let loose a string of high-pitched laughter. "Heavens, no! George would sooner bestow his fortune to the scullery girl than give my illegitimate child his name." A radiant flush rose to Mrs. Davenport's cheeks as her laughter died. She glanced nervously about her. "Milicent's father belonged to my Uncle, come south for the summer. He hung Sam the same day he was found in my bed, which also happened to be the day before my wedding.

"I'll not sully Sam's name. He was a good man. His only mistake was getting caught loving me." She blinked away what Phillip suspected were tears. "George married me anyway. For my fortune, he would have even if I'd told him I was with child. Now that you're the owner of my darkest secret, sir, I trust you'll be the gentleman and guard it well."

Her appalling admission took a moment to sink in, and when it did, he rushed to fill the silence. "I'm truly sorry for your...troubles, although the child—" He cut himself short, horrified that he'd almost divulged his feelings. "No need to worry. Your past is yours alone to share, although..."

She gazed at him expectantly, as he searched for a way to put his disjointed thoughts into words. "Your likeness to her will shout louder than any words you or I might speak." At least to those who had torn their eyes from her shapely form long enough to learn her face. "You bear a remarkable resemblance." Like a loadstone toward true north, the scrap of paper still within his grasp lured his gaze.

Mrs. Davenport hummed her agreement. "And you, Major Bailey, seem to take remarkable interest in a mere slave." Curiosity tipped her voice.

A mere slave? Phillip thrust the paper her direction. "Things aren't always as they seem. I, for example, would never have guessed that a finely bred southern lady would debase herself to the point of selling her own flesh."

She snatched the paper and crumpled it against her breast. "Davenport business is none of your concern!"

A fire lit within him, consuming every shred of common sense he possessed. "Is that all she is to you? *Business*?" His horse reeled, and it took him a minute to bring the animal back around.

When he drew alongside her again, he found that the anger that had puckered her mouth had vanished. In its place was a void. She stared into the distance, seeming to focus on something visible only in her mind. "Three hundred and twenty-three," her voice cracked.

"I beg your pardon?"

"The price of one, beautiful little girl. Same as the brood mare George bought with his earnings from the sale of my baby the day after my father died." Her face went slack as she stared into the past. "Did you know that mixed into feed, the shoots of a peach tree will kill a horse in under an hour?"

The sick turn of Phillip's stomach immobilized his tongue.

"I didn't know it would be that fast. Not that I minded." A new passion lit her eyes as she leveled them on Phillip. "But you're quite mistaken if you believe that even a day has passed since my daughter was ripped from me that I haven't grieved, haven't searched, haven't *begged* God to return her to me." Her chin trembled, but with what could only be practiced care, she stilled it and gathered her composure. "Do you believe in Providence, Major?"

Dubious of the reliability of his voice, Phillip nodded.

"Providence was my sister finding this clipping in a newspaper buried on her husband's desk. Providence is George Davenport lying on his deathbed so that his loathsome wife might act upon her daughter's needs." Her voice rose along with the certainty solidifying her gaze. "Providence is happening upon the man who might have the power and, dare I say, *desire* to help me set my daughter free?"

They fell silent as the troops, having reached them, marched past.

With his ill-conceived defense of her daughter, Phillip had unwittingly cracked Mrs. Davenport's carefully-erected shell, and the peek he'd gained inside had revealed a lonely and desperate spirit, not unlike Phillip's.

The difference between them was the years she'd had to plan, prepare, and pray.

Is this it, Father? Your answer? Your solution?

A whisper flitted across his soul bringing with it that unmistakable peace that only comes from Above. He let it fill his spirit, as a slow smile twisted his scar and reminded him of the workings of Providence in his own life.

He turned the smile on Mrs. Davenport. "You guessed right. I'd like nothing better."

Chapter Twenty

True Seeker took a firmer rein and gave a solid kick, forcing his mount into the middle of the swift creek. The roan was just as testy as its mistress.

His thoughts floated from Lillian to her father and his obvious refusal to come to Milly's aid. Now, she was on a northerly path heading toward whatever vile destination her master had planned for her. And every last one of them powerless to stop it.

True Seeker had never seen a man more broken than Bailey. It was an unbearable sight, and this morning, True Seeker was more than eager to light upon the Mobile trail.

Ahead, Totka urged his horse up the opposite bank. He'd kept them moving at a brisk, almost intolerable pace. Theirs was a full, four-day journey, but if they didn't reach Tensaw sooner than that, True Seeker feared the stout warrior's composure might crumble into a desperate, embarrassing heap.

In the minute it took True Seeker to climb the embankment and rejoin the path, Totka had dashed ahead and nearly disappeared through the trees. True Seeker grinned, shook his head, and spurred his horse back into a trot. Lillian's roan took the prompt with spirit and rapidly closed the gap.

"Why the hurry?" he asked between puffs of breath. "One would think a band of warring Choctaw in pursuit."

Totka slid him a cock-eyed smile. "Your day will come. Then you will wish you had kept your jaw locked and not pestered me."

True Seeker matched his playful tone. "That might be true, but today, I'm simply the loveless man forced to endure your reckless ill temper."

"Ill temper." Totka snorted, but pulled back slightly on the reins.

In truth, True Seeker doubted Totka suffered much with bouts of anger. He was as even-spirited a man as True Seeker had ever known, and even though only a handful of weeks had passed, they had spent enough time together for True Seeker to have formed a reliable opinion of him.

The two had often spoken into the night about topics ranging from the white-tailed deer to the floodwaters of the Tallapoosa, from the value of a plow to the absolute need of preserving ancient traditions, from the mysteries of a woman to the awe of her Maker.

For Totka, references to the Giver and Taker of Breath came like a steady heartbeat. Over the last days, he'd shared how he came to believe in the white man's Jesus, how he'd searched for someone who could read their Holy Book, how he'd refused to part company until he'd understood who this God-man was and what made Him worthy of Adela's devotion.

In True Seeker's opinion, Totka's love for the woman, as great as it was, was dwarfed by his love for God. It made True Seeker uncomfortable, yet curious.

He couldn't help his questions. Through them, he'd learned much about Jesus and had decided that He must have been a Native. The principles He taught were in keeping with their ways.

He deemphasized material gain, teaching that all land and living creatures belonged to the Creator, not man. With infinite power at his disposal, He exercised self-control and made himself meek. As the aged chiefs strived to do, Jesus wisely regulated his speech, not wasting words on the foolish. He spoke of the labor of love having no price, and He demonstrated it with his own life. And the loss of it.

True Seeker had recently concluded that he would be honored to know this Jesus on a deeper level. A wry smile twisted his mouth. With Totka as a travel companion, learning more would be inevitable.

Without warning, Totka grappled True Seeker's reins and yanked both horses to a dead stop. He cocked an ear toward the sound of approaching hoof beats.

"Riders, beyond that stand of trees," True Seeker murmured, dropping a palm to the butt of his pistol.

"How many?"

True Seeker tuned to the steady rhythm of thumping hooves. "Three, shod. Moving quickly, and they will already be aware of our presence," he said, pulling into the brush and checking that his weapons were loaded. After the war, this land was ceded to the Americans, and with sentiments still running hot toward the Indians, one could never be too careful.

"Well done. In these parts, to stand in a white man's path is to invite trouble. Remove your hand from your weapon." Totka leaned back in his saddle, and draped his wrists across the pommel.

Despite the unease churning his gut, True Seeker slipped his hand to his thigh and relaxed his posture.

The trio progressed, moving in and out of the trees in flashes of color. "Only traders ride this path. We will ask if they have—" Totka's back went rigid, his eyes intense and searching. Before True Seeker could open his mouth to voice his concern, Totka leapt from his horse and tore off, cutting through the woods toward the riders.

Fear gripped True Seeker by the heart. The man would get himself killed coming at these white men at a dead run. Without a plan, True Seeker drew his pistol and galloped down the winding trail, hoping to arrive in time to save his rash friend.

The forest broke open before him, exposing a scene he never could have predicted if the prophets had drawn it for him in the dirt. He dragged the roan to a harsh stop, matching its heaving breaths with his own.

"Adela." The name left his dust-coated mouth on a croak.

Atop a calm, gray mare, the woman didn't so much as flinch at the sound of her name or the ruckus True Seeker created at his arrival. Her wide-eyed gaze was pinned to the break in the shrubs and Totka. Hauling in chestfuls of wind, the man moved toward her with long, purposeful strides, heedless of McGirth's rifle aimed at his head.

Silent tears spilled down Adela's cheeks, and a tremble overtook her.

Without pause or words spoken, Totka grasped her around the waist, dragged her from the horse, and smothered her quiet sobs with his mouth. Her feet dangled as he clutched her to himself with one arm, while knocking the bonnet from her head with the other. Waves of russet spilled over her shoulders as his fingers dug through her hair, as though intent on rooting out every pin.

Still in possession of her lips, Totka shuddered and groaned.

Heat wicked up True Seeker's face. If someone didn't stop them, the two might soon be entwined on the ground.

A hearty chuckle disrupted his awkward thoughts. "Collect your jaw, boy. It's getting' away from ya," Caesar called.

True Seeker snapped his mouth shut and shifted his gaze to McGirth. His rifle lay across his lap, and patience softened his eyes.

"Will you not interfere?"

"I could try." McGirth pulled along True Seeker's horse and shook his head in a slow, sad arch. "But there's no stopping a raging river or love."

True Seeker had been referring to their open display of affection, not their future, but McGirth had a way of cutting to the marrow. "He will take her far from you. To his village." It was only fair McGirth be fully informed, and Totka was too preoccupied to give it much thought at the moment.

Their gazes traveled to Totka who clasped the base of Adela's head between his hands and murmured into her ear.

"If I hold her too close, I will lose her." McGirth's voice scratched out the words. Glancing back at True Seeker, he forced a smile. "And you seem to have lost something, as well." He stretched out his arm and dropped the pocket watch from his fist. It dangled from the chain wrapped around his thick fingers. "Crazy Fire was reluctant to part with it, but we finally agreed upon a price." McGirth grinned. "I should have been a courier, if they are all paid as well as that one."

True Seeker studied the fringes of the blanket protruding from beneath his saddle. "Forgive me for trading it. It was all I had of value. And Milly—"

"I understand, and I would have acted sooner, but I was away when the message arrived. I came as soon as I heard."

Gaze bouncing back to McGirth, True Seeker sat erect. "You've come to free her?"

"If possible, yes. Everyone deserves a chance at freedom. It was also an excuse to reconcile with my daughter." He jerked his head toward Adela. Hands clasped with Totka's, her smile rivaled the shine of her hair.

"Caesar," McGirth called.

The black man sidled up, a knowing smile on his face. "I reckon them two'll need a chaperone, suh."

McGirth sighed. "My thoughts exactly. Are you up to it?"

Totka was kissing her again, although less passionately, much to True Seeker's relief.

"Somebody gotta do it. May as well be me."

McGirth turned to True Seeker. "Think Totka'll mind escorting her back to Tensaw while you and I find and free Bailey's heart?"

An irrepressible smile worked its way up True Seeker's cheeks. "He might consider it."

"You have brought a new smile to my daughter's lips." McGirth lapsed into Muskogee. "One I have not seen since before her mother and sister..." His voice caught and the leathery skin of his face crinkled into a grimace. He loudly cleared his throat and pegged True Seeker with his gaze, his green eyes overflowing with intensity. "Will you take back the watch? As a gift of my gratitude?"

Without waiting for a response, he tucked the object into True Seeker's palm and slapped him on the arm. "Good." He swung a leg over his horse. "It's getting late. We'll camp here," he announced loudly then turned to True Seeker and winked. "No need for a fire, though."

They shared a laugh, and while McGirth began unsaddling his mount, True Seeker attached the watch chain to his shirtfront and dropped it in his pocket.

It thudded against his chest, and he smiled at its familiar weight. A hushed tick reached his young ears at the same instant that Grandmother Mahila's wrinkled voice flashed across his mind. For the rest of his days, whenever the tick of a watch thrummed his ears, he would always remember that in a world of mixed races and warring spirits, all things were possible.

***

A sudden noise yanked Milly from semi-sleep. Her eyes flew open to the hazy, pre-dawn glow that illuminated the stable where she'd spent a restless night. A disgruntled cow lowed mournful and long. From the barn rafters, a rooster trumpeted.

Morning, at last.

Her brain ground sluggish gears in an attempt to identify the sound she'd heard. Something falling? No, a slamming door.

He was coming for her.

She'd lain awake half the night knowing it was only a matter of time. After all these years, she knew Grayson well enough to be certain of that. She'd bet her next five meals it was the main reason he came for her himself instead of sending a slave hunter.

If Grayson hadn't been dead on his feet yesterday evening when they'd stopped at the wayside inn, she was certain she would have been forced to spend at least a portion of the night in his bed rather than on the hay strewn floor of the stall. Even with her hands tied behind her back and her ankles shackled, she would take the stall any day over that man's bed.

The place reeked of livestock, but at least she was its sole occupant. Every hour that she'd woken unmolested, she had breathed a prayer of thanks. God's comfort had been swift and all-encompassing—just enough to get her through to the next hour. And when the next hour had rolled around, she found Him occupying that one as well.

It had been an exhausting night, but one she would never forget. If anyone had been on hand to witness, they might have said she'd just spent the dark night utterly alone, but she would swear on her last chance at freedom that she wasn't.

No longer at war, her spirit had sensed God filling the filthy barn with His holy presence. His love had wiped away her shame, and although she had slept with the animals and been treated worse than one, He had convinced her that, to Him, she was the most cherished woman in Georgia. No, the whole world.

Voices neared, terse and unyielding. Grayson was angry. Perhaps bedbugs had tormented him, or perhaps breakfast hadn't been to his liking. Whatever the cause, it did not bode well for her.

The question of whether or not to fight him had plagued her from the moment he'd pulled her onto his horse in front of him and dug possessive fingers into her belly. She had never fought him before, but *before*, her mind had been trapped under the steel bondage of repression. Before, she hadn't realized she was someone worth fighting for. Nor had she savored freedom and love.

If she made a stand against him in her heart, would it be enough? Or did God require she resist and suffer the lash? In every prayer over the last hours, she'd begged Him for an answer, but He had yet to respond.

Shoulders aching, she tried to wiggle her fingers, but they had long ago ceased burning and gone numb. As the staccato of boots grew louder, so did the thump of her heart.

In an attempt to regain a bit of dignity, she floundered to pull herself into a sitting position, but when her arms screamed in pain, she flopped back.

Lids drifting closed, she expelled a weary breath. "You said you'd never leave me, Lord," she whispered, challenging Him to hold true to His promise. He'd been with her through the night, like a warm blanket tossed over her shoulders in the dead of winter. But now that she must face her persecutor, would He turn his back? He was a holy God. Surely, He couldn't stand in the presence of such evil.

The footsteps came to an abrupt halt outside her open stall.

You're my helper, Lord, and I refuse to fear what man can do to me. Warmth curled around her and eased the knot in her stomach. Peace filled her spirit and nudged open her lids.

Dust and bits of hay swirled in the first shafts of morning sunlight streaming through the slats in the barn wall. She blinked through the bright veil. Then blinked again. "Phillip?" It wasn't possible.

But it *was* him, from his scar-distorted eye down to his spit-shined boots, the man before her was Major Phillip Bailey.

Her heart leapt then crashed in shame.

The way he stood there, motionless, staring at her as though she were the most hideous creature on which he'd ever laid eyes, she almost wished she were seeing things. Almost.

Even with his face twisted in horror, the sight of him sprang tears to her eyes. "What are you doing here?" The words squeaked past the lump in her throat. "If you're planning to break me free, I won't go with you. I won't let you endanger yourself again." She scooted toward the back of the stall. The chains rattled, and she grimaced against the grinding in the shoulder that had supported her weight all night. Her humiliation was complete.

The movement propelled him into action. "Hold still. I'll get you out of here." He skidded to his knees in front of her and flipped her torso across his thighs. The immediate pressure releasing from her shoulder and arm elicited a groan of relief.

"I'm sorry, love. I'll be quick." His fingers ran the length of her back. Except for those around her wrists and ankles, he would find no welts or bruises, or any other fresh marks. God had been good to her.

"You shouldn't be here. It'll only make things worse." She tried to flip away from him, but he held her fast against him.

"Hush now. I'm almost done." He worked at the knot of her binding. "What has he done to you?" he muttered.

"Not as much as he will do, if he finds you here." *Please, God, don't let Phillip leave me.* The rope gave way, and fire burned through her shoulders as her arms bounced out of the constricting posture. She mashed her lips together and contained the cry within her mouth.

"I know it hurts. Forgive me." He eased her onto her back in the hay. "Almost there."

In a scorching race, blood rushed to her fingertips and set every nerve on fire. As she fought to withhold a sob, he fiddled with the irons clapped about her ankles. Within seconds, their weight fell away.

This escape plan was even more audacious than the last. Everything within her said she should scream at him to get away from her, but her tongue refused to form the words.

He moved back into her view, his beautiful, scarred face suspended above hers. Concern crinkled the skin around his eyes and mouth. Deft fingers swiped tears from her cheeks and picked straw from her lips. Moisture filled his eyes. "I knew God would do it, but I never imagined it would be this soon." His voice cracked, as he scooped her into his arms, and held her to him. His lips pressed against her forehead. "It's over. You can rest easy now."

"Over?" They hadn't even started running yet. Arms hanging useless at her sides, she twisted in an urgent attempt to stand. "We've got to get out of here. Help me get up."

He leaned back to look her full in the eye, a grin swathing his features. "Free five minutes, and already bossing me around."

She let herself fall against him. Her brow rose. "Free?"

Gold flecks, like sunshine, sparkled in his brown eyes. "That's what I said."

No, it wasn't possible. "Grayson would never let me go. He doesn't have the power to sell me."

"He didn't sell you, Milly. He found you dead. At least, that's the story he's going to tell your master." Phillip shrugged. "There isn't much a man won't lie about when offered enough money to do it."

She summoned strength to her arms and feebly pushed at his chest. "What cruel game are you playing? You can't afford me."

His hold tightened, as did his jaw. "You're right. My purse doesn't hold a fraction of what you're worth. Nor would it for years to come. But I'm not toying with you, Milly. There's someone—" His gaze wandered the stall as though searching for words hidden in the hay. "There's someone else who loves you dearly. Someone who paid your price. All you have to do is accept the gift."

"Someone else?" There *was* no one else. At least no one that cared enough. "If you're not my new master, then who is?" Confusion and fear tightened her features. A change of master could only mean uncertainty.

Scuffling feet and the rustle of silk sounded from behind him. He stiffened against her.

Fear spurred Milly's heart to a gallop. The uncontrollable urge to run overcame the pain in her limbs. She lurched for freedom from his arms, and almost achieved it before he could regain hold of her.

"Milly, no! Everything's going to be alright. I promise." Clutching her to his chest, he rubbed her back in a calm caress.

The fabric rustled again, nearer this time. Peering around Phillip's shoulder, Milly took in the sight of a lady, whose bright skirts were dimmed by the brilliant blue of her eyes—eyes that shimmered with unshed tears.

As Milly stared at the woman's silent, parted lips, something tugged at the back of her mind. "Who is she, Phillip?" Milly whispered.

Although she felt his gaze affixed to her face, his next hushed words were not for her. "We decided it was best you wait by the maple. If anyone learns of your involvement, it could—"

"Hang my reputation! I've waited fourteen years. It's long enough." The lady's rich voice filled the stall and unveiled a crevice in Milly's heart that had been long buried and forgotten.

"Momma?" The word slipped from her unbidden, yet as natural as if she'd uttered it last night.

Eyes wide, the woman lifted a pale hand to her throat. Why didn't she answer?

"Momma?" Milly's voice rose, insistent.

In a whoosh of stagnant barn air, the woman swept into the stall and slipped cool fingers against Milly's cheek. "Yes, baby, yes. I'm here." Her mother's assurances hurled Milly back to her childhood, to love and safety. No one would dare touch her, now. Momma was here. "Bailey."

A tense voice severed the calm. The man stood out of view, blocked by Momma shining face. "Grayson's demanding more."

Phillip snapped his head toward the man. "What happened? How much?"

"Someone must have seen Mrs. Davenport. Made the connection. It changes things, he says. Makes the deal riskier. He wants an extra two hundred and will go to Landcastle with the truth unless he gets it."

The chagrin in his voice told Milly something had just gone horribly wrong, but she couldn't pull her mind away from her joy long enough to make sense of it.

The cords in Phillip's neck went taut. "He already took every cent we have. We shook on it!"

Like a contagion, his panic leached onto Milly. With numb fingers, she grappled for his shirt. "What is it? What's going on?" She stared up at his twitching jaw. Was he refusing to look at her? "Phillip?"

A pat on her hand drew her gaze back to her mother. Not a hint of concern furrowed her brow. "No need for worry. A mother is always prepared. Mr. McGirth, if you'd be so kind as to escort me to my horse, I'll get the scoundrel his money." She brushed a kiss across Milly's forehead. "I'll be back before you miss me."

Before Milly could protest, Momma was gone. The lingering sensation against Milly's cheek assured her she had imagined nothing. After all these years, her mother had found her. And freed her.

"Momma…she…" The tears in her throat snagged her words. "She found me. She said she would, but I'd stopped hoping."

The tension in Phillip's face transferred to his arms as he held her closer. He let out a long, deep breath. "Thank God for that woman. And McGirth... Milly, if I ever doubt the Almighty again, feel free to lecture me at will."

A nervous laugh broke free of her throat. "You say it as though I'll be around long enough to witness it."

He pushed her slightly away and cocked his head. "You will be." He began to work her burning fingers between his own. "Can you move them now?"

Milly obeyed, barely aware of the pain through the myriad questions in her mind vying for answers. She frowned. "You're not making a lick of sense."

He chuckled, then stood and pulled her to her feet. "I suppose it's a lot to take in, but there's time. Come on. I'm getting you out of here."

Her ankles protested, but she ignored them as he slipped a supporting arm around her back and directed her out the rear of the barn.

Except for a group of horses tethered to a nearby post, the yard was eerily desolate.

She glanced over her shoulder, expecting any moment for someone to sound an alarm, but not even the breeze moved.

Phillip stopped at one of the horses and unwound the reins. When he turned back to her, it was with a gaze burning with love. "All you need to know Milly, is that you're free. As free as any white woman. Free to come and go as you please, to work and earn pay or do nothing at all." He slipped the reins against her palm. "Free to ride away from me and never look back, if that's what you want."

Confounded, she stared at the leather draped across her hand, until the sound of footsteps drew her gaze across the yard.

Milly's mother approached, her gait so smooth and light, she could be floating. An easy smile lit her eyes as she tucked her hand into the arm a ruggedly attired gentleman. The stranger from the barn?

A few steps beyond them, True Seeker strolled tall and confident, a massive grin rivaling the size of the bow slung over his shoulder.

"Just like that? I'm free?" Milly gave an unbelieving shake of her head.

Phillip tugged her chin to regain her attention then bore into her with steady, patient eyes.

"Do you trust me, Milly?"

"Of course." The answer emerged without an instant's hesitation and smoothed the lines on Phillip's forehead.

He swallowed her in an embrace and stroked her condemning hair. "Then you can trust me when I tell you that you're your own master now. You're free." The deep rumble of his voice vibrated her cheek as well as the thoughts in her brain. "Free to slap me for the audacity of loving you, or free to honor me by letting me care for you the rest of my life."

He tipped her chin toward him. With his thumb, he traced the outline of her lower lip. "Perfectly free." His husky inhale was cut short when his mouth covered hers, knocking the air from her lungs. The muscles of his arms hardened around her, trapping her against him and negating his insistence that she was free. Whether or not he'd paid a single coin for her body, he freely owned every square inch of her heart.

Questions scrambled for a foothold in her mind, but she had said she'd trust him, and she meant it. She let the reins slip to the ground then dug her fingers into the hair at the nape of his neck, allowing that trust to stake its claim.

With tears cool on her cheeks, Milly deepened the kiss and savored the first sweet taste of freedom.

About the Author

April W Gardner writes adult and middle grade historical fiction. She is also the founder and senior editor of the literary site, Clash of the Titles. As a proud military spouse, she has performed the art of homemaking all over the world. Currently, she makes her home in Georgia, the heart of ancient Creek Country.

To learn more about April and her books, please visit her on the web at www.aprilwgardner.com.

Acknowledgements

Thank you, Jesus, for your love and saving grace, for guiding my stumbling fingers over the keyboard, and for continuously soothing my warring spirit.

Endless gratitude goes to my dear family who puts up with my long writing hours, nutso in-character moments, and incessant verbal pursuit of the perfect story arc. I love you guys!

Michelle, Jennifer W, and Sarah, you were my right hands throughout this process. I owe much of this novel's completion to your patience, ready ears, and priceless input.

To my other critique partners and beta readers, Lisa, Jessica, Jennifer S, Jen-in-law, and Grace, I owe you big time.

Stephanie, editor dearest, thanks for hanging in there for me. Your trust in my abilities keeps me going!

Edna, avid student of Creek culture (a.k.a. guru!), your gift of time and knowledge has injected an element of authenticity into *Warring Spirits* that I could never have achieved alone. True Seeker thanks you, and I thank you.

An equal amount of appreciation to Chief Bearheart for passing along advice and wisdom. And character names!

Thanks again to Vinspire Publishing for taking a leap of faith with my stories.

To all my readers, thanks for believing in me, encouraging me, and uplifting me in prayer.

My love to all.

Author's Notes

When I sat down to plot out *Warring Spirits*, I had a goal in mind—to give my readers another book with a unique setting that had the same balance of war and love. It was important to me to continue the pattern I'd set in the first book in the Creek Country Saga, *Wounded Spirits*. Not only that, but I had to adequately tie off the romance I left hanging with Totka and Adela. (Dear reader, you were so patient with me for delaying that "happily ever after." Thank you!) It was a tall order! And one I couldn't fill for months. The story simply eluded me.

In fact, I wrote five chapters of Lillian's story before admitting to myself it wasn't going to work. Lillian might have her own book one day, but not yet. It was then that a bit of history in a research book I'd read half a dozen times over the years, suddenly leapt off the page and took a nosedive into my heart.

Negro Fort.

Within twenty-four hours, I had the basic plot sketched and knew there was no turning back.

When I finish reading a deeply historical novel, I always wonder which parts of the book were true to history and which were not. For those of you with equal curiosity, I've taken a few paragraphs to satisfy your questions. I've also included a few bits of historical trivia you might find interesting.

Many of the details and events (not including the main characters) in *Warring Spirits* are true to history. However, to stay in keeping with a workable plot, I altered the timeline of the army's arrival at Negro Fort as well as that of the sailors' deaths. I pray all you sticklers to accuracy will forgive me!

In regard to the runaways and their courage in the face of the joint army-navy expedition against them, Surgeon Marcus

C. Buck of the Fourth Infantry said, "We were pleased with their spirited opposition...though they were Negroes, Indian, and our enemies." (A number of Choctaw and Seminole were also in the fort, but for the sake of space, I chose not to include them in the book.)

According to one source, the hot shot (heated cannon ball) was guided to the magazine by William Hambly, who had previously worked for the British in the fort. The Negroes were overwhelmed and inexperienced and carelessly left the door open which allowed the red-hot ball to roll in. It was a one-in-a-million shot and created such a blast that it was heard clear across the water to Pensacola.

"You cannot conceive, nor I describe the horrors of the scene," wrote Surgeon Buck. "In an instant, hundreds of lifeless bodies were stretched upon the plain, buried in sand and rubbish, or suspended from the tops of surrounding pines. The brave soldier was disarmed of his resentment, and checked his victorious career, to drop a tear on the distressing scene."

Oddly enough, Chief Garcon –who was characterized as "lean, intense, hot-eyed and tight-lipped, cunning, courageous, and cruel" –was one of the survivors. As soon as the Americans learned the details of how he tarred and burned one of the sailors, they handed him over to the Creek who immediately shot him execution style.

As to the conflict with the Seminole, the battle brief I described was an exaggeration. According to Colonel Duncan Clinch, he "advanced with two hundred Cowetas (Creek) under the gallant Major McIntosh, to meet them (Seminole); but the cowardly wretches dispersed without our being able to get a view of them." Consequently, there were also no escaping slaves, but I couldn't help imagining what it must have felt like to have their allies come so close, bringing with them perhaps one last chance at freedom. What if the slaves had managed to escape...? What would have happened? How far would have gotten before being caught?

In the real-life situation, the runaways' last shred of hope must have been crushed when the Seminole scattered without a fight.

The joining of the American and Creek forces just two years after the Red Stick War was not only ironic, but tenuous. Still sparsely populated, the frontier was a rather small place and odds were great that at least one of the soldiers present knew someone who had died at Fort Mims. But what if an actual Fort Mims survivor was forced to fight alongside a former Red Stick? What kind of great conflict would that create? The storyteller in me had to know!

In the end, Clinch gave much of the credit for the campaign's success to the Indians. "I must beg leave to recommend to my Government the gallant Major McIntosh...(for his)...distinguished conduct during the whole expedition."

After such a bloody war as the Creek War, it pleases me to know there was at least one brief episode of friendly co-operation. But it wasn't to last. One year later, Jackson began promoting his policy to have the Indians removed to land beyond the Mississippi.

In 1816, at the time of this book's setting, the Creek confederacy was beginning its downward spiral toward destruction. Once set in motion, it would not be stopped. True Seeker's hunger and suffering were only a taste of what was to come.

Crafting this story cost more than I bargained for. A writer becomes her characters, lives inside their heads, in their world. This time, it was disturbingly painful. Milly and True Seeker dug deep, too deep at times. If the knowledge of what men can do to each other breaks my sinful heart, what must it do to God's?

Marcus', Adela's, Zachariah's, and eventually Phillip's blind eye to race was a rare find in those days. Having so many "good" characters together in one book borders on unrealistic, but my goal was to instill hope and strength in the reader and to drive home the fact that "in a world of mixed races and warring spirits, all things are possible." With God.

Your struggle might not be with racism or bitterness, but no matter your particular war, the truth remains that "with God all things are possible." Matthew 19:26b. I pray you've come away from *Warring Spirits* with that fact etched into your heart.

Because He lives,

April W Gardner

To learn more about the Creek Indians, Creek Country, and Negro Fort, please visit me on the web.

www.aprilgardner.com
www.aprilwgardner.com

*Quotes borrowed from *McIntosh and Weatherford, Creek Indian Leaders* by Benjamin W. Griffith, Jr.

Book Club Discussion Questions

Only Milly's African-textured hair gives away her heritage, allowing her to hide who she really is. In chapter one, Isum tries to remove her bonnet then says, "You don't need that no more. From here on, we'll be exactly like the Almighty created us to be…Your feet can run, but your heart, it gotta stop chasin' after lies. It's time you be who you's meant to be…A child of the King. And my girl. Nothin' else mattuh." For all Isum's gruffness, he makes an excellent point. At what place in the book does Milly finally believe this statement? What event/s bring her to that knowledge?

For personal introspection—What truth about yourself are you hiding from? What lies are you believing? Who does God mean for you to be?

Isum truly loves Milly, but her love for him is one of a different sort. How much do you believe his gruffness with her affects how she feels about him? Is there any other reason she might have for not being able to fully give him her heart? Was there ever a place during the book you wished they would end up together? Do you blame Isum for what he tried to do to Phillip?

Milly experiences a "treacherous yearning in her spirit" for unconditional affection. It motivates her to continue the lie that she's a white woman, like any other, and all for a few more respectful, tender moments with Phillip. God placed within women the desire to be tenderly loved and protected. Balanced with an accurate view of how God sees us, this is natural and good.

For personal introspection—Is there any area in your life influenced by the same yearning that drove Milly to lie? If so, is it healthy, or might you need to reevaluate your thoughts and/or behavior?

Major Phillip Bailey suffers with a form of post traumatic stress disorder as a result of his experience at Fort Mims. He is ashamed of his overpowering physiological and psychological reactions to certain things, such as the sight of gore. As an officer in the army, how do you think his commanders would react if they knew of his weakness? What about his troops? Do you believe Marcus to be correct in his approach to help Phillip hide his problem, or should he have used his authority as a medical officer to force Phillip off the battlefield?

Fort Mims took everything from Phillip. The Army is the only thing he believes he has left. His drive to advance in his career is so strong that he volunteers for battle despite his weakness. Along the way, his goal transforms. What did it change to and what event/s prompted this?

What is Phillip's view of slavery at the outset of the book compared to what it is at the end? How do his relationships with Saul, Enoch, and Milly play into this? Do you think Phillip still has room to grow in regard to his opinion about blacks and natives?

Was True Seeker justified in taking food from the McGirth's house? When he realized he had "stolen" the watch, he found himself in a sticky situation. Was there a better way he could have handled it?

An excellent judge of character, Grandmother Mahila gave True Seeker his name. During the book, in what ways does True Seeker live up to it?

Throughout the book, True Seeker strives to become a worthy man and warrior, as his uncle and father before him—a difficult task considering the war took his role models from him. What characters fill that position, and how specifically do they each help True Seeker? In his last scene, what statement does he make that hints at the fact that he, at last, has begun to see himself as something more than an awkward boy?

Plan Your Next Escape!

What's Your Reading Pleasure?

Whether it's brawny Highlanders, intriguing mysteries, juvenile fiction, illustrated children's books, or uplifting love stories, Vinspire Publishing has the adventure for you!

For a complete listing of books available, visit our website at www.vinspirepublishing.com.

Find us on Facebook at
www.facebook.com/VinspirePublishing

Follow us on Twitter at
www.twitter.com/vinspire2004.

We are your travel guide to your next adventure!